THIRTEEN
STORIES
AND
THIRTEEN
EPITAPHS

THIRTEEN
STORIES
AND
THIRTEEN
EPITAPHS

WILLIAM T. VOLLMANN

Grove Press New York

Originally published in Great Britain in 1991 by André Deutsch Limited.
First published in the United States of America in 1993 by Pantheon Books,
a division of Random House, Inc. First Grove Press paperback
edition, August 1994

"The Ghost of Magnetism" previously appeared in
The Paris Review.

"The Happy Girls" first appeared in a hand-printed artist's edition
of thirteen copies, complete with photographs, underwear,
mirror-glass, peephole, buzzer, electric red light and bra straps.
Copies are still available from the author at $4,000 apiece.
(Batteries and spare bulb are included.)

"Epitaph for Mien" first appeared in a lemon-gilded artist's edition
of one copy (acrylic on iridescent pastels).

"Divine Men" first appeared in *Grand Street*. An edition of
thirteen lino-cut copies is in progress.

"The Grave of Lost Stories" first appeared in *Conjunctions*. There
is also an artist's edition of one portfolio copy, illustrated with
the most poisonous pigments available.

Published simultaneously in Canada
Printed in the United States of America

Library of Congress Cataloging-in-Publication Data

Vollmann, William T.
Thirteen stories and thirteen epitaphs/William T. Vollmann.—1st
Grove Press ed.
ISBN 0-8021-3395-9
I. Title.
[PS3572. 0395T48   1994]   813' .54—dc20   94-790

Grove Press
841 Broadway
New York, NY 10003

10   9   8   7   6   5   4   3   2   1

For Ken, who kept the F.B.I. entertained,
for the F.B.I., who kept me entertained,
and for Greenglass, who is still being entertained

Contents

CONTENTS

THIRTEEN STORIES AND THIRTEEN EPITAPHS

UTHOR'S NOTE

THESE stories are all epitaphs; these epitaphs are all stories. (A good story is only a hearse to carry you to the ending where the epitaph waits.) —Such was my belief in writing this book, although now I wonder whether I missed the beginning. —No matter anymore; words are cold and dead. But wouldn't it be fine if endings could be abolished in favor of translations to elsewhere, if the story, the life, were an isometric exercise whose purpose was directed only toward the final glorious release?

William T. Vollmann

I

THE GHOST OF MAGNETISM

After running full speed through the green
segment of your route, you reach a point
where you realize that more care is needed.
An imaginary yellow light is flashing and
demands that you make more exact use of the
Orienteering skills you have learned. It is a
matter of locating and passing all the
checkpoints you have on your map that lead
you in the right direction.

BJORN KJELLSTROM, *Be Expert
with Map and Compass* (1976)

Tremblings of the Needle

Before I had even gone away, I started polishing San Francisco
as if it were a pair of glasses to look through and every *new*
thing dust and dandruff; so the day of the farewell party gleamed and
curved the world to the degree required by my nearsightedness: I
remember the breeze as we stood on the deck of the ferry; hot sun on
faces, shoulders and railings; my friends with their coolers and picnic
baskets; and the Bay all around and everything perfect (which is to say
ready-polished), Margaret smiling (she had arranged this ocean occasion
as a surprise), and the greenness of Angel Island just ahead with people
playing frisbee and the good smells of barbecue coming over the water;
while I stood so happy to be with my friends, wondering who else might
already be waiting on Angel Island as part of the surprise. As I looked
into their faces, they seemed to me so dearly lovable—in part, I think,
on account of the effort and expense that they had gone to for me,
which proved that they cared about me; but I like to think that had I
provided the party for them it would have been the same; I was already

7

burnishing them so delicately that their very failings had become endearing. —Beside me stood Martin in the sunlight, squinting and holding onto the railing with both hands. Too often I had considered him spineless, insipid, unintelligent. When he spoke it was difficult to pay attention to him, for he stuttered and rambled. But today he seemed to me submissive like Christ, with a gentle, timid childishness that needed to be loved and protected. How could I forget the journeys that he and I had taken together, the midnights when we had driven home through the Central Valley, when it was warm and the sky was greenish-grey, the fields greyish-black; and through the open window of the truck came the smell of alfalfa? We saw cars (very few, very late), and white road-dots gleamed in our headlights, and we played good old songs over and over in the cassette player and for hours our neighbor was the humid presence of fields. Now on the ferry he was quiet, for large groups intimidated him. I remembered ascending the steep gorges of dry mountains ten years before and being desperately thirsty, my lips grainy with blood and salt, and finding Martin at last and asking for water, Martin taking off his pack so patiently and handing his canteen to me, and the goodness and sweetness of that water. —Chubby Monique sat behind us, letting the wind flutter her sweatshirt, laughing and hugging her lover, Vera, whose narrow little face had sometimes been for me a banner of boredom, but which today suggested serenity. How limited I had been, that I had not always seen her that way! As for Monique, her laughter opened up her face in an unaffected way, and I suddenly understood that what I had sometimes mistaken in her for rudeness or selfishness was nothing less than honesty. I had never known Monique and Vera well, it occurred to me now, but I recalled the time when we had gone out to dinner together at some vegetarian Chinese place or other in the Richmond and I took a liking to them both because from appetizer to dessert they behaved as purely as butter virgins, feeding each other with the same spoon, nourishing each other with Calistoga water; then I felt a sharp pang as though I were excluded from something, and I longed to see them at home, where among the plump hard pillows of their futon, or condensing on the dark-lobed underleaves of their many houseplants, their innermost tendernesses must live, freshened by a thousand kisses, guarded and protected by the horned ram-skulls that hung on the walls; and although I could never see this it made me inexpressibly grateful that I might at least know of it; and the pang I felt, of loneliness or jealousy, was not unpleasing, because I imagined that these two and their love would at least dwell *near* me forever, increasing luxuriously like every other good thing. But presently Monique began complaining of not feeling well, and at dessert she scarcely opened her mouth when Vera lifted the spoon to her, but sat there drooping. —Baby, did you forget your pills again? said Vera. The other woman nodded miserably. Then she groaned, and pitched forward into her plate. —Vera cried out and half rose in her chair and said goddamn oh why did this have to happen again? She was wringing her hands, and her face was shiny with tears. I looked around me for the waiter, and saw that everyone in the restaurant had gathered around us staring with big spooky eyes like the cows in the south field would do when Martin and I had butchered a steer and the blood ran across the concrete floor of the slaughterhouse and through the corner drainpipe, sinking into the soft alfalfa of the south field, sinking, sinking underground to swell that dark black river of blood that must run beneath the Sierras and through the sewers of Sacramento and probably all the way to San Francisco but first the other cows smelled it and gathered around the slaughterhouse, staring with black-masked eyes from whitish faces in the hot twilight, staring at the trickling blood, at Martin and me—and Vera and I wiped the milky sticky dessert rice out of Monique's face with a wet napkin; we left some money on the table, and then Vera slung her friend over her shoulder and carried her out to the car; she did not want me to help. The willless arms and legs swung hideously; the Volkswagen shuddered home, stalling at almost every intersection. I sat with the unconscious girl in the back seat. Neither Vera nor I said a word. When we turned down the hill onto Mars Street, with the lights of San Francisco below us and then the soothing darkness of the Bay and the dense low ridge of lights that was Berkeley, Monique's eyes snapped open and then she closed them again, sighing and shaking her head and grinding her face in my lap, and I said how bad do you feel Monique? and Vera had turned off the ignition and was saying take it easy honey we're home now I'll put you to bed, and I lifted Monique's head as slowly as I could, but she had become still paler and her face and hands were sweaty and she said I'm going to be sick, so Vera rushed to open the door for her and carried her out and said I'm with you darling I'm holding you, and she laid her gently down where the grass was softest and knelt beside her and raised her head up into her lap, stroking her temples with such love and gentleness, and Monique began to retch and Vera was kissing her head all over and saying   that's a good doll that's right I'm here with you I won't let anything bad happen to you so go ahead and let it come out you'll feel better,   but Monique started moaning   no no   and she pulled away from Vera and sat up trembling with her eyes starting from her head and I heard a gulping noise deep in her throat and she was struggling feebly with her little hands to push Vera away and Vera said to me or herself   shit here she goes again this is the part I hate the worst   and Monique whispered *don't touch me I'm the Ghost of Magnetism!*   and I thought   what the *hell*   and I heard her teeth chattering and she said   no don't spin me   but Vera only said   come on honey you can't feel better till you throw up and Monique wailed   what have I *done* to you that you're trying to make me—oh!—   and she slumped in Vera's arms and Vera explained to me   you see she *hates* to throw up   and I said   ah   and I said   but what does she mean exactly by the Ghost of Magnetism?   and Vera said distractedly   it's not *her* it's Elaine Suicide   and I said   what about her? and Vera ran her hands through her hair and said   oh God that girl cracks me up she just *slays* me I wonder if she learned to talk like that at her rebirthing class   . . . but I knew that Vera was not telling me the truth, that this was some secret between her and Monique which their skulls and houseplants guarded like a rain forest's mystery; as for Elaine Suicide, whom I knew well, she had never to my knowledge taken a rebirthing class; nor had she confessed to any kinship with the eighteenth-century French physicists who played the compass false for the greater good; anyhow, Monique finally threw up and felt better. Now she and her lover were happy and laughing on the ferry, and I did not want to leave them and never see their Volkswagen again, whose windows were precariously held on with duct tape; I wanted to keep knowing them whether they laughed or cried, but even if I had been the Grand Demon of Magnetism at the center of the compass dial I would *still* have to vomit them up, along with the sweet water that Martin gave me, because I was leaving. —It was the same with all the others, who were spending the day with me for the last time, making a constellation of remembrance for me that I could not keep in my sky, no matter how much I wanted to, and they did not have and never had had any faults:—neither Margaret, who had never complained when I turned the stereo up loud, nor earnest Paul and Nancy who sat together as quiet

10

as Quakers and left early, nor Elaine Suicide who lay sulking prettily in the sun as she had done at the beach when I drew sketches of her naked; nor old Laddie the hobo, who was more lovingly patient than Santa Claus (when he was not drunk); once when he and Elaine and I were coming back from the beach and Elaine had to drive round and round the block looking for parking until she was close to tears, Laddie simply beamed and said well, how *nice* that we get to look at the view! Elaine, I sure hope you don't run out of gas! —yessir, Laddie was as perfect a being as Sharie the pathologist who let me eat all her ice cream or Painter Ben who had invited me to Thanksgiving dinner every year, because he was once lonely himself and so at holidays he had all the losers like me over for Thanksgiving, but I never went, preferring to get depressed alone over cheap and watery food in my chilly flat (although of course I was *never* as depressed as Elaine Suicide) and I wished now as I stood behind Ben on the ferry that I had come over more often to watch football on Sundays, that I had been at all his grand dinners (Vera and Monique always came)—as if I could *collect* them somehow in an album of imperishability, in which I could always see Ben's kitchen table where I used to sit down with him over spaghetti piled with the bright red meat sauce that he made by the quart and stored in the freezer along with packages of frozen spinach and squash puree, and the phone rang for Ben and the phone rang for Ben and I ate spaghetti to my heart's content; even Elaine, who seldom agreed with people, did not hesitate to say that when you ate at Painter Ben's house there was always more than enough to eat, which was both good and necessary as I had learned since Ben had once gone camping for six weeks with me and lost fifteen pounds on my food, which is why he now had another helping; and the phone rang for Ben and Ben said *that* one wanted me to take her climbing with me! and I said what did you tell her? and Ben grinned and said I told her no and I said she bores you? and Ben said *sex* bores me more and more and I said Ben you can jerk off to my girlfriend's picture anytime you want and Ben said I only jerk off to hundred dollar bills and the phone rang for Ben; after dinner he'd lead me down into his basement where everything smelled of paint and Ben said these paint-fume chemicals must sure be fucking me up but you know what? *I* don't care, because I don't *want* to be normal! and upstairs the phone rang for Ben and we played around at marbleizing and stippling his paints on practice squares of masonite because there

11

was *money* to be made in such projects, as evinced by the subtly marbled walls of the beauty parlor on Polk Street where the Handcuff Queen served you wine as she permed you; so Painter Ben, who made money because he bid high with calm conviction and worked very fast, had learned to make masonite look like agate or jasper or tiger's eye; he could turn a piece of cardboard into a vanilla tombstone; he could marbleize any rich bitch's fireplace into translucent mauve and porphyry and he was so handsome with his moustache, his iridescent blue-green eyes, his outdoor face whose cheeks creased widely whenever he smiled, that women were always calling his answering machine; yes indeed, in his way Painter Ben was perfect, like weatherbeaten blonde Megan, who had once been the beauty queen of Georgia, whom I had a crush on, so one very cold New Year's Eve in Berkeley I was doing everything I could to get Megan to go to bed with me like a magnetic flux line desiring to encircle the sweetest electric current and my friend Seth wished me luck and Megan spent hours cleaning her room and primping herself for her great date with me and my heart pounded *ba*-BOOM! *ba*-BOOM! with excitement at the thought that I would most certainly screw Megan, who had just graduated with honors from her safe sex seminar; and like all generals on the eve of victory I reflected on my long and cunning campaign of love-notes to Megan hidden in the closets, in the bathroom behind the toilet roll, in the kitchen under the nutmeg jar, to say nothing of love-notes boldly written summer and winter on the bulletin board or even on the back of Megan's junk mail—but always, it must be said, plotted and thrillingly accomplished when I was visiting Seth and Megan was out so that Megan would be surprised; and Megan had laughed and kissed me and her hair smelled like all the flowers of Georgia; therefore, as Seth and I strolled across the Berkeley campus that night passing the time by singing "Helplessly Hoping" and inspecting leaves and trees while Megan made herself perfect for me, I slammed my fist into my palm and said   Seth I've *got* her I *know* I do!   and Seth said sincerely   that would be *so wonderful!*   and Seth said   look at this pinnate leaf structure   and Seth said   Megan must really be smitten she's working so hard to fix herself up   and I said   I can hardly wait!   and the globe-lights shone hopefully through all the pinnate leaves even as we went jogging valiantly home where we heard the hair dryer purring Megan's promise and Megan called from the bathroom   almost ready guys   and Seth nudged me with his bony elbow and winked, right as Megan came out,

and she was so beautiful and Seth grinned and said   see you later pal
and I said   oh Megan   and hugged her and buttoned up her coat for
her and took her hand and we went running, running, with the New
Year's Eve darkness stinging and refreshing our foreheads, and Megan
was laughing and I thought soon I will be kissing this lovely face (a
privilege which in fact she was to refuse me over white wine in the Thai
restaurant as I sat looking into her eyes thinking well *that's* a fine how-
d'you-do which translates into *now* what do we do?—even though we
did have fun just the same, skipping hand in hand down Shattuck
Avenue at midnight singing "What Did the Deep Sea Say?" at the top
of our voices so that everyone stared at us) and when we got back to
Megan's house she turned on the space heater; sitting beside her close
enough to touch her cheek if that had been granted me I said   well if
you won't let me *sleep* with you can I at least *kiss* you?   and Megan said
no and I said   well if you won't let me *kiss* you can I *hold your hand?*
and Megan smiling said   you know I don't believe you can!   and I said
well all right   and went upstairs to Seth's absent sister's hard cold bed
on which I sat all night, the better to stare sulkily down at the floor
immediately beneath which my former beauty queen was even at that
moment (I presumed) sleeping happily alone with her face glowing pink
in the light of her space heater and her hair radiating away from her to
instruct her lucky pillows in all the directions; I felt so heartsore and
anguished and sorry for myself that I never even lay down although I
certainly longed for morphines and semi-morphines to close my swollen
eyes but the next day was next year and it was bright and sunny and
cold and I felt deliciously debauched with grief as Seth and I drove up
the coast singing "Chalk Up Another One, Another Broken Heart" and
walked in the woods chewing tree-sap and we astounded Seth's father
with the vampire-blood capsules that Megan had given me last night for
a present and I was as happy as could be; Megan was perfect, even if I
never saw her again (for you must not imagine that all these friends of
mine came to Margaret's surprise party or were even invited; Margaret
did not know them all and even if she had known them I don't think
she'd have asked them because they would have hated each other);—
speaking of which, I must not omit to praise the perfection of Mark
Dagger, who once said to me   if there's one thing I love in this world—
no, *two* things . . . *three* things!—it's **DRUGS, PUSSY** and **GUNS!** *I*
said it first: *FUCK* apple pie, baseball, a-a-and hot dogs! It's all about

drugs, pussy, guns!— while beside him Dickie swivelled his pale shaven head left and right, left and right, as if it were on greased bearings, and he clasped and unclasped his hands and said   now Dagger don't forget beer! And beer! and beer!   —*Beer!*   shouted Dagger.   —WHIS-KEEEEEY!   screamed Dickie.   —One ice cube,   sighed Dagger lovingly, make it a triple shot!   —Alcohol!   said Dickie.   —*Codeine!* said Dagger.   More alcohol!   said Dickie.   —But I *do* love acid, Dagger brooded, and Dickie said   yeah I remember you on acid, all right; you was yelling *General Lee! General Lee!* and then you was kicking soccer balls down the hall! The next thing I heard, you'd jumped through your window, CRASH!   and Dagger said   hey Massah suck my grits!   —and he was perfect, like Dickie, like Sheet-Rock Fred who sighed and had a beer and said   Hitler used to say the will is all; now I say the wall is ill;   feeling ill, he wrote poems sitting in his truck at lunch and then it was back to the mysteries of the mudding tray, the ladder and the bazooka; he was always sailing out past the Golden Gate into storms and talking about weighing anchor for India never to return; he was going to be a pirate, a Buddha, a samurai; he would commit *seppuku*; he broke his arm when a ladder caved in on him but he wouldn't stop working so they had to reset the bone twice, and Fred had a beer and said   I'm the plaster man with the master plan!   and he would say   you know all about Dr. Johnson don't you? you know about Mishima?   and sometimes Fred would just laugh, and you felt very sad looking at his long beard and his jacket that was white-smeared with mud from a thousand ceilings as if all the seagulls of life had crapped on him. He was my friend, and so was his sometime employee Sheet-Rock Seth who as I have intimated was skinny and tense and stopped the car every ten minutes to jump out into the dew because he'd seen some lovely plant that had to be picked and keyed and admired while Fred sat laughing to himself very quietly; likewise Seth shinnied up pine trees from sea to shining sea and vanished among the shaking branches as Fred sat reading again about the twenty-three hundred Japanese warriors who rode silently across the moonlit snow to avenge some humiliation or other of their lord's which had happened a generation ago and most of them would get slaughtered by the castle's defenders and the ones that didn't would have to slit their bellies open anyway to show their sincerity but the important thing was HONOR as Fred agreed, sighing and sighing to think that his beautiful samurai sword had gotten stolen

14

so how could *he* die like a warrior? . . . while meanwhile among the
thrashing bowing branches whose needles raked his face and smeared his
knees with sap, Seth was collecting and keying the biggest cone, which
he dipped in Varithane to make it last forever and when he had a bunch
of specimens rattling around in Megan's tampax box he mailed them to
the lab in Gatlinburg, Tennessee which was not far from where Seth's
friend Patricia lived, Patricia who slept all her nights with a stuffed
dolphin and loved Seth (hopelessly, because at that time Seth preferred
to walk the Berkeley campus looking the coeds up and down and then
go home to jerk off—he was not even interested in Megan!); Patricia
loved him because while there were many naturalists in Tennessee none
compared to Seth in thinness as she well knew and so did the scientists
at the lab when they put down the leaves they'd been holding to the
light and brushed the bark-chips off each other's shoulders and sighed
oh look here's *another* bunch of Seth's cones   and they said   that *rascal*
and they opened up the box like it was Christmas and juggled the cones
and called   hey *Elmer* look at this one yessir I've never seen anything
like it   and they said   is this a new *species* or a whole new *genus?*   and
they said   now *look* at the work that boy Seth's just given us 'cause the
darn pine tree textbooks will have to be *revised!*   —although had the
Tennessee scientists never said any of this but simply thrown his pine
cones into the wastebasket, Seth would not have cared because what he
enjoyed, you see, was climbing trees and finding things,—but you must
not believe Seth to be a mere harum-scarum conifer-thief who was
UNENLIGHTENED; no indeed, he went to see a shaman who groaned
ohh I feel so sorry for the ocean; the ocean is very angry with us because
we never give it anything good to eat; we only feed *garbage* to the ocean!
and everyone else stared at the shaman as blankly as subway tokens but
Seth went to the store and bought a dozen of his favorite candybars and
then he rode the streetcar all the way out to Ocean Beach, standing
very straight and stern so that all the old ladies thought what a nice boy,
and the driver said   Ocean Beach *last* stop!   and Seth got out and
walked slowly through the fog toward the ocean and the beach was
littered with thousands of dead little jellyfish that the ocean had vomited
up for an awful warning (what would poor weak-stomached Monique
have thought?); thus Seth stood all by himself in his falling-apart old
sneakers, right at the tide line, and the waves rolled foamily white
around his ankles as he endured, throwing the candybars as far out to

15

sea as he could, and the ocean swallowed them and gurgled happily, at which Seth was happy, too, because he always wanted to give things to people and spirits; once he found a run-over snake for me to boil so that I could make things out of its beautiful bones. Indeed Seth was my friend, and so was Bootwoman Marisa and so was Catherine and so too Ken the street photographer who went out with Elaine Suicide for years until he got sick of her for being so difficult (not that he didn't *used* to admire her for her extreme moods, as when the three of us would go down to the Mission some winter evening with Elaine weeping and bitter for no reason the whole black time, walking three discrete paces behind us, bundled up in her thick wool coat, her arms fiercely crossed while beside me Ken said proudly   isn't she *something?* isn't she *great?*); well, to make a long story longer, after Elaine moved away, sobbing it's not my fault you can't love me; it's only my fault that I found out, why, Ken rose into a whole new career: he screwed white girls and black girls and never changed the sheets so that his van reeked of pussy and Ken pissed in a juice jar and saved it until it was full (a practice he had in common with Seth, except that Seth dumped his out the window every morning, whereas Ken was certain that his was some golden California wine that increased in value with age) and Ken walked down the street with a denim cap pulled very low over his eyes because he said if you don't wear a hat then God *sees* you and *spits* on you!   but though his life was almost perfect the sad truth was that he had never yet *SCREWED AN ASIAN GIRL*, while I had my own Jenny Park who cooked me pork kat-su-don and was sweet to me and yelled at me and made me buy nice clothes and did my laundry, at which Ken said with true reverence,   *wow*, you better *marry* this one!   so once upon a time Ken happened to be driving slowly down a Tenderloin street looking for Brownie, his favorite black whore who wanted to be his girlfriend and had even offered to fuck him in the North Star Laundromat, but on this most momentous afternoon Ken saw, instead of Brownie, a young Japanese woman standing very mournfully on the corner and I wish I could describe the beauty of her smooth face whose eyes conveyed nothing and her black glory of hair, which fell down to her breasts as she leaned a little forward with her lips pursed, looking at Ken in a way that he had never seen before, so he assumed that she must be a hooker wafted to him by the spicy winds of chance and commerce, and pulling over he stuck his head out the passenger window with his faded cap very

16

low above his eyes like a cloud-bar, and he rubbed his unshaven chin and said   get in   and the woman got in and he said   hi   and she smiled very shyly and said   hi   and Ken said   you are *so beautiful!*   and she leaned her round cheek on her palm staring at him as she caressed her elbow and her skin was so soft and fine that Ken could hardly believe it so he said   how much?   and the woman just sat there because she didn't understand for as it turned out she wasn't a whore at all but something yet more still and secret who for some reason never to be known to Ken had just signed an eight-month lease on a Tenderloin apartment that smelled of insecticide while downstairs the old manageress kissed her pet bird over and over as it sat on one finger watching you with its little round eyes just as the manageress was to watch Ken and Satoko with such polite suspicion that the wrinkles radiating from her lips were like a zipper's teeth; and the manageress disconnected the front door buzzer at eight-thirty every night so that no visitors could announce themselves, which in the end was why Ken asked Satoko to give him a key, but I am now anticipating myself like a bad storyteller, for it is even possible that Ken had not yet learned these details when he banged Satoko that first day in his van and her pale shoulders trembled as she made small sounds and the next thing you knew he was buying her groceries and showing her how to cook because she knew hardly any English and was unfamiliar with American foods; Ken therefore became her mentor, pointing to a cat and saying *dog!*, pointing to a dog and saying *cat!* and at first Satoko believed everything that Ken said so he kept teasing her more and more until she laughed and hit him and Ken would say   aw *that's* my girl Tokyo!   and Satoko's father was in the Japanese Mafia and Satoko's upper teeth were false teeth because some medicine she'd had to take as a child had stained her real teeth brown, but for reasons of economy she had kept her lower teeth, which were brown, too, and Satoko lay in bed all day listening to heavy metal music very softly through her headphones while Ken was working and when Ken bought her a chicken she never bothered to put it in her refrigerator, so it rotted on the kitchen counter, at which Ken said   *wow!* she's *amazing!*   and Satoko, who sometimes lay on the bed looking at Ken like an animal with her hands dangling down from the edge of the bed like paws and her lips parted and her pale face shining in the darkness and her black eyes glowing and glowing at Ken, was very melancholy and cried a lot and hardly ever said anything and Ken would come in tired from working for Sheet-Rock Fred and take his dusty jacket off saying   aw *Tokyo* aw *girl*   until Satoko laughed and hit him and I said when was the war of 1812 Satoko?   and Satoko just looked at me; and my friend Bob said   how long have you been in this country Satoko? and Satoko just looked at him (so Bob said to me later in private indignation   why she's a moral pincushion!); and Ken said   aw *Tokyo* aw *girl*   and an enigmatic tear crawled down Satoko's cheek and she hung her head and Ken and I took her to stripshow bars and Satoko just sat there and the three of us rode around in Ken's van very slowly and Ken rolled down his window to yell whenever he saw a whore   *hey* don't you remember me it's *me* it's *Ken Photographer!*   and Satoko just sat there and I made funny faces for Satoko until she smiled.   —Satoko, I said,   are you happy or sad?   but Satoko just sat there. Later Ken said she told him   *I don't like these kind of question!*—   Ken gave her his denim cap to wear so that she would be protected even though that meant that God could see *him* now and spit on him. But Satoko rarely put it on. Ken gave her a sketchpad for Christmas and then she realized that she should give him something, too, and went out to buy him a shirt. Ken put the shirt on and wore it for five weeks straight. Sometimes when Ken was working I bought Satoko a beer in some bar and every washed-up Vietnam vet would say to me   you got yourself a *honey* she's from Saigon isn't she I can tell a V.C. a mile off   and I said   that's right and the vet would say   lemme buy you both a drink   and Satoko would stare down at the counter very peacefully as the vet called out hey Suzy a round apiece for Beauty and the Beast!   and I said thanks and he said   I'm telling you she's a *honey*   by which time I would be explaining all the jokes on the cocktail napkin to Satoko who laughed politely and then our two brown-bottled pledges of allegiance would arrive, thump, thump, and Satoko would say very softly to the vet *thank you*   and she'd drink very delicately beside me until four-o'-clock had come and Ken came bursting in with a big smile and hugged Satoko and said   aw *Tokyo girl!*   and Satoko nodded very seriously and cradled her head against his shoulder. —These outings gradually became infrequent as Satoko developed a somewhat cryptic coloration and withdrew more and more from everybody except Ken. She lived on Oreo cookies and steadily lost weight. If I came to see her (she could not be expected to respond to her buzzer but the manageress knew me by now and let me in if each time I promised never *ever* to do it again), if I went up the stinking stairs and knocked, I might hear Satoko stirring in bed, but she would not answer the door. Whenever Ken went to see his friends she waited in the van, weeping. Ken never knew why. —Neither of them used birth control once Satoko's weird Japanese contraceptives had been successfully used up, so Satoko became pregnant because as Ken said to me   Satoko just *loves* to fuck!   and he said   Satoko marry me and have our baby I'll support you I'll get you U.S. citizenship I'll get us a place to live   because he loved her so much—but Satoko just sat there and raised her chin at him with her heart-locket gleaming against her black dress and then she got an abortion, for which Ken paid half, *then* Ken took her to see his parents and said   hey Mom and Dad guess what this is my wife Satoko she's going to have my kid can you give us some money for a wedding present how about it huh?   but Ken's parents would not believe him, and Satoko just sat there staring expressionlessly at Ken's parents until her visa expired and she went back to Japan at which I said to Ken   why did she come here?   and Ken said laughing I never *did* figure that one out!   and he loved her and missed her so much that he could scarcely bear to screw other women—although he managed once in awhile, it is true, because that way he didn't have to sleep eternally in his van which he drove down to his post box twice a week or more hoping for mail from Satoko who at least would come back in the fall to fly to Bangkok with him, a plan to which she never alluded in the letters that she wrote, saying instead   *I thought I hate fuckin America but I hate more Japan cuz Japan's fuck'n small country. Fuck'n expensive. Fuck'n SAFETY country. I like New York. I love skyscraper. That was so beautiful. Especially night view*   and Ken cried   aw Tokyo what a girl!   and Satoko wrote him saying   *I'm really interested in Occultism, Eroticism, Cruelty, Violent and of cause Insanity. I think I'm mental masochist. Not physical! I don't like to think about happiness. I like dark side of human. I want to go to Greece someday. But I have a problem. Because I don't like Greek food!*   at which Ken laughed and laughed reading her words aloud to me over and over in his van and I was so happy for him and said   Ken don't let her get away I can see you really care about her   at which Ken laughed again because he was embarrassed to be caught caring for someone and Ken showed me a photo he'd taken of Satoko staring so dreamily at a poster of her favorite heavy metal band with skulls and skulls all over and Ken said   I hope she's saving up enough money to come back here   and Satoko wrote Ken   *I'm not alone*

anymore now. So long (Ken did not tell me this for quite a long time; I
heard it first from Painter Ben) and I told Ken I would go to Japan with
him and help him kidnap Satoko if he wanted, but Ken only laughed.
Once he called my answering machine in the middle of the night to
say *well* I'm photographin' the whores [he meant lawyers] in the financial
district! My agent is raisin' two thousand dollars for printing an' it's only
gonna cost me two hundred! I got my first closeup encounter of a
transsexual's pussy, an' I took a picture for you. It kinda caves in, an'
she says its always stays tight an' she can't get any diseases 'cause it
doesn't go anywhere—that was *so* beautiful! and I called the next day
to say Ken have you heard from Satoko? and he said I wrote her
twice but she didn't answer and I said that's a shame and he said
Satoko's *still* my girl and I *respect* her; I'm stopping in Tokyo on my way
to Bangkok and I sent her the flight time but she never answered and if
she doesn't come to the airport I'll respect her more than ever! —Ken
was a friend of mine, and so was stern and tousleheaded Lance in his
greasy black leather jacket who loved to build machines of attack and
destruction and spidery evasion and sat at the keyboard of his computer
smoking and drinking beer and the keyboard was black with grime and
he said now this here is a horse-skull robot that can only shake its head
no at all the *tortures* that this other machine will *judiciously* administer!
and I said well I'll be jig-jagged and he made me a knife out of horse-
bone and I hired him to make me a book with a twenty-pound steel
cover and it was the most beautiful book that I had ever seen and Lance
would always come with me to the transvestite bars and we'd fall in love
with the transvestites together until they would squeeze us and go *oh*
such muscles, at which we'd oblige ourselves to buy them drinks and I'd
try to buy Lance a drink and he'd say to the bar-girl better take mine
because *his* money's no good! then we'd swig and Lance would say
time to get back to work and he'd hop on his motorcycle and I'd wave
goodbye and stand on the corner where Ken first saw Satoko and I'd
lean against the liquor store wall until a pimp would say you got any
questions? and I'd say yeah when was the war of 1812? and Lance
always called me Commander and gave me good recipes for napalm. So
the day went through all of them, stringing them like pearls onto a
necklace of memories. This is why funerals have their place. My friends
were more beautiful to me than they had always been, simply because I
was going away. —But as yet I did not believe the fact. I could not

believe that this wide throat of sunlight that had swallowed us and the ferry so that we could sail to the island of light ahead must soon be strangled, that something would put black fingers on it and squeeze and squeeze until the sunlight choked and died and then the place that I found myself in would be a black place, which was where Elaine Suicide lived. As long as I had known her she had been crying, because although she was loving and wanted to be glamorous (unknowing that she already was) she could not help lashing out carelessly and childishly and selfishly, so she drove away the men she adored and then was miserable and dreamed about them and cried herself to sleep or sat in bed at night smoking cigarettes and watching the moon. I did not want to go to this Crying Place, but because I was leaving my home I knew that I had to; it was black in every direction.

The Compass Rose

I had to go away, and it did not matter in which direction; I would travel like a steady little wave, cool and clean and grey, sliding up the lighter grey sand of Ocean Beach and wetting it to my own shade of grey, and where the sand of memories was wetted it would be so smooth and grey and fresh (as if by licking Elaine's nipples you could make them new). It was summer and everything was hot and waiting for you so you had to expand in some direction . . . but I needed San Francisco to be the center for me when the time for contraction arrived later in the season and I wouldn't have that, I wouldn't—so how could I go in any direction when any direction only took me farther away? —I could hardly go such incorrect ways as west or north; going east would take me too far east; as for south, every step in that direction was a step away from perfection. But the enemy of human nature forced me to go that way. —Yes, I first gave way to the

South

. . . where the ocean just kept coming in and coming in, and black dolphin-fins slid out from under the water sometimes and the dolphins started playing and whistling as I remembered them doing when I was four in Los Angeles and my mother took me walking over the golden hills to see them at the research station and they seemed excited to see me and started leaping and jumping in their tank and the sun was hot on the grassy hill-shadows; so here in Long Beach a quarter-century later the dolphins were still happy and radios played loud in English and Spanish as planes flew overhead and long low tankers sat like the jigsaw pieces of some coastal horizon. Because of the dolphin recollections I could persuade myself for short intervals that I was still at home: anywhere in California, a state in which I had spent half my life, was almost as good as San Francisco. —If, however, I or rather *you* were to go farther south (it *had* to be you who departed; *I* was staying in San Francisco), then the Santa Ana Freeway would bear you through a bright white haze that made your eyes water; the sky was the color of concrete, the trees a quarter-mile ahead blue as in a washed-out snapshot, just like the blue outlines of skyscrapers in Los Angeles's downtown where Japanese restaurants hid inside hotels, pretending that bad air did not exist as they served you eel livers on lacquered red trays, but the one-storey Korean restaurants and beauty parlors sprawled bravely all the way to the La Brea Tar Pits, and although their air conditioners roared you could still taste hellish sulphur smog on your tongue no matter how many sweet rice-jelly desserts you ate—not that there was not a certain GRANDEUR of wide freeway-turns and vibrantly dirty evening breezes and shopping malls like cool clean palaces, but every afternoon was a hot misery to which you must pay reverence as your sports car lurched and shook itself while it sped down its lane, like a wet dog wanting to be dry; and the sunshine was searing in that poison haze and palm trees rose above the puny flatroofed houses and the traffic thickened on the freeway as more and more Buicks and campers and old

22

pickups and U-Hauls and snorting trucks merged, and white smoke came out of the factories and it got hotter and hotter and the air got worse and worse and you sped past a billboard for hair conditioner on which the woman's hair and face were spotted black with exhaust fumes and you made your breaths as shallow as could support life, and buildings were reflected in the shining flanks of the trucks you passed, and the sky glowed more and more angry-white and your eyes were burning and you sweated and felt sick and whenever you inhaled you felt a tickling in your throat and you felt so sick that you longed for the enemy missiles to hurry up and wipe it all out; but if you persisted past San Clemente the traffic would begin to lighten, drained off into the voracious new streets and houses in the former marshes and tawny-grass hills around San Diego, and you would presently come to the sign above the freeway that said MEXICO ONLY and the sign that said LAST U.S. EXIT and there would be the walkway bridge, the low, bush-speckled rises; then across the border in the blue haze was the dizzy glitter of Tijuana with its jumble of low white or grey houses on the hill, with scarcely any space between them, its upholstery and body shops saying WELCOME in case you had gotten into a collision already, its taco stands on wheels at the street corners, its men in billed caps wheeling carts of smoking meat through the traffic, its boys running through the lines of traffic hoping to wash your windows, and the day was hot and the men in tank tops swung their big brown arms. At a corner, a boy guarded a shopping cart full of watermelon pieces. You saw fat women with beautiful orange faces. A man stood in the street waving propeller-toys for sale so hopefully, and there were men in cowboy hats, and fat women and more fat women and so many more, and in the heat there swam the silvery glare of the honking Mexican buses. Sad-faced Indian kids with dirt on their cheeks sold gum, five packs for a quarter. Sitting at a sidewalk café a block down from the burlesque show, you drank Cuervo Gold out of a big red plastic cup and nodded at the men trying to sell you plastic-wrapped bunches of flowers, while from the second- and third-storey patio cafés the music came booming and booming, and you saw bottles gleaming yellow like smilodon tusks in the liquor stores. —How *many*, guy? said a man briskly, holding up a stack of bracelets. —*Zero*, you said. In doorways, Mexicans stood with their feet apart, watching you, rubbing their moustaches, stroking their hair. You pretended that all your friends were there, but you didn't believe yourself; you felt very lost. You longed for San Francisco as Ken still longed for Satoko with her little mouth and glistening white upper teeth and the dear little hairs in her nostrils and the freckles on her nose, her pale broad cheeks, her black eyes watching him as she kissed him—but Ken would have known what to do in Mexico; he'd start taking pictures and in five minutes everyone would be eating out of his hand. Margaret, on the other hand, would have bought things. She had come here with you twice, once to buy a leather pocketbook and once to purchase an extremely handsome grey blanket which you could remember seeing on her living room couch with the sun shining on it as Margaret sat listening to the radio and working and waiting for her boyfriend to take her up to Sonoma for the weekend where the two of them would drink wine and go hiking behind a waterfall that he knew about, and Margaret was humming very softly in the sun; she had sipped a beer at this very table with you and a girl had tried to steal money from her purse. —But Margaret was in San Francisco now, where you would never be again. Best not to think of that now—you were HAPPY! After all, everybody was a whore here; you liked whores. You gave a child some money and his sister came up to the table with her chin in her hands; then came *her* sister with the mahogany face, and their eyes were shining, and the kids all put their arms around you and the boy came back to try to sell you gum again and the girl tried to steal the gum you had already bought and the little girl selling roses patted you sweetly on the back, pulled at your chair. American servicemen with mirror-goggle glasses walked down the sidewalk with their gum-chewing girlfriends. They owned everything. They huddled like crewcut football players in the streets, yelling: *Let's go! Let's go!* —You wondered how the Mexicans could stand not to kill them. The little rose-seller flicked her finger in your face and, smiling, hopped up and down the street on one foot, clutching her four bunches of roses; if you had been in San Francisco you would have bought them all and offered one to each cardinal direction, but here you could not do it; you were spinning and puking; you were *not* at the Center. —You went to a shop where laminated pork sizzled on a spit, and you ordered a taco. They cut off nice slices of the meat that was tender and crunchy like bacon on the inside; they added relishes; they piled your taco with fresh green guacamole. —Yes, *everything* seemed very nice here, but everything was nice only because you beguiled yourself into standing, so to speak, on one leg, with the idiotic self-confidence of the flamingo, who will *not* realize that any passerby could kick the remaining leg out from under him; now suddenly you felt an itch of sad sick anxiety, knowing that even if you were one of those birds who can rotate their heads right around to peck for mites between their own shoulders you would be powerless; you could not quiet yourself even by buying a dozen pigskin wallets, a hundred snakeskin belts, a thousand switchblade combs or drinking horns or knives, but you tried to pretend that you could by wandering desperately down the long tunnel of the bazaar and hoping that the loud stupid music could drown out your thoughts; you proceeded from one shop to the next, from magnet M_{32} to M_{33}, admiring the severe brightness of patterned blankets that partitioned them, noting that the casings of the stilettos seemed to have changed since last year when you had bought one for Ken and he took it everywhere going *click-click!* with such happy brutality that everyone watched him out of eye-corners and Ken laughed and laughed; you remembered this when you looked at some South Korean army handcuffs and you felt good again for a minute; you thought about the Handcuff Queen standing naked with a diamond ring on her long veiny finger and her pubic hair sticking up crackling with electricity and her head bent back for a good hearty yell and her wrists straining ecstatically in the loops of her Taiwanese pair, which were the same kind as the pair you had bought here in T.J. once for three dollars, after which you drove home to promptly and happily handcuff a jug of maple syrup to the refrigerator door to make her laugh, so, wafted Queen-ward on a wave of handcuff nostalgia, you admired the South Korean apparati and made them click eerily through themselves like their own ghosts and asked how much for these?   and the quiet serious Mexican behind the glass case said   fourteen dollars,   and you almost bought them to make up for last time when you went through the bazaars with Margaret and bought nothing but a bottle of vanilla—unheard of!   —You want service? a Mexican had said. —No, thank you, you said. —WHY? the man screamed in despair. A Mexican cried to Margaret: Get this big purse! Big enough to hold *all* your money!   and Margaret laughed and said nothing, so the Mexican turned to you and demanded from behind his big wide sunglasses: You don't want *anything* in this store? —Nope, you said. —You want this purse?   the Mexican asked Margaret.   —Yes,   she said,   but it's too expensive.   —The Mexican looked you up and down in disgust. When he looked away, you knew that you had failed him forever. —Get a Mexican boyfriend, he told Margaret heavily. *He'll* buy something for you! —You still wanted nothing from any store except . . . except . . ., so the operative word to describe your activities was *brachiation*, which is to say the swinging by alternate arms of apes from branch to branch; at some point you would miss and fall because San Francisco was the only tree in the jungle that you knew—no, turning yourself into other animals wouldn't rescue you; you could be a ring-tailed lemur and diddle yourself with the lushly black-and-white-striped appendage that named you, but that wouldn't help in the long run; you could become a bird with an orange head, a bird whose head was crowned with green feathers like berries; but even the most shining of all peacocks must eventually fold his fantail, exhausted, and let it drag on the wet and dirty grass; no, nothing could help you, not a prayer to Jesus at the cathedral with its three yellow domes, each with its cross (you were not pure enough of spirit for your anguish to rise even as high as the clock tower); nor would a prescription for sleeping pills, filled at your parking garage's Farmacia (*fundada en 1950*), be of use even though you inhaled the smell of fresh-baked bread that rose up all the yellow-painted levels to your car—no, not even your car could help you, for you were not allowed to drive in any direction but south—remember?—; you had left your home and could only get farther and farther from it and new things were happening to your friends that you would not find out about because they were not important enough matters for the telephone, only important enough to change your friends just as you yourself were mutating by going south, no matter how exactly you tried to conserve yourself by stopping at Rosarita Beach with its clean sea-clouds and lime-green houses, up against which people leaned and watched you, or at Ensenada, an hour south of T.J., where the restaurants had views of the sea and the prices were still American prices and the menu was in English and the songs played by the live band were in English and the beer was fresh (in the story that surrounds this parenthesis the word "beer" occurs exactly thirteen times, and the word "death" never—drink, then, and live!) and the band played on, but in San Francisco at that very minute restaurants were closing down or opening, and someone else was existing in your apartment and Satoko would never live with Ken in the Tenderloin anymore and Seth had moved to Tennessee where he fell in love with a woman as skinny as he and the weather in San Francisco was different and your friends there were forgetting you or at least doing without you; everything was different. The Handcuff Queen would be eating ice cream now, saying, *So much has changed!* sitting with her legs close together and her bangs down almost to her eyes; and her elbows were drawn demurely in against her body. She would be wearing a blue dress and a white pearl necklace. Her thighs were soft and plump. She finished her ice cream and sat clasping her hands tight between her legs; she was rubbing her thighs together and looking for someone to beat her nicely and you weren't there . . . The farther south you went the worse it got. It is true that Sheet-Rock Fred had sometimes spoken of living in Mexico City for half a year or so; if you went there and waited for a very long time and were lucky you might conceivably see him (if he didn't go to India instead to get cremated beside the Ganges), but then what about Megan? or what about the Handcuff Queen? Once you had gone with that ever so special woman (whom even Ken was afraid of) to the South Pole Bar—a bad dismal place where there were holes between the stalls of toilets so as to pass money and commit other dirty work, a place where it was always dark and the drinkers talked in low voices except when there was a sneering match or a fight; once you had gone there with Fred and the man beside you knocked your Budweiser in your lap and said to you *now smile you sonofabitch!* and Fred smiled and said to you *smile* and you smiled—which later set you afire with shame and rage; it was in this bar that the Handcuff Queen began playing pool with you and everyone laughed because you were such a poor player; everyone was friendly to you and tried to make time with the Handcuff Queen, who taught you things such as NEVER LEAN ON THE EDGE OF THE POOL TABLE OR YOU'LL GET PUNCHED and you thought to yourself *it's really possible; if I try hard enough I can be at home anywhere—look; she does it!* —But later you discovered that she had been born in the Tenderloin. She was not at home elsewhere. —Nor could you ever be at home in Mexico. At night, dark figures stood with bowed heads at the side of the road. They stood beside the shops of baskets and curios; they sat on the sidewalks in three-legged chairs, and there were black hillcurves above the road and the sky was virtually starless; the white road-dots jerked by, and you drove down steep dirt hills where stretches of dingy yellow lights waited to entrap you, and families were standing outside their homes in the hot night; you saw odd long sweeps of white house-wall; you saw a very young pregnant girl crying like Elaine Suicide; you saw a woman pushing a baby carriage, smoking a cigarette whose end glowed in the darkness. Presently you would run out of gas, and then the dark figures would get you. There was nothing you could do about it. You were not allowed to go back home. If you tried, if despite the rules you did turn the red north end of the magnetic needle back toward Bathurst Island,* then they would force you to buy a toy boat, a Madonna, a model of a three-masted clipper ship, and a woman would be moving her lips silently outside your window, with her sleeping baby's head dangling in space behind her, as if its neck were broken, and she stood holding out her beggar's cup . . . If somehow you were to get beyond *her*, either because the car ahead of you had given up or for some more inscrutable reason, such as the fact that the Compass Rose is *empty* in the center of its petals, you must face the man selling fake seagulls, the man selling Corona T-shirts (and the passengers of other cars hunched away from his smiling); and if you inched past them until you were in sight of the border lights that glared grim and white ahead, you would meet the Indian girls who sold brightly patterned wristbands, the big men lugging huge baskets for sale, while other vendors crossed their legs behind them, waiting to lure you into quagmires of fake elephants and horses, lace tablecloths and luggage, a ceramic quadruple-decker hamburger, ceramic peppers, ceramic strings of garlic, in which you would probably be lost forever, trembling and wiping your forehead as men serenaded you in hopes of money, as men walked up and down the frozen lines of traffic with guitars for sale slung over their shoulders like fruit; as men spread thin lace tablecloths before your eyes like wings; as men tried to sell you seat-covers that resembled giant biscuits; and all the vendors nodded and waved to each other and called out loudly to each other while the Americans in the cars talked soundlessly, sealed in glass worlds; women offered you bouquets of roses; a tiny Indian girl, very nicely dressed, tried to sell you vials of dairy creamer and when you said no she shook one at you. —Oh, you were long lost already! —I do admit that the border was getting closer and closer; now you could hear the helicopters that hovered over the fence to keep Mexicans in their place; sometimes their searchlights gleamed on the scale-plates of abandoned cars in No

* The land mass closest to the North Magnetic Pole—*i.e.*, the direction of San Francisco.

Man's Land; now you could read the gleaming white signs that said OPEN/ABIERTA and the darkly glittering glass of the second floor offices ahead looked blankly down at Mexico. Men tried to sell you plastic wedding cakes, blankets, fluffy muppets, erotic playing cards like Painter Ben's; and through the feast of red tail-lights ahead you could see the blue computer screens on the second floor of the border station, and each car was suffused with the jelly-red fog of the car ahead's tail-lights, but you would never get to the border, and if you did the Americans would not let you through, and if they did you would get stuck in traffic forever in Anaheim; and if you didn't, then anyhow as I said San Francisco would have become *different*.

West

Well, so maybe it would hurt less if you went west to Hawaii, where the air was so richly humid that from a thousand feet up, among the steamy trees, it seemed that there was no dividing line between sea and sky, the blueness only becoming richer and richer as your eye descended, as if the air were thickening, hydrogen and oxygen mixing in the breeze and slowly combining like ice cream in a milkshake. The wave-foam rolled in slowly and did not break against the black lava but smoothed sideways along it like bubbles in pumice. It was not too different from San Francisco, where there was an occasional freeway-side palm and at sunset the trees were black against the orange sky, so you should have felt at home, even in this slightly alien sunset that gave the grass a soft color somewhere between silver and gold, even beneath this big red sun, banded like Jupiter, that hung in a vein of pink beside the big blue fatty fog, where the remains of the rain forest lived, but when you turned on the TV you saw a newscaster whom you had never seen before and for that reason you had a bad dream that you were home and in your apartment again in lovely San Francisco but somehow the city had become dangerous and thugs had shot your friend Martin and thugs had smashed Ken's camera and vandalized Painter Ben's best marbleizing jobs and stolen Sheet-Rock Fred's truck and poisoned Monique in a vegetarian restaurant—she died in agony because she couldn't throw up in time—and Vera sat rocking herself and weeping in her Volkswagen that now went nowhere and Elaine Suicide pulled down her pants and stuck her ass out the window hoping the thugs would shoot (but she closed her eyes and winced); as for you, you were being followed by thugs whenever you went outdoors so you had to go to the Communists south of Market Street for help and plead your case with many twirls of a red flag, like a devout Tibetan turning a prayer-wheel, until at last they agreed to render fraternal assistance and then you sat very quietly with the Communists in your room while the military adviser set the charge. He had promised you that nothing in your room would be hurt; the bomb would blow up all the thugs safely and efficiently and inevitably. But you felt uneasy because everyone was staring moodily down at the floor and sipping water from the bathroom sink and whispering. Your ethical double-champions had told you that once the bomb went off you would have to run to escape from the police. Quietly, you got your pistol from the bureau and strapped the holster on. One of the Communists wanted to see it. You kept the gun, but thumbed the magazine release, and the magazine popped softly into your hand and you passed it to him to admire, at which he smiled with a sort of virginal shyness so that you understood that he would now demonstrate the folk arts of his native autonomous region; he put the magazine to his mouth, he placed his delicate brown fingers over the bullet indicator holes and began playing it like a flute; and all the other Communists came and sat on your bed beside you with their arms around your shoulders—yes, it was certainly beautiful, but you felt more anxious than ever because you were disarmed now except for one bullet in the chamber of the pistol; and suddenly the sentry at your living room window hissed and everyone held his breath as the adviser came in smiling; he had set the charges; everything was ready for the thugs—but a woman clapped her hand to her mouth in horror because she saw blood slowly staining his shirt; the thugs had gotten him. Nevertheless no one said anything about it; he had only been a Spartacist who defended bureaucratically deformed workers' states. He sat down heavily on your bed; a compass fell out of his pocket and the needle was pointing west, which was the direction the thugs were coming from . . . now your heart pounded like a string of concussion-bombs because you could see your enemies goose-stepping up the street in their black shirts that said N and S and E and W, and

in their arms they bore a great nuclear compass in a concrete housing—
it was stolen, no doubt—and they threw it down and stamped on its
thick glass face with their jackboots until it cracked inside with many
spider-tracks like the patterns on a frosted window and the thugs
stamped harder until it shattered and then they wrenched the long thin
black sharp radioactive compass needle out of it and strode laughing up
to your window, getting ready to hurl their nasty spear, but then the
dying Spartacist's bomb went off, and there was a silent flash, and
confetti was raining down on the street. Something had gone wrong.
The thugs ran off with their tongues lolling out of their mouths like
dogs. Then the shockwave of the blast struck; your house trembled and
began to move. It slid slowly down the street. (The acceleration vector
is parallel to that of the magnetic force.) You rushed to the window and
screamed to people to stay out of the way, but no one could hear. The
Communists sat on the bed confounded. Your house was going faster
and faster, past the running police and down a hill and up the next one
past the white mansions of Pacific Heights. The Spartacist was dead.
You sped past a May Day procession, a funeral; you slid down Divisadero
Street and up the next hill and down into the sea; the Communists
screamed and tried to shoot out the windows but it was too late; you
were at the bottom of the ocean, a thousand miles down, in a cemetery
of rotten ships and escaped houses; you could never come home again.
—You woke up in Hawaii; you went walking on the lava, which
resembled freshly turned soil in a house-lot in San Francisco, with the
grass running weedy riot; you drove along the coast, on a narrow road
along which yelling teenagers sped in old cars; you visited the ancient
Place of Refuge where the trees were big-leaved and steamy; you drove
on and on until Hawaii seemed to be a part of California, with its sun
and long dry roads along the coast as if it were San Diego or even maybe
Mendecino on a hot day, but there were no smoothies and the
passionfruit juice was not fresh-squeezed the way it was in Berkeley and
there were no helpful toxic-warning decals on the gas pumps although
in Hawaii things were not *all* bad because you *could* suck on rum-soaked
sugarcane whenever you felt like it or pick green coconuts from the tree
and smash them open to drink the milk or mix the milk with rum so
that you forgot that you were not in San Francisco anymore and might
never ever live there again (which meant that you had no home); you
staggered along some black-lava breakwater or other which was guarded

by screw-pines and tree-ferns; you had another belt of rum and there was a warm wind to turn your shirtcuffs into sails; and there were so many red and lavender flowers bursting out of the wall of wet green leaves around the waterfalls and tree-ferns roofed you over graciously, creaking thickets of yellow-green bamboo providing their own flavor of shade so that the air was cool and refreshing to the skin, and your tears of homesickness felt very cool and precious and the bamboo leaned together to make a many-stalked tunnel through which a stream flowed and spiderwebs strung the tops of the banana trees together and everywhere you looked, stalks and leaves made some elaborate shade pattern, and little falls trickled in single or paired streams down the laval wall, rebounding from pool to pool; and there were leaves like spiders, leaves like frogs, leaves wide enough to sit on, taro-leaves like lions' teeth, and you were enchanted with all the shapes but then you came to the top of a great waterfall and the liana-wall was behind you and the fall was before you and below you like a wake, a jet-trail, white within white, passing strata of lava and grass and moss as it rushed down the lava-wall with a sound like gravel; it fell down and down into a black lava-cup that you could not even see into because the ground was very muddy and slippery, and all of a sudden you knew that you were going to fall as your house of dreams had fallen and to keep from falling you had to stand a few feet back from the edge, back behind the Hapu'u ferns and the spiderwebs, and you cried like a baby among the heliconia and the pale orange ilima blossoms.

North

So you blew the dust off the sighting mirror of your compass, whose precision lines framed your face as if you were looking at yourself through the reticule of a sniping rifle; you corrected the black dial for declination and lined up the needle with the baseplate so that you were going due north from San Francisco, and you followed your nose. You knew that north would hurt when its fists began to strike you, but maybe it would hurt less than west. *Never until now have American men and machines*

struck directly at Communist North Vietnam!—DOD newsreel, 1965.
—So you left the beautiful round-faced Vietnamese children rolling marbles in the streets of San Francisco; you left Elaine Suicide rocking herself, smoking cigarettes and saying, I'm *so* sick of myself . . . you left the green hedges of Union Square where the couples sat on the benches holding each other's hands and people sat on the grass that was cut as smooth as pool-table felt and pigeons fluttered over that happy greenness and the shrubs were blossoming in their boxes and the palms rose high in the evening; you left the whores (from whose cunts electricity shot out like maple seeds) on Ellis Street begging you for needles saying   if you ever want a few extra dollars you can get $3 *apiece* for 'em!;   you left the conclaves of sheet-rockers meeting in bars on rainy nights with their yellow slickers white-spattered with sheet-rock stains and the sheet-rockers said to each other   how ya pullin' through?   and they answered   just fine, that's why Walgreen's sells vaseline—haw!— which reminded Sheet-Rock Fred of the one about the difference between eating out a Jewish girl and eating a bowl of Jello; you left home, in short, and went north to Gualala among the blueberries and the huckleberries, and you liked Gualala because it was only half a day's drive from San Francisco and the smell of sun on the clay of the pygmy forest was so good; you loved the way that trees leaned against trees and the way that tree-twigs fared downward like the ribs of fishes, and you fed your compass sweetheart the pale young needle-shoots of spruces and hemlocks because those were the sweetest, and the earth was so luxuriously giving that you could run down an almost vertical slope without fear because your heels sank deep into the loam with every step to make steps for you; you hugged the azaleas for fun; you ate some miner's lettuce, and there was a breeze and the soft hills were like birds waving their fern-wings, but then the blackness that Elaine knew so much about was clawing at you and your heels slipped and you tumbled down the hill cutting your face on prickers and falling farther and farther north, past Willits where you and Seth had set up a tent one night and been scared by a racoon, magnifying it into a brown bear, a black bear, a grizzly bear, a polar bear, a softly terrifying monster of immense cunning preparing to smother you with its night-bulk; you left the state of grace, which is to say the state of California, and continued north to Oregon and Washington; you now dropped entirely out of our great nation, suffering considerably from the speeding helplessness imposed

33

on any particle moving in a circle perpendicular to a uniform magnetic field, and you tumbled into British Columbia with the rivers of the Fraser Valley roaring in your ears; you passed the Canadian Rockies that loomed snowy and tree-bearded high above you; you bounced into the soft wet tundra of Chetwynd, where years before you and Seth had camped and listened to the wind and everything was mossy and lonely; that was the summer that Seth had borrowed your copy of Sir Walter Scott's *Old Mortality* and read it studiously while you both waited at the roadside for a car or truck to come by, to stop, to take you farther north; and Seth would be laughing so hard over the first page that he'd have to put the book down to get his breath, and then he'd chew a little beef jerky and drink condensed milk and look around at the greenness and loneliness and pick up the book again and start all over because he'd lost his place, and before he'd found it again he'd be laughing even harder than before, gasping for breath at the quaintness of the old schoolmaster; roaring and wheezing, he finished the first page and laughed so hard that he had to sit down, and then the two of you got a ride north and Seth put the book away; the next morning by the roadside he took it out of his pack, where it had become dogeared, and read the first page again and it was even funnier to him than before; he read it over and over, and sometime it rained as he stood there, and big raindrops spattered the book and the print ran a trifle, and sometimes you and Seth had to ford rivers and the book got soaked in Seth's pack, and later on you and Seth hiked the Arctic snowfields and the pages froze and stuck together, but enterprising Seth pried them apart with his knife and found page one again and solemnly he stood there perusing its smeared print and the corners of his mouth began to twitch and you could not help but grin as you watched him and the first whinny of laughter burst out of him despite his concentration and he snorted and chortled and chuckled so hard that you were both laughing until your sides ached and the book thawed and froze and got waterlogged and moldy over the weeks and strata of stuck-together pages peeled apart:—although the book was half a thousand pages long and only once did Seth get to page two, it is evident that of all the book's readers, students and devotees Seth was the best and most faithful. —But you and Seth had returned to San Francisco in time; now doing that was against the law. (Seth's housemate Megan still lived there; once she had told you: you know, some of my favorite books I've never even *read*.) Wearily, you impelled yourself deeper and deeper into Canada and it was snowing loneliness all about you and you were in the Arctic archipelago with angled waves striking the shores of islands whose black snow-ridges and snow-knobs swirled with snow, whose big wide gorges were sinewed with snow (once in San Francisco there had been snow at Sutro Tower for a day, so you and your sweetheart, Clara Bee, went excitedly up to see this new thing, stopping at the corner store on Parnassus to get garlic bagels and smoothies and smoked oysters, and you went up hills and hills and the view got prettier with every step; you walked along Ashbury or was it Clayton Street and looked down 17th Street at the Castro and Noe Valley spread out below you in the sun, with Mission Dolores and the palm trees and churches, and you turned up narrowing twisting streets and passed the house that looked like a Spanish dungeon and Clara Bee, who would later drop you like a compass with a stuck needle, was holding your hand and you were thinking about the snow and feeling very happy and here it was, almost a finger-width of it, so chilly, so pure and white, and you two laughed and sprinkled it in each other's hair and had your picnic and agreed to get married and went back down to the sun as the snow, abandoned, melted sadly behind you). —In the Arctic there was all the snow you could eat. The shores of the fjord curved back and forth, and the green-grey water widened until it became the Arctic Ocean. Three white hares with up-pricked ears went bouncing and leaping across the snow in silent anxiety. A great white snow-pyramid stood at the head of the fjord, opposite Skull Point with its low orange sky-bar on the horizon (soon the sun would go away for the night, for the winter; you would not see it until April), and the sharp translucent purple ridge of Axel Heiberg Island was like a knife-edge slicing the evening, slicing your heart open with its beauty, and the sun was painfully orange, about to vanish into the V in the island's last ridge, and there was a purple-grey sea-calm below you despite the freezing breeze; the snow was knee-deep, and a tiny white iceberg floated before the great white headland that you stood on, and the island went on and on northwards through the pack-ice that got more and more contorted until it was mountains to struggle over on the way to the Pole where you could stand homesick and frozen stiff while the world revolved around you . . . Every night in your sleeping bag you put on your one dry pair of socks, a soft white pair that Elaine Suicide had given you, and they felt so soft and warm on your feet that as the nights of whiteness and glare wore on you came to think of them as meaning warmth, and you thought of Elaine and kissed them. But of course you wouldn't see Elaine anymore; you were so far away from her that her suicidal glamor seemed as warm and homey as Sausalito. You remembered Melissa the whore who one day was downcast on Jones Street because she couldn't get any business and the kids were making fun of her; and you loved Melissa, so you gave her a pep talk: Remember, Melissa   (you declaimed),   remember that you are the •prettiest, •sweetest, •most intelligent, •SEXIEST whore on Jones Street, and all men love you and want to date you, but you're only going to date the richest ones, which means that by tomorrow you're going to be a millionairess; you'll have all the dope and crack and smack you want; then I know you'll buy me a giant burger with mushrooms and grilled not raw onions and San Marino relish the way they make it on Clement Street   —and Melissa was smiling and laughing and brightening like a shirt on Haight Street being tie-dyed, because one moving charge does really truly exert a magnetic force on another moving charge, and sometimes two people can even help each other; so you felt good and you felt even better when Melissa hugged you and gave you a kiss for free. But Melissa would not like it up here. No, you would never see her again, either. —Now the wind began to blow and you had to lie inside your sleeping bag for days and days, just as you did when you were up here with Painter Ben and he smoked two packs of cigarettes a day out of desperate boredom and played solitaire over and over while the tent shuddered and strained and he cried out   this is the most idlest trip I've ever been on!   and the water froze and the toothpaste froze and your boots froze solid and all your socks except for Elaine's froze and you licked your lips suffering from California orange juice withdrawal and day by day the wind nudged your tent and shrank it around you because the ground had been frozen so hard that you hadn't been able to stake the corners down so you'd had to hold them with rocks which the wind rolled closer and closer on all sides and then the six-month darkness came and you lay trapped in a frozen scream with a film of ice over your mouth and eyes like the Franklin Expedition seamen in their graves on Beechey Island, and as your blood slowly turned to a reddish-black popsicle you dreamed of escaping south but your feet had been so long frostbitten that they were gangrenous and even if they weren't, even if you could start running south and south across the frozen sea, you would eventually fail the test

36

of Orpheus and look behind you, whereupon you would see a white speck sunning itself on greenish ice—a polar bear! and even as you looked at the bear the bear looked at you and began following you; he was gaining on you, grinning a black grin at you and you could see the darknesses inside his ears; he smelled you and saw you all too well; he was running toward you to devour you; and even if you were to cut a hole in the sea-crust with your ice-axe and dive in, you would not much postpone your fate; the polar bear would wait beside and a little behind the hole so that you could not see anything, waiting to swat the life out of you with his paw, and hypothermia was getting you in the water anyhow, to say nothing of oxygen starvation, and you knew that life was only going to get worse. —No, north wouldn't do at all, so by default you had to proceed

East

On this longest day of the year you were going away from L.A. on a warm desert evening with houses all around, sucking up the water like vampires, and you kept going through the dry mountains and down into dusty blue valleys, heading steadily east, and as night fell you sped down and down to Needles and the air got hotter and hotter as if you were going to hell and the motels glowed with neon lights, one color per customer, and you crossed into Arizona and there were ocotillos and chollas and lightning-flashes all night as you lay naked in the hot hills and yearned already for San Francisco as Ken yearned to kiss the stubble in Satoko's armpits as she stood there in her black nightgown looking at him with her hands on her head and Ken said   Tokyo? Tokyo? Are you my girl?   and she smiled and said very softly   yeah   and the next morning you continued east along Highway 40 and the blue mountains and mesas rose like dreams above the yellow grass. North of Flagstaff, in the San Francisco Peaks where the Hopi kachina-spirits live, lightning flashed like a snake's tongue. It was sunny, and it thundered. Little raindrops fell upon your lips. You lay upon a rock, and red ants crawled there, and black ants, too, as big as your toe. Again you chewed the tender tender needles of evergreens. (When you brought a handful home, Margaret thought them too bitter.) Dandelions and blueflax danced in the meadow; in a sandier spot you came across the reddish-orange treasures of Indian paintbrush. You ran uphill through the tunnels of white aspen and reached another hot yellow meadow browsing with bees, and more aspen forest whose creamy trunks were as smooth as poles, and then a steep slope of evergreen forest, which was littered with the grey trunks of windblown trees, some hollow, some swarming with ants, and after much labor among the snapping twigs you came to the crest of the hill and there was a grassy dome where mulleins grew as high as your head and inside each one was a white moth and the blades of mountains rose purple-grey, high above the rolling hills, whose grass was soft like yellow corn-dust, and the smell of dust was good and clean, and there was snow on Humphreys Peak; and you ran laughing down and down again, past a dead black witching-tree with branches like ribs, like the branches in Gualala, like the branches everywhere, and you continued east, with flat ridges in the distance speckled with greyish-blue shrubs, and it was night and then morning and the patches of sunlight on the chaparral made it gold; and there were clouds over the mountains with cloud-stuff eternally bursting from them in a frozen explosion of purity, and you saw a purple scorpionweed and then trees and dust and mountains. But the San Francisco Peaks were not San Francisco . . . Continuing east, nonetheless, because you had to, you traversed the Painted Desert with its many distances of blue and grey and yellow; you stopped at all the diners you could, so as to look at the proud darkskinned waitresses in their silver-adorned belts, with their black hair that fell loose or braided to their waists, hurray! They brought you red chiles and green chiles; they tossed their heads in a glitter of turquoise earrings. Their Spanish accents were sweet to your ears. As they served you, you pretended that you were home and it was sunny and foggy as it so often is in San Francisco, as it was that time when you tried to drum up business for the Handcuff Queen so you brought Martin to her beauty parlor and the Handcuff Queen poured you wine and started cutting Martin's hair as strangely as she could, so that it hung down over his forehead like a wet braided root, and when "You Only Live Twice" came on, she hummed along and said, *oh! turn it up!* and meanwhile one of the other girls said   I have a date to get my earlobes sewn up this afternoon   and the Handcuff Queen said   are you for *real?*

and Martin said   I want my ears to show   and the Handcuff Queen cried exasperatedly   *why* do you always wait till the last minute to ask that? It's like waiting till the last minute to ask for a rubber!   and Martin said   you see I just don't want my boss complaining   and the Handcuff Queen drank more wine out of a paper cup and said coolly that's *his* problem   but then she asked tenderly   so can you handle having a little more fullness down there or should I take it down more? and the music was sunny and spicy as the Handcuff Queen cleaned a razor and applied it between head and ear, as meanwhile Lisa beside her finished with her last customer;—   usually I take a bike ride after work but today I don't think I will,   said Lisa, frowning into the mirror and spraying her hair with delicate toots of the atomizer, and you yawned and had another cup of the Handcuff Queen's wine and Lisa said   aren't you even going to ask why not?   so you finally said   why not?   as you looked out at the sunny street and Lisa said   'cause I've been *drinking* since ten-o'-clock and I'm going to take a nap!   and the Handcuff Queen said   you sure can't hold your liquor girl you must've been in that bathroom a dozen times!   and Lisa walked with little wriggles and hip-thrusts whenever your eyes or Martin's eyes were on her and you had another cup of the Handcuff Queen's wine and you were perfectly happy, like Elaine Suicide when she was a little girl at Catholic school and she sang the Pied Piper song so well that the nuns gave her a whole string of lollipops. Now you wouldn't see Elaine or the Handcuff Queen or Lisa or Martin anymore; nor would you meet any of the Arizona or New Mexico waitresses again, but precisely because they were vanishing they reminded you of home, so you enjoyed thinking of them just as you used to do with Painter Ben while you and he zipped along in his white Gem Top, a long trail of dust pointing the correct direction behind you, the direction opposite to yours, and you tried to occupy yourself by visualizing the waitress at the Four B's Diner (*Be Hungry, Be Happy, Be Healthy, Be Back*), even though you remembered less and less of her; you could barely see her hair spilling down her back anymore, streaming like a Hawaiian waterfall from its wide beret (and you fell down the waterfall into the black cup; your house fell into the ocean; you fell onto the North Pole and were impaled); you could barely see her sad, stern face, and you had never known what she was called. —What do you think her name was?   you asked Ben.   —Maria,   he replied,   they're all Marias. She had a nice little beer belly on her,   he added unromantically. But you were sure now that she had been glamorous, like Elaine Suicide . . . In Albuquerque Ben bought glass Christmas tree ornaments at the crafts fair to give as presents because, he said, I resent it when people give *me* gifts—if I can't eat it or use it up, at least let it be glass so I can break it! —He was going to give them away in San Francisco. But *you* weren't. You were travelling too far, too fast, because you were travelling away. You had to go this way; you had been a butterfly of the four directions and this was the only one left. San Francisco westened and westened behind you . . . In Utah, Suzie the blonde waitress smiled at you as she brought you your fried chicken and buttermilk, and she asked you if everything was OK and could she bring you anything else and she really meant it and when you were finished she said to *please* have a *good* night and because she reminded you of Megan the Georgia beauty queen, who reminded you of home, you drew a heart with an arrow through it on the check and then you paid and went out, peering shyly at the mechanical bear across the street that raised its arms ever so slowly as if to bless you, and outside the town the red buttes were dotted with green . . . In the twilight, when the deer came out, and a hot evening wind blew your tent like a tumbleweed so that you had to run to catch it and stake it down, the cliff-castles of Utah darkened and the grass became pale and vague and the cicadas sang and the crag-walls far away were purplish-blue and the sky was a glowing bluish-yellow like a lantern slide of a faded watercolor, and the shape of every leaf was black and perfect above the ridge where the sky was, but below it the trees were inkblots on sticks; and the light in the sky became darkness, and everything was so beautiful that you were miserable because you were going to leave it. You had to keep going east. For a long time you sat in the darkness, feeling the warmth of it and the space of it, watching the lovely desert stars until the sky began to glow again and the northern rim of the canyon began to be visible again in all the deceptive detail of moonshine, and the cliff-wall to the south was so solid black with moonlight behind it that you wondered how you ever could have tried to go south; and the night went on and on around you . . . Yes, you were going east. But you would resist. You would not set your watch forward, ever; you would stay on San Francisco time. You would always tell people that you were from San Francisco, even ten years from now. You would call San Francisco every day; you would call the people you knew there and make them wave their receivers out the window so that you could hear the fog and the clouds. You would never buy a bed; you would only sleep in a sleeping bag inside a tent in the exact center of whatever living room you might be forced to rent, with your head facing west. You would keep your possessions in a suitcase; you would maintain your compass at San Francisco declination. —You would do none of these things. You would take the plane and get it over with. (You were pathetic because you could not keep what you loved the way it was.) You would fly out of Las Vegas because that gave you an excuse to go a few miles west again, back toward the center of the Compass Rose, San Francisco, with all its lovely pistils and stamens . . . Rolling west through the Virgin Mountains, brightening with every spurious mile, you rode the smooth freeway past gas station-casinos whose signs said things like   NO BARE TOPS   NO BARE BOTTOMS   NO BARE FEET   and you drove past the exits that vanished eerily behind desert ridges so that you could never see any of the towns to which they hypothetically led. Enjoying the heat on your elbow that rested on the frame of the open window, you came to a rise and suddenly saw the dim blue skyscrapers of Las Vegas, and mountains very far behind them, riding the haze as though whatever connected them to earth had been dissolved; and presently every exit led to houses and trees and condominiums and hotels and then you got to the Strip. —The airport was surrounded by obscenely green grass watered with sprinklers, every drop of which should have been worth as much as a drop of blood; and inside it was air-conditioned and there was a ripply pattern on the carpet so that you felt like Christ walking on a coolly buoyant sea, and the slot machines sang songs like two-note electronic xylophones.

Leaving

My T-shirt is dirty from travelling, so I decide to buy another. How many exiles, after all, have you seen disembarking from the military jet without a suit and tie to cozen the press crew that stand scuffing their feet in the gravel of the strange runway? I see an extra large shirt that says LAS VEGAS and I think it would make me belong to own it, so I pay the ten bucks and take it into the MEN's room, where I strain and strain to pull it on, thinking, my, these foreign customs! and all the MEN are looking over their shoulders at me as they piss, making me more and more embarrassed until I finally wrench that uniform of alienness down over my head there in front of the mirrors where the MEN are washing their hands and staring at me, but the tail will not even reach to my belly button. Maybe this means that I should not have left San Francisco. Please, Sheet-Rock Fred, where are the twenty-three hundred Japanese warriors who will ride silently across the moonlit snow to avenge me? —Oh, we only sell children's T-shirts, explains the saleslady, and there are *no* cash refunds; I'm *really* sorry. Maybe *this* one would fit, sir—unless you'd rather exchange it for a baseball hat. —Like Fred, I have no samurai sword with which to let the anguish inside my belly loose upon this unsuspecting world. I could slit myself open with my Buck knife, I guess; instead I take the other shirt, which does fit, just barely, but burdens me from groin to clavicle with the giant countenance of Mickey Mouse leering at the world like some wide-eyed buck-toothed Big Brother. Seth's friend Patricia, the one with the stuffed dolphin, might now admire me, but I cannot admire myself, and the MEN stare at me as if I am retarded. —Indeed I am, for thus accoutered, I have thoughts of seeing Las Vegas. Maybe I'll find some easy fifth direction, some *something* about the place that I can adjust my needle to. —If not, then I can deny the future a little longer (not that I don't know how silent everyone will be on the airplane during the silent movie and then they will be restless and go back and forth in their seats so that they'll hurt each other's knees and they'll gobble sandwiches and thrust their heels into each other's knees—how madcap!)—deny it, I say, by peering round me at this glaring blaring present so bereft of associations. I don't care about anything.—Las Vegas it is.

First things first: Downstairs.

Where can I go where I can sit and have a drink and not be bothered? I ask the lady at the ice-conditioned limo concession.

Well, she says slowly, the drinks at the Barbary Coast aren't *too* expensive.

Does Mark Dagger go there?

Mark Dagger? Oh, you mean the one with all the rhinestones? Yes, I believe I saw him there the year before last, with Johnny Carson. That's the Mark Dagger you mean, isn't it?

That's the one. How about Satoko?

Satoko? Can't say that rings a bell. You know how it is; there are so many stars coming through here. Sir, there's a line behind you. Do you want a ticket for the Barbary Coast or not?

The Barbary Coast it is!   I cry genially.

The ＿＿ look at me and shake their heads.

I pay, I go out, and thanks to all my practice with orienteering north and south I soon locate the line of people, owned by their leaden suitcases, who stand wiping their foreheads and hitting their children and waiting for the limousine.

You going to the Riviera?   inquires the "starter," a wolfish tallish tanned lifeguard type whose blond haircut must be worth at least a hundred bucks. His skull is derived from the primitive diapsid condition.

Not me, I say.   The Barbary Coast.

The ***BARBARY COAST!?!!!!!!!***   cries the "starter" in horror. What *do* you want to go *there* for?

People are shuffling and coughing. My indecision is wasting their time.

I just want to sit down and drink and be left alone,   I explain weakly

but the "starter" shouts: *No one's* going to *hassle* you; Vegas is *not* that kind of town!

and one of the tourists says disgustedly   what did you *come* here for if you don't want to spend money?

and I say   well, uh, I *do*, maybe even five or ten dollars . . .

and he looks away from this shamefully unflushed dissident turd called me, and everyone else looks away, too

and he pretends to puke

and he claps me on the shoulder and says: how about it, *pal*? The Riviera or not?

The Riviera it is!   I say bravely. (Would that the Handcuff Queen had shackled my tongue!)

Into the limousine. The "starter" snaps the rope behind me; I am the last passenger on this crossing to Paradise and the others must wait. The driver opens the door for me. The back seat appears to be full, although I cannot say for sure because I have not gotten inside yet and so my science-fiction sunglasses have not undarkened. —Well, I had just better swivel my butt in (hoping that my raggedy bluejeans, which hang very loosely around my hips [because despite the many plate-heaps of green and red chiles served me by the afore-mentioned Arizona and New Mexico waitresses—whom I can never forget—I have lost ten pounds in the desert], will not slide down to my ankles, thereby revealing that I am not wearing any underwear—for the sufficient and simple reason that all I own is dirty), but as I thus position myself as close to the window as possible, I hear a scream, and nerve-messages speeding to my brain make me understand within mere seconds (such is the speed of the average neuron) that I have sat down on a child sitting in its mother's lap.   —*Sorry* about that,   is all that I can say, but there is only icy silence, so that I wonder if perhaps I didn't say it at all, but only thought it—but then it would be even worse if I *had* said it and forthwith said it again like some smart-aleck from Nowheresville, so I keep silent, with my ass sticking out the open door while I wonder where to put it. —Disgustedly, the driver comes back and flips down a special seat for me like a baby seat that was right in front of me all along, but I would never have discovered it, because it was concealed in the black vinyl complexities of the front seat and even now my glasses are only half-undarkened. So I sit down; my pants do slip down an inch after all, and there I am half bare-assed in the baby seat with my Mickey Mouse T-shirt on and I am definitely in Las Vegas.

It is very dark inside the limo, which is only allowed to be air conditioned when the driver has passengers and is in motion, which is to say now. The driver pulls quite rapidly away from the curb, at which I stare as if it were long-lost San Francisco; I want to imagine another farewell party at which my best friend, the "starter," is the honored guest; for I am leaving him now, too, leaving, *leaving!* and the driver thumb-stabs the most powerful icy-cool button available so that the air conditioner shrieks in my ears as if I were back in the Arctic and in despair I ask myself   now why didn't I go *that* way?   forgetting that I already did, forgetting the terrifying magnetic storms—but then oblivion is my heart's desire; I admire the wind-scream of this limousine precisely because it mercifully masks whatever any of the other passengers (whom I still can't see) may or may not be saying about me; meanwhile it is still very hot. —Off we go.

Between the streets are sand dunes and desert shrubs. We pass by the Pussycat with its SEX ACTS, and more sand dunes and scores of other places that say *SEX SATIONAL* or **TOPLESS** (now I know where the BARE BOTTOMS people who aren't allowed into the gas station casinos must come: in these places, I am sure, the B-girls' breasts are the size of other girls' buttocks; nothing would be more American and directionless than to squeeze those sweetnesses), and we pass more sand dunes and then we're on the Strip and there are green lawns everywhere.

Outside the Riviera, where the air is hot enough to give me hyperhidrosis, everyone gives the driver a two or three dollar tip. I reach into my pocket (which has a hole in it), hesitate between two pennies and a dime, and finally give him a quarter.

Thank you, sir, he says very stolidly.

I am not sorry for him. After all, I am an exile; after all, he'd never helped with *my* baggage!

The limo departs. I reach into my shirt pocket, pull out my compass, and throw it down on the sidewalk. It does not smash until I grind it under my heel. I kick it into the street and a car runs over it.

Now for **GAMBLING**. That is what you do when you have been expelled from San Francisco—which has happened to me! This is the most hateful place that I can imagine—because I am in it. (I remember a breeze, and Margaret smiling, and decide never to remember it again.)

Where can I get change for the slot machines? I ask the bell captain, whose flaming livery and upturned moustache, upon whose ends I half expect to see balanced a pair of glass balls, proclaim him more a man of the world than I in my Mickey Mouse shirt could ever hope to be.

Thirty yards to the left, he says, troubling himself even so far as to point in that direction, which I still know; all the same I am grateful to him, for I hope not to know it much longer.

I take a sighting on a change machine, and try each of my dollar bills, but they are too dirty; the machine will not take them, and so as usual, like Ken saying Tokyo? Tokyo, why are you crying?, I am defeated. I walk on into the dim coolness, stunned by the thunderous percussions of jackpots, the suspenseful reveille-tootings and hummings of slot machines, and I see a fat man playing electronic poker and the colored lights are glaring on his glasses; I see a woman pull the lever and win two quarters and purse her lips very tightly and look both ways like a bad dog shitting on the carpet; I find a human-operated change booth at last and request ten dollars in quarters and the woman (whose cheeks have been marbleized as if by Painter Ben) gives me a roll and says ten

45

dollars!, and *winks* at me and I smile back and start putting them into a slot machine one by one. The machine eats four dollars and then chokes and turns red and vomits a dollar fifty into my hand, and I am quite elated because I have *won*. A cocktail waitress who happens to be all legs comes by, but I do not want to drink standing, like a needle that does not dare to spin; suddenly I feel that something terrible and secretly expected is about to happen to me, striking me from that hypothetical fifth direction or some strange angle previously unmeasured by my compass clinometer; so I turn north and east and south and west (the known and therefore useless directions), searching for danger; needless to say, with my compass broken as in my dreams I am not aligned for any use, and there is nothing to do but listen to the paunchy corpses cheering at the CRAPS table (everything here reminds me of excrement); and after that why not go out and sit by the pool, where beautiful girls and ugly girls dive into the shimmering blue water, cleaving it with their hands and swimming true west toward my former home while I think about the shit and bowels inside them? They dive and dive; out of habit, or perhaps in Ken's memory, I look between their legs. I am becoming evil.

Cocktail? *hints* a new waitress who's also all legs.

A margarita, please, I say.

Knowing that it will be $3.50, I have the money already counted out from my change cup, plus a 50¢ tip to display my graciousness, there being nothing left to aspire to any longer but the noblesse oblige of the bell captain, who has assuredly forgotten me. I will never see him again. —Miss Legs returns with my margarita, which is to say my chilled heap of salt-topped white slush in a plastic goblet, and it does not look at all promising, but then neither do I, for I am wretchedly sad, weary and bestubbled; I am an outlaw—or would be if I were not the Ghost of Insignificance.

Three-fifty? I say.

Exactly, says Miss Legs, bored.

I give her the four, and she sweeps it into her apron without counting it, which grieves me and makes me wish that I hadn't given her any tip—for at the end of the day how will she know that it was *I* who thought so considerately of her? (Already I am falling into old habits: I seek to make friends and become KNOWN. Why don't I go fuck myself? —But I'd asked myself that in Tijuana.) Not only that, but the margarita tastes like sugared pool cleanser. Shaking my head like Lance's horse-skull robot, I peer down through the sweet and translucent waste of liquid that must go inside me now that I have PAID for it and I can see the bottom of the goblet bulging out like the lens of a magnifying glass, and that makes me queasy. Probably the anticipated awful thing, whatever it may be, is starting to happen to me already. In this hot white place, enclosed by white hotel walls, I watch the women in their bathing suits and try to forget how stupid everything is. (Nobody's as beautiful as Megan; no one has the class of the Handcuff Queen.) The rest of my life, I know, will be much the same: a uniform magnetic field. I will sit and drink these chemically flavored chemicals called margaritas until I *know* that I am about to be sick; come to think of it, I will do that NOW; this will not be one of those sustained binges in which I keep breaking through into new states east of California, as if I were falling through layers of ice too thin to bear my weight, having drunk the strength out of them—no, this will not be any such noble thing; but rather a purgation simple—which is all that Riviera margaritas are good for anyhow. In short, I am going to be sick. I want to be, need to be; I welcome the third margarita, the first burning belch, the bubble stuck in my windpipe, gluing lung to lung, the belly-twitchings that wriggle Mickey's big ears derisively against me like melting cocktail stirrers, like the nuptial tubercules of snakes; this thought certainly makes me sicker as I order another round from Miss Legs (no tip), and drink it down and then the next, which convinces me that there is indeed no difference between Las Vegas and Tijuana; now for Number Five, and everything is empty like Satoko's bed in the Tenderloin beneath which the dust grows higher on the gigantic heart of barbed wire which one of Painter Ben's girlfriends made for him (the night before Satoko left for Japan he brought it by as a farewell gift, and she said thank you and abandoned it); the sixth drink conflates Hawaii with Canada, and the sweetness of the seventh is so successfully disgusting at last that I stand up proud and tall and sneering and I vomit into the pool, just like the ocean puking up its thousands of jellyfish like translucent little abortions when it was misfed, for which Seth's candybars could never have been enough recompense even though he spent the nethermost nickels in his pocket on them; I lean forward and vomit all over the swimmers and everyone screams and the brownish-green slush of margarita-puke begins to diffuse itself gently throughout the pool and I puke again—BLOOD this time, very dark

47

blood; something is stuck very fast in me—oh, I do not *want* it to come up!—but I puke again and feel a human head expelling itself through my throat, and I know that if I had a flashlight and a mirror I would be able to see that wet drowned scalp glistening behind my tonsils, just as a baby's head is "crowned" in the mother's vagina during the penultimate stage of birth; I am choking and retching and finally I vomit Monique out, in little heaves and stages, and her corpse floats face-down in the pool, with a cape of hair swirling around it, and her limp arms stretch out ahead of her, pointing west to San Francisco, so that, as cool as a scholar in the midst of my grief and anger, I deduce that she must have been the Ghost of Magnetism after all; and the beautiful swimmers have rushed out of the pool and are shrieking in horror and here comes the bouncer; I am sick again; I have to be, and I vomit up dead white Vera in sad white bits that float and mingle with her lover as they mingled with her inside me; I vomit up the stream of pure water that Martin once gave me, and it splashes into the pool and sullies itself with blood and booze and memory-flesh; it was fresh only inside me. In a series of horrid papery retches I yield up Seth's candybars at last. I vomit back all the meals that Painter Ben ever gave me, and the hands that Megan never let me kiss; there they float in the pool, with the dead fingers curled, bleeding from their stumps, and it is a wonder that those gracefully tapering fingers of hers didn't choke me as they came up. I upchuck a cup of wine that the Handcuff Queen poured for me once when I visited her in her marbleized beauty parlor; I cough up all the Thanksgiving turkeys that I never had, and they splash into the blue water one by one, floating with beseechingly upraised drumsticks. Now I feel emptier and San Francisco is not pulling me and hurting me quite as much, but there are so many more memories still inside me that must be given back before the compass bearing can be adjusted!—and the bouncer is HERE.

You're going to have to leave, sir, he says.

Ohhhhhhhhhhhh-KAY! I reply jauntily, snapping my finger in his face. He is a family man; he has a home; he won't dare to do anything. He will hush up the fact that I have eaten human flesh.

I walk out into the hot sun, wiping my mouth on my sleeve. My sense of direction is weaker. As Laddie the hobo would say, how *nice* that we get to look at the view! —I wander up and down through the Strip

48

and at last find a casino called Golden Memories. —What a *perfect* name, I say to myself. —Here I will enter; here I will have done.

My pockets are bulging with quarters—I am weighed down with change! Everyone from San Francisco is in my pocket. How wearily heavy they are! I must get rid of them. —I rush to the bank of slot machines and no one even looks up and the slot machines are blinking and glowing and chirping and popping with a magnetic flux of at least 937 billion webers per square meter and I close my eyes and spin myself around so that I will be dizzy and not know *right* from *left* from *wrong* and my outflung wrist strikes the corner of a 25¢ machine with a thud that hurts and blood runs down to my hand from a harmless little triangular cut (but although to others I seem unsteady, an increasing steadiness of *perception* comes into play, so that I know I could go on forever, weary, aching, but perfectly alert, ready to sip at still another margarita) and I take out my first quarter, with Margaret's face on it, and she is beautiful and smiling as she was on her thirtieth birthday when there was a surprise party for her in Golden Gate Park and I kiss her cheek but the quarter only tastes like sweat and dirt and tarnished cold metal. With remorse and deepest sorrow, I nudge the quarter into the slot and pull the lever. (None of this is voluntary.) There is a clang, and pictures whirl meaninglessly around behind the tiny rectangular window, halting at last with a display of three not quite identical bottles, probably because Margaret and I once drove up to the wine country and tasted three different kinds of Sonoma wine on a humid sunny day when everything smelled like grapes and I thought then that I would keep that day in my heart forever. —Surprise! —Martin's quarter wobbles and trembles on the edge of the slot, but I flick it in and pull the lever, losing him forever with only two stylized roses and a pistol remaining behind the window to remind me of the time he set me up with two women, one after the other, whom I took on shooting dates, and so never saw again. No, they had not cared for me; but Martin had done his best. —Paul and Nancy, when spent, send the picture-symbols clanging and clicking about, stopping at last, with a quietly definitive click, upon a Christmas tree, a blue droplet and a mountain—the three memorializing, I believe, the forest path that Nancy and I walked along on a summer afternoon when the streams were wide and we both agreed that we were going to live in San Francisco, the blue tear being one of those that ran so soundlessly down Paul's cheek on the night that he and I parted; as for the mountain—what a shame to give up that glorious mountain! White Mountain Peak it was, and Paul and I clambered up it stone by stone from the hot desert through the sandy tree-wastes and the sloping meadows, all the way to its rocky icy shoulder, from which the two of us looked down at the Sierras and the Owens Valley and the whole world green and blue below us; we imagined that we could almost see San Francisco, and we slapped each other's shoulders proudly;—but now, alas, White Mountain Peak is only a stylized purple triangle with a jagged fringe of white—living dead behind that narrow window (in a slot machine memories become cartoons), waiting beside its brother symbols, the droplet and the tree, for the next pull of the lever that will make their relation vanish, and I turn away so that I can see neither mountain nor tree nor drop anymore; I want it that way. I close my eyes; I see circles with crossed lines inside them whirling and wheeling in the darkness (a magnetic flux line has no beginning, no end), and a lady pants beside me as she crams her quarters desperately in. I gamble away Laddie and Sharie and Painter Ben; but when I try to spend the Handcuff Queen my machine goes *ding-ding-ding-ding!* and the display says **BAR BAR BAR** and a choking rush of quarters clatters in the pan. There are Paul and Nancy again, frozen-etched smiling and waving on their two-headed quarter; I must say goodbye again now; but happily the other quarters awarded me are new ones, bearing only the blank profile of George Washington. —I move to another machine; I do not want to risk getting any more of my real quarters back. (These alien quarters, they're fine: I can spend them on drinks on the airplane.) —Goodbye, Paul and Nancy! Now I drop Mark Dagger into the slot, and pull the lever, and get two knives and a needle—*ding-clunnk!*; Dickie yields a knife, a needle and a bottle (but what a pity it was to spend those skinhead quarters; the stern bald profiles were so patriotic, so special); Sheet-Rock Fred scores a **BAR BAR BAR** again because that was where he used to drink and Seth gives me candy **BAR BAR BAR** as he did the ocean and my friends are vomited up again and I have one more chance to keep everyone whom I fed into this machine, but I cannot do it. —Seth whirls into the slot never to return. Fred hesitates on the lip of that maw for a moment because his edge is scratched and burred, but I roll him in and the eagle on his back goes whirling and tumbling with outspread wings like Fred sailing to India with one day's supply of food and I pull the lever and the slot machine goes *g-chunk-chunk-chunk!* and comes to rest on a white bottle, a red bottle and a turkey, because over Christmas turkey Sheet-Rock Dave once said to Sheet-Rock Fred I hope I got the right color wine, because you see I'm not a real wine *connoisseur,* and Fred smiled a little and rubbed his beard and said: well, Dave, there are only two rules about wine: number one, the color of the wine should be the color of the meat; and number two, whatever you do you're going to be a *fool!*—and *anyhow* Dave there's no such thing as a wine connoisseur, because a *connoisseur* is just an *entrepreneur* on a heap of *manure,* since he's just *conning* a *sewer,* don't you see, and a sewer is what most people are! Marisa and Melissa, Catherine and Ken, Megan and Satoko I gamble away, shoveling in a handful of George Washingtons like clods upon the grave, and then I am done—except for Elaine.

The Angel of Happiness

Elaine Suicide often wore fingerless gloves. She had big movie-star eyes and fine brown hair with reddish highlights. When she was bored or sad she put her hand on top of her head and stared into her elbow or somewhere else that nobody including her could see, but we used to draw pictures together because Elaine was always into art of one sort or another, taking photographic self-portraits (Ken let her use his dark-room) and composing xerox art and drawing herself having her period shaking her pale fists with blood storming down from the black cloud between her legs and blood popping out of her nipples and jagged blood-lightnings flickering in her screaming mouth and black shockwaves streaming out from every part of her like sunlight, and she saved clippings from the *San Francisco Chronicle* about women's sexuality and adored Madonna and for that reason went to see Madonna movies over and over. She took herself very seriously; she made lists of things to do to perfect herself like

Stop biting my nails * continue to dance every morning * see movies movies movies * walk the dog when you don't want to * do the

51

dishes when you don't want to * only buy what you need when you need it * decide what it is you want (pertaining to all levels) * draw a design with water color ideas * begin notes on a very interesting film * stop eating between meals * clear up complexion * always be nice to people on the phone * don't sulk * don't whine * be cool—fire and ice * shave legs and armpits regularly * cry when you feel like suicide is the only answer because crying is better * kiss Mom hello

and Elaine made calculations to determine approximately how much time she had left in this world in top form, taking account of her twenty-three day physical cycle with her peak at day six, her twenty-eight day intellectual cycle with her peak at day eight; and Elaine wrote **Figure out days alive: Age × 365** and she thought and added **1 day for each leap year you've been alive** and she smoked cigarettes all night lying naked on her bed looking out the window at Sixth Street with its winos sleeping and the financial district's towers and pyramids being cemetery-beautiful in the moonlight and streetlights and all the flat roofs below her scrunching down so that she could look out over the world and she added **1 day for your last birthday** and she added **the # of days since your last birthday (don't count Feb. 29 if it's there; don't count your birthday; don't count today)** and she went through the algorithm and concluded **Round this off to a whole # and that's the day of that cycle you're in.**

For awhile she was reading Goethe, which she pronounced Goath, and I never corrected her because I thought where do I get off telling her how to pronounce the guy's name when I can understand perfectly what she means and anyhow I hate it when people tell me how to pronounce things, so when Elaine said I think that Goath is so *profound* I just said I agree a *hundred* percent, Elaine; I agree a *thousand* percent— but when Elaine found out that it was actually Goethe she was so angry at me that she called me up just to cuss me out.

I'm sorry, I said.

I can't *believe* you'd let me mispronounce it in front of you for *weeks!* stormed Elaine.

Well, I said, I guess I'm just a very conservative person. I would never tell you to change, Elaine, because change of any kind makes me sick to my stomach.

Getting to know Elaine was like listening from start to finish to the Suzanne Vega compact disk that she bought in order to record one particular song onto the soundtrack of her film with maximum fidelity and then Elaine was finished with that compact disk forever because she did not have a compact disk player and never would since she had given up being an Assistant Media Buyer in the advertising office on Market Street and so would *never* have enough money to buy a compact disk player and I listened to the compact disk without knowing which track was the one that Elaine had used because I had moved away from San Francisco, you see, before the film was completed, so I had to listen to each and every song whispering to me so intimately through the headphones about things that I could not understand, not being a woman with big dark eyes that sometimes had circles under them as Elaine's most often did as she sat on her bed glumly smoking cigarettes and I looked at the photo of Suzanne Vega on the cover of the compact disk and looked and looked and *really* looked at it to see if Suzanne Vega's face told me anything about Elaine and it sort of did because I was listening to or had listened to or was about to listen to the song that Elaine had used, the magic key to Elaine Suicide that would explain things about Elaine because Elaine had chosen it just as Suzanne Vega must somehow look like her songs and something about her face must correspond to *that* song that explained Elaine and in a way her face was not so different from Elaine's in its quality of entranced distance.

Elaine had a very nice low throaty laugh, and there was nowhere she wouldn't go. Sometimes she kept me company in whore bars. But then the whores stayed away from us because they couldn't understand why Elaine was there and then Elaine was very disappointed.

I cannot recall without pain how Elaine shone so shy and eager around Ken and how he ignored her and Elaine kept smiling at him and asking him how he was or what he was doing or other things which would not require much effort to answer and which would therefore be less likely to irritate Ken and Ken told her to get lost and she would not let the balloon of her desperate faith be punctured and kept smiling because one of the things on her list was * keep smiling, like Ken says * and Ken said   is that a pimple on your cheek or is that herpes that is so ugly   and Elaine said   why do you have to be like that   and Ken said shut up you fucking bitch or I'll slam your head against the wall   and Elaine's head dropped and Elaine said   why do you have to be such an asshole   and everyone else pretended that nothing was happening and we all had more beer except for Elaine who kept drinking grapefruit

THIRTEEN STORIES AND THIRTEEN EPITAPHS

juice and vodka and got very quiet and drunk and Ken left and Ben left and everyone started leaving and I said   how long will you be staying Elaine   and Elaine said   I'll stay here to the end   and I said   hey Elaine can I put my hand down your dress   and Elaine said   no way and I said   aw just this once   and Elaine said   all right   and so I walked Elaine home and she was crying silently so that I could see the reflections of streetlights and carlights in the tears that streamed so steadily down her cheeks and I said   well Elaine let me stop and think of some advice to give you while I piss   and Elaine laughed a little through her tears and I pissed between the bars of a fence and thought as hard as I could and put my arm around her and when I crossed the wide ribbon of light and noise that was Market Street I said   Elaine Ken doesn't love you anymore he loves Satoko but all you need is someone to respect you someone to take care of you you can't live on your own you can't live with someone who depends on you you need someone to depend on someone happy who will make you happy,   and I felt so bad for Elaine and wanted so much for Elaine to find someone and I was awake with the controlled weary watchfulness of alcohol that can keep you and fuel you all night if you need it to and I wondered if the bus were still running and when we got to Elaine's house before I could kiss her goodnight she said   you can sleep here if you want   and my heart started pounding and I said   with you?   and she said sadly   yes we might as well have some fun.

And I thought to myself I'm leaving San Francisco tomorrow and here I am about to fuck Elaine Suicide and why shouldn't I? Aside from the fact that it's not me that she wants to fuck at all, why shouldn't I? Aside from the fact that she might give me some disease, why shouldn't I? Aside from the fact that she won't enjoy it as much as I will and that she's feeling miserable and that by saying yes to her I'm taking advantage of her, why shouldn't I? Why shouldn't I kiss her all over this once and be close to her before she finally does kill herself? Why shouldn't everything be a part of everything for one more night before the translucent baseplate must be rotated and the red needle spins as sickeningly as a stomach churning and I don't even know the declination anymore? Why shouldn't I love her because she's my friend? And I could think of no reason not to do it, and I knew how nice it was going to be, but even then I had no inkling of what I *really* wanted to do it for.

Elaine's body was so light and lovely and perfect. As soon as we were in the bedroom I took off my clothes; I started pulling her clothes off so eagerly; I kissed her and kissed her.   —Take it easy,   laughed Elaine. —She fit just right in my hands. Everything about her tasted good. Elaine said   you know we really ought to use a rubber   and I said oh let's not   and I stuck it in. It was perfect. It was still perfect in the morning even though neither of us had slept much and there were bluish circles under both our eyes and Elaine lay puffing cigarette smoke down at the dawn but we went out and I bought her breakfast at the Mexican coffee shop around the corner and I was so happy that I could barely eat and on the street I saw a pimp I knew who said to me   hey bro, 's up? and I said   just keeping *this* lady company *if* you know what I mean and I think that you do   and Elaine laughed and laughed and it was very sunny in San Francisco and the birds were singing and it got warmer and warmer until the sun was so bright and I felt brave at last and Elaine was running down the streets with me, holding my hand, and I did not want to say goodbye; I could not believe that my feet were still on the ground, I was so happy. But later Elaine said   oh shit I forgot I'm ovulating. I think I'm going to get pregnant. I really think so.

And I was filled with joy. It all made sense: the sweetness and perfection of her had been just right because she was ready to make babies. And I said   if you want to have a baby you go ahead and have it; if you want an abortion I'll come back to town and pay for half of it and hold your hand while you're having it   and Elaine said   you're so sweet   and I kept thinking   yes if she has an abortion I'll be able to come back to town and be with her and so I won't have left San Francisco yet and if she has the baby I'll still be here, too, growing and dreaming inside of Elaine.

1

Epitaph for

YUMMY AND KEN

✻ THAILAND ✻

You said to him: you walk walk walk I say sit down please. I
shy; I say to you sir please sit down welcome.

You said: I want tomorrow you stay with me. I not have everything.
I know happy. I want you stay with me. I love you. (Too much, you
know.) I don't tell lies you! I *stay* you! I not pay everything. I know now
I love you. I want you stay with me. Maybe we have baby. You go clean
now. Take shower. Go for me. I can for you *everything*. I like you too
much! You drink Thailand very good. You make love very good. Very
very happy. Darling smell very happy. I like you love you make love
very happy. I want to go voom voom with you now. I clean shirt for
you.

You said: I cannot you walk alone. You hungry I buy for you.

You said: I happy happy happy. I love my Ken.

You took him to See Sar Ket, where you were from, where they sang
beautiful songs to him while he slept. Angels of love descended into his
soul. Fish swam in rice fields, and pregnant women smiled worked ate
salted fish rice.

He said: She is not a whore. She is a good Rice Girl. You would do
real good with the whores here. Her friend Marlee will know where we
are. She is a whore. You can stay with her. We stay in the adjoining
shack. Underneath at night when all is quiet, the rats play in the dirt.

II
THE BAD GIRL

Guidone's story ended here,
Not with a smile, but with a tear
That he'd proved to gents—and *ladies* too—
His virility, prowesss, and derring-do.

ARIOSTO, *Orlando Furioso*
(1516), xx.65

In Thailand the whore he married always got the men she went with to take her shopping. She always got them to buy him a shirt. She'd come home so happy, saying: Look new shirt I buy you! You so handsome!

Her name was Yummy.

She wanted bigger tits because she thought she could make more money that way. Everyone believes in something. So she popped hormone pills. Night after night he heard her retching into the toilet hole. He said   Yummy you're beautiful the way you are—I'm telling you straight up. Do you understand? You're my wife; you don't need to take anything!   and Yummy said   OK Ken for you I stop now. —Later she retched and he found more pills. She lied and said   *no* Ken *no* Ken they belong Marlee   and talked very fast in Thai to Marlee until Marlee nodded and said   yes Ken mine mine.

You don't want me,   Yummy said.   I'm a bad girl.

She said: What you want, Ken? I can for you everything. My eyes for you, my hands for you.

He met her on his first night in Thailand, when passing by the bars he saw so many naked legs on a platform, so many ankles, so many feet in high heels that it was like looking into the window of a shoe store. There was more female flesh than he could eat. But he did not want to go into one of those places because that would cost him money (he didn't know how much). Anyway, he did not want a girl just to take to bed; he wanted a friend—for he had had so many innings with women!

They came whenever he wanted them. Victorious warfare is a routine business. Every two weeks, it seemed, he used to say to me: I have a new one. I have to show her pictures. She wants to look at pictures. Usually they fuck me *after* they look at pictures. —At dawn, when a girl whom he had fucked told him a dream that she had had, he wanted to slap her in the face. He hated dreams; there was very little that he liked. So he came to Thailand.

The dream, as I understand it (although it is difficult to know because he hated dreams) was to be with people he could not understand. Then people would not bore him so much. —I would have stayed with Satoko forever, he told the women that he fucked. *She* never talked back to me. —He said it in this way, of course, to hurt them. But while hurting them was the main reason for saying it, while the hurting ice of Satoko's shadow was very fine because it hurt, his dream of her burning their dream of him, his dream really did mean something. Satoko was a beautiful vampire who said nothing, did nothing, absorbed him like a lake into which he, a stone, fell with scarcely a ripple. There was nothing about her to understand: she was the infinity of emptiness.

He was going to meet Satoko in Thailand when she sent him the note saying that she was with someone else. He went to Thailand alone.

In Thailand, he prayed to himself, *the girls truly love you. The girls in Thailand are really something. I believe that in all their acting there is a whole bunch of sincerity.*

He saw Yummy in one of the open bars, watching him as he came around the corner. He was somewhat unsure of himself. It did not seem possible that it could be this easy to take a woman home. (In his way he was very innocent.) She had a big smile on her face. She got off her stool. She stood looking into his face, smoothing her long glossy hair down across her shoulder, brushing her snow-white T-shirt to be clean for him, and over her shoulder the other girls watched, ready to take their turn if she should falter.

He didn't even mean to take her home. He was just going to buy her a drink. He bought her a Coke, and had the same. She liked that. She was happy that he wasn't drunk. Then they went out to dinner.

Her kneecaps shone like peaches.

She took his hand. Her arm was longer than his. She led him into a taxi, and they went to his hotel.

She said: Go, take shower.

He took a shower, and then she did, too. She wrapped herself in a sheet, because she was shy. Ken stood with a towel around his waist.

By then he wanted her to stay as long as possible. He wanted to keep her all night like some treasure. He loved the mystery that defended itself successfully against him behind that sweet shield of forehead. Almost crazed by that face he came so close to, loving its lips and clear black eyes, he opened his suitcases and began to show her his belongings, as slowly as he could, so that she would have to spend more of her life with him. She looked at everything politely and said: I don't understand. OK.   —She was trying to be nice to him.

He had a map of Thailand, and she politely moved her eyes across it. She said: OK. Get into bed.

She said: Turn light off.   —She didn't want him to see her.

She made noises as if she were enjoying it. She rubbed his chest and said: Small here, big down there. Hee, hee!

She said: You handsome man. My friend at the bar, she say you handsome.

At four in the morning she said that she had to go back to work.

He said: Stay.

She said: OK.

They ate breakfast, and he took her to the Bank of Bangkok. They went upstairs, and he changed a thousand dollars into Thai money. She was very shy. Everyone in the bank knew that she was a whore. Ken sat her down on his lap in front of everybody and held her tight and put the twenty-seven hundred bhat in her hand. He wanted her to know everything about him, to trust him. She turned her face away. She did not want to look at the money.

Whenever they passed a beggar, she always put one bhat into the cup.

Ken thought he might love her now. He suspected that she felt sorry for him. He didn't even know how to take a *tuk-tuk*. If he went anywhere by himself he could bargain with the driver until he was hoarse and it cost him thirty bhat. When Yummy was with him, it cost twenty bhat. She looked out for him.

When it was dark he said: I want to see where you live.

She said: OK.

They took a *tuk-tuk* to the edge of the slum where she lived. Then he followed her, like a dog whose eyes were white moons in its black head, while weak streetlamps made other moons down the tree-roofed street.

He saw jigsaw walls and houses. She led him between the wood-box shacks, the night sky slit by wires.

Four families lived in her shack.

She said: This my room. Very small.

She said: Come on down we make love. We make love very happy.

Children's faces watched him from other shacks. Sheets of corrugated roofing lay among the weeds. Beautiful Thai songs that he could not understand were on the eternal radio.

He said: Can I live with you?

She said: OK. Up to you.

She showed him how to take a shower, there on the rotten boards with litter all around. You poured water over your head from a barrel. Whenever he showered, the children would peek from between the slats, and Yummy laughed and said: baby watch *falang!**

When he brushed his teeth everybody watched.

Then she said: OK. I have to go. Go to hotel. Go to work.

He handed her a thousand bhat, and three hundred more to buy her out of the bar for the night.

She said nothing. She was thinking.

I have to work,   she said.   —She wouldn't tell him why.

Stay,   he said.   I'll give you money, Yummy.

No no,   she said.

She stayed with him for a week. Then she said: I loves you too much. I loves you make love.

Ken thought: I must really be something.

When she lay tranquilly naked on her mattress, he touched the lovely bottoms of her feet, and she gazed upward, and he made love to her.

There behind those narrow streets walled not only by houses but also by laundry and children, his love for her increased, in the same way that the crotchpiece of a bar girl's gown would work itself more and more snug between her legs.

She said: I likes you loves you. Maybe we have baby.

She said: I your girl, Ken. My lips for you, anything for you! Morning me, night me. Same same heart. I wait you. Me good heart— *good* heart!

* Foreigner.

66

He kissed the wide flat nose-bridge, the deep high cheekbones that thrilled him.

He looked idly between the slats that separated rooms, and saw the boy whose chin was black with snot and dirt, the girl as small and slender as a banana-leaf.

He said: I want to go somewhere with you now. Someplace new.

You want go to village?

OK.

Mama-Papa say no good. We must be married.

Ken looked at her levelly. —How much?

No I *no* want your money. You no love me? OK.

No, Yummy. Tell me what to do. I'm just a *falang*. You have to tell me.

You must buy me gold ring.

OK.

Her brother Singha was there. Ken looked at him and thought: Is this my brother-in-law? It almost seemed possible that Yummy was his wife, but he could not believe in this brother-in-law.

When it was time to buy the ring, she knew where to go. She must have been there before.

Ken said: Any ring you want, Yummy. —But she did not take advantage of him. She bought the least expensive ring in the shop. Ken paid a hundred and fifty dollars and put it on her finger.

He made love to her, she encouraging him with her little fingers on his shoulders.

It was at this time that he met Number One, who lived in the next shack. She was the whore with the arm raised as if to strike (but all she held was a cigarette), the proud nipples riding the crescent of the pulled down brassiere, the navel deep as darkness, the mound of Venus so soft in his cupped hand, the other wrist, so densely lined with parallel scars as to resemble tree-bark. Her mouth glistened and her nostrils were wide like a priestess's. She threw her head back and raised her arm higher and higher and threw the cigarette away and the hand came swooping down for his penis in the sarong . . . He laughed and ducked her. She was a junky. Later she began to steal money from him. She took it from his pants when he was in the shower. He never slept with her. He wanted to be faithful to his wife.

On the train to her village, she ordered food she thought he'd like. In the country she bought him sweet rice. They took a bus past the rice fields and she said: Look, Ken, look, see! Before, I work rice fields, bent over, sore. No good. Mama-Papa very poor. Baby very poor. No money.

She introduced him. —Mama me, she said. Papa me.

So these were his parents-in-law. He was determined to put on a good face to please them, like some girl working in the street, her knee bent, her elbow cocked like a wing, her fingers so prettily resting in her hair.

The father came very close to him and stared into his face, saying nothing.

The mother had an old woman's heavy eyelids, half-closed over dark-glowing pupils, the eyes themselves clenched wearily in the struggle not to be dragged down by the weight of those deep-creased cheeks.

Yummy had one daughter, who lived with Mama-Papa. —Baby me! Yummy cried. —Throughout the visit the little girl was watching her, already cocking her head and smiling knowingly; she would be like her.

Every day Ken asked her when they were going to get married.

Today, she said. —But it never happened.

Sometimes they walked through the village and the children would stop playing to follow them and Ken would make faces until they all shrieked and laughed. Yummy's friends always smiled at Ken, and Yummy said: Say Thai thank you. They say you handsome man.

He took her to a Thai movie in town. All the teenagers were snorting glue. He had to go to the bathroom but she said: Go here, between seats. Bathroom too dangerous.

Watching the children, she said: Before go to school I no have shoe.

Finally it was the wedding day after all. Yummy put the ring into a silver bowl. She dropped in some jewelry, which she said to everyone that Ken had given her. She started drinking whiskey. Ken bought beer and whiskey and Coke for everyone. He gave her parents money.

The priest picked up the cauldron and weighed and counted everything. He called out the numbers. Ken's drunken wife shouted out: *One million!*

Kiss me now, she whispered.

He kissed her, and everyone clapped. Then they made him sing a song.

She said: Ken we make love. Then I clean shirt for you.

She said: I happy happy happy.

Then they went back to Bangkok where she lived, in her rickety ship upon the sea of rubble slopping against the walkway boards. Her dresses hung neatly in the sun.

Sometimes they had parties there, and the fat girls who were not pretty enough to work in whorehouses called: Ken, sing song, sing song! and he'd sing a Woody Guthrie song and they'd clap. They said: Very good! You number one!

No! shouted the junky, Number One. *I, I!*

Ken was happy with his wife. —We have baby now? he said.

She covered herself and sat gazing at him with liquid animal eyes.

The muddy yard was littered with plastic bags, oilcans, tins, palm-fronds . . .

Number One smiled.

One day Yummy was patting white powder on her face, and she stood in the doorway looking slightly downward as the night-light shone upon her from between the slats of the back wall, and a lock of hair was against her cheek like ivy, and she said: OK I go work now.

Number One smiled.

His confusion crowded upon him, like propositions between syllogisms between G-strings between the multitudinous moons of buttocks crowded between smiles.

Yummy went back to work where Thai girls sat at the bar laughing through open oval mouths, Thai girls showed themselves in profile with succulent lips. Before they went up to the stage to dance, they passed by the glowing bas-relief of Mickey Mouse and prayed to the Buddha.

That first night, he strode into the bar and bought her out for the evening. Three hundred bhat. It was the equivalent of twelve dollars. She went with him without resistance, saying: Ken, I no want to take your money. —They climbed into a *tuk-tuk* and she gave directions. The driver let them off where another dog leaned forward proudly like a stiff corpse tumbling out of some niche, and the dog's ears were raised in the darkness as it listened to them coming, and then they were in the slum, home again.

I loves you too much, Ken. I happy happy happy.

The next night she went back again. Again he came there and stood among the Western boys who stood shoulder to shoulder gazing up at the constellations of dancing girls; he bought her out before another man could get to her.

Ken I loves you.

On the third night they were home in their room of the shack and she stood in the corner looking at him with one hand behind her back, as if she were hiding something from him. She had already attached her bar number to her breast, to make it more convenient for men to pick her out. Her shirt was buttoned up to the neck. When she stood thus, so straight and serious, she did not seem to be the same person as the girl who held herself with thrown back head and glistening lips, waiting for men to kiss her eyes. But she *was* the same: the number proved it.

They said nothing to each other.

He waited until she had gone to work, and then set out to claim her.

She sat on the bar stool looking at him, with her hands crossed in her lap. She was wearing big earrings that night; her hair was blacker and fluffier than the purest thing.

She said: Why you no understand? I have to work. You go home, stay with brother me, sleep. I don't want to take your money.

He said: I don't want you to work. I buy you out.

She said: No Ken I *no* go out with man! Ask Marlee. I just say please sir sit down welcome.

The other girls watched him, leaning against each other. They were waiting for him to go home. Around the corner of the big long bar, a bald white man, perhaps a German, gleamed his eyes at the girl laughing in his lap.

He got into the *tuk-tuk* alone. Thirty bhat.

The next night they were at home, and Yummy and her girlfriend had showered from the big jugs and were already dressed to go to work. (Number One could never go. Her arms were so slashed with the underlinings of her sadness that she was not attractive to men with money.) They stood looking at him, folding their arms across their flower-patterned breasts. Yummy still wore her bathing cap, which was speckled like a toadstool. She looked very knowing.

Goodbye, Yummy, he said. Have a good night at work.

Bye, Ken.

Yummy?

She waited.

Why do you want to work?

She laughed and lectured him: No, why, no what, no where, no when, no *he*.

He waited until she was gone. Then he set out past the children standing hungrily around the vendors of sizzling meat and got a *tuk-tuk*. He went to the bar with the money in his hand to buy her out.

She said: OK, go home now, Ken. Go for me.

He went to a massage parlor and got a hand job and a bath, relaxed, talked with the girl, who put on the TV for him . . . He felt like a king. As soon as he left, his heart began to ache.

When she came home he said: Yummy, are you my wife?

She was crying so hard that deep wrinkles seared themselves on either side of her nose. Her thin lips curled apart, and she howled. —Oh, what pain! There was no way that he could help her.

She wouldn't even tell him why she was crying.

The next night she went back to work, back to the place where the bar girls laughed into each other's cunts.

He did not go there. He had no proof; he did not want to know. He went to another bar where all the girls went straight for his pockets and two of them said: OK, we smoke you?

How much?

Three hundred.

You both?

Your choice.

He picked the uglier one. She got down and sucked him off, right in front of the bar, while the other one brought him a beer. Everyone laughed. (Most men went into a private room.) He grinned around defiantly. He couldn't come. Later they took him into the private room and he still couldn't come.

He wanted to take one of them home, but he couldn't since home was where he lived with his wife who was at that very moment selling her pussy.

That night she didn't come back.

The next night she came in cringing. —You want to boxing me?

No, no.

Ken never hit anybody, no matter what he said.

Ken? she said so sweetly. Now I sleep at Number One's house.

Why, Yummy, why? Why won't you stay with me?

OK. We take shower. We make love, very very happy.

71

She spread her legs and giggled.

When she got up afterward, she covered herself. Ken pulled the sheet away. She whispered   no Ken no Ken no Ken.

Next, being a tourist, he took her to the islands. She was shy among the white couples. He fell more and more in love with her.

She never went into the ocean above her knees, so he would drag her and she would laugh and splash.

She was always trying to fatten him up. She made him eat barbequed barracuda, rice salad, milkshakes . . .

They returned home, and he tried to convince himself that those good days had not been exceptional days to baffle him as he lived among her sun-hung dresses, her brother Singha coming and going, Number One watching him when he took showers, and every day clung endlessly to the underside of its evening until it was time for him to leave the country in order to renew his passport. That was how you had to do things. You had to go to Malaysia, so that they could pretend with you that you were visiting all over again, just a *falang* who didn't belong anywhere. He told her he'd be back in three days. She said: Ken, only Ken, my arms for you.

He hated Malaysia. They loved him too much. Too much, you know! They loved him so much they fixed his passport instantly. He hated everything about it. There was a night plane and then the *tuk-tuk*. He got home at four in the morning and heard a man coughing inside Yummy's room.

He stood still.

He thought: If I bust in on them, she won't get her money from him.

He thought: I don't want to embarrass her.

He hid in the shadows until she came out with the man, a white man, to see him to a *tuk-tuk*, and he could see the oval moon of her face in the darkness, the shadows of eyebrows, nostrils, lips, like the inky smudges of the moon; he could see the ghost of her hand in the darkness. It was as if the night were her nakedness.

Number One was at his shoulder. Number One said: Where's Yummy?

Walking a man to the *tuk-tuk*.

She see you?

No.

Why! Why! Why you no tell her, hit her?

It's her business, Number One. Nothing I can do about it.

When his wife came back, her eyes went wide.

Yummy, he said, aren't you glad to see me?

Number One began screaming at her in Thai.

Yummy turned to him. —You no see me! Number One tell on me! Don't believe Number One! I no tell lies you! I no have man in there. I show man room. Only! Number One no good!

She refused to let him in until she had tidied up. He stood breathing the night stenches while Number One winked at him and smiled.

When Yummy had made the room into home again, she said: I go to Marlee's house.

Then he felt as if he were one of the little boys with shaven heads who ran barefoot among the rubble, playing with toy pistols, unable to kill or be or have.

OK, he said wearily.

But she was not like the child who begged on the sidewalk. She did not need money. He would give it to her. If her family needed it, he would give it to them, too. He wanted her to love him. What didn't he understand?

He just wanted her to trust him.

He said: Please stay please.

OK, she said.

They took a shower together. The next day he wouldn't let her go to work. He offered her money but she wouldn't take it.

He took her back to the islands, and she lay sleeping with her wrist dangling down upon her breast. A mosquito whined. Her legs gleamed with light. Her hair tumbled down across her forehead. It was very hot and still.

She whispered: Why am I sick? I been good. I pray to Buddha.

He went to the next bungalow and got the man there, who had a thermometer. Her temperature was a hundred and four degrees. The ferry had just left, and they ran shouting along the beach until it came back. They carried Yummy onto it. Ken shook the man's hand and told him to watch their belongings. Now the ferry departed again, into the hot blue sea. He sat beside Yummy all the way, not knowing how to help her. Her eyes never opened. It was low tide when the boat docked, and he had to carry her through the mud, sinking sometimes to his

73

waist. She was very heavy. The sweat splashed down from his forehead to her forehead. He said to her Yummy Yummy, but she couldn't hear. Once he was compelled to put her down. She lay gently upon the slime; she did not break its skin. When he had caught his breath, he raised her again and held her firmly against his breast.

He got her to a doctor, who prescribed sleeping pills. Ken said nothing. The next day he took her to a hospital and bought her the medicine she needed. Then he rode back to Bangkok with her on the train. There the doctors laughed: Your wife, she's OK now. No problem. Just Thai girl, just malaria!

She said: OK. I wait wait OK now.

Ken said: Let's go back to the islands. I'll take care of you there.

She said: You go Ken please. I come Thursday.

OK.

On the islands he told everyone that she was coming on Friday.

They laughed. —You love her, Ken?

Yes.

She your wife? What she do?

She's a whore.

On Thursday she didn't come.

On Friday she still hadn't come.

He said to everyone: She's my wife. She does what she wants.

On Tuesday she hadn't come.

They all teased him and moaned so lovesick: *Yu-u-u-um-mee!*

On Wednesday they shouted: YUMMY! and Yummy was on the ferry with her hair so beautiful and she said: Oh Ken hi. I tell you I come. We go bungalow, make love very happy.

They sat on the floor and got drunk.

The man who had watched their belongings was there too. He drank very steadily, never looking at Yummy. Yummy winked and belched and said to him: You stay. You very handsome man.

Ken went out to get more whiskey and left them alone.

The next morning he asked the man: So, did you fuck my wife?

The man's eyes dropped. No no, he said.

After that, Ken didn't much care anymore. They went back to Bangkok. Sometimes he didn't see her for days.

In the mirrored bars where he now slouched as if moonstruck, a young head with straight black bangs nestled against his shoulder. A slender brown arm grew across his chest like ivy, even as his finger trailed absently upon a brown hip. His eyes and her eyes locked upon the dancer's bottom and naked ankles on the platform; and on the face beside his own the lips parted slowly in a painted smile; the eyes shone; but she did not look at him because he was dreaming his way inside the dancer; she kept her glance carefully smiling and parallel.

The next thing that his wife told him was that she was going to America. She wouldn't say where. She kept saying: Ken, I go away. What *you* do? —She was worried for him.

When he heard this, he lost sight of his love for a moment, and when he saw it again it was like the dead rat on its back by their bed, its mouth down-curved in sadness, its four little hands dangling, its tail limp like a fresh-killed snake.

Then the American went back without her, and the Austrian came.

She said: Ken, I go Austria. What you do now? I cannot you stay alone.

He said: Up to you, babe.

But he had her passport locked in his safety deposit box.

She said: OK. I go now.

They went to his safety deposit box, and he got it out and gave it to her. What a gentleman I am, he said to himself.

He said: Yummy, I'll give you a thousand dollars if you stay. You go to your village with me. We do whatever you want.

She stood holding her keys and crying. Her cheeks were chased with long vertical lines, and she vomited grief between her teeth as the tears trickled slowly out of her black eye-slits. A lock of hair fell across her face and was drenched with tears. Such sadness as he saw in her he had not believed it possible to see.

Beside her, on the wall, a Thai calendar girl smiled demurely.

The next night she went to work.

(If she was strong enough to make her own decisions and feel good about it, I think I could have really helped her out, Ken said later. I would have felt good about that. But she was so broken and hurt.)

And the night after that she went to work.

Goodbye, Yummy, he said.

She stopped and looked at him. Standing there in the darkness, she appeared to be a starched doll in her long white frilly dress.

I'll give you all my money,   he said.   I'll buy you forever, give your family anything.

I no want your money, Ken. He buy ticket. I have to go.

She went on into the darkness, past the squatting men and tumbled scraps of metal. Almost instantly he lost her in that maze walled with corrugated metal and laundry, where skinny little men walked barefoot down narrow streets whose walls were crowned with broken glass.

He went out to stalk a woman, being now one with the one-eyed dogs who slobbered between their glowing teeth in the darkness of the streets. Now his love was like a skirt pulled up to show the little polyester-covered mound of his desire, his only desire; he didn't care about love. He found the bar girls touching each other's bathing suits with tender fingers. Their hair was permed and frizzed and fluffed like new-baked bread. Girls' navels were steadfast stars above the upcurved moons of panties. Girls smiled politely, watching with neutral eyes.

He sat down at the bar and took a girl. She put her arm around his neck and pressed her nose against his cheek.

I am becoming more and more like the rats mosquitoes lizards and dog shit! he shouted.

She smiled.

He thought: I really like these people. They lie all the time.

His wife had certainly begun to divest herself of him, in much the same way that a G-string can be slid down one hip with the tug of a single ringed finger. She didn't sleep at home much anymore. She had her brother Singha move in, so that Ken would have somebody to take care of him.

Children laughed and stuck their tongues out happily at him from between the slats of other shacks.

She said: Ken, I see you, I don't know I want to cry.

She gave him her passport again. He locked it in his safe deposit box, and the next day the Austrian put his fist through the wall because now Yummy couldn't go to Austria and he couldn't find Ken. Yummy was protected. It wasn't her fault that Ken had locked up the passport. So the era of the Austrian came to a close, as he thought. (By now it was Ken's habit to want to put on the pure mask of another woman's face, pulling it down to him, its lips on his lips, its soft clean hair tickling his neck, the gold chain on its neck slapping against his neck as he reached for a breast . . . Then he would forget his wife.)

76

Ken come on Ken,   said Yummy.   I worry about you with the people that are no good! Maybe they no good; you not know everything. You *no* talk to everyone!

Ken said: Sorry. I sorry you.

Yummy said: What you do, where you go, I don't know.

Which of the umpety-ump million flavors of pussy would he taste tonight?

They prayed to Buddha before they danced. They prayed for a good man.

He went to the worst part of town there was. He considered the girl with the butterfly tattooed to her thigh, who glittered hopefully with earrings and brassiere-armor and jeweled panty-armor, waiting for the number on her breast to be called.

He said to himself: This neighborhood is really a scary place, so if Yummy is sincere then she won't be able to sleep right now.

He went home. Yummy was out.

Not long after this, he went with his wife to the hotel where they had first made love. They made love once more. She drank a pint of whiskey. In the middle of the night, she started weeping. She said: Ken, I have to go now. Gunther is crying next door. I go for him. He want me go Austria tomorrow.

Ken shouted: You want to go? Go! There's the door. Leave me alone.

Twin streams of tears ran down her cheeks. She stared into his face, clasping her hands tight in a little steeple, as if she were sacred.

Ken, you come tomorrow? Say goodbye?

No.

I for you everything, Ken, Ken. Everything for you. My eyes you want? I take them, give them you. I chop my hand for you, Ken. Ken, Ken, you are like Mama-Papa, baby me, Ken. I worry you, Ken. (She was biting her lips.) Maybe you meet lady no good. Wants money too much. Not same me—me good heart! Ken, what you do? I do Austria.

Up to you, Yummy. Stay with me, I love you. Go, up to you.

She got on her knees and prayed to Buddha. Then she stood up and dressed to go to work . . .

The next day she sent her brother Singha to bring him to say goodbye.

Okay,   Ken said.

They got in the *tuk-tuk* and Singha gave the directions. Twenty bhat.

Singha said softly: Ken, I sorry you! —When they stalled in traffic by a crowded bazaar, Ken threw thirty bhat into the driver's lap and ran away.

Singha cried: *Ken! Ken!*

Ken went to a matinee and bought a whore.

Singha stayed on with Ken in the shack. He never asked Ken for money. —You smile and hold real still, said Ken. He had no need for shackles. Sometimes he would forget to give Singha anything, and then Marlee would say: Ken, give Singha money! He no eat today! —Then Ken would strike his forehead and give Singha a few bhat. — Number One laughed. —Singha was a very good person. So gradually Ken started thinking that Yummy must have been a good person, too.

Later, he went around and asked every whore he met: Can I go home with you? Can I live with you? —They all said no.

2

Epitaph for

PEGGY

* U.S.A. *

Y ou, having been well recommended by Jimmy (one of your better clients), were giving Code Six a blowjob and trying not to smell the stench of him; and Code Six was grunting and grinning to beat the band when a man strode toward you in the darkness. Code Six looked up. You got up, rubbing your tired knees, searching for your knife. Last month another girl had been skullcracked here, in this place between hotel towers. Across the alley, a window creaked open and a Vietnamese boy stuck his head out. The man came closer. Then you saw that he was your man Titus.

Can I have a word with you?   Titus said. He paid no attention to Code Six.

Not right at this moment,   you said.

Why don't you come by and see me when you get through.

And where might that be?

You know where I'm gonna be at waiting for you.

I'm not gonna go back to the hotel room,   you said to him. (You were so tired of him.)

Where you goin'?   he said.

Gonna rent a hotel room,   you said. (You said it not looking at him. You said it hating him, happy that after one more trick you would have enough money to sleep free of him, grief-pierced that you would not ever be beside him again.)

I'm going home then,   Titus said. His face was tear-wet, shiny like new glass.

Your heart broke.

Well I don't got a key there or anything,   you said,   so . . .

I'll *be* there,   he said. (He said it to you. He would be there for you. You loved him.)

Well I'm not gonna go to the hotel,   you told him, looking down at Code Six's incredible shrinking cock so that Titus would not know how much you loved him.   —If I don't got a key,   you said,   I'm not goin' out. You can't stand out there and wait?

I'll wait,   said Titus. He turned and strode away.

Now finish me off, said Code Six, and after him came Jimmy who said well now tell me about love, who said tell me a happy story about love that I can keep with me and remember.

You're not too happy are you? you said. You sure you're OK?

Oh I'm happy I'm happy, Jimmy said, that's why I only like to hear happy stories.

Well I love my man, you said. I guess that's happy, isn't it? I don't just *service* him, I actually *make love* to him.

III
THE HAPPY GIRLS

Keep the bait (spinners or wobblers) moving; it attracts the fish more readily.

ANONYMOUS, *Never Say Die: A Survival Manual* (1979)

1

When tax-time approaches, the receipts and check-stubs buried without obsequies in last year's folder suddenly become valuable: dead men have sprouted flowers. They may even *save money!* Well, what will my pleasure be? Shall I first kiss these mouths whose mold-blooms are the purple-inked slips once awarded me by weary postal clerks, or would I be better served between bedshrouds stamped **PAID** or **CASH**, redeeming which I might **PAY** less **CASH** later? Certainly no skinflint should neglect to unpeel eyelids, which have become double-page rosters so painstakingly ballpointed, veinpointed, by old ladies who, being Museum employees, never make mistakes! (although it *is* true that they gnaw their pencaps at each subtotal.) —Invoices, tickets, consummated bills, I must regurgitate them every one. (Save a dollar, and you can buy ten cents' worth of happiness!) Thus I reap my pathetic harvest with scissors and stapler; I calculate, dismember and verify until new flowers bloom in schemes and totals: I am going to nickel and dime the tax collectors to DEATH. (Squander a dime, and get a dollar's worth of pain.) If—perish the thought—they ever choose to *audit* me, I will smite them with smiles as I sit them down in the living room; I'll bring out this year's illuminated financial album, every page of which will be beautiful, will attest to my innocence.

But this is only practice: the most earnest tax to pay falls on nights when memories march in their dismal column one by one, like ants across my pillow: from them the Grand Total of guilt, shame and sorrow must be rendered. At least, delights (so they say) will be deducted from the reckoning. That is why every New Year's I pry the nails from lead caskets, and begin forthwith to appraise the sticky lips of stale joys. — What was the happiest day of my life?

Again I become an archaeologist who would learn the Secret, excavating with the picks of plus and minus (for by now flowers are but fossils, their faces also dead and calcified). Have I already lived so long? What sad accumulations! . . . Here beneath the phone bills are love-records, with their profits and losses attached to prove that every agony was a joy, every joy an agony—a situation whose novelty goes far to redeem it. Despite inevitably itemized deductions of mistrust, so that even then my dollar was not quite worth a hundred cents, I did figure sweethearts as highly as I could in the currency of meaningfulness, wanting them so much that I *believed* in them; and everything was accordingly perfect—or appears now to be as I flip through yellowing folders; but what about the tears and the ugly little disappointments that lived in the closet and under the bed? —Deduct ten cents. —Adjusting, then, for these our cannibal children, I must credit solitude more highly:—the sunny times of footsore joy on Arctic islands, for instance, when I reached ice and could glide almost effortlessly through coolness more dazzling than music. Motion seemed then to exact no penalty (which may be computed on form IT-2109.5). —Net sum, then: a transparent dime of ice. —Or how filled with martial pride I'd been when I bought my first pistol! *That* was a new green dollar whose eagle screamed beneath the dandelion-seed-sun of stars! (I had not yet learned that I would never be able to hit the target at all, much less get bull's-eyes. —*I* see, you like to save paper! chuckled the old shooter beside me at the magnum bench. You'll be able to use that target over and over *again!*) —I had death in hand; what could be happier than that? —Perhaps the time when I was three or four and my mother took me to the San Diego Zoo (which I do not remember) and on the way the sun was so coin-bright through the train window that I thought I could touch it and I was so happy to see that gloriously shining ball riding through the sky beside me, at exactly the same speed as the train, warming me and gilding my mother's hair. —A dollar ten!

But now the tax collectors demand the final sum; it is almost the day of judgment, and weary accountants have closed up their offices, anticipating their first long sleep in weeks (*this* is the joyous time for them), and so I must make my declaration at last: The happiest day of my life I spent in a massage parlor.

2

The place was on the corner. At first glance it appeared to be a little restaurant, or perhaps a nightclub. Girls and fish swam brightly in the painted sea around the door, which was glass, and you smelled cooking when you came closer, because next door was a Thai café where the girls sometimes went between customer-bouts to have a bowl of noodles or a skewer of beef satay with peanut sauce, or they ran in to gulp down ice-cold leechee-fruit juice, standing at the counter, talking very rapidly with the waiter in Thai, paying in paper money and running out without waiting for change, while on the walls the huge travel posters from Thailand made those hurrying girls seem much less real than the dancing-girls of Bangkok or the perfect little bronzy girls who rode alone in high-prowed canoes down jungle rivers, looking out at the café tables (each with its squeeze bottle of red sauce and brown sauce) with leisurely submissive smiles; so it was not unreasonable at first to think that the massage parlor was also a restaurant, but when you reached the glass door it was only a mirror that gave you back your face, sweaty and a little baffled, and there was no menu and the door was locked. To the right of the door was a buzzer. If you rang this, you would have to wait for some time while they scrutinized you from behind their two-way mirror. They usually let the businessmen in. The businessmen stayed half an hour or an hour and went out (a little furtively, it seemed to me) by the other door, the unmarked door around the corner, between the photo shop and the lobby of the transient hotel. This money-engine, in short, was carefully run. If you called, an Asian girl would answer   *yes?* and if you did not know what to ask she would hang up.

They let me in because they knew me and they were bored. They sat beside me and served me tea and fanned themselves. Inside the cool massage parlor on that sunny afternoon, the girls peered out from behind the red curtains into the bright day to see who was ringing the bell.

Oooh, a customer! cried the Asian girls. A *beeg* one!

A sofa curved round the walls of a room filled with mirrors.

Hey, bay-bee, you want massage?

A red bulb shone down on a multitude of colored fish, swimming motionlessly high above a glass table.

The customers came in. They did not say much. They sat and smoked. The girls laughed and gossiped among themselves. Whenever a new businessman rang the buzzer, their voices became very low and slow and melting:

You want massage? I take *real* good care of you.

Everywhere you turned were naked legs and high heels and the smell of permed hair.

Tosany, where's the key? said Suzy. I'm bee-zee. —And, yawning, she took her businessman by the hand and led him down the hall. He was young: he was a little sheepish.

The girls laughed and practiced thrusting their hips out and said, *Hon-ee!*

You have to make me smile! mourned Tosany. I cannot smile! I cannot smile because I have braces!

On the sofa, another businessman waited, getting more and more impatient. Tosany had lured him in with her hoop-earrings that glittered with all the seductiveness of gold, with her lush hair that fell over her naked shoulders like a scarf. Now that he was with the girls in their world of tea, water, mirrors and dimness, they knew they had him, and bewitched him into a state of fretful impotence. From time to time he looked at his watch and made as if to rise, but they ignored him. He was their captive now. He knew it, too; he glared and sat back down. Tosany was sitting by the water jug in her fake satin nightdress that was so soft and smooth and shiny; her fingernails were silvery-pink, like mother-of-pearl. The businessman sighed and drummed his fingers. His secretaries never dared to keep him waiting like this; they bowed their heads when they brought his correspondence to be signed. But Tosany only crinkled up her narrow black eyes slyly and cocked her tongue in the corner of her mouth. At last he swore and leaped to his feet. The girls stopped laughing and watched him. He strode to the door and took hold of the handle. At once Tosany rushed over to him, pleading and begging in a soft steady whine; she drew the bolt on the door and pulled him away and he did not resist; she led him by the hand and took him down the hall.

I'm *bee-zee*, baby, she called laughingly back to Burmese Donna.

In fifteen minutes he was through. I saw him going into the bathroom, naked except for the white towel around his waist and the smile that bespoke pure profit.

—Ah, the next man on the sofa said. A *beau*-ti-ful girl!

Someone rang the bell. Suzy peeped around the curtain and saw a man in sunglasses, shading his eyes, peering anxiously through the glass.

Bee-zee! We are bee-zee! she shouted. I don' want him.

You know him? said Donna.

Yes.

A man rang the buzzer. He was dressed in a suit and tie, and carried a hand-tooled leather briefcase. His hair was parted; he was well-shaven, and his shoes shone.

You want me to take care of you? said Tosany.

He laughed. —No, not now.

He wanted someone else.

The girls admired Tosany's striped dress. —I *love* that one! they said. Shit, I want to buy that one so bad!

Another man swam up to the glass.

Who want to take the customer? laughed Tosany. I'm too lazy to open the door!

No one came to the door for a very long time. The girls drank tea and fanned each other. Sometimes they went into the dressing room to amuse themselves putting on red shoes, white shoes, black shoes, dresses, lying on Regina's mattress beside the black slip and the black bra on top of the pillow that they never touched, putting on gold shoes, playing the latest blue slip like a harp and then letting it drop on the floor, playing with all the colors, wrapping themselves in the blanket with peacock eyes.

A man rang the buzzer. He bowed to the coercive striping force of Tosany's dress. *Hon-ee!* she said. Sure I'll be good to you! Tosany's *always* so good to her man!

Suzy, she said, where's the key? I'm bee-zee now!

Half an hour later, when she had come out of the shower and changed into a new dress, she was tired of men. Whenever one rang, she called

from behind the curtain: Bee-zee! Sorry, we are very *bee-zee* now! —
And all the girls laughed. A man rang, and they stuck out their tongues.

After that, they did not let anyone in. They giggled and poured each
other tea and tried on each other's dresses all afternoon; they did up
each other's hair; and I *knew* that they loved each other and loved
themselves; and I was so happy to see them luxuriously happy. At the
zenith of the afternoon, when the windows of the bar across the street
glowed like squares of black fire, they began to perform their masquerades
for each other. Tosany sat by the water jug and waggled her tongue at
imaginary customers again, her hands crossed virginally in her lap, that
fine gold chain glittering against her throat, and Suzy doubled over
laughing and Donna cooed *ooh* Tosany *hon-ee*, *ooh* Tosany *bay-bee!*
Then Donna changed into her green-barred pants suit with the wide
stomach sash, and combed her hair very carefully down on her forehead,
with many side-glances into the mirror, while Tosany and Suzy watched
in open-mouthed suspense, as Donna said modestly I am really shy! I
feel so nervous! and now she entered her act of leaning so pale and
pensive in the back doorway, stroking the glass bead-curtains that men
had to pay to pass through, crossing her plump legs, hand on hip, and
her eyes so sadly inviting and her lips so pink and juicy that the other
girls laughed until they gasped, and Suzy said yes Tosany that's just
what she do all the time—make those rich men feel *sorry* for her! —
And Tosany grinned like an imp. Then Suzy put on her black slip and
pulled it up just over the knee; while Tosany and Donna stripped to
their bras (the cups of which were embroidered with patterns like
cabbage leaves) and they made their eyes as wide as they could and
said *make me happy bay-bee!* and they fell down laughing. It was Thanksgiving behind the mirror. They were home in laughing water despite the
men outside an inch of glass (it was twilight now), despite the drunks
smashing bottles beneath the pink neon curves of whore-signs, despite
those poor cousins, the high-heeled street workers with drug-scarred
arms and pimply undernourished faces who stood on the corner and
smiled so gratefully when men agreed to use them, who sometimes came
to check their makeup in the mirror-window (behind which the Happy
Girls paid them no glance); despite the pimps, the lords and masters,
raging and hitting women right there on the sidewalk as darkness seeped
down. Here inside it was safe. Tosany in her long green dress with big
hooks and ovals embroidered on it, so that she seemed to have python-

skin, Suzy with her smiles and smiles, Donna with her face of shy restfulness inside its block of straight black hair;—they had made exemptions for themselves. Their time, their bodies were their own. These ladies, so adept at inspiring passion in others, exalted me. Their performances demonstrated a sublime and spontaneous art.

3

Seeing them happy, as I said, I was, too, when I did not yet understand the taxes and fees that they had to pay.

Tosany's surcharges, for instance, included her father in Thailand, who'd promised to kill her if she ever came back. When she was fourteen, a Cambodian boy too shy to greet the rotten skulls to whose number he had been assigned began to run. He ran through the jungle with a deer's silent terror. He had almost reached Thailand when he kept his appointment with politics after all—by tripping a hidden wire. He dragged himself across the border without any feet. The doctor had to amputate his legs to the knee. Tosany's family nursed him, out of charity. Tosany wanted to make him a happy boy. After that, of course, she was not good for anything but to be a whore. So she became one. She became an American lieutenant's happy girl until the citizenship papers came through. In divorcing him she did not laugh because she was cruel, but only because she was nervous. Now she began to make her money. Money came and money went. Finally she got a letter saying that her father had died. By the lieutenant she had had a little son, whom she loved and who had never seen Thailand, so in her flat she said to him   you will like it there hon-ee you will see!,   but the boy just looked at her with big black eyes and drove his toy jeep soundlessly across the carpet, and Tosany said: be a happy boy bay-bee!   and he threw his toy against the wall. Tosany poured herself some tea and cried because she did not want to see her father's grave. Sometimes she pretended that he was alive and had forgiven her. But all the time she knew that she would take her son home to the cemetery, where they must prostrate themselves.

Suzy's lover beat her and took her money every night that she came home. Whenever the phone at the massage parlor rang, she peeped at it as if it might be her jackal-prince, and said Tosany you say to him please I am *bee-zee* I am working good money *very bee-zee!*

Donna laughed so easily like an innocent child who did not yet know that she would forget herself as she had forgotten her diseases.

The greatest payment due, however, was exacted by Regina, who owned the black slip and black brassiere on the mattress in the changing room. Regina also owned the massage parlor. She would not have permitted the costume show which made my happiest day, but she had taken that afternoon off as she did every now and then which made the girls so happy because on such days she could not terrify them as usual when they sat in the waiting room in silence as if they were listening to a piano recital whose success or failure would determine all too much, and whenever the buzzer rang Regina made them let the man in if he had money, no matter how ugly or cruel he was, and sometimes Regina came into the room where they had fucked the customer, and searched the bed for money; sometimes she searched their purses; sometimes made them come into the dressing room and searched inside their bras with her nail-bitten hands; she had made Donna fuck her twice, and sometimes Regina slapped the girls and sometimes she pinched them, and Regina also had a razor (which, however, she used only as a threat because she did not want to damage the girls, and in any event using the razor would have been too much for the girls to bear, unlike the mere *threat* of it that was made ever so occasionally on those particularly bad days when Regina's face was like a steel door with something molten behind it). I could not believe in any of this until I met Regina, and then at once I believed in everything.

In addition to these local taxes, whose sum can only be estimated, must be added the national line item of men, the other kind of men who did not dress in suits and ties, and once or twice had gathered in front of that locked mirror-door at times of darkness that nothing but automobile-lights crawled upon; and the men threw bottles against the glass and smashed it with boot-toes and bricks and then came running in (that was another reason for that unmarked side-door, which Tosany hoped that she would never have to use).

In spite of various credits, these tolls contributed to the way the girls were, so that if I met Tosany in the restaurant next door she would be too busy drinking leechee-fruit juice to have any time for me;* if I met her on the street she would not see me, and in fact the longer I knew her the more unseeing of me she became, because I never gave her any money.

And yet, knowing these things now, and knowing that there are probably other worse things about that life, worse even than the caress of Regina's loving razor, I cannot say that that afternoon was not one of the happiest and most beautiful of my life. (I will swear to it when I am audited.) I remember how the girls clapped when Suzy put on a striped turtleneck shirt that made her look quite pale and delicate and magnificent when she raised her chin and folded her bronzy arms; I remember Tosany in her snake-green dress that glittered with scaly diamonds, smiling with such innocent happiness, like a girl at the movies. The old cliché of the doomed sailors serenely playing cards in a sinking ship may apply here, but isn't the happiness more coppery and shiny for that? Everything was OK. For two hours the girls truly *were* happy.

---

* I admit the probability that I myself was another of these tolls exacted from her. Nor is it fair for me to judge her more severely than any other professional: what she sold were the trappings of affection, so why should she give them away?

3

Epitaph for

MIEN

* VIETNAM *

Your lover drove fast. The old car rattled.
I said: Thanks for the ride.
I said: Sure is hot.
I said: You get many hitchhikers around here?
He said: Would you believe too many?
He had a steel plate in his skull.
He said: I was in the Special Forces. I know how to kill. I could kill
you in two seconds.
He said: Sometimes I get so crazy. I think it was the Agent Orange.
They put us in the rice paddies crawling in the shit for two weeks three
weeks and the choppers kept spraying it like mist and rain. You could
see the jungle shrivel up.
He said: I was in Demolitions. Once they had me blow up a Catholic
church to get some V.C. After it went up, they found out they had the
wrong guys. I was a Catholic, too, before that. Killed a hundred people
praying.
He said: This steel plate aches.
He said: I killed Mien, too. She was only fourteen, but she looked
twenty-one. They would have served her at any bar in the world.
He said: I didn't believe it when the C.O. said she was fucking the
radio operator. Couldn't believe it.
The C.O. said: She's passing on codes to the V.C.
The C.O. said: She's Charlie.
The C.O. was black.
Your lover said: You're a nigger, sir. Your father was a black man,
sir.
(As long as he said sir it was between the two of them. As long as he
said sir they could just both step outside.)
The C.O. said: It's OK. I know how you feel.
The C.O. said: Do you want me to take care of it?
Your lover said: I'll do it myself.
He took you to a park on a hill high above Saigon.
He wanted to kiss your breasts. He said: Are you Charlie?

You trembled, turned milky yellow. You were his, beautiful.

He brought his face against your face. He said: Are you Charlie?

You said: You—no belong here . . .

He took his knife and stabbed you in the throat. He cut your head off and brought it to the C.O. He threw it down on his desk. He said: If you ever find out you fingered the wrong girl, don't tell me, you nigger motherfucker sir.

He said: My steel plate aches.

IV
THE BITCH

. . . as if to say that only men could be silly
enough in society as we find it to indulge in
rhapsodies of the untrammeled Feminine.

ROBERT HARBISON, *Pharaoh's*
Dream: The Secret Life of
Stories (1988)

Blackwell sat with one hand on his knee, the other palm against chin as the fingers drummed slowly against the visor of the baseball cap, and he stared straight ahead through his fingers thinking how 'm I s'posed to get money?   —Right then he hated his wife. Hated her like poisoned shit on broken glass. What he wanted, what Naomi surely wasn't, was a Somebody Chick who'd stop him from making money the way he made it, which was to go through the wall. Naomi *never* said   Blackwell baby there got to be another solution;   Naomi *never* said   you listen to me motherfucker I be *leavin'* you if you don't stop with that crazy shit—   well, she was young, just starting to find out what life was all about; Blackwell knew he had to get his own head together, but he had to *find* MONEY to do it and Naomi sure knew how to *lose* money on dope and silver stretch pants and you name it, not that he ever saw her bringing *in* money—'course all she'd be good for was to ho anyway, and she'd do that regardless; she'd do that money or no money. Why, once when he'd driven down the street he'd seen her standing in shiny silver leotards, staring at the cars with clasped hands— not that that was proof, but it was something. Another time he'd seen her with her sister Marietta, both in ankle-length dresses with more layers than wedding-cakes!, Naomi in yellow, Marietta in blue, and they wore those you know Egyptian kind of sandals and dreadlocks and *bigass* plastic-gold bangles and rings; Marietta had on a bracelet with a crucifix like she was trying to be *righteous* or some shit like that; and Naomi had a golden crown and Marietta had a sky-blue headband dangling with blue plastic beads; *he'd* seen the bloods hanging around, like they didn't know if they were there to get their cocks sucked or WHAT. When he remembered that, he got to feeling sorry for himself, and sat drinking and panhandling in the park, where it was hot and gangly guys walked with white shiny grins. He hated Naomi. Hated her like stink.

Two men started fighting.

You better leave my baby alone,   said one of the combatants,   or you gonna have *problems.*

Within a minute, a fat cop had shown up.   —Break it up, break it up! he yelled.   Get going!   He leaned against a trash can with crossed arms, crossed legs, waiting until everything got nice and peaceful. Another cop joined him.

Got *two* of 'em now!   Blackwell said.   If they shit on me, I'll try *anything!*   —His pulse raged through his chest and shoulders until he wanted something to happen, but then the second cop finally left, and his colleague walked up and down the rows of benches, looking intently into everyone's face. The gentleman of the streets beside Blackwell nodded to him and ambled off before his turn came.

Blackwell looked right into Whitey's eyes.   —I wasn't doing nothing, he said.

Didn't say you was,   said the cop.   Didn't say anything, did I?

Blackwell stared him down. That time nothing happened, so he went over to some kids and started playing catch.   —Not so far, boss, not so far,   he said when one of the kids ran way out.   Too much for me!   — But he could always lob the ball the whole distance just the same; he was a strong man.   —Maybe I throw more powerful than I *thought* I would,   he said modestly, and the kid was wide-eyed with worship.   — Come on, boss,   laughed Blackwell.   You gotta *develop* your pass!   — What it came down to, he thought to himself, was that *she* didn't stop him, so why should he stop himself if she didn't even fucking care? Anyhow, what he did was inside jobs. He didn't hurt nobody. Sometimes on pigeon-winged nights he sneaked a truckload of fancy women's clothes from some warehouse and drove them to the Projects, where he went through them very very quickly with sure hands, picking out whatever he wanted, taking whatever he could carry in his borrowed van, and it was like Christmas for Blackwell and he was grinning and smoking rock and life was good and he was shouting to himself   oh *baby!*   When he was done, the Project people would descend on the truck with all the respectfulness of vultures and pick through what was left, Blackwell watching them through his rear-view mirror as he drove slowly away into the darkness, with clothes bundling him warm and secure against the night, and Blackwell was laughing because he knew that by the time the cops showed if they ever did there'd be so many people running in so many directions that they never *could* figure out who had done it. When he got home Naomi would be sobbing oh my God and what're we gonna *do* if they put you in jail, but Blackwell had noticed that a brand-new dress that was some snazzy black-and-red and just the right size to cover her smug little ass would sure shut her up. He sure had noticed that. Anyhow, *he* wasn't hurting *no* one. Why, if he stole a truckload of some fancy women's parka that was selling about as good as fried dogshit, then it was *advertising* for that parka; that parka would sell *great* in all the stores a few months later, just you wait and see. —But Naomi never understood that. She thought that Blackwell was *badass* or some shit like that. Well, what was he supposed to do? It wasn't *his* fault he had to go through the wall. It wasn't *his* fault that whatever happened happened. Once he broke into a safe and only expected to find a couple hundred bucks but there was *eight thousand* there, all in twenties and hundreds, so he shoved it into his car and started driving toward the Projects and the police went after him and he went faster and faster and got out of it leaving some pig in a squad car as mad as Naomi when he slapped her face but then he heard the sirens of more *more* police cars coming at him and he ducked in between two big Project towers and parked the car behind the other abandoned cars and jumped out and crawled under the edge among the broken glass and beer cans and hid there all night. In the morning the cops were driving up and down the street looking for him because they *knew* he was there, but they didn't find him and he thought for sure that he could get away with it and he imagined her waiting up for him and wondering where he was and crying again and a big grin split his face; this was SHOWING the bitch!—and then he thought how great it was going to be when he got home and turned the key so quietly in the lock that it didn't wake her and there she was sleeping in her clothes with her head down on the kitchen table and her eyelids red and swollen with crying and then he'd yell *Boo!* and she'd wake up with a little scream and stare at him and he'd watch the anger flood into her face and then as she opened her mouth to scream at him he'd start stuffing money in it! ten dollar bills, twenty dollar bills, cramming all the money in her mouth to gag her and shut her up and astound her so that she'd love him. Oh, how *he* loved *her*—truth was, he couldn't find a single line more in her face than that time when he'd first seen her, her skin *so* soft and fine, lips crimson-wide and glistening so that when she started kissing him his face and body was smeared with her lipstick as if she could smear her taste all over him, and her lashes were as gracefully deadly as the tooth-hairs of Venus flytraps (but lately her eyes had gotten bigger in the narrow mask of her face and the way she looked at him was neither friendly nor unfriendly). So he had his hopes, and it would've *been* that way, too, except that there was a lady who'd seen Blackwell go under the hedge in the night! She looked at the hedge and saw Blackwell's liquid eyes looking at her so trustfully and she looked away and looked back at him with a scared determined merciless face and stepped back and Blackwell prayed   *Oh Lord let her drop dead right now oh Lord don't let her open her big fat mouth AMEN*   but Miss Snitch was already running toward the squad car yelling   *Officer! Hey officer!*   and a cop came and told her to get the hell out didn't she *see* this was a *dangerous area* right now and Blackwell prayed for a jet plane to crash into her heart but the cunt *still* wouldn't mind her own business and she ran down the street to where the other cops had been huddled with their walkie-talkies crackling like bacon, but now there was only a woman cop nosing around there when Miss Snitch yelled   *hey, officers, I seen him!*   and the pig listened to her yabbling for a minute and then pulled her gun and strode up so fast she thought that maybe Blackwell would think she wasn't afraid of him, but *hunh!*—*he* hadn't been born yesterday even though his heart went *bomb-bomb-bomb* because Miss Piggy was looking straight *at* him as if she saw him (which she couldn't) and she said   come out of there   and Blackwell lay still knowing she didn't see him even though her big blue pig-eyes were staring right at him from behind the plastic goggles and he could see her eyeballs getting bigger and bigger and Blackwell crouched perfectly still behind the thorns thinking to himself   I'd like to make *you* oink you bigass honky pig ho   and Blackwell's heart was beating very fast; he was feeling so alive, and he thought to himself   she doesn't see me   but then Miss Snitch called   HE'S RIGHT THERE I *SEEN* HIM   and the lady pig put her finger on the trigger and told Blackwell again to come out of there and he knew she saw him now and he could almost feel her breath on him; she was breathing very fast and hard and he said   don't shoot   and started coming out and the bitch cop went to her car, never looking away from him, and radioed for help—oh, she'd been *coy* about admitting in front of Blackwell that she was the only cop there, huh?—*huh?*—but he knew what was going down and thought it was pretty funny; he wasn't about to try anything, though, because she had that gun, so he just crouched there half out of the hedge with his head out like a turtle's and his hands on his head and the other cops came running and told him to come out and Blackwell said   I'm coming and then he saw the cop he'd gotten away from in the first place back on the freeway and the cop was mad that Blackwell had escaped and gotten caught by a goddamn *cow* instead of him—imagine that!—so he got Blackwell in a chokehold that fucked him up for two weeks and they put the cuffs on and threw him into jail. All Blackwell could think of right then was   it's all my wife's fault god*damn* the motherfucking *bitch*.

4

Epitaph for

A JAGUAR

* BELIZE *

You did not know that you were born so that your teeth could be a necklace. Ricardo did not know that he was born to girdle trees.

When he asked to go to high school, his father said: I'm sorry to disappoint you, son, but I don't have the money to send you. You'll have to become a *chiclero* like me.

At first the boy felt very sad, but he became strong. Nimbly he ascended the dark-greened cliffs of trees. He could tap eight or a dozen of them a day.

Now he loved to work. School was far on the road behind him. He loved the jungle whose veins he opened.

He became a hunter, whispering *tch-tch!* for silence as he chambered the slug. He held up his hand to say *wait!* and slipped away, scarcely ever returning without your predecessors: a bird already half-plucked, or a little reddish-brown deer slung over his shoulders with the neck hanging down perpendicular to the body, the head nodding, the black eyes still shiny, the ears still alert . . .

His father said: Good, Ricky. Now tie the feet. I will show you how.

High above, frond-shadows played up and down the animal's ribs, as if she were still breathing. Ricardo's father cut a *tikai*-vine and brought the hoofs together in a series of half-hitches. He adorned her with a collar of leaves, to keep the throat from opening at the bloody hinge.

Ricardo learned how to skin an animal perfectly, slowly, with the back of the blade so that the inside of the hide was pearly-white. He gutted game in the hot sun by the greasy river as white butterflies flickered around the glistening scarlet neck-meat, and doctor-flies bit the backs of his hands (the barely visible welts would burn and itch).

His father said: Clean this part good, Ricky. Clean it very good, all the blood, so that the meat don't spoil.

There was only one rifle among them all. They let him carry it. Sometimes he became lonely, especially at night, and then as they sat around the fire they pretended to be musicians for him, playing rubber leaves for their guitars, blowing grassblade flutes until he laughed. They said: You are our hunter, Ricky!

He laughed for pride.

Then passed a time when he never saw anything to shoot, and you lived your life to the last morning when the sun was three-quarters of the way up into the ferns, which curled closely over the trail, and the whine of the flies was louder and louder.

Ricardo was on his way to girdle trees. The birds hushed hearing him and then began to cry again; and all around him were pattering sounds, any one of which could have been made by an animal, or a hunter, or a blowing branch, but Ricardo had learned in the jungle school, and so he listened on the grey mud of the old road; he slipped into the jungle, his way never barred by the dogs, and saw you.

You were almost lost in the blue-green tree-shadows, but he saw you. (It would be presumptuous to imagine you. I wasn't there. I only know that you were beautiful.) Now you were doomed. Ricardo came from people who did not know how to give up.

You streaked up a tree. The dogs ringed around shouting.

Ricardo lifted his gun. His face was shining. He took aim, thinking: how proud my Dad will be! and pulled the trigger.

The cartridge did not explode.

He tried all his other cartridges, each in turn. None exploded.

You snarled.

He ran to get his father and the other *chicleros* and when they came the dogs were still crouched on all sides of you, barking up at you, and you growled and scratched the branch.

They sent him back to camp to get a knife and a file. Anxious, he thought that he knew a shortcut, but got lost where palms rose on straights and various diagonals fifty feet high, and fallen fern-tips drank the grey water in the deep tank ruts in the mud, into which he sank ankle-deep, calf-deep even though he avoided the pools covered with dead leaves, the pools of clear water in which little white blossoms floated like stars. He pulled himself out and kept running. He was so excited that he could not stop smiling. Now he saw where he was. He recognized trees by their gashes. He was chasing your death down cool humid tree-tunnels whose air was made up of biting gnats. Yellow warblers flickered among the trees as he ran. When he reached camp at last, he found that someone had already gotten the tools, so he ran back to your tree and you were still snarling.

They cut a new firing pin for the rifle. They filed it well. Then a man took aim at you as you grinned hate. He pulled the trigger. Still your death did not come.

They took the gun apart, aimed the barrel at you and hit the cartridge with a hammer. You stared the bullet down, and it did not come.

At last Ricardo's father said: Ricky, it is time for school. I will show you how Mexicans kill.

He said: All of you—bark like dogs!

He lashed the knife to a stake and climbed up the next tree, a fat mossy tree thinly vine-veiled. The men were barking like dogs as loudly as they could. You, confused, afraid, enraged, crouched watching them, turning your head from side to side, as meanwhile Ricardo's father got within range, and then he stabbed you.

You screeched and leaped agonized to end him, but were caught in the tree-crotch. Ricardo's father pulled the spear out and stabbed you again. Then he jumped down. You opened your mouth. Then you tumbled down dead.

They sold your skin, but Ricardo wore the necklace made from your teeth until his own son was born.

V
DIVINE MEN

By their tombs we know them . . .

National Geographic,
"The Eternal Etruscans"
(1988)

Everyone that I know would like to be God. Everyone is *almost* God. If there is a God, shall we praise Him or blame Him that this is so? (If I had the answer to this *I* would be God and I would not have to tell stories.) —"You desire to be filled with the supreme Good," says one writer, putting these words into the mouth of Christ, "but you cannot attain this blessing now. I am that Good; wait for me . . ."*—I have been waiting all my life, and (by definition, I suppose) will have to wait at least until the end. In the meantime, there are stories to be told, for I have seen Him on this earth.

1

Declassified Army Footage
(25 May 1970 Airstrikes Report)

A man in a plane flew along the horizon, firing bullets. The casings glittered in the sun as they spattered against his shoulders and fell down into the sky. —A plane was rushing low, with many little white globes

---

* Thomas à Kempis, *The Imitation of Christ* (*ca.* 1413). I quote the translation by Leo Sherley-Price (New York: Penguin, 1952), p. 160.

of fire speeding ahead even faster to show it the way. —A plane hovered over a river for a long time, until you came to believe that the plane was like a cloud. Then, shockingly, a white bar of light fell out of the plane and exploded. A soldier shot bullets at the village across the river. White dots sped away from the plane across the sky; they fell and became death. —There was a plane and a long white whirl of bombs, the jungle turning red and pink, and white puffs bursting at random, white mushroom puffs, new ones forming between old craters, their fire-rings expanding and thinning with tremendous speed. White gobs of napalm fell. Bombs turned end over end, forever it seemed, falling forward as well as down, until at last they burst, sometimes just missing houses and roads, sometimes not; and the frame of reference kept sweeping on as the plane flew on so that whatever happened happened far behind in an unreal patchwork of green and brown, the junglescape unrolling steadily like a magic carpet into which the plane wove its bullet-trails so that it would be able to rise above itself.

Was the soldier God? —No, because he would never know exactly what he had done.

2

A man with a hooded face walked in an alley crying   *Coke! Coke! Coke! Smoke! Smoke! Smoke! Smoke!*   and I said   oh no thanks man that's not my thing   and the pusher said   aw c'mon got some heavy duty rock for you to try   and I said   no that's OK.   The pusher said   watcha tryin' to do then get your dick wet?   and I said   that's right   and the pusher said   listen I don't *ever* pay for no pussy; I just give 'em a sniff of crack, give it away to 'em, you know, and then they go *oh* I didn't *get* that sniff and then I get *hard* with the bitches and say oh yes you did but I'm late for an important 'pointment gotta be goin' so long bitch, and then the bitch goes no no wait, and then I go all right you can have another but not before you suck me, and man I'm telling you I never used a rubber in my life.

Was *he* God? —Well, almost. But he could not create crack *ex nihilo.*

There had to be Somebody Whom he bought it from, Somebody Who could crush him if he crossed up or didn't pay, Somebody Who had made him.

3

Once when my sweetheart Jenny backed up into a package truck and destroyed her car's backside and sat sobbing hysterically, I said   well Jenny let's look in the yellow pages and see who can fix it.   There was a body shop not far away, and we drove mournfully down the street, with glass-shards tinkling so musically out of the rear window to gleam like mica on the asphalt; we turned the corner and ascended the ramp from the tire shop to the body shop where it was cool and greasy and professional and very very serious. The German came over and inspected the car, sighing and shaking his head to let us know in advance that Jenny's little mistake would cost her, and Jenny got out and I got out and the German walked around the car very slowly, and we followed him with reverence, and he said   eighteen hundred   and Jenny shrieked no way!   and the German said   well if we use salvaged parts I can make it thirteen hundred and once we repaint it no one will be able to tell the difference   and Jenny sobbed   can't *believe* it! I was just gonna sell it!   and the German led us around the car again and said   yes Miss you are lucky twelve hundred yes   and Jenny said   twelve hundred! And I took it to a 'spectable joint! So pissed off! Well, I'll just pass on costs to whomever I sell.   —So it was settled. —Jenny and I started to take everything out of the car, maps and scattered cassettes and both boxes of kleenex (one of which Jenny was now drawing from to dab her eyes, kleenex after kleenex with marvelous regularity) as the German accepted the keys into his hands with stern authority. There remained some books in the trunk, but that had been half-crushed by the package truck and pinched more forbiddingly shut than the entrance to some brass tomb of the sixteenth century, so Jenny started crying again and said   what are we gonna *do* about this?   but the German said   do not worry Miss   and the German said   Jaws! Come here, Jaws!   and Jaws looked over from behind another naked automobile and came striding up to us, wiping his hands on the knees of his coveralls, and he was very tall and wore dark sunglasses even here where the lighting was not so bright and his face was pimply and he grinned and his teeth were full of fillings, and he wore shiny black boots like a thug although there was grease on them now as there was all over his coveralls and he came close to us nodding and looking at us with no thought of intimidating us but Jenny ducked away from him with wide eyes and her mouth fell open and she forgot to dab at her eyes and the German just stood there with his hands on his hips, glorying in Jaws, and the German said quietly now Jaws   as he pointed to the shattered trunk, and Jaws walked up to it and ran his tongue across his lips smiling and took the trunk lid in one hand and the bumper in the other and flexed his arms a little and there was a sound of metal going *urrrrrrrrrrrrrrrrrrrrrrrrreeeeeeech!* and then something went *spoingg!* and the trunk flew open and Jaws was not swearing, not a bit.

Was Jaws God! —After all, the German owned him; the German could fire him at any time. And yet it occurred to me as I watched Jaws opening the trunk for us that he had no thought for the German at such times, that his strength was his happiness—yes, he was *happy* in himself as he did this; and if the German fired him it would make no difference; he could take the German's face in his hands when he got his pink slip and slowly squeeze it with his palms, so happy when the skull burst and shattered, so happy that no consequences could touch him . . . Unlike the soldier, he knew exactly what he was doing. Unlike the pusher, he was not restricted or defined by his allegiance. He had attained the blessing. He was the Good that I had waited for. And as I loaded the books from the trunk into my pack, as I put my arm around Jenny, leading her down the ramp into the sunlight, I prayed that Jaws would never crush me—but Whom was I praying to?—and I kept my worship secret, to be out of hearing of whatever God might be greater still.

5

Epitaph for

LIEUTENANT VYACHESLAV OSDCHI

✳ AFGHANISTAN ✳

The women were then herded into a house,
into which the Soviet officer in charge, Lt.
Vyacheslav Osdchi, threw grenades.

MERCURY NEWS WIRE SERVICE

My late soldier, now deadbound with one steel bolt:—Diminish. Slip through the lock. (You need to, you want to; it's safe inside.) My late soldier, now hellbound, did you have time to descend your downfall?

My late Lieutenant Osdchi, you marched to Hell, where women without bones whirled about you in an autumn of flaming flowers, and Lieutenant William Calley, the hero of My Lai, said   hallelujah it's you!   said   *now* we'll solve the world's problems!   —In Hell, Lieutenant, you forgot what houses are, and how to herd women, and even (last to go) how to pull the pin of a grenade. You forgot the screams of shattering glass, then the other screams that took black root in the hothouse of flame-flowers. When I die I'll forget them, too. Until then, even until then, I'll be standing with my foot on your sandy grave, kicking you back under whenever you try to come out of Hell for air, or wriggle up into the dirt to get away from Calley and his bad breath, to escape that wind of women-leaves that sticks to you like napalm. I'll be herding you back to Hell, Lieutenant; it's safe inside when you're dead and shrieking; I'll be lobbing grenades at you; and after me, someone else will come to tread you back under again, and blow you back to Hell.

But the dead leaves I walk on, I'll walk on them tenderly; I'll caress them with rain's cool fingers; I'll rest them on rivers. My boots are sanctified with dead leaves; my feet aren't worth the dead dirt I walk on.

121

VI

THE HANDCUFF
MANUAL

We are surrounded by eternity and the uniting
of love. There is but one center from which all
species issue, as rays from a sun, and to which
all species return.

GIORDANO BRUNO, letter to the
Inquisition (1600?)

1

Waterless Swimming

Forty-five minutes before she mailed her prepackaged goodbye
into the hot, feculent depths of Gun City where streams of
filthy rainwater carried cigarette butts down gutter-grooves, Elaine
Suicide sat alone in the theater between movies, feeling INSPIRED and
singing to herself a little song that she had made up: *He left me, left
me, left me high and dry*   until the usher said   I'm sorry but you gotta go
or else buy another ticket   so Elaine went to the lobby where she sat
eating popcorn and feeling important because she had solved everything.
Then she wrote in her golden book   *This is a death (female). A (male)
finds the body, lays it out, covers it, and then, as a last thought, thinks to
touch its genitals or breast.*   —I'm almost almost finished!   she said to
herself. (Elaine sought to keep herself light and bright: she was always
cleaning up her possessions and getting rid of what she no longer
needed.) She closed the book. It was an afternoon so cloudlessly blue
that it felt a crime to be hurrying back home as she was now doing
so as to feed her cat Sad-Eyes an extra large bowl of pet chow, after
which, those machine-shaped ocher-colored nuggets having clattered

successfully out of the sack, she took Sad-Eyes into her arms and said aw poor *baby* I wonder who's going to feed you next   and Sad-Eyes lay quite still against Elaine's chest and stared up at her with greeny-green triangles that seemed much more curious than sad, until finally Elaine, feeling peevish that Sad-Eyes did not miss her in advance, plumped her down on the floor and pouted. Then began to laugh at herself because in fact she didn't feel ANYTHING!   *Left me, left me, left me high and dry*,   she sang softly. She threw herself down in bed and smoked three cigarettes with the window open, and got up at last with a yawwwwwwwwwwwwwwwwwn which she caught sight of in the mirror and considered ugly. She stood looking at herself. Suddenly she grimaced. She reached under the bed and took out a roll of electrical tape. She tore off a piece and slapped it down across the mirror so that her reflected eyes were covered. Then she laughed again and went to the post office (peeking at her watch from time to time as she stood in the queue because she did not want to miss her appointment with herself), and under her arm was the package heavy with the weight of sins, sealed many times with silver tape, to which she had glued a photograph of a woman with black hair and black eyes and a black blouse (or perhaps it was only that the photograph made her look that way), and a very strange collar went loosely around the woman's neck like a snake. This package traveled slowly but very surely, so that six days after the burial service (to which he had not been invited) the yellow slip was posted on Abraham Yesterday's mailbox and he signed for it and the doorman brought it out of the room where the vacuum cleaner was kept. There were no stamps on it. How the postal service had been induced to carry it across the country was a mystery. As yet it would be incorrect to say that Abraham had any premonition, for although the envelope was wrapped round with transparent tape, as if to contain something from leaching out, that was how Elaine always sent her packages. He slit it open. Inside there was no note. At once he began to feel nervous. There were three books, each gold in color. The first was a little New Testament. Abraham swung its covers open and looked in between them for the secret message like a glint of sunlight on dingy cloud-cobbles roofing the narrow pillar of sky between two skyscrapers. (Robinson Crusoe used to do this, too, in times of trial. Abraham had picked up the habit from him.) He saw the lines about Mary washing the Disciples' feet with her long silky hair that was so warm and soft as it swallowed up their ankles like a field of golden grass; and he was happy, but closing up the book, he thought a moment later to verify the message, so he impudently opened the book again and found: *But if they cannot exercise self-control, let them marry. For it is better to marry than to burn with passion.* Then Abraham was afraid. Turning to the beginning, he read the message of the Gideons, which compared this most shining of volumes to a mine, a sword, a river, and warned him: *It involves the highest responsibility, will reward the greatest labor, and will condemn all who trifle with its sacred contents.* Now, because she was dead (although he did not yet know it), because she had sent this book to him, the responsibility had become his, and his anxiety increased, for this was only the first of the golden books.

The second book was entitled *The Golden Book of Attitudes*, by Father John Doe. It was for alcoholics. It said: *The correct attitude: The knowledge and conviction that God is the Author of sex and therefore that it is something good in itself . . . Self-control outside of marriage is possible, but only with God's grace.*

Now at last he took up the third gold book, whose cover was imprinted with red circles in which black chicken-skeletons sniffed at their own assholes (or so it seemed to Abraham, but other souls might have considered the chickens to be flowers). Inside, Elaine had glued triangular pieces of photographs of herself. It was half-filled with writing, which went sideways, very large, as if she had become bored with the very first word and sought to use the book up as quickly as she could. One page said:

I abuse the hum of nothingness in the air, with my empty head echoing my empty heart. It's dark. Click! say the handcuffs. Sad-Eyes doesn't hear. I turn the light switch on and see my clothes hanging in the closet waiting to put me on. You abused me; I abuse myself; the sun will always go down and

Abraham did not want to go to the end yet. He was definitely afraid of that. He opened to another page, which said:

2 lovers meet the morning. One attempts to seduce the other who lies uninterested but not protesting. Seducer quietly lays down his head and stops trying—then rolls onto her as if he's beginning again—but actually continues rolling, right out of the bed and onto his feet and into the bathroom to pee and relieve his desire. The other gets up from bed. The two meet in the kitchen with friendly smiles.

I remember that, he said. I rolled right *through* her, like the jaws of empty handcuffs.

At the end was a Polaroid of Elaine split right down the head from forehead to chin, with a twitchy smile of self-consciousness on the left side of her mouth (the only side that remained), and Elaine's brown left eye looked very knowingly through the transparent tape that sped so soundlessly across it like a film of ice, and there were rainbow fingerprints all over Elaine's half-face but Abraham was not certain now whether they were hers or his; and beside herself Elaine had written *continued→* so he turned the page

and the next page said *Abraham I'm sorry to give you this*

and the next page had the right half of Elaine's face from a different photo when her hair was long; and an earring like golden fishing-gear descended from her ear into a cloud of hair and the right side of Elaine's mouth was lipsticked very red and her right eyebrow curved glamorously like a movie star's and a strip of transparent tape shot across it

and the next page said *These 3 gold books found themselves stacked on top of each other for no good reason*

and the next page had two pieces of Elaine's face from two photographs, one eye apiece, one eye naked, round and brown like a bird's, the other half hidden by hair, and between them Elaine had drawn a line with an arrow at each end, as if she could connect them that way

and the next page said *And I'm trying to get rid of shit. RID*

and on the next page was a slice of Elaine's face with very pink lips, she seemed to be wearing a blue wool beret which blended into the smeary darkness in a straight military way that made Elaine seem dead because her face had been laid down on its side with the shroud of transparent tape wrapping around her single eye and strapping her head down against the darkness; beneath the photograph it said *But there's some stuff I just can't*

and the next page said *THROW AWAY*

and the next page had two parts of Elaine's face cut from different photographs, as usual, cut to different shapes so that they could

128

never be put together, and there was a margin of page between them, and one piece of Elaine was smiling so fiercely that her cheek was wrinkled up but the band of transparent tape ended halfway across her eyeball and its serrated edges looked like tears, whereas in the other piece of Elaine a face that had never slept stared through tape and her sweatshirt was soft and grey; beneath the two Elaines it said   BUT YOU CAN

and the next page said   *This ½ a book has been eating pieces of me for years here*

and the next page had a tiny piece of Elaine and beside her it said *Now it's yours. Lock it tight. Thank you. ELAINE*

and the other half of the book was blank.

He closed the book and watched the pages very slowly settle, like the black flakes of soot that sifted ever so often down between buildings. Suddenly, just before the gap closed irreparably between the two halves of the book, he seized the cover in a panic and threw it open, as if there were something that he could still do. The page said:

All morning long, in my dreams, I have been trying to swim laps with no water.

Then he knew that Elaine was dead. That was her epitaph. Later, when Painter Ben told him what had happened, he wondered if she had swum a little in her blood, there in the cast iron bathtub.

The Handcuffs

Painter Ben said that Elaine had been found with her wrists handcuffed together, apparently so that she could not change her mind. She must have clicked the cuffs on once her veins had properly opened; the razorknife lay on the bottom of the tub beside her. Hearing this, Abraham opened his new golden Testament and read these words *He said to them, "Come and see."*   —But how could Abraham do this, when she was buried? —He reflected until it was dark (aside, of course, from the tiny yellow squares of light from distant towers that stood stacked like illuminated punchcards), and at last he thought that he understood the words. His Bible was telling him to discover how and why she had died.

But he already knew.

Out with the handcuffs black and cold. He clicked them down over his eyes like spectacles, as he had done with Elaine so many times; through them he peered at the last photograph, hoping that it would now be somehow talismanically enhanced to glow more intelligibly than his guilt.

No such luck.

For he who speaks in tongues does not speak to man but to God, said the Bible, *for no one understands* Him; *however, in the spirit He speaks mysteries.*

But what can I *do* then, if I can't even understand? Abraham asked.

And with many other words he testified and exhorted them, saying, "Be saved from this perverse generation."

The Apparition

It was late on a snowy night. In the skyscraper next to his, Abraham saw the orange trapezoidal glow of a lampshade behind metal blinds, a chair-back like a cartoon tombstone, and then a woman's bare leg; then there was darkness for three storeys up and another window with the blinds drawn at a more guarded angle to the pane, so that only a feeble yellowish-greyness escaped. —What a slideshow of diversity! —He looked away and then the blue square of a television shone; he looked away and then a woman was pressing her nose against the glass, staring at him. Across her face (he could see it very distinctly) was a pane of transparent tape.

2

Civilians

To understand this matter of handcuffs you must first be reminded that Abraham lived in Gun City, U.S.A., that noisy place of canyon-like streets bridged by concrete overpasses beneath whose tunnel darkness the smells of urine and fear hovered as unregarded as the odors of hamster cages, which everyone knows from the news; and when Abraham went down into the subway there would always be a pool of filthy water at the bottom of the steel-tread stairs, shining with an eye's brightness. He joined the line before the ticket booth, with its two fat women behind two windows; one window said **PERFORMING CLER-ICAL DUTIES** and the woman behind it stared sullenly into space, listening, perhaps, to the rumble of bread trucks and armored cars just above her head; the other window was open, which is to say almost entirely sealed by bulletproof glass, but there was a narrow grimy gutter beneath the pane, through which the customers passed their money and then fished out their tokens one by one with successive crooks of a forefinger. These brass disks were still warm from the fat woman's hand, so Abraham felt that something intimate had happened between her and him, as if she had extruded them from some specialized commercial anus upon receipt of the money in her slot, but she had not seen Abraham at all; she had seen only his money, and now as he walked away from the booth, rubbing the pair of tokens absently together between thumb and middle finger (he really should have bought a five-pack or a ten-pack, but because he never *would* admit to himself that he was compelled to live in Gun City out of soldierly honor he bought only two tokens at a time: one to travel, one to return), other people were already sliding their money slyly through her slot and then scooping up their tokens (which were as heavy as bullet casings, with round graphite centers that smeared their fingers), gathering them toward themselves by twos and threes upon the sill, until they had double handfuls to scoop into their breast-pockets and mouths—oh, yes, their mouths, too; he so often saw the jowly clerks peering over their shoulders like hunted foxes, their jaws working, their cheeks bulging with tokens, for they had come to crave the taste of the graphite upon their grey tongues—a nuisance to the public, of course, for that meant that the tokens one bought were so often sticky with dried saliva, but at least they had been licked half-clean. He put one token in his left coat pocket as usual, buttoning it securely; then he waited behind the man behind the woman who was waiting her turn, which came as quickly as the man's, as his, so he pressed his token firmly into the turnstile slot; he strode into the entry chute while ten people stood behind him; he nudged the metal bars with his hips and they grudgingly creaked aside. It was dark and dirty on the platform. Teenagers were shouting and chasing one another through the crowd, knocking down whoever was in their way; oafs blew bubble-gum and burst each other's pink balloons with a flick of a dirty fingernail, so that the noise was like gunfire; schoolchildren scuttled among the newspapers and paper bags that lay on the concrete like last year's autumn leaves; boys and girls popped plastic bags in each other's ears, and he heard one bald guy whispering to another we *conditioned* those warders! As far as the fucking screws, we *had* them! and the loudspeaker bellowed something scratchily inaudible. The others jostled each other (or at least the big ones did, the ones with bull-shoulders); they read their newspapers (although they were wedged so tightly together that they could not turn a page); they faced the subway track; their eyes flickered sideways to watch for danger. The air was intolerably close and foul. At last the train lurched out of the tunnel, hissing and rattling deafeningly, its scrawls of graffiti shining like bones, its cracked windows shuddering in their sockets. The doors opened, and people streamed out, forcing the others aside with their concentrated force, like jets from a riot-hose, but soon the strong ones had gone through the turnstile, and the rest dwindled in purpose and numbers, so that the boarding passengers could sweep them back into the car, elbowing each other in a grim struggle for seats. Abraham boarded the train and sat focusing his gaze on the official red triangle on the opposite wall above the handrail, the triangle painted just for him, so that he would not have to inadvertently look another person in the face; all around him, the other seated passengers did the same, focusing wearily upon their designated triangles; as for the dozens of standees, however, they were supposed to look upwards, where the ceiling was peppered with a constellation of little bright circles, but no one did, for that would have meant leaving oneself unguarded to the attacks of pickpockets.

The Mirror

Originally (by which I mean in the days before her golden books) Elaine also lived in Gun City—a fact which you might have already deduced. She'd just moved out of Bomber Towers after an argument about rent with her flatmate Sondra, whom she hated because Sondra said things like   I would *never* tell a lie and my Mom is my *best* friend,   so Elaine acted as ugly as she could about the rent until Sondra's lip started to tremble and then Elaine said   anyhow I'm moving *out*   and took a cheap studio on Empire Avenue which was now mainly unemployment blocks and drug pushers so Elaine had to get about seventeen locks to put on the door, but when the last niobium plate had been fiercely screwed down, she felt very happy and began humming songs and lit a cigarette. She poured pet chow into a bowl for Sad-Eyes and watched her pick at it. When it was gone, she scrubbed the grime off a banana that she had left too near the window and ate it.   —Well, there's a lot about me that isn't any good,   thought Elaine, looking at herself naked in the mirror.   But that's not *all* of me.

Elaine loved men who didn't love her. She had once tried to go out with a perfectly nice average guy, she'd really tried, and she could see him falling in love with her by the minute and it was all she could do not to start laughing.   —When can we get together again?   he cried. *Tomorrow?*   —I don't know,   Elaine sighed.   Maybe next week.

He called and called.

Finally he even came over and said: What's wrong with me? Why don't you like me?

I don't know,   said Elaine, bored.   You make money for all the wrong reasons.

She went to a party of lawyers where a very sweet boy asked her to go for a walk with him.

Eat me up, Elaine, he whispered in her ear. Come on. Bang me. I mean, it's Gun City after all.

CAPITALISM is just eating everybody up, said Elaine mercilessly. It makes me sick.

She went to a bar and there was the most *sexy* looking guy there, but he wouldn't even notice her, so Elaine went home and cried.

But her life turned around like a wheel in a squirrel-cage when she met Abraham.

He was a tall, well-built youth, with pale circles on his wrists. He seemed very shy and grateful. He had been discharged from the Army for medical reasons, he said.

What did you do last night? said Elaine, trying to make conversation.

Dully, Abraham rubbed the white circles around his wrists. —If you remember what you did last night, you didn't have fun.

Elaine gazed into his eyes. —You are so weird, she said. But I like you.

But have you ever *done* anything weird before? he insisted.

Well, said Elaine, thinking hard, there was this menáge à trois experience between this couple and her girlfriend. I was the girlfriend. His idea of sleeping with two women was humping this one for two minutes and then humping the other one. And we didn't want to have *anything* to do with him.

At this, some life came into Abraham's face. He winked at her, just like the blind man whom Elaine sometimes helped cross the street. — Elaine giggled.

They went out for a drink, and Abraham said: There's too much freedom in this world.

Oh, give me a break, she yawned, getting bored with him again.

It was midnight on New Year's Eve, and from the top of every building, hundreds fired off their revolvers with roar and flash, and swarms of bullets greyly eclipsed the moon, and the aluminum cases came tinkling down with the sound of wind-chimes, weightlessly pelting the bookies in their baseball caps, ornamenting the hair of high school girls who ate too much hamburger, striking the steel curbs, getting squashed as flat as cigarette butts beneath the trampling of friends and lovers who cried Oooooh! at the red gun-flashes. Suddenly a body came streaking down through the darkness, decaying from the excited state to the ground state. It smashed the awning of a grocery store and burst on the pavement. —He was the *scapegoat*, parents explained to their children grimly. He had to die for us.

I never liked that part, Elaine said. It never seemed fair to me. And if you've seen the expressions on their faces on TV, the way they hide and hold on to the bars of their cages . . .

Well, *someone* has to be a scapegoat, said Abraham reasonably. That's how it's always been.

I know it has to be that way, Elaine said. I just don't like to see it, that's all.

It doesn't bother me, said Abraham. You know I come from a military family.

The Dog Tags

That was true. Abraham Yesterday had been well prepared for life. A soldier's son, he became a soldier like his two brothers and distinguished himself in Vietnam and Nicaragua, receiving the Order of the Screaming Skull for disabling an enemy bunker single-handed with two grenades, and being recommended by his commanding officer for entrance to the Theoretical Ordnance Division. There he was chosen to study with the great Doctor Bacteria, whose pupils, as is known, are sparsely distributed upon this earth. Abraham proved exemplary at dehydrating various hydrated chlorides, and won the praise of his teacher, who wrote of him, "This soldier is extremely intelligent and motivated, and *can be relied upon*"—italics Dr. Bacteria's, meaning that Abraham was to be assigned forthwith to the Special Team which was coordinating a massive attempt to reduce the intelligentsia of the enemy to basic sulphates. So Abraham soon found himself leading his battalion along a dyke, the men balancing themselves like drunks, with mud and water on either side, Abraham holding aloft his poisoned bomb, which was glassy and pear-shaped, with many veins running around it, and Abraham felt so powerful because he was going to annihilate the

Nicaraguan command centers that he ran onward laughing, with 'copters chattering their laughter behind him; and his men were happy, too, because this was The Real Thing. The Nicaraguans shot at Abraham, but he only laughed; he was wearing bulletproof armor. The Order of the Screaming Skull was black and crimson and yellow on his chest, and his stars and epaulets made him even more glorious than he was. As he ran, his lucky dog tags slapped against his chest. *They* would protect him—how could they not?—for he had INHERITED them.

3

In the Days of Yore, *or*, How Old Colonel Yesterday Won the Quest

Far away, you see, there had been a battlefield, where an American soldier was sent. It does not matter exactly where it was; in the east, long columns of defeated German soldiers already marched across the silver-grey photographs in the history books, with their hands upon their heads, and the Russians with their rifles walked on either side, shepherding them to their deaths. The Siegfried Line was still quiet; blossoming trees, planted when its concrete was poured, still made gardens of the places where German soldiers went down into its tunnels, so that it could be pretended that Germany was also a blossoming garden. The barbed wire was not yet cut; the tank traps waited new-clean, and within the walls were secrets as promising as unwrapped Christmas presents. So the soldiers marched down into the smooth damp darkness, with their funny helmets and their rifles at their shoulders; but they felt despondent; they had no hope. —And the Americans came. They landed in West Africa; they landed in Italy, and they landed in France. They were really happy now; they shouted and laughed and their faces were well-fed. This soldier was one of them. —Kiss me! he cried to the girls who threw down flowers in front of his tank. —Bring wine and sausages!

he cried to the men. Then he liberated them all. And he loaded his rifle and pressed on, shooting Germans along the way.

Oh, he is a *brave* young soldier! said one of his grenades to the other. Then the soldier threw them both, and they hissed with pleasure and sent out sparks of excitement from their fuses and exploded grandly.

What a *steadfast* fellow! said his helmet, and it stopped all the bullets that the Germans fired at him.

How *good* he is! said his rifle. I will always aim myself true for him!

As for me, said his pistol blushingly, I will see to it that he fights to the last man.

And the soldier pressed on until he came to the Siegfried Line.

Now some of us will be killed, said his comrades, shaking hands all around, to say goodbye in advance. They were still very well-fed.

That's as may be, said the soldier, but some of *them* will die too, I think! and he pulled his helmet on tight and reloaded his rifle.

Everything around him was shattered and ruined and bristling with wreckage. His comrades shot down all the trees with their machine-guns; they shot their mortars into the dark bunkers where the Germans lived, and the Germans began firing back, and now the soldier was a free man and he began shooting and shooting into the dark places; he killed more Germans than anyone.

Kicking Back on the Mattress of Memories

Later, when the war was over, he married, and (since the story must conform to the rules of fairytales) three sons issued from the port turret of his naval wife, their names being Sherman, Douglas and Abraham. As even the wars of twenty years ago are seen so distantly, heard only behind the humming and cheeping of video transfers of old Defense Department films in which jungle leaves shimmer and bombs go off in high grass, with a somberly exotic memory-odor like coffee, so old Colonel Yesterday (now merely a Mr., but not to his friends) left behind

137

his calling year by year as he crossed a miracle of civilian bridges whose complexity of lines seemed to be constructed using a Spirograph. Once when business took him to Gun City and in the subway station he passed by two G-men pounding each other on the back going well I'll be GODdamned if it isn't my old Hoover Pal! Say what've you been *doing* with yourself all this time? then Mr. Yesterday felt something like homesickness for the bunkers whose inky rivers he had navigated bomb by bomb, and he slowed his pace listening to the G-men saying ah, played the arms market. Won a little, lost a little, and had sense enough to quit. —Well, at least you've *learned* something, Sam. Say, remember Singapore, '52? —You mean '51? —'51, you're right. You always did have a good memory, Sam. Boy, weren't those belly-dancers something, the ones with the little manacles in their navels? —By GOD. But this new crisis is bad news. —You're right there! Boy, if I only had a line to the Bureau again . . . —Same old Sam! I sure wish you could. We just don't have the backing we used to. We're getting soft, Sam. —I just don't understand it. Everything some fifth-rate agent says gets in the papers! . . . and then the two G-men saw that Mr. Yesterday was listening and came sprinting after him yelling FREEZE, *you!* I said FREEZE! and Mr. Yesterday *whizzed* his senior citizen's discount card into the turnstile and took the Marshall line quick as a wink, transferred to the 3 Truman and the 4 Kennedy straight to Cuba Station until he was sure he'd lost them. His chest ached. He kept saying to himself: Never again. I just can't do that stuff again. —Nonetheless, he had kept the dog tags of the last German that he'd killed, one minute before Hitler committed suicide. They were two cold black strips of metal, joined by a chain; they were heavy and slick with gun-oil; they had the smell of handcuffs about them. Sometimes, when the rest of the family was watching the blue adventures of Lone Shen on the old television and everybody got killed in action all over again, he went out to the garage to hold them in his hands. It was strange, the way they could suck the warmth out of him. He told no one about them, least of all his wife, because they had power and were magic. A houselight from across the featurelessly white-walled driveway shone green in the window, which was grey and of a varying texture, like pond ice. He held the dog tags up to the light and watched them glow. But they sucked him dry, somehow. They left him so tired that when he pissed he could not even tell whether the ringing in his ears was piss striking the bowl or a sound in his head or maybe the ringing of the telephone. And then Mrs. Yesterday would be waiting outside the bathroom saying Winston, is something wrong? Winston you always take so *long* in there! and Mr. Yesterday said can't a man even have privacy when he takes a leak? and Mrs. Yesterday said that old Sergeant-Major had those symptoms, you know, when his prostate trouble started and Mr. Yesterday said I *don't* have prostate trouble! and Mrs. Yesterday said are you *sure*, dear? and Mr. Yesterday said what's for dinner? and Mrs. Yesterday said Swiss steak and frozen succotash and Mr. Yesterday said I think I'll go lie down in the den for a minute and Mrs. Yesterday said I'll send one of the boys in to wake you when it's ready and Mr. Yesterday said fine, dear, fine and he sat down in the olive-drab armchair where he could daydream again about the Battle of the Bulge with the newspaper beside him for him to scan in case he wanted to check the obituaries which he was now the proper age to do because almost every month, it seemed, there'd be some item like

> PATTON, George, S., Corporal, Ret. (A.P.) Corporal Patton died early this morning at Torquemada Naval Hospital, of complications following an engorged intestine. Decorated for valiant holding action in the Battle of Verdun, Corporal Patton is today most often remembered for his close friendship with **Colonel Winston Yesterday, U.S.M.C., Ret.,** whom experts predict will kick off any day now.

and old Mr. Yesterday sighed and scowled and saluted at the group portrait on the wall and then folded down the paper to read **UNEMPLOYMENT UP IN GUN CITY** and suddenly he didn't feel at all sleepy anymore, so he slipped out into the garage to hold the dog tags in his hands, and when Douglas said *gee*, Dad, I've been looking all over for you! he said sheepishly yes, son, I'm trying to decide how much gasoline to put into the lawn mower.

The Recruitment of Sherman

When Sherman the eldest son was twenty-one, Mr. Yesterday called him into the den with its quiet dimness and racks of hunting rifles and grenades and skulls and antlers, and Sherman sat down on the folding chair because nobody but Mr. Yesterday sat down in the armchair, and Mr. Yesterday poured them each a tumbler of Burning Patriot Sour Mash and Sherman said *gee*, Dad! and Mr. Yesterday rubbed his belly and said: Well, son, and what do you want to BE in life?

A soldier, Dad, like you.

When you close your eyes at night what do you see?

Well uh I see islands of brown and uh green inside khaki seas and rivers like the Yellow River or maybe the Yalu River where we're fighting the Communists now and I want to be there swimming through that ocher mud firing at them Dad like *you* did until they surrender, over and OUT.

What you're seeing, son, is the sleeve of your camouflage uniform. I think you'd better apply to Special Forces.

Gosh, Dad, do you think they'll take me?

Sherman, your old man still has a little bit of pull with Canine Senior down at the recruitment office. I'll take care of that. But now there's something I want to ask you.

Dad, I know what you're going to say. I promise you that Marnie and I will wait to go steady until after I come back, because both she and I agree that my career has got to come first.

Good boy! But that's not what I wanted to bring up; I knew that went without saying. Marnie's a good girl; she'll wait. —Now, have you ever seen these?

And suddenly there they were, cold and black and dangling, the little neck chain like the tail-bones of a dead rattlesnake so that the tags were loathsomely machined and there was still dried blood inside the grooves of the swastika and the German boy's name yawned in etched black rivers that ran deeper and deeper inside the metal.

140

Wow, Dad, those are really NEAT! Where did you get 'em?

Killed a man for 'em, son. I want you to wear 'em, and wear 'em with *pride*.

Wide-eyed, Sherman took the tags from his smiling father, and he felt so alive, so alive (his heart was pounding; his penis was hard as a rock); he felt so alive that he wanted to die right then . . . but as he began to put them around his neck a strange expression came into his face. He looked down at the carpet; he shook his head stupidly from side to side, like a horse beset by flies; he looked anywhere but at his father. Suddenly he burst out: I—I can't do it, Dad! I want to do what I'm told but they're too strong for me; they—they *hurt* me . . .

There was a long silence.

I expected more from you,   Mr. Yesterday said at last.   Get out.

Sherman joined up the next day long before breakfast, and went off to war, where planes flew serenely like hornets, each in formation, each in its turn dropping a bomb, turning belly up and veering back (these were the grey silhouettes that he knew from World War II). A soldier was reading the Bible to soldiers sitting in the dirt: *Every sin that a man does is outside the body, but he who commits sexual immorality sins against his own body*   and Sherman thought   does that mean that Marnie and I—*gosh!*   and Sherman thought   but what about the immorality I committed when I couldn't take the dog tags?   and his face flushed with shame which he knew his father also felt; shame was the only bond between them now; his photo would never hang on the wall of the den where Mr. Yesterday sat reading **Bureaucrats overrun Gun City** (U.P.I.); and in the rec. room, where the two other boys stood dispiritedly casting noosey horseshoes around the neck of a Communist figurine, Douglas was saying: You got to accept it, Abe. Dad said he's not our brother no more.   —For Sherman the landscape was all grey. A soldier was painstakingly writing as he sat in the grass. A soldier adjusted the strap of his comrade's pack. All around him, Sherman saw platoon boats and planes, platoon boats and planes, a grey machine rushing steadily along a blue horizon. He was in the **SPECIAL FORCES**! But even though Hegel and Schlegel and the other bagels proclaimed through their empty O-mouths that things were getting better and better, he did not have much confidence. He remembered the old rule that if you make a long-distance call to someone you have a crush on (Marnie, for instance) and there's a long interval between the click of the connection and the first ring, your nerve will fail. Something like that was going to happen to him. It had to. Marnie sat watching television day and night weeping, hoping to catch sight of Sherman among the other soldiers who smiled and waved from the bluish-grey screen and the planes moved forward slowly, shrewdly, one by one, each plane's exhaust smoking around the soldiers' ankles, and soldiers stretched out their arms to point and then the planes leaped into the air. Sherman wanted so much to go soaring up from runways, but he was wounded first. He expostulated on his stretcher, gesturing, but they carried him into the medical hut anyway. Later he died and became just another white-draped body to be carried away by the Red Cross jeep . . .

Prop-Serity

Meanwhile old Mr. Yesterday sat reading the newspaper year by year and the headline said   **GUN CITY'S MAYOR PROCLAIMS "WE ARE THE FUTURE"**   and Mr. Yesterday said   I damned well hope so and his youngest son Abraham said   Dad, what's prop-serity?   and Mr. Yesterday said   huh?   and Abraham said   it was a word I learned in school   and his mother said   oh, you mean *prosperity*, Abraham!   and Abraham said   oh   and Mr. Yesterday laughed and went back to reading the paper   and Abraham said   Dad, what does nuclear mean? and Mrs. Yesterday said   Abraham don't bother your father while he's reading   and Mr. Yesterday said   it's like a gun, Abe, only bigger and better   and Abraham said   does it have more prop-serity?   and Mr. Yesterday said   yep, you hit the nail on the head that time, boy!   and Abraham ran off imagining that prop-serity was something dark and black and red-glowing that you fired out of guns, so when he was old enough to take the subway in to Gun City with Douglas for the first time and he breathed in the black air he said   wow, so this is prop-serity!   and Douglas said   aw, grow up, Abe!   and later on Mr. Yesterday would say   Abraham, run in to Gun City and buy one of them new reloading presses, would you?   and Abraham would take the subway down to Victory Street (it was still safe for children to ride alone then) and place the order in one of the crowded hardware stores (there were new ones going up every day, double-decker, triple-decker hardware stores, revolving hardware stores even, due to the construction boom), and Mr. Yesterday said   Abraham, run in to Gun City and fetch me some thumbscrews, would you, boy?   so he took the subway in, rattling below the pool tabled basements of bedroom communities where the lovely loveless housewives took phenobarbital and lay curled in bed all day like frozen shrimp, then past the stations of Hinges, Informerville and Slammer to Victory Street where there was now a hardware store as high as he could see with square yellow-green windows whose incandescent lamps resembled double rows of molars. The metal regime sustained him unthwarted, holding him up, binding him tightly to himself.

The Recruitment of Douglas

Then (it was the year after the tank factory in Gun City closed, and the year before the submarine business really started going underwater, and the recession widened in the same way that the hem of a woman's dresscoat is spread when she widens the gap between her ankles, striding unfreely along) Douglas the second son reached his majority, and Mr. Yesterday asked to speak with him privately.   —I thought you might like to have these,   he said.   See the bullet hole where I shot him in the neck?

Father, father,   sighed the son,   those things are so old-fashioned. The way we kill people now in the R.O.T.C., we turn their entire skeletons into little black pellets that we can carry with us for souvenirs. —Catching sight of himself in the mirror, he forgot all else until he had adjusted his collar. He was very vain.

So he was not the destined one either. The old soldier sat very still, disheartened.   —But, Douglas,   wept the mother,   I'm not going to hear about you getting hurt down there,   and Mr. Yesterday said: he did not take what I offered, so I will not see him again.

Douglas became a soldier and went off to war to try his luck. He saw the long columns of refugees, the little boy wiping tears from his eyes. He saw soldiers in trucks and boats, soldiers patting little brown children for the newsreels, soldiers distributing food behind the security of barbed wire, and yet he could not enjoy himself. He became one of many soldiers at a gun, laboring at it, one of many soldiers hunting, soldiers briskly trotting through shoulder-high grass, soldiers fording streams; green-clothed soldiers creeping through forests, adjusting the straps of their heavy helmets as they went. The officer with the pointer touched the patrol area on the map. The other officers nodded earnestly. The officers assembled their men and moved their jaws up and down. Soldiers were taking packages out of a steel dragon and stacking them in a hole in the ground. Soldiers strode slowly through the jungle, rubbing their helmets as the grass went whipping across their eyes. Soldiers were sitting and firing their big gun. The recoil made them jerk back as if they weren't sure they liked it. Soldiers were shooting at a green hill. There was a report, a wait, a glowing circle, and then a smoke-puff. Then a gun on the green hill fired back, and Douglas was killed instantly.

The Recruitment of Abraham

Now Abraham the youngest grew older (it was the time when lead pushers first made headlines in Gun City although there was still so much skyscraper construction that drill-guns fulfilled the acoustic functions of woodpeckers) and he saw his father looking at him and two days before he reached his majority he dreamed of being uncertain whether or not he were going to some cold dark island that might be fatal, so windy and scary, but in the morning he said to himself just one more day before my father asks me and that night he did not dream of anything and then it was breakfast time and his mother said happy birthday, Abraham and they all sat quiet over cereal and bacon and soft boiled eggs with Sherman's picture and Douglas's picture grinning tightly from the living room through black ribbons and streamers (his mother had had her way there; they'd held funerals) and then Abraham's

144

father said   son I want you to come into the den for a minute   and his mother blinked very rapidly and began to do the dishes.

I had meant to give these to one of your brothers,   Mr. Yesterday said,   but one refused it and one was too weak for it. Abraham, will you take it and wear it?

Yes, Father, I will,   said he.

Then his father was content, and delivered unto him his power, his legacy.

Abraham joined the army, where soldiers walked one way, and little dark people in conical hats walked the other. A man in a conical hat was hoeing his field as soldiers walked across it. Trampling rows of crops, the soldiers waved at a smiling Vietnamese child. It was all prop-serity to him. The trampling went on so long that it turned into a business. Two big soldiers walked a little blindfolded Vietnamese into a building, and the door closed behind them forever. Afterward, Abraham was ordered to fall in with the sunglasses-wearing soldiers shouting and chewing gum as their PT boat went down the canal.

4

Abraham's Last Campaign

Just as a green tank may blend in with the jungle, raising its snout questingly, rolling up to a lagoon and waiting and then firing so that a big white smoke-puff rises on the other side of the water, and the tank now emerges boldly from its thicket, crushing down trees and rolling slowly along on the flats to see what will happen next, so magically equipped young Abraham led his men past every obstacle—at least until he came to the place where the young Nicaraguan soldier lay hiding in the grass, looking around, lighting a cigarette, watching a low horizon across which an American 'copter flew, tail up, bubble down, watching an American flag waving, watching Abraham's soldiers ranging across a fluffy field (**KILL** written on all their helmets), watching Abraham's face dodge jerkily behind the reticule of his sight picture; and the Nicaraguan soldier waited until Abraham's cheekbone was centered and then pulled the trigger and the bullets went *dit-dit-dit* toward their target. Abraham as I said was wearing his impermeable armor, so that he had nothing to fear, and the Nicaraguan soldier could not understand what was happening as Abraham continued to lead on his shock troops (who had flipped down their crystalline visors after the first casualty), and the Nicaraguan soldier could see Abraham's grainily magnified face grimacing and twitching a little in his scope, but Abraham did not fall; no blood shot out of him; his head was not sawed off; Abraham only brushed at the bullets from time to time, for they itched annoyingly as they grazed his armor. Then the Nicaraguan soldier was confounded and enraged, and aimed at the bomb in Abraham's arms—which through a lucky hit went **POOF**, which it was not supposed to do until tomorrow. —Dr. Bacteria said that it was perfectly all right because those things happened, but Abraham noticed that he was not placed in command of the next commando party. Thereafter he was placed on "active reserve," so that his tour of duty became like one of those stifling nights at the opera when you cannot let your head roll onto your shoulder because that would block the view of the ladies behind and you cannot stand up and leave— that would *never* be allowed between intermissions—and the music creeps and crawls and the singers take one step forward and two steps back and stand and kneel to pass the time while the phony castle rotates stupidly, until at last you cannot stand it anymore and long to gallop into the aisle and down the cushioned steps to the railing of your balcony and pull yourself up onto it kneeling, clasp your hands in front of your head like a good diver and launch yourself down to the first tier of heads; because you want to escape the opera, you cannot believe that it will even hurt; you are almost certain that it will be like plunging into cool water whose wave-music is the murmurous xylophones (for you do not object to the music itself, only to your own uselessness there). —He called his father on Family Day, and old Mr. Yesterday said gruffly: Don't buck it, son! and Abraham hung up wondering what this was supposed to mean; he kissed the dog tags until he could taste the old blood on his tongue, but his fortunes did not improve. Soon thereafter, Abraham resigned his commission. Just before he stepped aboard the camouflage-colored van in which he would ride to the Demilitarization Ward, he took off the dog tags, and flung them into the waste can.

5

The Four Resolutions

What goals do you have? asked the staff psychiatrist. You don't want to kill anyone anymore?

Not when they won't die, said bitterly prudent Abraham.

Well, what then? —The shrink was impatient. —You realize, don't you, that you're a sick man, that you need treatment? If you weren't sick you wouldn't have failed. Stick *that* down your Adam's apple.

Doc, that's not how it is, said Abraham. I trusted Dad's dog tags and *they* failed.

Dog tags, eh? said the psychiatrist disdainfully. Wear a rabbit's foot, too? You'll try handcuffs next, I bet. That's what the washouts do—go into police work. But remember this, boy: you can make yourself into anything. If you want to be a nightmare, go on ahead. I can't stop you.

Just as eggnog drips off a blender-blade like mucus from a tonsil, so the shrink's words went *pingggg-gaplopppp!* inside Abraham's mind, and he thought handcuffs, eh? Handcuffs. Mmmph. Everyone needs something to hold onto.

The Peace Offensive

So he returned to Gun City in the discharge van. (When he heard the news, old Mr. Yesterday died of a broken heart, **pop!**—taking his spouse with him locked in his bony arms.) Things weren't the way they used to be. The Israelis were making better guns than anyone, boys; they had the R & D. The Russians weren't making enough tanks to match our output anymore, so the prices we commanded tumbled into the pits with

147

greased pungi-stakes. Unemployment, trade unionism, and other spots
of blight had flecked the red-white-and-blue curtains now drawn across
the dusty windowpanes of the Colt Smoothbore Factory. Abraham
hardly recognized the home front anymore. He squeezed his wrists
alternately between thumb and forefinger, wondering what successor to
the dog tags he could enshrine at the center of his life, and handcuffs
seemed possible, and yet . . . —Well, first of all, a man wore dog tags
himself. But handcuffs were made to be locked around someone else.
And he had no one else. Hence Elaine. General Wolfburger, more
understanding than Mr. Yesterday had been, pitied Abraham and strove
to interest him in medals, replica black-powder cannons, flag pins and
slingshots. When these things failed, there was nothing left to offer him
but girls. Hence again Elaine. Meanwhile they boarded up Assault Rifle
Towers; they closed down the Nerve Gas Herbarium; they laid off a
whole division at Old Faithful Nuclear & Co. Although on the street
corners recruiters cried Gitcher JAWBS! JAWBS now! JAWBS that'll
feed ya!, the nuclear technicians did not take their handbills because
they did not want to work on anything except bombs, so they never
became sheet-rockers with sheet-rocker bosses writing verses to them
such as:

I

Skim down the stairwell from
the front door up to the Radio—use
the disc. for the inside ceiling corners at
the entrance. —LOOK around to get it
ready to Sand tomorrow.

II

Tues.—go to 681 ALVARADO +
First coat everything.

III

TALK to you tues. night—
TRY to do a good job—don't let
anything go.

As for Abraham, he didn't want to tape or sand, either. Instead he saw fit to collect his disability pay and fondly cherish Elaine who at that time loved war movies because he did, and had just begun to write in her little golden book although everything was wonderfully demilitarized during those first evenings together in Gun City when the taxis went squeaking and glowing by and the homeless people were smart enough to be quiet and the miniskirted secretaries rushed with the sound of shoed horses to stand in line for SON OF METALLICA or SADISTIC RULE at the theater where the white constellations of light were so elegant beneath black marquee-skies, and Elaine took Abraham out for dinner, the two of them sitting on coppery stools not seeing the men at the next table lift upper lips and flip back sap-brims already flipped back, resting their cheeks in their hands, muttering   Gun City sure has gone to hell;   shuffling their feet on the floor as they argued over the check; Abraham saw only Elaine; Elaine saw only Abraham even when the place caught fire and then the automatic sprinkler came on to drench them and the waitress and other shattered operators, but at least Abraham could go on kissing her; at least he had that. *She* was his prop-serity (I use the word for the last time but one).* He took Elaine out for dessert . . .

I just came back from the ranch in California and it was *beautiful* sighed the chiropractor, jerking Elaine's neck back and forth in slow whipsaw motions of immense ferocity and power so that Elaine's neck popped and clicked as Elaine lay smiling so starrily beneath the sign that said **PLEASE WAIT TO BE SCENTED.**   —And what's new with *you*, Elaina dear?

Oh I have a new boyfriend.

I could tell it was good, because your spine is so straight and radiant today. I'm so happy for you.

Her spine straight, his shadow horned, Abraham went down to the place where night sounds were the pulsing breaths of air conditioning ducts and the even, lethal breeze of automobiles all around him as Abraham ducked into the courtyard of Franklin DeMott Towers and waited as a greenish star sped overhead, a satellite or some new

---

* One rule, indeed the first, is that the kissing game can be played out almost forever, like the tortures of unrequited love, ever more bitter, less sweet; the second rule is the "almost"—for eventually the well does run dry, and then the handcuffs clatter tight against your wristbone.

experimental bullet, and listened to the elevator inside, the cables of which screamed suddenly, like an alarm, although the tremor of that scream was symmetrically modulated, and then someone came out. Someone could always be counted on to come out.

Hey, bro, you want some bang?   said the pusher.

Abraham looked both ways.   What kind?   he said.

Oh, *listen*, bro, I got me the BEST, got some forty-five caliber bang. Arizona lead.

OK. Two shots.

The bullets tumbled into his hand. Abraham gave the man his five and went off happily, thinking how much fun it was going to be to shoot up with Elaine . . .

. . . as meanwhile Elaine was making a special bracelet for Abraham out of gunmetal scraps even though that was kind of nationalistic or ballistic but she knew what he liked, and Abraham put it on and then said   you know, Elaine, I bet *you'd* look good with it on . . .

Immutable Processes

Now she was watching him, so anxious that he would find her desirable; she pulled his head down between her breasts with desperate happiness. (Yes, Elaine had begun to watch Abraham lately. Actually she had done it for a long time. But she was coming to the conclusion that she shouldn't be doing it because it made her unhappy. On the other hand, as she wrote in her golden book, nothing *kept* her from examining his position in the world, and its relationship to her.)

Don't worry honey,   he said.   I can get something.

Something to . . .?

That's right,   he said.   You know. Then we won't have to worry anymore. It takes all the uncertainty out of it. It's a lot better than an operation. A lot of people I know use one.

But what about *me?*   she cried petulantly.   You think you have it all figured out, but you never checked to see if it would even fit me or if it's what I want.

Oh, it'll fit you, he said. It fits everybody. And I know just where to go to get one. Somebody wrote it in the men's room at Veterans' Hospital . . .

6

The Purchase

It was a blue day in Gun City and the tan-colored bricks of the more genteel apartment buildings supported one another's weight as well as the weight of the terraces whose windows looked into steel shutters rolled down against the day; and skyscrapers stood on end like corncobs, and beer cans rolled down the stepped roofs of skyscrapers and fell a hundred stories to smash like meteors upon the sidewalks, not hurting anyone who mattered because *they* were inside, at work; and the sounds of rumbling and hammering rose between buildings and ascended as an offering into the sky, and the melodies of police sirens floated on the chilly breeze, and from somewhere came a steady cracking noise as if work gangs were beating on the skyscrapers with chains. Accompanied by this symphony, Abraham emerged from the subway warren and walked down a narrow street of boarded up windows. Foamy little gobs of spit squashed under his heels. The door of a bar was open, and he went in and looked up the dark rotten stairs, but it was too quiet; he did not feel safe. He came to a more crowded place where the Munitions Union was on strike and the same old scab agitator with the bullhorn stood calling out Gitcher JAWBS! and strikers were throwing lead slugs at him that tumbled into the depths of his bullhorn like unlucky insects falling into a pitcher plant and the rattling and booming of those heavy bits of lead inside the bullhorn's ribbed caverns was amplified to the sound of a gun battle. The strikers were aiming for the scab's face, but they could not yet reach him because he held the bullhorn in front of him so that it seemed to grow out of his face like an elephant's trunk; yet insensibly the bullhorn got heavier and heavier with the slugs inside it, and the scab's message became more and more muffled. At last he could not hold the bullhorn any longer, and it fell from his hands. Then the strikers opened fire with zip guns and pistols whose disassembled parts they had stolen over years and years of shifts on the riot rifle conveyor belts, where hollow-nose bullets and revolver cylinders and speed loaders had been known to slip between the moving plates and fall onto the lead-slicked floor beneath until the factory workers looked both ways and stuffed them into their pockets. At home the union leaders had miniature sub-factories inside cabinets, with special lathes and mashers and rifling presses that could turn a silver spoon into a pistol barrel; whatever hammers and recoil pins the rank and file had scavenged were brought here on Tuesday evenings when the union secretary called the rolls and the treasurer collected dues payable in subway tokens so that the graphite centers could be punched out and made into bullets cased in the brass doughnuts that remained; meanwhile the union members sang songs from the Golden Testament such as *Truth is in the inward parts, justice in our noble hearts* and as they sang these songs the union machinists rifled those inward parts for better accuracy, bent low over the secret humming cabinets so that their butts stuck high in the air, and later when the whole caboodle was arrested by agents of the D.A.'s office they were put to the torture and asked to identify the machinists but nobody could because all they could remember were those butts in grey denim trousers quivering away like grimy cloven apples; and the TV was on loud to catch all the industrial news and the screw-turners sat around the coffee table making every subassembly snug with incredibly skilled fingers so that later when the arrested machinists were asked to identify them they said   sorry Officer but we really can't 'cause all we remember is those dirty fingers wiggling fast as you please and the big ammo men were in the basement leaning on their reloading presses to seat and cap each bullet firmly, snorting with effort, so that when the arrested screw-turners were asked   now who were your confederates downstairs? all they could say was   gee Yer Honor I can't rightly say 'cause when I close my eyes to recollect all I can see in my mind's eye is flapping nostrils and I'm looking up deeper and deeper inside them like twin black gun-barrels but I can't see the renegade at the other end;—   and this phenomenon, ladies and gentlemen, is called DIVISION OF LABOR. So anyhow they blew the scab's head off and while they were so engaged Abraham, who was wearing grey coveralls just like them (for he had learned the tricks of the covert penetration trade under Dr. Bacteria), passed through them saying   Amen, brothers and sneaked around the corner to the back of the factory where the Police Division was still going although the union there had begun a sympathy slowdown and Abraham ascended the kneebreakingly high steps by the loading dock and went into the little office with the silver badge in the window and said   yes fine day isn't it well I'd like to buy a pair of handcuffs, please.

You a peace officer, sir?   said the clerk.   We only sell to peace officers.

How much does a pair go for?   said Abraham.

Thirty-two dollars retail,   said the clerk.   We wholesale only to departments in Detroit, Washington, Houston and Los Angeles.

Abraham took out fifty dollars in ones and fanned them on the counter. The clerk just looked at him, so he threw in a ten. Sighing and shaking his head, the clerk disappeared into the storeroom and came back after a moment with a cardboard box that said in big letters

"Lock – Rite ™ **"**   and then below that, in smaller type, "The Cuff That Won't Quit".

Just you look outside and see if the Inspector's coming,   said the clerk.

Abraham went to the parking lot, looked both ways, saw nobody except a few hooligans, and returned.   —Coast is clear,   he said.

The clerk heated a blunt stylus in the flame of his cigarette lighter until it glowed cherry-red. Then he took the handcuffs out of the box and obliterated the serial number, expertly kneading steel shavings into the hot metal until it was perfectly smooth where the digits had been. At last, with a wink at Abraham, he filched a bottle of blueing solution from the storeroom and applied three drops. He spat on an eraser and massaged it vigorously across the stain until it matched the color of the handcuffs, blew on the spot until it was dry, snapped the handcuffs folded again, and popped them into the box.

Use them in good health, sir,   he said.   And, like I always say to my customers, *do* read the manual.

First Pleasures

All the way home, Abraham's heart beat fast with excitement. It was only with difficulty that he could keep himself from opening the box. How nice it would be to clench his new cuffs around two other subway riders' wrists, leaving them to go through life together willy-nilly! Would such a pair forge a brotherhood stronger, in the end, than the steel that bound them? Or would they take the cheap way out and end their troubles at a locksmith's? It depended, Abraham supposed, on the individual. —But HE would not use his handcuffs cheaply: they were for Elaine.

He ran up the creaking stairs of his building to his apartment; he unlocked his steel-plated door and threw down the box on the kitchen counter; he popped open a Bullet Beer in the rounded silver can; then he lifted the top from the box. He wiped the storage grease from the handcuffs and unfolded them like wings. Ah! He would never have to remember prop-serity or the dog tags anymore. Then, sipping his beer, he unfolded and commenced to read

The Handcuff Manual

He skipped to the part after the congratulations to new owners:

> We begin with yet more proof (as if any were needed!) of the diversity that adds zest to our national life, like a thousand square black windows in a brick building: Each Department teaches its VERY OWN handcuffing techniques. —Our allies have spoken to us with unbefitting contempt

154

of the *primitivism* of this practice, thereby showing their own stunted development (have the Russians ever achieved *their* visionary dream of the frictionless rocket-launcher? —Oh, impossible things and far-off places!); for as long as handcuffing procedures are not completely standardized, even the most case-hardened suspects can scarcely hope to anticipate, and thereby to escape, every Surprise and Peculiarity. Of course, that fact adds complexity to this discussion by a kaleidoscopic number of permutations. This here manual, however, is intended to be a general guide only.

Hmmph, he said to himself. Get to the part that makes my dick hard.

To handcuff your suspect, position one of her hands behind her back with the palm facing outward (this is the most crucial phase of securing your prisoner). Maintain control of her by keeping her off balance. A bitter but expectant skepticism is the best means of accomplishing this (see manual FM-36: "Sexual Trapping"). Hold one handcuff with the keyhole facing away from her hand and toward the small of her back. Now place the jaw of the handcuff against her wrist, at the extreme termination of the ulna. Press the jaw firmly against the wrist, causing the jaw to swivel through the cheek and re-engage. Press the jaw into the cheek to tighten the cuff against the skin, being careful always that the skin is not pinched in the jaws or that circulation is not restricted. (Suck your own cheeks between your jaws if you wish to resemble a skull.) Now you or she should bring the other hand behind her back so that the palm is facing outward. Kiss her hand and read her her rights. Now constrict her other hand and double-lock both cuffs, thanking God that it has not turned out to be one of those days in the office when, suddenly realizing the triviality of what you are doing, you feel too big for your own shoulders . . .

Abraham could stand no more. He dialled the long distance porno number in Bangkok to learn how his javelin of glory ought to be polished and it said   *Dear soldier!*   and the woman said   watching you in the interrogation room   and the woman said   I know you're a V.C. bitch   and the woman said   I'm pulling up your skirt   and the woman said   You're glaring at me with your big black eyes; you're shouting: My taste is poison to you, imperialist pig!   and the woman laughed and said   but *I* know that just like Comrade Lenin says, socialist corn tastes the same as any other corn, does it not?

Oh Elaine oh Elaine oh oh.

Later he took the handcuff manual up again and finished the essentials:

> When you have become proficient at double-locking, the next step is to develop confidence in the use of imaginary handcuffs. These may be purchased in the three standard sizes (please specify when ordering). Imaginary handcuffs are applied by means of certain spoken algorithms not dissimilar to the so-called "spells" in the Grimoires of the ancients, their function being to constrict and constrain the volition of the suspect (ideally, without her knowing it). As the techniques involved are complex, we have thought it best to develop an intermediate model, which still has weight and substance but lacks visibility; this is ideal for covert operations. Neither invisible nor imaginary handcuffs will be of any use to you, however, until you master the fundamentals of metal swallowing metal with the proper number of graduated clicks.

Yes, just as vanilla is the standard at the top of every signboard of flavors, so the handcuffs of peerless metal began everything. What a divine hourglass shape they had, narrowing like Elaine's waist where the hinges joined them, then widening again for a ring of hollow hips that could clamp tighter and tighter . . . And what *weight* they had (although weight was something that he must be weaned from, if he were to graduate to those imaginary handcuffs). He liked to hold the handcuffs

156

against his wrist, to just touch the jaws to his skin in an electric prick
. . . There he stayed, to use the simile of Babur, as long as milk takes to
boil. —Now at last he let the loops close upon him and tighten, and he
smiled to feel that coolness rushing up his arms and into his shoulders.
He became stolid, immortal, unaware. When a siren went screaming by,
he opened his eyes and found that two hours had gone by.

Abraham and Elaine

I have something SPECIAL for us,   said Abraham, opening the box.
Just like I promised.
    Elaine bit her lip.   —I'd rather just do it the way we did last time,
she said.
    Try it. For me.
    Oh, all right. But we have to remember to "become very very rich
and retain forever our youth." I read that somewhere, but I forget where.

Abraham and Elaine

Isn't it silly how we make this so important?   Elaine said.   It's like me
hanging pictures on the walls and admiring the shadows they make.
    Oh, no it isn't,   said Abraham in a threatening voice.
    Anyway, most of my life I spend sleeping or working in the office,
said Elaine.   Tomorrow's Monday, so I have to go to bed early. I really
hate that. But I don't stand to gain by fighting it, do you think?
    Just put the handcuffs on,   said Abraham.
    The idea of money in the bank is a good one,   said Elaine.   I can
almost smell it cooking on the stove like dessert for the kids. If I ever

have kids, but now I don't know. It doesn't seem like there's any place for them to play.

Impatiently, Abraham lifted the top from the box and pulled the handcuffs out, staring avidly as they hinged open into two rings.

No, I don't think I will have any,   said Elaine.   But the sun will always go down and my alarm clock will go off and Abraham will be waiting with his pet handcuffs.

7

Abraham and Elaine

Sometimes on a Friday noon after Abraham got his disability check from the little Army window that was just big enough for him to pass his identification through to the patriotic eye behind, and Elaine had bought a sixpack of wine cooler from Mr. Rat's Super-Duper, they took the bullet train to the city limits and went picnicking in one of the wrecked cars in the brown grass by the river, he gallantly brushing the broken glass from the driver's seat for her, she sitting there, hanging her handbag from the gearshift while she got the handcuffs out and locked his wrists to the steering wheel with a nice breadstick in his mouth for him to gnaw on at his pleasure, and sunshine came bravely in through the wrecked windshield.

Well, so I let you do it to me once,   Elaine said.   But it was only once. If I'm lucky it won't happen again. Should I scratch your nose for you? Is the scarf tight enough around my neck?

Because she always spoke this way, there came one outing when after peering up at the rusty clouds Elaine saw him sitting free-wristed and exclaimed: Where are the handcuffs?

I didn't bring them,   he said dully.   I thought you didn't like them.

I don't.

158

Well then,   he said, finishing his bottle of cooler. He hurled it through what was left of the windshield, and it shattered on a hood ornament.

Well, why didn't you bring them?   she said.   Of course you have every right not to explain why.

In that case I won't explain why. Cigarette?

Tell me.

I thought you said I didn't have to.

Tell me.

Well, if truth be told,   he grinned, very sure of himself at last,   I have them right here, in my shirt pocket.

Well, you can.

I can what?

Honey, put them on me,   she said.

Her voice was rich with love.

Fireless Swimming

Yes, reader, we just saw a TURNING POINT for poor Elaine Suicide! Slowly the handcuffs had taken on credibility for her because they meant so much to Abraham that they had quickly become a part of him like his hands and penis so that she almost loved them—and yet every day, it seemed, she knew less about him than she had the day before.

But don't let me assume things,   she said to herself.   I'm not talking face to face with you, Abraham. I'm just thinking these things all alone, lying on my bed smoking cigarettes and scrubbing the grime off the windows so I can watch the sky. And it's also true that when I watch you I *want* to know more. I can't figure you out. I want you to give me an answer, but I don't know if I'd recognize it when you came out with it. I want to know why you're the way you are.

Elaine Alone

First she had a dream that she was trying to get out of England with everyone who was important to her, a busload of ex-lovers and just friends and unjust relations, and at the first of the many passport stations she filled out the form but nobody stamped it, so she filled out another form and again nothing happened, and all her friends were getting on the bus to the next station already so she gave up and ran after them and boarded at the last minute, pretending that her form was stamped like theirs, but she knew that after all the intermediate stations were completed, she would come to the last station before the ship and then they would find her out and keep her in England forever all by herself. The next night she dreamed that she was in a bus terminal in Montréal waiting to interview someone important day after day until they started watching her from the adjoining room, which was a barber shop, and finally they came to her and said: We're going to give you a head start, but you'd better begin running, because if we catch you in town we're going to kill you and Elaine said but it's snowing outside! and they gathered around her and gave her a gun with three shots in it and then a sick feeling of reality began to get her and she was gasping with fear and she said how long will you give me before you come after me? and they said we're coming after you tonight and they coolly examined her belongings (scarves and notebooks and fingerless gloves) before handing them back to her, and Elaine wanted to take everything because it was important to her but she was afraid she'd drop something in the snow every now and then which would leave a trail for them to follow, so she sat turning her belongings over and over in her fingers, her mouth dry with fear, and she said when tonight are you coming after me? and they said oh, about ten minutes and Elaine threw everything down on the floor but one scarf and her golden notebook and started running through the snow and it was very dark and the wind chilled her as if she were naked and the snow was knee-deep and she came to a bulkhead that said **TRANSIT AUTHORITY** and the ten minutes were

160

almost up so she scrabbled in the snow making a trench so that she could get the door open and as she dug she thought   oh no I forgot the gun!   and she was sobbing and gasping for breath and at last she got the door open and it slammed shut behind her and she felt her way down a flight of steep narrow steps as if she were descending a pyramid in total darkness and came at last to a basement where tramps were lying against the wall, and she leaped over the turnstile because she had no subway tokens and went down more stairs until she came to a cave of sulphur bricks where a sewage waterfall spewed under arc lamps, and in the slimy pools below the falls many vagrant families stood fishing lead slugs out, and on a newspaper that fluttered by the headline said   **WOMAN, 24, RAPED, THROWN DOWN ELEVATOR SHAFT IN GUN CITY (U.P.I.)** and Elaine said   thank God I'm home in Gun City   and she woke up but her heart was still pounding. She said to herself   this has something to do with the handcuffs. But what? What does it mean?

She said to herself: Why, that place was my insides!

She said: But was it always like that inside me or did it just get that way?

She opened up her *Golden Book of Attitudes* but could find no answer there.

Abraham and Elaine

You have dark circles under your eyes,   he said.

Pretty soon they'll go all *around* my eyes,   laughed Elaine.   Then they'll click down tighter and tighter.

8

Phase One Plus

Taking these words of hers as permission, Abraham put his token into the dirty slot and let the crowd feed him into the magazine of the subway car. Now he was speeding through the Colt Auto Tunnel, which was like an immense narrow bathroom, like the inside of a snake plastered with bathroom tile. Now he passed Victory Station, and he thought of the dead hardware stores there; then he reached Informerville, where he (1) left the car and (2) climbed the broken escalator, (3) passed through the turnstile, (4) ascended the dirty stairs to Security Street, (5) crossed the parking lot of the weapons factory, (6) went around to the back entrance with the silver badge in the window, and (7) looked both ways to make certain that the Inspector was not in the parking lot.

Back again?   said the clerk.   I was pretty sure you'd come. The customers always want a second pair, for the ankles.

Look here . . .   Abraham began.

Oh, two pair, is it? You're one of those.

I guess you could call me that,   said Abraham.   But I'm sincere about all this. I take it personally, you could say. The others don't generally get as far as imaginary handcuffs, I bet.

You're right,   said the clerk very slowly (for some reason he reminded Abraham of the newsreel of Operation Blind Bat, the pilot with his big headphones meditating, absorbing),   but not for the reason you think. Actually it's the expense. The imaginaries cost more than you might guess.

What about the invisibles?

With each stage the cost goes up, of course,   laughed the clerk.   I hope you're a rich man. You're not getting those today, are you?

No, my wife's not ready yet.

They never are. But you're working on her, aren't you, you clever little bastard? Bide with me a minute while I fix those serial numbers.

9

Abraham and Elaine

The worst thing about it was that it had all been done before. (So it seemed to him, because he could not quite forget his father's dog tags.) How could it be that people had been on this earth for so long that every person *must* know that when he took off his clothes he would be naked; and yet so many people were shocked by a drawing of a naked body? Why should anyone be horrified by handcuffs when it was rigidly apparent that policemen used them efficiently? By the same token, and worst of all, why should he be titillated? —But he didn't really want to think about that. Nothing had been enough ever since the dog tags failed. It would be cheaper and more convenient if he felt differently, but that was just how it was, so he took the subway to Elaine's and on the way another subway car went past, in which he saw himself looking out the window at himself through huge grey-green glasses and he was thinking too bad it's not one of those cold nights when Elaine used to put on her fuzzy pajamas (now that the winter was safely gone, he could be nostalgic for it; maybe in three or four months he'd pretend that today had also been fun); and a man in a baseball hat snored on the subway car, holding a piece of cardboard that said **I NEED YOUR SPARE CHAINS** and meanwhile Elaine waited for him looking out the window. She saw a couple walking down the sidewalk, and the man's hand was on the woman's shoulder. He smiled at his partner and turned toward her to let his smile come into her face and be registered and then sent back to him buttered by her own taste, but she moved her face away involuntarily, as if his breath smelled; so he dug his fingers into her shoulder, at which she twisted sharply away, at which he gripped her hard enough to bruise; he surely must have bruised her,

Elaine thought. She picked up an orange which she left on top of the refrigerator to ripen but it had turned black with air-grime; making a face of disgust, Elaine creaked the window open and lobbed it into the air and it fell thirteen stories to the pavement. Elaine expected it to burst, but it didn't. It bounced like a Superball and then rolled into the nearest sewer.

Guess what I brought?   said Abraham.

New ones?

New ones.

Not so long ago,   said Elaine,   when a man asked a woman he hardly knew to marry him, he was simply asking her to sleep with him. He would fuck her like a doll.

What are you saying?

You don't care what I'm saying. If you did you would have asked me or maybe taken me with you. There are special things in those places, you know, women's special things. Don't you see that those are just *your* things?

Elaine, you know you put them on sometimes without my asking you.

That doesn't mean anything. It doesn't!

They're not the invisible ones yet, don't worry. They're just accessories.

Like me, I guess.

Oh, no,   said Abraham.   You've got that all wrong. You're not the accessory. You're the reason.

Abraham, I don't think I love you anymore.

So that night, on the roof of his apartment tower, Abraham sat alone, with all Gun City below him: the arches of streetlamp reflections on the Remington River, the blinking airplanes sliding down invisible ramps in the sky between blinking smokestacks, the peaceful inhumanity of cars streaming under and over on bridge necklaces, car-light making grey street-canyons yellow, the random squares of lighted windows . . . A cool breeze, almost clean, blew against the back of his neck.

Well, that's over,   he thought, feeling bitterly sorry for himself. Turned out she was a failure just like my brothers. I know her so well. If I'd said she was only the accessory she would have licked my hand. —Am I the only one left to support America on my shoulders?

Witnesses

So it came to pass that two girls named Darla and Carmella were wandering through the women's holster store trying to decide how Darla should spend her vacation.

Elsie could take me to Gunbridge Mall,　said Darla.

Well,　said Carmella,　I'll ask my friend and if she wants you to come then you can come.

Whatever.　—Darla picked up the latest pink snug-tight Robopath trigger-snuggie design and put it back without looking at it.　—Or maybe I should go see Elaine. I haven't seen her for a long time. Have you seen her?

There you go!　said Carmella, relieved that now she would not have to ask her friend to do anything for Darla.　—I bet if you ask Elaine she'll show you around.

I'd be so *psyched* if I could see her!　glowed Darla.　I mean I'm not asking her to take me around the *world* or anything . . .

See, there's this *awesome* park that Elaine can take you to,　said Carmella.　They've got steel trees and steel benches and when you put a quarter in these steel fingers come and fold over your lap so you're protected. And they're putting in pay TVs. I bet she'd be thrilled to see you.

I didn't need this vacation *honestly*,　confessed Darla.　Originally I was thinking of going to Guntown or Gun Village but then I thought why not see Elaine.

Poor Elaine,　sighed Carmella.　I wonder what she's gonna do.

Maybe she'll move.

I think she needs a full time restrainer coming every day. Especially after the way Abraham treated her.

You said it. When I heard about their relationship I said that's sick I mean that's weird. I guess he was even talking about INVISIBLE HANDCUFFS when she broke it off. Can you imagine? I can see the steel kind because that's halfway accepted although when I saw my sister and her boyfriend I said that's not right I mean with those young kids—

Have *you* ever tried it?   asked Carmella.

I'm not telling!   said the other girl, and they both laughed.

10

Abraham and Elaine

Now that she didn't have him, she loved him. She called up and Abraham said   if I come back will you still turn your face away when I kiss you?   and Elaine said   no   and Abraham said   will you still refuse to let me buy the invisible handcuffs?   and Elaine said   no   and Abraham said   all right then but I'm going to go buy them now and I'm going to click them on good and tight.

Second Pleasures

The clerk winked and slid them over. Now Abraham could feel them in his hands, so cold and heavy and oily, but he could not see them. In awe, he realized that this was how it must have been for his father all those lonely nights in the garage. Now he wished that he had kept the dog tags, so that he could have buried them in his father's grave.

He went home. He turned out the light and sat in the darkness holding the handcuffs, because in darkness when other objects were invisible he could almost persuade himself that he saw them in his hand; so he sat on in that holy stillness, like a father watching by the crib of his newborn baby, careful not to disturb the infant's sleep.

Abraham and Elaine

You know what I'm going to ask,   Abraham said.

No,   said Elaine.

But by now he had her wrists invisibly handcuffed together behind her back; he had her ankles individually cuffed with guilt and tenderness to bedposts so that her legs were spread, and she was wearing a diving mask with the mouthpiece of the snorkel dangling wetly between her breasts (he had asked her to lick it) and her hair was very coppery in the glow from the bedside lamp, and her eyes were huge and blue behind the lenses of the mask (which were, of course, of the very highest diopter), and the nosepiece made her nose look very fat and white, and her lips were parted a little so that she could breathe; he leaned forward and breathed the breath that issued from that sweet pink darkness; he pulled down her lower lip between his fingers and kissed her teeth. — How he smiled to see her lick her lips again and again, because the mouth-breathing was drying them out!—and he wondered how the surgical quality silicone felt against her face: was it comfortable? above all, was it natural?—and now he lifted the mouthpiece from her chest, kissing it where it was still wet from her saliva; he bent it and put it into her mouth, lodging the bulbous terminus firmly behind her teeth, which she obligingly clenched; then he began to tack down the strips of black electrical tape across her lips (which snapped something sticky over Elaine's mind just as the army psychiatrist's words did for Abraham when he mentioned handcuffs), sealing the snorkel in place, wrapping the tape round and round; and every turn put her further into his power. He brushed the hair very tenderly away from her mouth as he taped; he did not want to pain her. The snorkel was warm from her breath now; he could see little droplets of condensation inside it. He held his palm an inch above the top of the tube and felt the skin becoming moist with her exhalation. Then he put one finger across the outlet. There was a whistling sound. She tried to smile at him. Now he pressed his hand down firmly to seal the tube. Her breath hissed out through the blow valve; then he felt the vacuum pressure of her next inhalation against his hand. Her eyes widened. She began to struggle. He smiled down upon her . . .

When he had gone, she sat weeping at the way that he had degraded her. She looked at herself in the mirror. For the first time, she took the electrical tape and slapped it across her reflection, gashing her face with blackness—

Abraham and Elaine

He took the subway home and kicked aside the all-expense-paid coupons that had piled up in front of his door, as they had by his neighbor's and everyone else's and unlocked the door and lay down with the invisible handcuffs squonched down lovingly on his erection, and he dialled the long distance porno number in Bangkok and it said   *If you're not eighteen, please hang up now*   and he forgot Elaine in her black coat and wool socks and then the woman said   watching you in the detention room   and the woman said   I know you're married   and the woman said   I've seen the dress you wear, with the little jaws and circles like the mistaken faces of young poets   and the woman said   I saw how you smiled when the policewoman spread your cheeks   and the woman said   I pick up my handcuffs, and I run in there, too   and the woman said   you're just pulling down your convict panties when you see me   and the woman said   a smile crosses your face   and the woman said   I'm sucking each of your toes one by one   and the woman said   I bury my tongue deep inside you, licking you in perfect episipentagons   and the woman said   the handcuffs go around your thighs, biting into your soft plump flesh   and the woman said   call back after six o'clock for an even *hotter* story!

Abraham and Elaine

The handcuffs continued to do their work, Abraham's kindness being now half-strangled, Elaine's confidence deeply incised by metal ligatures. Furious with one another, they were walking round and round Gunmetal Pond, which was rather more brown than grey in the sunlight, and between them (for they were a good ten yards apart), the professional dogwalkers followed their charges in the same inexorable circles, being pulled so fiercely by the big marmadukes that they had to dig in their heels to keep from being yanked down on their faces, and like clusters of helium balloons the long low sausage-dogs yapped after rats, darting between the marmadukes' legs, getting tangled in each other's leashes, biting each other in a stupid panic, and a sausage-dog got in Abraham's way and he kicked it and it screamed and the dog-watcher came chasing him, at which the marmadukes bayed and surged and dragged him down and Elaine said   it's just like that scapegoat when we met, on New Year's Eve,   and Abraham said   I guess it is   and he took her hand and they wandered away to where the tramp in wraparound sunglasses stood playing the violin, not noticing as hordes of sausage-dogs crapped on his foot, and the skyscrapers towered all around and curved and bent in Elaine's glasses.

I'm sorry. I just want to cast a golden attitude,   whimpered Elaine. But your black steel attitude keeps hitting me like you're throwing horseshoes and I'm the post.

Don't kid yourself,   said Abraham, pulling his hand away.   You crave those cuffs just as much as I do.

(He was right, in a way. She had never reached the realization that people really *are* rather rubbery and NEED handcuffs, such as the good citizens who took special classes so that they could learn to become more like their dogs—just a few of the many successful graduates being the big fat lady whose partner was a poodle huge and round like a dark balloon; the nervous man who yapped like his terrier . . . all of them schmiegling and beagling along.)

169

I don't want to get hooked, Elaine said. If you do that to me, it's your responsibility. Abraham, I'm talking to you. Do you hear me?

There's nothing to worry about, he said. You can't get hooked on them unless you lose the key. Then you just go to a locksmith and it's all over.

And Elaine was standing in her bedroom by the open window yawning and watching how her nipples shrank when she put her hands on them and grew again when she let the breeze flow over them and Elaine thought to herself I'd rather be bored like this than be at work. And Elaine wrote in her golden book without knowing exactly what the words meant *before my insides spill recklessly.* She liked the sound of it. She wrote in her golden book *I miss all those New England snow blizzards like nobody knows here* and she wrote *Imagine a young girl. Conversations and all her daily activities before she is abducted and molested and murdered by a senseless killer.*

I want a warmer heart, Elaine said. Did you ever wish you had that?

Sometimes, said Abraham.

. . . And Elaine sat on her bed picking her toenails and flicking them down on the floor.

Well, said Abraham, how about it? Are you ready now?

Elaine looked both ways and then wandered nude into the hall and went into the bathroom, and then she came back and lay down beside him and she wondered is this inter-dependency? and Abraham thought ah look at them clicking so nicely around her ankles and Elaine thought it's like trying to swim laps without any water and Abraham thought now for the big ones that go around her tits and Elaine thought am I going to be made happy from this? and Abraham thought now and Elaine thought I really don't like this and Abraham thought now and Elaine thought I think the party was outside.

What are you doing tonight? said Abraham.

I'm going to scrub the bloodstains from my underwear, said Elaine.

and Elaine wrote in her golden book *Image/Theme: A woman and her lover. She needs love and comfort but does not get it. As time passes and she sees her lover's failure, she accepts it and builds a room filled with warm things to soothe and satisfy*

170

but she could not for the life of her imagine what those warm things were.

and Elaine was singing in her room alone   *he left me, left me high and dry.*

Then it was late and dark and Elaine was lying down on the floor with her eyes closed but not asleep. Abraham came in and turned the light on. He glanced at her, undressed, turned the light out and got into bed. Soon he had fallen asleep. Elaine opened her eyes and imagined that he had just embraced her passionately.

11

Abraham and Elaine

I would have liked to know what it would have been like without the handcuffs,   Elaine said.   And it's not one of those things you can just do someday anymore. 'Cause time passes, you know, Abraham. Things have happened. Why aren't you saying anything?

I don't need to say things. The handcuffs say them for me.

She took a deep breath.   —Believe it or not, there are some things I don't want to talk about, either. But sometimes I have to say them.

He ingested her words like a bloodsucker, so that whatever she was going to say next drained into silence. His eyes were dull. Both pupils and irises were shrinking. She pulled him down onto the sofa, and he lay on top of her, his serrated edges rasping against her sweater.

Have you drunk anything tonight?   she said at last.

No,   he said.

That's good,   she said.   I thought you'd been drinking a lot.

He said nothing. She laughed suddenly and threw her arms around him.   —Want a drink now?   she whispered.   I bought us some gun oil single malt. Why not?

He lay very still, breathing in sadness like polluted air. Finally he began to button his shirt.

What are you thinking?   she said.

He sat up and tucked his shirt into his pants. He zipped up his fly.

Speak to me,   she said.

He was putting on his shoes. He tied the laces and got to his feet.

Are you hostile?   she said.

He patted her arm.   No, I'm not hostile.

You're hostile.

He smiled very widely (maybe she would see the grief keening behind his teeth) and patted her other arm.   —No,   he said,   I'm not hostile.

Once more he touched her, and then—to his own immense surprise— he let out a groan and rushed toward the door. She bounded in front of him like a lioness and threw herself against it, glaring so fiercely at him that for a moment he was cowed.

No! she shouted.

He went to the sink, opened the cold water tap as far as it would go, and thrust his head under the stream of water. The chilly shock of it restored his peace, and he began lapping at the water very tranquilly.— Elaine stood watching him, with her hands on her hips. She uttered an odd little laugh.   —All right,   she said at last, stepping back.

He went to the door, opening it inch by creaking inch, looking now at it, now at her. He could not for the life of him understand his own self. He was fettered in the brain-dungeon of a stranger the consequences of whose behavior he must suffer without recourse. It was three in the morning.

Will you be all right?   she said.

I'll be fine,   said Abraham.

He wandered home in a daze. It was a wonder that no one molested him as he strode heedlessly through the grim shadows between the deserted buildings, thinking to himself   so why can't I cherish her?

12

Witnesses Again

It was a bright evening in Gun City, the sky glowing like a white hot manhole cover; but brightest of all was the fleet of rivet-studded armored trucks that squatted along the curbs of Security Lane, their drivers staring dimly out through brown-smoked windshields. In the shoe store, the girl with cat's-eye glasses whose crossed legs showed the marks of manacles met the girl with pink flamingo earrings who kept putting them in her mouth; and they mutually exclaimed DARLA! and CARMELLA! and Carmella said you heard about Elaine?

Of course I heard, said Darla. What do you think I am, stupid?

She almost died in the hospital, said Carmella. She wasn't eating.

Isn't that awful? said Darla. I mean I can't believe it.

Why would she want to do that? Trying to hang herself like that. How could she leave that beautiful house behind? I mean a *perfect* location.

I know you don't feel sad about that guy Abraham but I do. A goodlooking guy. I was against him before but I'm not anymore. Because once you open yourself up to those invisible handcuffs like Elaine did then you lose all your rights. It was like Elaine couldn't make up her mind whether to put them on or take them off. Just the way she was when she was on that diet shit. She cracks me up. Well, she never was a brain surgeon.

Gone through hell, though, said Carmella loyally. I'm never gonna be like that.

I mean she's not exactly the most stable—

You know, I knew there was something funny about that relationship. Those two could never be dressed casual. I hate that about them.

And there was something competitive about them, too, said Darla.

Just the way they interacted. Like she was determined to cling to him tighter than he could put those cuffs on her.

Disgusting,   said Carmella.

Crazy,   said Darla.

Meanwhile

Elaine Suicide was in a grocery store, not knowing anything but pain.

Touch me,   said Elaine so drearily.

I don't like no one to touch my face,   said the salesgirl.   'Cause their doin' that, that's how I get pimples.

13

Home Again

Of course Abraham and Elaine made up, being caught in each other like the linings of suitcases in the jaws of suitcases. It's not as simple as a subway ride with the conductor's hair cut very straight across the back of his neck. Abraham was guilty and loving, shining and sparkling— although he may not seem so to you. What was his difficulty? It cannot be said that he had no feelings. Now that familiarity and PROP-SERITY had been reestablished he did (it is true) concern himself less with Elaine's feelings than his own, but how could anyone compete with Elaine when it came to having feelings? (Elaine always wanted to color with crayons; she remained shy, and went to movies to hide. This was part of the broad range of actions from which darling Elaine selectively chose contrary actions.)

They had Thanksgiving at his uncle General Wolfburger's. At the beginning of the meal everyone was expected to utter some personal mantra of grace and all those introductory valences, so Elaine, who was an occasional animal activist, said: Thank you for all the turkeys, chickens and pigs . . .   —at which everyone laughed pleasantly—and Elaine went on   . . .who *weren't* killed for this day—   at which everyone got quiet.

Something stinks about that,   said General Wolfburger after awhile. I don't know what. I smell liberal vermin in the pantry. We need a good economocide!

Elaine hummed and paid no attention. She was invulnerable to people she didn't love.

Later, Mrs. Wolfburger called Abraham into the kitchen and said: My dear, are you sure she's right for you? She needs a TIGHT REIN.

Don't worry,   said Abraham.   She'll get it.

A Summation

At first, as we have seen, Abraham was as self-satisfied as a fat girl who enjoys the feeling of her own soft thighs rubbing together when she walks. New ones, new ones! After all, he said to himself, Elaine was a girl of incredible pudency. Abraham thought to himself   her breasts are as beautiful as twin smokestacks spewing and blinking in the night.

But it didn't take long before it was time for the imaginary handcuffs. He was ready for them. He needed them. They would overcome the disappointing tastelessness of Elaine's breasts. That is the sad thing about fetishes: that they wear out. He had a long trail of discarded weapons behind him as like his father he descended into those final bunkers. We who already know how Elaine was to kill herself may believe, if we choose, that perhaps the purpose of Abraham's life lay not in any one charm or token, but precisely in that discarding of tokens; hence Elaine must be discarded to death. But that is too glib. Abraham cried when he heard the news; he really did.

What are you thinking?   said Abraham, clicking and unclicking the imaginary handcuffs (he made the sound with his tongue).

Oh, thinking about how I feed on jealousy and unfairness.

Are you jealous of the handcuffs?

Elaine shook her head. Later she went to the movies alone and cried. What else was new?

Home Again

So with money in his pocket he rode up out of the subway graves with the rest of the swarm, and he came to the factory. The strike had been broken; he saw nothing but pissed-on leaflets struggling against each other in a stinking breeze. A newspaper blew up against his leg; the headline said: **EPIDEMIC OF SHOOTINGS IN GUN CITY.** — Abraham looked both ways. The Inspector wasn't there. (The Inspector was never there.) He strode up the steps by the loading dock.

Ah, the clerk said, it's you.

He had been drinking from a squirt can of some kind of solvent. His eyeballs were grey and reflective.

Pull yourself together, said Abraham contemptuously.

Pull myself together! the clerk laughed. With what? Your hand-cuffs? Oh, you filthy little pervert . . .!

Abraham spread ten twenty-dollar bills on the counter.

Don't you see how you're holding it all in? the clerk shouted. Don't you know the story of the man who could postpone his drunkenness?

I guess *you* couldn't, said Abraham.

He could save it all up, said the clerk. He could drink as much as he wanted in the bars and spy on the other drunks. But he had to let the drunkenness come later; that was the rule. It could be done at his convenience, but it had to be done. Do you follow me?

How much money do you want?

Somehow he never got around to it, said the clerk. Even on his deathbed he didn't have time; he was too busy dying then. So he became a drunken ghost. You remind me of that guy. I saw him on TV. He's running for President. You have those same Presidential features, and you have money like he does, and you . . . you . . .   —His voice was breaking.

What exactly's on your mind?   said Abraham. He had a bad feeling now.

Would you—could you?

Could I what?—Oh, fuck, no! Use your own goddamned handcuffs! What do you think I am?

The clerk looked at him appealingly.   —Well, if you ever change your mind you know where to find me. Here. I'll get the new pair for you. Invisibles again. On the house.

I came for the imaginaries.

I got to tell you, those imaginaries, there's been a crackdown. We can't sell them anymore.

14

The Quest

Again they went picnicking in the outskirts of Gun City, where the boarded up hotels, yellow with white trim, reminded Elaine of omelettes. All around them the windows of orange brick towers were shimmering. People leaned out panting and stifled to enjoy the urine-smelling sunshine. But Abraham scarcely paid any attention to Elaine now; she was only camouflage. He was looking for the imaginary handcuffs. He was just as he had been the time that he came home from the screwdriver store, glowing with the single yellow eye of a technological purpose. He watched everyone who seemed to have anything to do with nothingness. One day he and Elaine were sitting on a bench behind two likely specimens who passed emptiness back and forth in their hands, and one said   where jew git it?   and the other said   down on Gun Street   and the first said   well, shit. That pair's a purty good one!   and the second said   yew go ahead an' look at it. I'm gonna go to Milo's and git me some see-gars. Yew know, right around the corner   and Abraham kept thinking   how am I going to see those? No, I *can't* see them or feel them!   —And he felt very despondent.   —He visited the Gun Library with its long steel tables, upon which stood double rows of dingy lamps whose metal shades were scratched with firearms obscenities. Behind the tarnished balconies were rows of uniform volumes chained to the shelves; these, if any, might tell him about imaginary handcuffs and which of the four possible deadly pathways of copper-64 he must walk to find them. But those pages had been torn out of the relevant volumes.   —He went down to Fanny Alley where the fat whores stuck out their dimpled doughy behinds and made kissing sounds with lips that fluttered faster than scarlet hummingbirds' wings, but although he carefully watched the men come and steer them away like cars, the whores leaning giant sturdy hairdos against the men's rigid shoulders as the men went straight-eyed down the street, he saw no evidence of handcuffs real invisible or imaginary.

He closed both Elaine's hands in his and whispered: I'm almost there. I feel that I'm almost there . . .

Elaine looked away.   —Keep being perfect until you *are* perfect, she said.

Oh, go to hell,   he said.   I only need you a little longer.

The Palm Reader

The cardboard sign said **OPEN** and the green neon sign said MADAME STALINA : PALMISTRY READINGS – TAROT READINGS. The white curtains were drawn against the window, but a light was on behind them. He went up to the door and opened it.

Just a minute,   Madame Stalina said.   Let me calm the kids down.

The kids sat watching TV. They were fat boys. Madame Stalina's husband was a used car salesman.

All right, so you want a palm reading or what?   said Madame Stalina.

That's right,   said Abraham.   But first . . .   —and he opened up the box and began to put the handcuffs on.   —You see,   he explained,

I just feel more comfortable with these things on. Is that a problem for you?

Madame Stalina squinched up her face in disapproval. —I always say what a person does in Gun City is his own business, she said. Not that I care for that sort of thing myself, but if you tell me to take your money I'll take your money. It's fifteen dollars.

Now, said Abraham, I want you to look at these handcuffs and read them like you were reading my hands. They *are* my hands in a manner of speaking, my second pair of hands.

All right, said Madame Stalina wearily. Whatever you want. Just let me close the door. I don't want the kids watching this kind of thing.

She was a fat greasy woman with shiny teeth.

Well, I can see you're in some kind of crisis right now, said Madame Stalina, taking one of Abraham's shackles between two fingers. But things are gonna clear up. I can tell you that. There's someone in your future, and you have to act decisively.

How decisively exactly?

I mean *decisively*. Things are coming to a head. A stitch in time saves nine. He who hesitates is lost.

The children had pushed the door barely ajar and were peeking at Abraham. He winked at them. Someday, if they wanted to, they could grow up just like him.

I can see this is a matter of life and death, said Madame Stalina. But the spirits still aren't visible yet. They—

They're supposed to be invisible, said Abraham. In this case, at least.

Madame Stalina laughed. Oh, shit, she said. So *that's* all you want. Melvin! Hey, Mel!

A grumpy man came in. He wore a T-shirt that said MEL'S USED CARS, GUARANTEED ALL THE WAY TO THE PARKING LOT. —When's dinner, anyway? he said. When you gonna be through with this guy?

He wants the imaginary handcuffs, she said. That's what he's looking for.

Mel looked Abraham up and down. —Him? He don't look the type. 'Course he's got the steel cuffs on, but in my 'pinion he don't appear to me to be one o' them *Power Users*.

Well, he is, snapped Madame Stalina.

Are you sure that's what you want, mister?   said Mel.   I kin sell you a pair, but they're not guaranteed. An' I'll tell you something else, too. They're about to be discontinued. Too many complaints. An' I can't discount 'em. Five hundred cash. No way you're gonna jew me down.

Abraham tried to get his wallet out of his pocket, but the handcuffs made it difficult.   —Honey, you want me to help you with those? crooned Madame Stalina.

Yes, please.

Two turns of the key, and his wrists were free as pink flamingo-birds. Out came the wallet.   —Five hundred, you said? Here you go.

With a wink at his wife, Mel made the motion of reaching into thin air.   —Got 'em!   he cried.   They was just now tryin' to swim into the air conditioning. Hold out your hand, mister.

And so the moment came when Abraham's palm lay yearningly outstretched, and Mel's fist descended inch by dramatic inch and then opened at last just above Abraham's fingers. Although Abraham could not feel anything, triumph and well-being thrilled in his heart.

Don't forget,   said Madame Stalina.   The five hundred was for him. You owe *me* fifteen bucks.

15

The Imaginary Handcuffs

I said that no one could see them or weigh them. But they tightened as inflexibly as reality . . . Consider cattle guard lines painted on the road, which fool the cows, then prison-bar lines printed on spectacles, which fool the convicts, then imaginary spectacles, which fool the blind . . .

16

Abraham and Elaine

Now there was no manual anymore. But all he had to do was look at her in a certain way for the tightness to lock across her face so cold and hard; and she sat on the rug and leaned against the door with closed eyes, her earrings barely quivering, her brows curving down as disdainfully as limp wrists. Consummated, it was over. With her other belongings he enclosed the handcuffs and the razorknife (but imaginary handcuffs only; it was a nasty joke, because she couldn't see them. Actually the joke was on him because she could.)

I wish he'd come back and visit, Elaine said to herself. It's too much to expect to have him forever.

I don't wanna just love love love and not be loved.

I still have a pattern of being attracted to those characters. I— But the handcuffs, I never liked *them*. The only reason I tried to like them was for his sake. But I have them now. I'll always have them.

She moved away. One morning, with any addict's failure of self-knowledge, he called her, but she didn't answer. All afternoon, all evening when he called her, the phone rang and rang, with that long and bitter echo that proves conclusively that telephones can see and hear and seek to give us their terrible news, for she was lying in that bloody bathtub as her kitten meowed and licked so gently at the blood. And yes, she wore her handcuffs.

But he truly didn't know. He had not yet gotten the package with the three golden books. Then that came, but he had not read the golden books. Then he had, but he had not yet called Painter Ben. He knew only that something was wrong with Elaine. Again I insist that he cried. In one of his panic dreams he was bombing along in a rented old junkmobile, trying not to think about Elaine, knowing that there was nothing beyond the imaginary handcuffs, no God or supercuffs, desperate to go somewhere just the same and find the thing that would save him before he perished in unworthiness like both of his brothers and everyone and everything that he had trusted, shivering the other station wagons aside in the narrow chute of dirt-colored concrete in which cars flowed like candy wrappers in a rainy gutter; between two rusty elevated freeways he was speeding toward the smoky yellow sky of Gun City that always smelled like burning, and a plane shot along his trajectory, lower and lower until it seemed just above him and he was in its shadow and a wing nut fell off it and shot through the roof of another car, and then the plane sped forward and began to recede between two paupers' towers whose hue, which was that of dried menstrual blood, brightened under the angry sky. Abraham accelerated as he went up the freeway roller coaster, his heart pounding sickeningly—

—but Elaine had slit open her veins which were long twin galleries, and underground loading docks whose rusty tracks were the color of the reddish darkness; trains passing dead trains whose square windows appeared reddish-black; and the lights gleamed purple on the blood-tracks and bare bulbs in brackets bleached the walls behind them in quadrilateral sections as if the darkness were dust and they had somehow worn it away in those little bare patches. Inside Elaine there were brick walls with arches as in Poe's wine cellar; there the telltale hearts had once beat like trembling liver-colored water balloons, bulging through the opening like Mishima's intestines when he committed *sepukku*; but everything was dry now; Elaine had let the blood out.

I can't forgive you for not letting me be the one,   he said to her when he knew.   You did it—you, with your knife and handcuffs. I would have used the same tools; I would have done it gently for you; and when you started to bleed you could have looked at me and seen your face on my shoulders.

6

Epitaph for

A RAJASTHANI PALACE

* INDIA *

Mornings of pale lakeweed speckled the surface of your doom like the pulp of fresh-squeezed juice.

Were you dead?

The Maharajah was, but birds lived in your arches, which proves any contrary. Your lily-pond terrace remained an open wound in your marble chessboard floors, in which water trembled like your beating heart.

Weren't you dead? Tintinnabulations of pigeons proclaimed it.

It was no pigeon who said *No man is an islande.*

You were yourself the island, water-stained around the edges, windowed and domed and caped with gazebos, indented with corridors, walled knee-high with marble planters for red and purple flowers spiderwebbed, fresh with wisteria and bougainvillea and potted palms and plants with leaves like swords. Islands are dead.

Yet your round marble tables were still reverenced by green-uniformed, yellow-turbaned servants polishing in the early morning. They swept and bowed; they bore trays on their shoulders to feed the squishy mollusks that lived in your innermost chambers; they were your corpuscles, but your blood was embalming fluid.

Pigeons murmured death in your arches white-pillowed with stucco like wedding cakes, tipped with colored glass points (green and red the luckiest). They said you were a sea-urchin's shell: adorned with proud spicules, but empty inside. In your gazebos of stucco and white marble, spiders had spun hereditary tangles beneath the tables.

But marble lions roared in your railings. On top of your head, a dark green parrot mocked the pigeons.

Of course there was porridge and curry and sitar music in your marble restaurants, sunrise coming through your windows; rich French families rubbing jowls, clutching purses. At every moment, the waiter was there to say: *More tomato juice, please? Thank you!* as he filled the glass.

(Waiters were always there. When I meant to love your marble nook, sun on your slowly trickling fountain, your emerald of grass and single tree guarded by your marble minarets, waiters brought me an Indian beer. Then I loved the beer more than you, and forgot to consider whether you were dead.)

Your lake was sliced by the motor-powered gondola with its black smoke. Water was greenly kerosene-slicked. Across it, white-lamped fortresses puffed up their envious turrets, their arches like negative vertebrae in rows on rows. *They* were dead, their bones a negatious urine-bleached yellow.

But you lived your genteel doom as pure and silent as a single vulture at sunrise.

VII

FLOWERS IN YOUR HAIR

Belief in such magic died hard: Coronado
searched in vain for El Dorado, and Ponce de
León died in his pursuit of the Fountain of
Youth.

RICHARD SLOTKIN, *The Fatal
Environment* (1985)

1

When I was seven I had to run away from home, so I went to
the clover meadow behind the houses and started up the hill
which was the boundary of my knowledge. The bees dreamed aside as
easily as they might dream back, and I searched for four-leaf clovers
because they'd bring me luck which I could store in hand against trolls
and other emergencies (luck must be the same as money). I didn't find
any. The clover flowers were purple and white; in my head the words
to that old song: LORD, I'm one; LORD, I'm two; LORD, I'm three;
LORD, I'm four; LORD, I'm five hundred miles from my home, with each
hundred miles (which were really a hundred steps) bringing the day
closer to night, the leaves blending insidiously into each other's dark
greenness like hours so that despite the desultory nature of my progress I
was lured from leaf to leaf more rapidly than I imagined, until suddenly
I'd been caught by the top of the hill, beyond which stretched a world
more adequately designed to test my boldness. This was another field
whose milkweed and thistles and goldenrod reified a direct contradiction
of me, especially now at summer's end when the goldenrod was tall
enough to overshadow me and the milkweed had begun to puff up its

189

downy pods of loneliness, not yet sad and brown and crackly but on the verge of something like sexual failure or the dissolution of Parliament. Because the goldenrod was so high I could see past this realm only indistinctly, but there seemed to be a pond whose shallows would crispen soon enough into grey ice, then a house by itself, and lastly a road of utter dismalness, dwindling away into the forest, where, I supposed, I would sleep tonight, as exiles always do in fairytales, haunted by wolves and witch-lights. Not that anything would ever stop me from running away . . . !—so it astounded me to find how strongly I desired to look back—just once, of course, and only as a goodbye to my toys. But as soon as I did turn around, my sight sped straight to that white box among all the other yellow and green and pink boxes; the kitchen window was open now; the car in the driveway . . . and with a speed calculable only by a supercooled electronic brain my hilltop became a place of the most intolerably fierce loneliness which stung me more bitterly than any thistle ever had, so I fled home. —When I left San Francisco, on the other hand, I went unwillingly, which meant that I looked back from the very first step. And I went much farther than five hundred miles. That Canaan of ominous milkweeds had been no more a wilderness to me than was the city in which I dwelled so sullenly, refusing even to name it by its name. Towers tricked with square eyes stood in my way on every side, the curses that I heard in the streets were like thistles, and the eyes of the living dead were yellower than goldenrod. As long as I could, therefore, I maintained my resolution of keeping my watch set to San Francisco time. I refused to learn the routes and destinations of the subways, being convinced that if I did the new geography would crowd out the old. I met people only for professional reasons, pitying and fearing them when they insisted that relocation was an equilibrium reaction, that just as I must now replace my inner San Francisco with an inner Gun City, so later—at any time!—I could replace Gun City with San Francisco, without tax, toll, or diminution. —But what about thermodynamics? I said (never to them). Nothing is frictionless. —An acquaintance who fancied himself learned began by admitting that when a chemical reaction is reversed, the equilibrium constant becomes the reciprocal, but he denied that that proved anything. Two places could go on being each other for all eternity, he said. —Possibly, I thought, but why put it to the test? It was like saying that a three-leaf clover still retained some luck! —You're not very hardboiled about things, said one of my occasional lovers, who was allergic to all metals except silver and gold. You ought to be more hardboiled, being in Gun City and all. I was pretty hardboiled by the time I was twenty. —I'll do better with you, I said mechanically. You'll see. —Well, she replied, sometimes one comes out as being better than one expected in these situations, and sometimes one comes out worse. —I wasn't sure what she meant, or if that had anything to do with looking back, but that is the way of it with lovers: your lips begin to discuss double lives; the ambiguities which once seemed momentous only bore you: you long for the clear speech of home. I was continually occupied with questions such as the following: If you get a seat on the subway and then the car fills up and you see a tired old lady in the crowd, not looking at you, ought you to rise and give up your seat, hoping that (a) you will be able to force your way through to her and tap her on the shoulder and point to the seat and that (b) she will not cower away from you in fear and that (c) she will struggle to the seat and that (d) the seat will still be free? —But then, before I could answer, the radio would play the song about how if you go to San Francisco you need to wear some flowers in your hair because flowers are the code for love; San Francisco is the city of love; that song had been young in the time when I thought to run away from home (I had never heard of San Francisco then). So I made up my mind to go back for a visit. —It won't be running away, I said to myself. After all, I'll have to come back here.

2

At first I had the same feeling as when I first visited Dinah the whore and her pimp Jack so early one morning that everything was still dark and I went up into that sad ugly wicked place where they did business and saw things which I didn't realize until too late that I hadn't wanted to see, and then I came out of the room with the smell of Dinah's smile greedy and hateful around me (all my money already inside Jack's arm) and I went down the stairs and came out of the hotel into morning brightness with office workers streaming immaculate and bland so that neither I nor they seemed real, and the sky was so clear and the whole day mine with all its sunny hours. I felt this way, as I said, being back in San Francisco even though it was not my San Francisco anymore and must therefore have new secrets like four-leaf clovers that I would never find. When I ran home from the bee meadow I must have sunk immediately into the heart of the good world once more, because I do not remember anything that happened after I got home; it was all dreamless like the knife-edge of an orgasm; so at first in San Francisco when I thought nothing and remembered nothing it seemed to me that the same perfection had taken me. —My optimism became still more extreme, therefore laudatory, when Elaine Suicide picked me up at the airport because she loved me, and I felt on top of the world, especially since I was carrying two guns in my suitcase, so I kissed her trying to suck spit from her mouth and she pushed me away laughing and I kissed her again and she said: stop that! you're being selfish!   and I thought well of *course* I'm selfish which was why I continued to want to kiss Elaine just as I wanted to have each day two of my favorite milkshakes which were unavailable outside of San Francisco; for similar reasons we went to the same vegetarian Chinese restaurant in the Richmond where she and I had gone five years before; I used to go there with my friends Vera and Monique, too, but Monique had died of AIDS and Vera was in Arizona trying to heal herself with crystals. I knew that Elaine got upset if anyone mentioned Vera, so I said nothing of what I was thinking and Elaine looked at me with an expression between hurt and merely inquisitive and said   why are you being so quiet? Are you being HONEST with yourself?   because honesty was important to Elaine who was no longer Elaine Suicide but Elaine Pure Light (with *her* a few days later I got into an argument about honesty so stupid and miserable that I avoided her for the rest of the visit); and I said   yes   and I told the waiter that Elaine was my wife so she had better have the best possible service but unfortunately the waiter did not speak English. Elaine looked around as if she'd never been here before and said   this dark place doesn't love me at all   and I said   it's not so dark in here   and Elaine said   I can't even see myself burning in the candle flame   and I said you look tired   and she said   it's just that I keep thinking of this dog that I've been trying to save.   —She paid for lunch and tried to give me the leftovers but I was afraid they would only sit in one of my friends' refrigerators until they went bad (as food will do even in San Francisco) so I said no and Elaine said she would drive around and find a homeless person to give them to. She was very nice that way, episodically. Once a retarded man who loved her had saved up scraps from his lunches over a whole week to make a ***special lunch*** for Elaine and when he gave it to her she said no thanks but then he started to cry and Elaine felt terrible so she took the composite lunch and kissed his cheek to make him happy again and then she spent an hour searching for someone who needed that lunch because she wasn't hungry and it wouldn't have been right to throw it away. She was now worried to a point far beyond action about a dog who'd gotten half-crushed by a car in the middle of the Bay Bridge; the traffic had prevented her from stopping, but through her rear view mirror of sympathy she'd seen him crawl bleeding to the shoulder of the freeway where I had once stood watching my friend Catherine swim from Alcatraz Island with the Dolphin Club and Elaine attempted to get into the righthand lane so that she could stop and lift the dog into her arms no matter how much honking and swearing and yelling might come about but the vehicles to her right, an olive-green Dodge and a big truck, would not part for her, so the dog dwindled, standing there on his front legs with his hind legs dragging and he was whimpering, and Elaine's wheels rolled her all unwillingly away from San Francisco, over the summer fogs that milkened the water, and then she was in the East Bay, so with the utmost feeling she turned round and got back onto the bridge, writing off her appointment in Berkeley, which wasn't so important anyway, and writing off this return trip as well since it must be conducted on the other deck of the bridge; but *now* at last she could loop back toward the East Bay again, past the last exit and onto the bridge that carried her smoothly over the fog, Elaine pressing determinedly to the righthand lane all the way, but it took her an hour to get to the bloody spot and by then the dog was gone. Who knew where he was? Elaine had borrowed her boss's cellular phone and was calling all the dog pounds as she drove around looking for the animal, whom she never found; and I felt strange to see Elaine looking for anything when she already lived in San Francisco which for me had become a static fresco of gold-leafed fulfillment. *Traveling is a fool's paradise,* says Emerson, but Engels says in the *Anti-Dühring* that *Necessity is blind only insofar as it is not understood,* suggesting most hopefully that there was a reason why we all blew hither and thither like crimson leaves. Was the dog the same for Elaine as San Francisco was for me? Monique and Vera always used to talk about being "centered," which I never liked at the time because it seemed to be merely the current fashion of flowers in your hair. But there was no reason not to admit that Elaine was dog-centered and I was self-centered and Ken was whore-centered. Elaine dropped me off at Ken's house, and Ken's eyes lit up to see me and I felt so good to be shaking his hand and we both knew right away that we'd go get some whores just for old times.

Stay real still, Ken said. This is a good picture. Oh, you're moving your head.

The whore kept wiggling.

You better do it quick, 'cause I can't stand up like that, she said.

Ken was under the black cloth. He zigged the lens in and out. — That's beautiful, with your head between your legs. Let me get the light in there better.

See, said the whore, that scar, that's my bullet hole. That's where I got shot last month.

As soon as she said that I started feeling sorry for her and wondering again why I had come back to San Francisco when really it was no different than any other place in this nasty world.

She smiled and brushed her skirt. Her tits hung down.

3

Everything was going on about me, just as it would go on around my grave after I was dead. On a sky-blue Saturday a whore stood on the corner of Eddy and Jones, lovely, expectant, and in the park the winos shouted as always. I went into a Vietnamese place for lunch; green cardboard cutouts of Tsingtao bottles rode the walls, but I got a fresh orange juice instead since San Francisco was associated for me with citrus beverages, and I watched the Vietnamese ladies working happily because it was their place and they were grandmother, mother, daughter—look, the daughter had a little baby! and they took turns holding the bottle for her to drink from. I squeezed the good hot red sauce onto my barbecue; the young waitress smiled at me and made me another fresh orange juice. She sat down with her mother at a corner table for a moment to drink tea; business was slow. Then she leaped up to refill the salt shakers, while a canned Vietnamese girl sang on the radio, so tranquil and cheerful. So this day had the same blue purity as the morning when I'd come out of Jack and Dinah's, but I knew that I wouldn't go into this restaurant again (and if I did there'd be some other restaurant I wouldn't go into again), and so even though the waitress looked after me sweetly as I went out I saw only the forgetfulness that was already coming on her like a smile's end, the mouth-corners trembling very faintly, relaxing, shrinking like an erection that's done its job, and then there is blankness again, the neutral face, the dead face that recognizes not. I went up the street past Satoko's old apartment to where the massage parlor still was, and almost rang the buzzer to see if any of the Happy Girls were there, but I knew they wouldn't be:— Tosany in Thailand; Donna gone to become unknown; I wasn't even sure I remembered Suzy's face. —So I went on down the block and saw a skinny woman grinning like a vampire and then I wandered back to Jones Street where I sometimes used to see my friend Melissa, showing cars her tits as tasty as chocolates, never wasting herself in smiles of phony love, which was why of all the people I'd met in the Tenderloin, I liked Melissa best. I asked the other corner girls if she was around, but they only said: I don't know her. I never heard of her. —That was what they always said. —I owe her five dollars, I said, and I really want to give it to her. —Nobody gonna be givin' it to Melissa no more, said one of the gum chewers (and I remembered *her* from the time I'd been at Ken's photo lab where the favored option for cutting negatives was **SNIP NORMAL** and I'd just gotten a short haircut and Ken and I were rolling slowly up Jones Street in his van and the gum chewer came to my window and asked if I wanted a date and I said: Where's the Tenderloin? I'm looking for the Tenderloin and she put her hands on her hips and blew a bubble and said well, baby, here you are and I said but is this San Francisco? and she said who *are* you, anyway? and I said: My name's Snip Normal and she laughed so hard she practically fell down on the sidewalk, and all the other whores on the corner split their sides and Ken was grinning and I glowed like the god of stupid laughs); Melissa O.D.'d, she said. Right up that alley by the Hob Nob. We all went chippin' in and buried her in the cutest pink coffin with a silver liner, I'm tellin' you. I took some pictures but they got lost. I was so PROUD to be there, 'cause she and I went way back. And we called her mom and told her she'd died in a car accident. You can gimme the five dollars. I'll say a mass for her. —OK, I said, and I gave her the five and went on still not knowing whether she'd ever met Melissa, whether her Melissa was my Melissa, whether Melissa was alive or dead. That was the thing about short visits.

4

Permit me to keep belaboring the point, with the same vigorous ferocity with which I belabored myself: Because I'd refused to be at home anywhere else, I didn't have a home anywhere. I'd thought that if I maintained my affections with rigid concentration, embracing the altar unsleepingly, everything would be all right, but somehow the altar had been made of butter and the heat of my love melted it into grease while meanwhile someone bent over me from behind and picked my pocket. I felt pretty sorry for myself. I was locked out of Paradise. I'd thought it pretty good when Ken locked others out, coming back snickering from another opening or seminar and giving me a full report:—*viz.*, People are always asking me why I take these kinds of pictures. I always just say, *I . . . don't . . . know*, but I'll spend the rest of my life trying to find out! What idiots, man! —and Ken and I would laugh over how their mouths fell open when they saw the latest cunt shot. —These pictures are REPULSIVE! a woman shouted, and Ken beamed with pride. It would be unjust to imply that Ken ever sought to hammer the tender toes of others (although he did, of course); no, I would never in nine eons imply such a thing when the truth was that Ken's pride was one of the most admirable traits in his character, consisting as it did of a defiant and alienated homelessness which though willed took on additional magnificence when others spurned him and he lounged leering and shouting like Satan after the foreclosure of Hell; offered the chance to repent and be adopted by a million gentle Jesuses, Ken was not the slightest bit

196

tempted to make *that* mistake. When I'd found the milkweeds and thistles blocking my way I'd run back, but Ken had gone in without a rubber. So now he amused himself by locking others out of the heart that fettered him. —Once a whore didn't like Ken and me very much. We were locked out of her San Francisco even as she lured us with hands up down breasts, flicking up folding back behind her head. — Let's take all that off, said Ken. —That's all I'm takin' off, she said. —Was Ken crushed? —Hardly. —But when *I* and I alone was locked out, I was despondent. —My favorite narcissist! said my friend Paul, shaking his head. (But he'd moved to Pittsburgh.) I felt the same malaise as any tourist who's seen the sights and still has a day or three superfluous until the plane. And I thought to myself: The way I used to feel here, was it imagination or was it just blue light? —What was the point of it? What was the point of any of it? —I was staying in my friend Greenglass's apartment, Greenglass being away, Margaret packing her furniture for storage because she was going to move out of the apartment she'd had for ten years and the new place didn't have much room, Elaine looking for animals, Painter Ben wielding brush and roller at China Basin Monday through Sunday with everything figured out by him among all the miles of dropclothed latexed rooms that smelled like toxic bubblegum, the same smell as the breath of that whore I'd given the five bucks to, and the rooms glistened with paint sweat while Ben stood on the bucket to do ceilings and add new axioms and propositions to his personal philosophy, such as: With girls NO usually means MAYBE, and MAYBE means YES. Why *is* that, I wonder?—even as Martin finished his DNA research at the lab, not thinking about his research at all but rather about the fact, now verified with loving cunning, from no to maybe to yes, that his girlfriend would never ever love him again, that that was finished, that while he might charge her depreciation for her half of his mattress and then relocate across the street he could never get her half of his years back to give to someone else as young and fine as she had been before she started getting weak and sick and weepy and saying leave me alone; the girlfriend coming to as if from a long nightmare; Seth now reestablished in Tennessee, loving someone more each day precisely because she'd never love him again; Ken in the middle of something if you know what I mean, but taking a moment to call from a pay phone and say: Well, the good news is I just got my dick sucked by this nineteen-year-old prostitute. She was *perfect.* She was really HARD and MEAN. Man, I love San Francisco! It's a nice dry cool place to pick up whores. And it never snows. And you can scream in the streets and nobody else cares or listens!— and even as he spoke my own true Brandi was whoring like a shadow black on black, arms curving, body curving, head back where the world curved, belonging everywhere because she had nowhere, and on those summer Haight Street nights you could see the lovely pubic hair spreading like a stain around her panties while meanwhile Bootwoman Marisa raised her baby daughter to be good and hate blacks (if you ask me, said Marisa, with that same anger that I so often felt in my other surroundings, if you ask me, it should be illegal for white people to have abortions, except in cases of incest or rape or birth defects, and it should be mandatory for all half-breeds and mixed breeds to have abortions after one child and I said uh huh and she said are you still with that Asian girl? and I said yep and she said to Ken [who'd married white] well Ken give my love to your wife and she said to me don't bother to give my love to Jenny but she kissed me goodbye just the same and gave me a persimmon and I rode away with Ken, thinking how happy and sad that visit had been because she was twenty-one now and had hair, beautiful red hair, which I'd never seen on her skull before, and her dragon tattoo still glowed and she was beautiful and her baby was beautiful and I cared for Marisa and was sorry for the way she hated people just as she was sorry for my ignorance and softness about racial matters and the way I was whoring myself into an early grave, so she said; at which I said will you come to my funeral? and she said of *course* I will and held up the baby to see me and said to her he's pretty weird, but he won't hurt you I *think* and the baby stared at me and began to scream), while at that very moment, on the summit of Russian Hill, Sheet-Rock Fred was rubbing his beard and sighing to himself about Alaska and the world's embroidered robes and then laughing very very quietly while he exercised his trade in the misinterpretable hallways of the rich, there being plenty of new cracks in homes since the earthquake, and Fred presented the mudding tray to another ladder in another foyer of this grand house such as he would never live in—why, he was doing better and better!—now for the Fix-All, which had to be applied with *finesse*, glop, glop! . . . let's see, Laddie the hobo was dead;—life going on without me, in short, as it should, sunlight on Greenglass's blue backstairs, plants reaching high for that sunlight, the same announcer on the radio, the same cat staring away.

The cat lay on her side, tail straight back, rear legs sidewise, head between front paws which gripped the carpet soundlessly, ready to pounce at once. Her eyes were half-closed, but her ears were erect, turning slowly and constantly to follow the sounds of the world.

The phone rang.

Hello? I said.

You're not supposed to answer the phone, Greenglass said. I need to check my messages.

Sorry, Greenglass. I forgot.

The phone rang.

Hello?

I thought I told you not to answer the phone.

Sorry, Greenglass. I forgot.

The phone rang.

Hello?

Hey, a drunk said. Is this the number fer gettin' yer dick sucked?

Well, sir, I can't make any guarantees one way or the other. You see, I don't live here. I'm just staying here.

Awright. Hold on. I'm tryin' to get disconnected . . .

I think I'm disconnected already, I told him.

Oh, yeah, smartass? Well, how come I can still hear ya? Huh? *Huh?*

You can't hear me. I can't hear you. So I don't know why I'm trying to tell you anything. I sincerely don't.

Look, the drunk said. You trying to apologize for something? You think you got something to apologize for? I got more to apologize for than you ever dreamed. You try and pull a fast one and apologize first, I say no way, Jose. I say you better listen, cocksucker.

All right, I said. I'm listening.

Aw *right*. Now, the first thing is—ya see, I useta wanna *be* something, only here I am. Just a lousy drunk. You don't haveta tell me I'm a drunk. I know I'm a drunk. Are you tryin' to tell me I'm a drunk?

I said that I wasn't.

Better believe I'm no drunk, he said. I know whereof I'm speakin'. I useta travel around. You know. In the container ships. And every time I came back fewer people knew me. They didn't *wanna* know me. And all that hippie stuff. Wear some flowers in yer hair. Yaaah, and a thumb

199

up yer ass! That hippie stuff ruined the neighborhood. What the fuck did I do it all for when there's no home left to come to? It's like I was nobody—

Please deposit fifteen cents, said a recorded voice.

I'll give ya my deposit! shouted the drunk fiercely. He slammed down the receiver.

The phone rang.

Hello?

Didn't I tell you not to answer the phone? I need to check my messages.

Sorry, Greenglass. I forgot.

Why do you keep answering the phone?

Sometimes it's for me. Sometimes I just hope it's for me.

Well, don't do it again. But notwithstanding that, I'm glad you're staying at my place. You're always welcome. Is everything OK?

Sure. I'm sleeping in your bed. Just wish you were here with me.

You shouldn't say things like that. My mother's listening.

Actually, Greenglass, now fortyish and not in any way dependent on his mother's opinions, was worried about the F.B.I. It was strange for me to be here in his living room without him and to see the little absences, such as his computer, which the F.B.I. had carried off like a trophy, certain now that once they printed out all the personal letters and address files inside it they would be able to send him to jail; such as the big orange envelopes of photographic paper that said **OPEN IN DARKROOM ONLY**, but now lay spread like a raped girl's legs in the F.B.I.'s special crime investigation chamber; such as Greenglass's sixteen-by-twenty prints of mothers and daughters on the nudist beaches in France (five hundred felony counts of child porn for exposing those five hundred pictures with five hundred clicks, and five hundred counts more to import them, because Greenglass had brought them home to San Francisco after he'd made them); like the enlarger, which they'd also rushed away for scratch match tests similar to those of ballistics labs (accidentally destroying the lens) because if they could prove that this was the evil enlarger which had printed Greenglass's evil pictures then that would be another CLUE for the F.B.I.; and meanwhile they called up all the pubescent girls in his address book to tell them that he was not only a child *pornographer* but also a child *molester*, and had he ever touched them in slimy ways? Greenglass was spending thousands on his lawyer. And his negatives, his reified memories, were gone. Whenever I was lonely for San Francisco I'd look through Ken's pictures; how much more Greenglass's images must have once staved off his own homesickness!

Greenglass? I said.

What? Make it quick. This call is costing me. I just wanted to check my messages.

Well, I said, I just wondered why it is that when I lived here and everything happened with me in it I felt like a goldplated compass needle.

You didn't.

Maybe I didn't.

You have a very sick way of putting things, said Greenglass. Now, what are my messages? I've got to meet with the Committee for Artistic Freedom. I continue to be assailed by the indelicate attentions of the Federal Government. They've just been to my European publisher and confiscated all the prints for my monograph, so that puts the kibosh on that.

Greenglass, I'm honored to be associated with a noted child pornographer like you.

Oh, shut up.

And don't don't let them run you out of San Francisco.

Are you kidding? I'm leaving the country. I've had it here, amigo.

Greenglass, I said, I really am your friend and I'm sorry I tease and abuse you and I'm sorry about the F.B.I. and I'm sorry you don't feel at home here anymore and I'm sorry you never have time to talk to me, and . . . but I'd only gotten as far as green before he'd hung up.

5

The day went by as insidiously as that afternoon in the clover field. It was blue outside but that meant nothing. I didn't make any effort. It was clearly my plan to run away from running, but modestly, to avoid being enshrouded in new difficulties, so I sat on Greenglass's sofa being beyond caring whether the phone might ring again or when Greenglass's new flatmate might come home or what exactly the temperature was on any of the orbiting planets. Where were the milkweeds? (But I wouldn't even have the enterprise to drink their poisonous juice.) A bill from Greenglass's lawyer lay where the computer had once been, and I could see the name GREENGLASS persisting tirelessly on the form; yet despite that comforting permanence I suddenly felt a chill as the true meaning of my friend's name obtruded itself upon my eye's supplications:—namely, a sealed glass of greenness, that clover meadow without lucky clovers, which had been cupped down on my ears from birth to drown me in the sea of emptiness when all the time I'd thought myself happy—no, I didn't know Greenglass at all!—and it seemed to me that the milkweed choice would have been less frightening; but I was and always would be in the glass; I knew my place—

Maybe the phone will ring,   I said to myself.

6

The phone rang.

Hello?

We stayed up in Seattle for about a month,   said a whore's voice. (I'd given her Greenglass's number and told her to call any time.)   — Mount Ranier, it's so beautiful,   she said.   All that snow and then that dirt.

Uh huh.

It's so beautiful. When I die I hope I go there. That's the only place for me. That's home for me. To be buried in that nice clean snow where no one can see me.

Do you remember me, Keiko?   I said.   You calling me for money?

I just needed to talk to you. Lot of times I thought about killing myself, when I saw those needle marks I have. But you have to be strong, like my counselor told me. You have to be strong.

Do you remember me? It's important to me. Do you know me?

I found this number in my purse,   she said.   I don't remember why I was supposed to call. I don't feel so good. They said I had to call or I couldn't be with my friends anymore. I want you to hold my breasts up like this, OK? Hold them both up and show like this.

Keiko, I'm sorry; I'm looking through all the little holes in the phone but I can't see your breasts.

That's OK. You're not a bad guy.

I want to ask you something, I said. Look at your tattoo right now. When you see that little coffin so nice and black on your arm and you know that all your best friends wear the same coffin from the same day, does that make you happier? Does it make you feel like you have something to hold onto?

(Keiko's arms were not just scarred but lined, patched, painted and folded with purple scars. Her face was serene. I remembered her glistening eyes; her hair, originally cold Asian black, dyed brown, but greying at the roots, her buttocks flabby and scarred in ovals like bruises, her face suddenly stiff and weary, her breasts hanging down so wearily when she lay on her side to be sexy with what she called her "sleepy look." She was forty-six and looked seventy. She'd been born during World War II, in an internment camp for Japanese Americans. As soon as she married, her husband had dropped dead. She'd married again, and her second husband had died just this year. She and some other Japanese whores had all gotten tiny coffin tattoos together in witness of eternal friendship.)

Keiko? Did you hear me?

I'm looking right now, but my coffin is gone. My home is gone. I don't know. That means all my friends are dead. They're safe under that dirt. But you're not a bad guy at all. That's right.

7

The phone rang.

Hello?

I used to travel around the world, Keiko said very dreamily. I'd go to all those different countries. And now I'm back in the Tenderloin, each person I meet is like a different country, although I only go from hall to hall.

203

7

Epitaph for

A COWARD'S HEART

✽ U.S.A. ✽

So I boarded the Greyhound bus to Los Angeles that stopped in all the little desert towns along the way. My seatmate was a gentle old baker. Eighty years of age, and all his life he'd baked pies. I suppose that he is dead now. He came from one of those towns in the Owens Valley where the fields sang water from the whirring brass nozzles of the rainbirds that made rainbow mists across the hand-lines and wheel-lines and standpipes and green green alfalfa, but the streets of those towns were always dusty like the back yards of the little adobe houses where tumbleweeds blew, and the storefronts creaked, and air-dust faded the Whites and the Sierras to the color of his denim overalls. I suppose he knew almost everything there is to know about making pies. Pies went into the oven cloud-white and came out brown and crisp and sweet with the smell of California fruit. On his seventy-ninth birthday the previous summer, he'd retired, but even now he still loved to make pies. I saw him now for what he was: a Buddha of doughy perfection, soft-spoken and serene like a fan turning very quiet and cool on a hot desert night. So I added him to my pantheon of divine men, being prepared to worship him as the god of pies and whispers. His best friend was in hospital, so he'd baked a batch of apple pies for him. They were still hot and oven-fragrant; all the way to Los Angeles I inhaled the freshness of them. He told me about his decades of early mornings by the oven door, and I kept thinking what a fine man! here is one person at least whose life has been useful and pleasant to all; and we came to Los Angeles in the darkness and he shook my hand. I thought that I would never see him again. But probabilities are odd. Just as it is very likely that in a group of only thirty people (not three hundred and fifty-odd, as one might think) two will have the same birthday, so it turned out that as I returned from Los Angeles, this time in an almost empty bus I saw my friend, and happily went to sit with him. He too regarded me with pleasure, and the hours passed, happily fraught with pies, until we had almost reached my town. —Suddenly he pointed in the distance. —Look, he said, there's Manzanar, that concentration camp where we put all those poor Japanese. —I had never been there, and so I followed his finger, but the distance was too great; I couldn't see much. —I still cannot understand how we could have hurt those poor people, said the old baker. —It was an awful thing, I said. — The baker gazed into my face, and I saw something rising up in him to be said: —If only it had been THE JEWS!

I gazed at him, speechless. Then I got up and changed my seat.

What had he seen all those years, when he worked upon those pale faces of dough, scoring them with his fingernails before he gave them to the gas fires?

We came to my town, and I took my duffel bag and stood up. I was tense because I was going to have to pass by him. When I came to his seat, I said goodbye in a low voice. But he did not answer.

And I wondered what I should have done. Should I have kept my seat and argued with the man? Should I have withheld my goodbye? Whatever I had done, I had done wrong. Otherwise why would I be ashamed?

Ten years passed, and I was sitting on the steps of the New York Public Library with my friend Garth, each of us eating a hot dog and enjoying the hot spring afternoon. Beside us was sat a young white girl. I did not see her very clearly, because Garth was sitting between her and me, and I was talking to Garth and listening to what he said because he was my friend. In fact I scarcely noticed her at all until a black man walked up to her and said you shouldn't be showing your legs like that and I thought that he was joking or that they knew each other or something because she laughed, and with mild interest I looked at her because the thing was happening next to me and I saw that she looked very young and was from one of those Catholic high schools which require the girls to wear uniform skirts, and the man looked her up and down and started walking on his way and shouted suddenly: That's right, show your pussy, bitch! Gonna carve it up; gonna stick it to you till it comes out your mouth! How ya gonna like that, ya fucking white bitch? and then he walked a few more steps and turned back again baring his teeth and then walked away. From the girl there was only silence. Garth and I looked at each other. Then we started talking again. But I remember neither what he or I was saying nor why we were saying it, because I felt so ashamed. I looked at the girl and saw that she was sitting staring down at the steps with such misery and humiliation on her face, and I thought to myself: well, maybe she was miserable before but I did not believe it. I wanted to go up to her and say: I'm really sorry about what that man said to you but I thought: maybe it's better to say this just before Garth and I get up to go, because otherwise if I hurt her by reminding her of it, then knowing all the time that we saw —so I didn't say anything to her, but to Garth I said: I'm so disappointed in myself and he said: I feel the same way and the girl still sat beside us and he said: but you know it happened so *fast* and he said: I was still just *registering* it when it was over before I could *react* to it and I said: I wish I had punched that man and he said I wish I had yelled at him "Get OUT of here, you asshole!" and we both sat wishing what we hadn't done while I kept the girl in my side vision thinking soon now I will get up and say to her I am sorry but then time passed and the girl got up and walked slowly away and I could have gotten up and run after her but I thought how can I when she wants to be alone and it has been such a long time now since it happened and I did not turn my head to watch her go because I did not want to invade her in any other way and I felt grief that she was leaving before I could say that I was sorry but not until she had left my line of sight did I suddenly know the loss of the opportunity that might have put something a little right and Garth and I continued to talk, staring straight ahead of us, and I felt then that I was damned.

Yes, cursed am I. But cursed beyond possibility of cursing are those two men (so I'd like the last word to run). In Hell they will have to wear the edges of broken glass smooth with their tongues . . .

But that cannot be the last word, being now as irrelevant as that girl whose integrity I did not repair, those burned ghosts whose memory I did nothing for . . . Have you ever seen a heart beating inside someone's chest? My heart was like the whore who looked so beautiful from across the bar and then when I got closer she was old, with scales of pink and white powder flaking from the quivering wrinkles of her cheeks; and her *eyes*—so lonely and glistening and old, like those of a monster out of time; of course when I got away from her again, her form, grandly ladylike, impressed me as before (one cannot easily spy out the craters of the moon); but although I should beyond all measure have admired her skill at passing herself off I could not forget the hideousness of her, which was beyond comparison with the simple plainness of old women who were what they were. —So I said to myself: that is what the difficulty was, that I thought my heart was loving and beautiful; whereas if I simply recognize its fadedness I will be content . . .

Which perhaps is the worst cowardice of all.

VIII
KINDNESS

Place there is none: *we go backward and forward*, and there is no place.

AUGUSTINE, *Confessions*,
X.XXVI.37 (*ca.* AD 420)

1

I am afraid that the following story may well seem to have a moral that I do not in the least intend, for I do believe in giving assistance to others. Admittedly, whatever help I have offered has rarely succeeded in accomplishing anything; yet I myself have benefited so much from the generosity of friends and strangers that I have never seen reason to be pessimistic about what one human being can do for another. There are always instances, good and bad, that prove that the world does not work the way we expect it to. I remember the case of Sheet-Rock Mark, who went with my friend Ken to a Vietnamese restaurant, and Mark kept yelling   what the fuck do you want to take me to this *gook* place for? why do you want this goddamned *gook* food?   and I imagine that the Vietnamese lady who served them understood very well the drift of Mark's words and feared and hated Mark, and then after lunch Mark saw that the door was broken and he said to her   oh you want me to fix your door?   He got his tools and worked on that door for a good hour, and when he was finished the door was fixed and the Vietnamese lady was happy. It seems to me that Mark did more good than one of the people who would have despised Mark for calling her a gook, who would have been polite to her and smiled at her encouragingly when she tried to speak English, but who would never in a million years have repaired the door. —What you make of all this is your business. But let me tell you the story.

2

Laddie was a hobo.

My grandfather worked on the Union Pacific Railroad all his life, so I asked him what the hobos were like. He seemed a little reluctant to talk about them, but I kept asking.

They were average people in my day, he said. They were just broke. They'd jump on a freight train. Some of 'em were really fine people; some of 'em were bums. That's how it always is. Most of 'em there was nothing criminal about. On the railroad we used to have a sandhouse where we kept the sand warm and dry. That was a good place for 'em to sleep. No one was after 'em except maybe the Railroad Police. There might be a hundred or more in the course of a week. Before Roosevelt, you'd starve to death if you didn't have a place. These were awful days, Bill, awful days. You can't imagine.

3

On the day that Elaine Suicide agreed to drive to the beach so that I could draw pictures of her naked, she invited Laddie along, and he sat between us, so that that squinting Santa Claus face, with the plaid cap roofing one eye as he smiled, with that beard finer spun with goodness than cotton candy, was like our reward. Elaine said oh Laddie you're so cute! and Laddie smiled so that his eyes beamed and his nose wrinkled up and later said to me all those *beautiful girls* make me so HARD! Why, that Amalia Carlotta at Ken's, every time she hugs me I get so HARD! . . . —Elaine, hearing, laughed and said Laddie you're a funny one.

Laddie, I said, who's more beautiful—Elaine or Amalia Carlotta?

I love 'em both the same,   he said.

Look at this traffic,   said Elaine.   It's going to take forever to get there. Shit. Well, I'll just take my time.

Take your time but hurry up,   said Laddie.   Take your time but hurry up. Dere was an old Jewish guy and he always used to say that. A hide merchant with a tannery. Always rushing around buying up hides. Some people they just can't stop. They always got to be going somewhere. One night he got in his car and drove too fast and got killed. Had two brick apartment buildings. He left his wife everything.

We both had to help Laddie down the root-grown cliff to the beach where Elaine took off her clothes and lay down on a towel saying   you can look but you have to promise not to touch!   and I promised as meanwhile Laddie, meaning to be polite, had wandered around the promontory to a place of new wet sand where he ran throwing crumbs of sourdough bread to the seagulls. Elaine had bought the bread for his lunch. Presently he returned to his driftwood log to sit in state, licking the rolling paper of a nascent joint, his fingers so worked and leathery in his beard.   —Laddie, you silly, your shoes are soaked!   cried the lovely Elaine, whose breasts and eyes were the joy of our sandy neighborhood, and Laddie looked upon her with the utmost benignity, saying,   yes, yes, Elaine,   and he sighed heavily as the seawater oozed from the toes of his loafers.

Laddie said   when my time comes don't put me in a hospital. I'll escape and die in a train yard.

Yes, Laddie dear,   said Elaine,   but what about your shoes?

Dat's no tragedy,   said Laddie. All the same, at long last he took them off and crammed them each full of newspaper, which he then lit most magisterially with the tip of his reefer. Soon smoke and foot odor began to come out of them, and the leather toes wrinkled and sizzled as Laddie sat thinking so that his head rose like a cloud of white beard and white locks above his cowboy hands that rolled joints without him; and his irises seemed to spiral inward in continuation of the trios of wrinkles at eye-corners that hooked out like rays, that curved around like claws, and his face was very very dark brown with the sun-years, and he lived in a halo of fine white hair as if he were the sun, and his lips were half-hidden by that white moss-fire of moustache and beard that glowed like the stare of his far-off eyes. —Now Laddie blew out his shoe-fires in

215

triumph, waved the scorched objects around until they were cool, and stuck his feet in.

Still wet, he said.

Elaine giggled.

He thought some more.

Maybe I can dry them out in Ken's oven, he said.

But then his doubts came home to roost. —Do you think Ken will let me? he said. I hate to be asking Ken for dese favors alla time.

Ken won't care, I said.

Sure enough, when Laddie got back to Ken's he was granted permission to plunge his loafers into the oven at 350°, after which he sat down over the paper reading it once and twice and said: Dese articles are so *interesting*. Dey went to a lot of work over dis, so why *shouldn't* I read it twice? —Then with shagged-down lids and lips parted to receive the joint, Laddie seemed broodingly tender, and his hair shone white like the lighter flame, and the plaid cap cast the shadow of peace across his face; and the next thing you know it was the proverbial morning after and Ken grinned I think your shoes are done, Laddie and Laddie said my shoes? MY SHOES! and rushed to the oven to gape at the charred black things in wonder, and then poor Laddie raised his half-closed hand in a vague salute to his dead shoes, God rest you well . . . but then his face lit up and he cried: I know, Ken—I'll use 'em for *planters!* —So saying, he filled them with dirt and beach weeds which he had providentially picked with Elaine and me the previous day; then he took his brand-new flowerpots to the window-sill and his face was radiant and Ken cried admiringly Laddie you sure are SOMETHING.

4

Laddie was staying at Ken's because Ken had gotten kicked out of his studio for making too much noise with skinheads, bums and whores, so he'd lived in his van for awhile until his ballet friend Greenglass took pity on him (as it was very easy for Greenglass to do since he was about to go to the Rhine to film some bathing beauties), so Greenglass said: Ken, you can stay here while I'm gone as long as you respect my place   and Ken said: sure, pal   and Greenglass said: I'm trusting you not to go into my room or bring any derelict characters up   and Ken said: sure, pal   and Greenglass said: because I don't want fleas in my place when I come back   and Ken said: sure, pal.   As soon as Green-glass was gone, Ken moved into his room and brought Laddie in, to the eternal glory of Laddie's nine-day hobo salads which were never refrigerated because Laddie liked them to taste strong. Laddie usually hopped a freight every month to go up to Sacramento and then Reno where he gambled and lost, but now he decided to take a month off. Greenglass would be gone for a month. Laddie bought the groceries and cooked the food, because he was grateful to Ken, and anyhow Laddie was the kind of man who would buy lunch for a total stranger without worrying about his own. I don't know how many times Laddie bought me lunch. And whenever I asked about tattoos, Laddie would show me the fly tattooed on the head of his dick. He told Ken all his stories of riding the rails for half a century, and his eyes turned beautiful and wild when he told about the wind and the mountains and the hobo camps and the Indians. He'd ride a boxcar into the Central Valley and spend the day picking apples or cherries or walnuts. Then he'd blow his wages on two-dollar whores. Cocaine was five cents, the same as a haircut. You bought it just behind the barber shop. And Laddie said: When my time comes, let me die on a train.

Ken's girl Mary said: You should just let him sleep outside in the cold, 'cause that's what he's used to. You're not going to do him any good.

Ken said: You're not doing him any good, either. You're not even doing yourself any good.

5

Laddie could be sweet to anybody on the street, especially if he didn't know them, but when he knew them and got drunk he could turn a little nasty. Ken said: well you know Laddie's been through a lot; he's gotten hurt and robbed and beaten up for no reason; I said: yeah I suppose there's hate in him that needs to come out like in everybody else.

When he drank, he'd begin to raise his voice. He began to declaim his toast, which went like this:

> Here's to the gal dat can but won't do it.
> Tie her ass down and make her do it.
> 'Cause birds do it and fly;
> Bees do it and die,
> Dogs do it and stick to it,
> So tie her down and make her do it.

Then he started talking about niggers, cunts, spics and no-good Injuns. Once two Indians had tried to kill him on a train because he bought them a sandwich and they saw his roll. He wrapped himself up in cardboard at night because they were crossing Wyoming and it was winter and the Indians called him a goddamned paper rattler and one of them knifed him. Laddie still had the scar.   —Mebbe I shoulda died then,   he said.   It's no good to die indoors. Well, soon I'll be seein' that blue sky again . . . Goddamned no-good Injun bastards!

6

Greenglass was due to come back in three days. Ken and Laddie cleaned the place bareass-shiny so that Greenglass would be happy, and Laddie bought all new spices and paper towels for Greenglass; and Ken said: let's take a walk, Laddie   but Laddie said: Dis sofa is so nice, Ken; soon I'll be seein' that blue sky again. Tell me dat story again about why you don't eat out girls no more!   and Ken said: Laddie, I've told you that story a hundred times!   and Laddie said: Awright, then I'll tell *you* a story. Like dis guy dis salesman is goin' to Mexico, see, and goin' down the old route and it's so *bumpy*, and a long way to go, see, and dere's dis little town, not even a name yet, so the neighbors get togedder and have a picnic to figure it out. Just them and dese big-eared sheep, and they want to have a name 'cause the postman's already comin' 'long, see, and dis leedle girl, she about eight years old, and dere's dis old man with dis white mule and she look behind and said why don't you call it *My Ass?* and dey say that's a fine name, and that's what they call it, see. Well, dis travelling salesman was coming down all dis time, and when he got to town he checked into dis hotel and took a tub bath and then he said he wanted some crab, an' the lady said sorry mister my husband look all over My Ass and he can't find no crab! —Yeah, but not all the stories are dat funny. I remember Billy, Curly and Larry. Larry had dis girl and he choked her with a Turkish towel in Stockton, so dat was a terrible tragedy.

Ken said: Laddie, you've told me that story a hundred times.

7

Greenglass was due back in one day, and at last Laddie did succeed in getting Ken to tell the story about why he'd more or less given up on eating women out, which was that he had once done it to Elaine Suicide when Elaine had an infection, after which Elaine went blithely to Greece, not knowing that Ken was starting to get a sore throat, which became worse and worse until Ken's tonsils were coated with white stuff, and when James the Engineer drank some of Ken's orange juice (which Ken always drank straight from the carton), he got it, too.

Dat was good, to hear dat once more,   said Laddie, gazing benevolently through his hair.

Tomorrow we'll be out of here,   said Ken.

Dis sofa feels so good,   said Laddie.

You'll be seeing that blue sky again. And I'll be sleeping in my van again. Or over at Mary's house—

I'm afraid now, Ken. Dis life has spoiled me. I feel old. Dose no-good guys are out dere layin' for me—

Ken allowed Laddie to stay in his van for a night, two nights, a week, until Laddie got drunk and ugly and Ken kicked him out. Laddie said he was going to ride the rails. But a week later Ken saw him dead drunk in Golden Gate Park, lying in the dogshit-smeared grass, as pale now as his fine white hair, his eyes closed so wearily. —

8

Epitaph for

PEGGY'S PIMP

* U.S.A. *

Say brother, you said, can you help me raise fifteen dollars for my lady's bail?

I'm all out of money, Jimmy said, but you can ask my friend Code Six here.

Sure, laughed Code Six, I'll give you a five. What the fuck. If your bitch is stupid enough to want out of jail she needs all the help she can get.

Thanks man, you said. I'll never forget this.

Only ten more dollars to go, said Jimmy.

You gave him a look. That's right, he said.

You went up the street and everyone heard you ask another man for twenty-five.

IX

MY PORTRAIT, MY LOVE, MY WIFE

The theologian may indulge in the pleasing
task of describing Religion as she is descended
from heaven, arrayed in her native purity. A
more melancholy duty is imposed on the
historian. He must discover the inevitable
mixture of error and corruption which she
contracted in a long residence upon earth,
among a weak and degenerate race of beings.

EDWARD GIBBON, *Decline and
Fall of the Roman Empire*

First I must tell you that I love my wife and am proud of her,
that I have looked into her face for so long now that it seems to
be my own reflection. No doubt that is why she makes me feel tired.
You should also understand that I work very long hours at my job, as a
result of which my concentration has increased by kangaroo-bounds,
while my patience has departed at precisely the same rate. —But now
already, like all complainers, I am beginning to seem an odious blowfly
(I know that if someone unfamiliar to me had written these lines I would
dislike him); so let me give a *précis d'histoire*.

One morning when my wife and I were on vacation, we lay in bed
before breakfast and she said: Now let's plan the day.

I have one activity in mind,   I said, putting my arm around her
naked waist.

She pulled away and sat up. She began to brush her hair.

So what activity did you have in mind? she said after awhile.

Guess.

Going to the beach.

No. Guess again.

227

I don't have time for these games,   my wife said.   I'm going to take a shower.

By the time she stepped out of the bathroom, fully dressed and shimmering with makeup like some disturbingly gorgeous moth, I had yielded to her massively determined unconsciousness. I often did. My wife had a certain problem. If I did not love her so much I would call her frigid.

So I became one of those fellows who admires a fine female leg. I enjoyed thinking on this and related subjects, and even in subdividing my desire into two categories. The first was entirely pleasant: I enjoyed the thought of the woman's body, without a trace of guilt or intention, and so I cleaved the water and swam on and the water closed behind me without a memory. The other kind was equally without any real intention, because I knew that it would be futile, but my heart was agonized and I looked into the woman's face admiring it and drinking it as if I could lap it up like milk, but I could not and I knew that; the beautiful face remained unknowable so that as soon as I looked away the precious image of it was gone (except perhaps for a residue that was less perception than yearning); as soon as I looked away I would not have it anymore; I would not have her beauty anymore; I knew this and it superseded everything else so that I enjoyed every moment I spent with her; I paid scarcely any attention to the conversation, such was my overwhelming joy and fulfillment in looking at her—of course I knew, too, that she and I were performing our lip- and tongue-service perfectly well. These words were what held us together so that I could continue to admire her. Later my heart ached.

My wife never noticed these gazes. She was too busy.

Of the women in the second category there was one whom I had known much longer than my wife. My wife did not like her. They had nothing whatever in common. If fucking my wife (on the rare occasions when this was possible without rape) had become an exercise in narcissism, because my wife's face as I said was mine, then fucking my dear dear friend must be something different. Such was *my* religion.

Once she'd wanted to know how it would be when we were married. I said that it would be very nice; my only regret was that she and I would not be married to each other.

Almost daily I kissed my air-portrait of her face as it had been when she was young and glowing with the fresh blood within, her eyes on me

neither blue nor grey nor green as her mouth formed a smile for me, a
perfect ellipse offering me darkness between her handsome white teeth—
no, none of this describes at all what I felt to gaze upon her freckled
face, so smooth and soft (so my eye said; I'd never caressed it), such
healthiness and tranquility that I wanted to swallow the breath from her
nostrils as she stood cocking her head and gazing up into my face to
study I know not what; the edges of her veil of hair cut the sunlight so
that they glistened with golden blood like gold thread or new gold grass-
tips trembling on California hills; her face made me realize for the first
time the wondrous art of flesh and bone, the gorgeous colors of a face—
all doomed to change so quickly that five years after I had first met her
people were telling me: I don't know why you think her so beautiful!
—at which, amazed, I tried to see her as they did, her skin now
approaching ash-grey in its tone, the flesh beginning to shrivel and
tighten on her skull even as the wrinkles came—I exaggerate; she was
not yet forty, but no one could deny that she was on the way to forty—
no one except I, because I *could not* see in this faithless way of theirs,
remembering as I did that time when she had had her loveliness, which,
having had, she must always have no matter if she became as wrinkled
as one of the Bog People presented to us in that book by the possibly
eponymous Professor P. V. Glob . . .—am I making sense? I remember
how I looked at her face in those sunny summers and it was so beautiful
that I could not know it! It is my earnest hope (for I once studied
science) that a sufficient measure of these gluey words will enable me to
at least make a cast of her face, a deathmask of that perfection of hers
which must be better than nothing; and yet as I *see* her face before me
now I know that I do not see it on this page . . .—but if I had a
photograph to give you here, would you see her even then? —Oh, a
nice young woman, you might say; I can tell that much; she looks shy
and tender—quite ordinary. —Well, suppose I were to describe with
precision her bone structure and heavenly pigmentation, excluding from
the ranks of potential comprehenders all but the most technically
minded anatomists and anthropologists . . . ? —No, not even these
exalted beings would understand; no one would or could (if they did,
then all of us would see the extraordinary beauty of everything); not
even she would understand—how could she when she did not even
value the hairs that remained on her comb? Therefore, since only I can
see her in her glory, I *must* requite myself of my duty toward that glory,

knowing that you, reading this, will never see the heavenly mask comprised of these words! What you see is an admission of failure. But listen. It is not that.

Never had I kissed her eyelids or freckle-fleshed cheekbones. Never had I drunk the warm breath from her nostrils. I had not put my mouth to the dear creases which put her mouth in parentheses when she smiled. Once, it is true, I kissed her lips, on her thirtieth birthday. But that was in between many other well-wishers—best not to think of that.

This friend of mine, in other words, whom I loved beyond clouds, had always been my secret well-spring of exaltation—and no doubt the fact that I had never drunk from her increased my desire for the water, which reflected clouds so pale and strange . . . For years she made my heart ache. For years I thought that this waxing of our relations was a progression; then I *hoped* that it was; then I became confused; at last I became weary and disgusted. It was as if she were my wife.

But when I saw her more frequently, my feelings began to rise, and pretty soon I'd be sneaking into the living room as my wife squeezed pimples before the bathroom mirror, and I'd be dialling my friend's number and my heart would be everywhere and I'd be saying to her: You know what I'm going to ask. I can't help it. Please say yes just once. Come with me! I was whispering into the phone like a hypnotist.

Lying both to herself and to me, my good friend (whom I forgot to tell you was also married) said: Whatever do you mean?

We'll go out for a nice dinner and I'll pay for everything, I assured her (looking over my shoulder to make sure that my wife was still popping her pimples).

I love you so much I can't stand it, I said (and it was true).

She began to say something which I knew would be negative, so quickly I added: You don't have to love me.

I was enjoying seeing you so much, and now I'm getting so upset, she whispered.

Just make me happy.

I don't think we should talk anymore.

I won't hurt your life. I'll never tell anyone, I promise. You know I feel so alive when I'm with you.

I'm going to have to hang up now. I'm really sorry.

Please say yes.

Goodbye.

But this dismissal, final as it might seem, had now happened several times.

So one night when she called me and asked to visit, I said: My wife will be out of town next week.

Oh,   she said.

My heart began pounding, and it was not an excruciatingly beautiful sensation as it had been when I first fell in love with my wife, but a sad and impure excitement. I had to keep my voice flat when I replied, in case my wife in the next room (who had very keen ears) might be listening. So, hearing the eagerness and tenderness of that other voice on the telephone, my heart ached because I must sound so cruelly cold to her. —Yet who knows, after all, whether she even noticed? — Nonetheless, I will never forget the remorse I felt for the wrong I was doing to this innocent heart (never to my wife, who sat reading in the next room, so coldly and sarcastically alone).

That week I was so excited that I could barely sleep. I watched my wife packing with pleasure which I could barely conceal. But as soon as I kissed her goodbye, I began to feel a terrible ache like white party-favors blowing down from cottonwood trees. The thing that I was about to do made me feel desolate.

My wife left, happy and trusting.

The doorbell rang.

As soon as I had put my arm around her waist, I became dizzy. My feelings were so powerful that I almost fainted.

I was happy even in my toes.

We went to see the animated broccoli, and I could not take my arm away from her. I said her name. I said: If you get tired of my hand on you just say so. If you don't I'm going to keep it there all day.

She smiled and didn't say anything. She never did.

My happiness was as green as English apple juice.

Now it was an evening the color of marbled paper between the skyscrapers. Somehow the bruised clouds reminded me of her skin. I got her drunk and I got drunk and I said her name and said   I can't help it that my voice is breaking   and I said her name and said   I really love you   (and I pulled her to me and started kissing her throat, saying her name, saying: you're getting older and your neck is getting more wrinkled every year and every year it looks more and more beautiful;

please let me kiss your neck)   and I kissed her neck, sucking it, tasting her skin-taste of milk and salt.

As I put my hand up between her legs I said   please let me kiss your knees   and I pulled up her skirt and pressed my lips against her and she kissed my hand once and said   I have my mother's legs.

The sublime moment was now approaching in which one's partner in adultery, having permitted one to slide her underpants down to her ankles, has freed one foot, so that the panties hang from her other leg, like the flag of a captured garrison about to come down, and then at last she drags them down with her other heel and they dangle from her toe for a moment before she wriggles her foot and they fall hushedly to the carpet.

Her slender arms both caressed me and held me rigidly away. When I kissed her, she seldom opened her mouth to me, so that it was like kissing a skull. Her cool skin smelled like salt and milk. She said   please stop now or I'll be so lost.   Shrieking with laughter she said   this is *wrong wrong wrong!*

She was all sugar and butter and cream. Her soul had a rich butter taste. Her breath was like plums.

. . . Proof positive of some mystery or other: that morning could stream in upon the bed in patches, warming me before I was awake. How strange that such a thing can be! One moment there was nothing, and then there was warmth felt without a me to feel it, and then I was there as if I had always been, and finally, without premeditation, she was there. A past, either real or just now invented along with me, had unrolled behind me with instantaneous speed. I knew already what the sun was, and who I was, and who was beside me. I found myself still cuddled against her, which surprised me, since when I shared this bed with my wife I would roll away in my sleep. It seemed that I had changed my position hardly at all in the course of the night.

The first action of the day: I put my hand on her breast. It was very soft. At once, I felt her heart begin to beat beneath, with the tremulous speed of a hummingbird's. The first realization of the day: she was terrified.

For a long time she did not move, but at last, having understood that our nakedness and my hand would not go away, she fluttered open her freckle-colored eyelashes and said,   *Well!* How did I—what happened to my *clothes?*

I took them off.

Did I—did we sleep together?

No.

I don't remember. What did we do?

I—kissed you—

It was hard for me to say this.

She looked at me. I thought that I was not understanding her face, but of course I was. Only then did I understand how hopeless it was, and the hopelessness immediately hid away again because it knew that I could not bear to see it. Months later, when I thought about what had happened, it seemed to me that from the moment I woke up beside her my sadness steadily deepened, like water dripping into a bottle drop by drop, because I knew then that she would leave (and how could it have been any other way?), but when I remember that time now I feel only contentment perfuming me forever with the smell of her hair which I'd slept with, she curled naked around her plumpness as she slept. I'd loved her flesh as soft and easily bruised as mushrooms—

There was a big hickey on her neck where I'd kissed her.

She went to Macy's to get some skin bronzer to cover it, and I split the cost with her. I was generous that way.

Her husband was having dinner at the house of his father, the well-known Dr. Faustus, whom she feared. She begged me to go with her. I did not know what to say. She was sweating with nervousness. The hickey was showing again. I didn't have the heart to tell her that.

She seemed to feel that it was my obligation to come. I agreed, dreading it terribly. I said to myself: Today is the Day of Consequences.

The day passed. Every few minutes, she went into the bathroom and put on more skin bronzer.

On the bus I asked her to kiss me one last time, but she refused; she was already in Dr. Faustus's neighborhood; someone who knew her might see.

At dinner Dr. Faustus led a discussion of compulsive gambling, at which I said: *that* must be an exhilarating vice!—   entering the conversation with superbly witty alertness while, never once looking at her, I put my hand on her knee and she pulled her knee away and the conversation was now about spies and I said to her husband: it would be so *strange* to lead a double life—   as meanwhile I slid my hand up my beloved's skirt and my beloved looked down at her plate and said to

233

everyone at large: I'm sorry I'm not more *vivacious*; you see, I have this stomach cramp . . . and once or twice she glanced at me sidelong with an expression which might have been miserable longing but was more probably fear, and Dr. Faustus said: You've been to Jupiter? And, pray, what is the political situation there? —Well, I said, draining yet another tiny Mexican beer in a single gulp (and as I did this I remembered how on the bus I had said to her: what can I do when I get home to distract me from pining for you? and she very quickly looked out the window and said: well, you could always rent a video and I said: I could and she said: or you could drink Grand Marnier like I did and I said: well, that's true; I could put my lips on the bottle you poured from and pretend that I was kissing your lips and she said: I hope my lips didn't taste—never mind and I said: do you mean did they taste like alcohol? and she nodded and I put my arm around her and said: your lips tasted so good—), *well*, said I to Dr. Faustus, the situation in Jupiter is improving . . . —at which her husband said: but from what I read in the papers they're fanatics up there at which Dr. Faustus thundered: anyone who uses the word fanatic is a fanatic! Remember that through a sheer accident of astro-geography it's possible to be located between two hostile superpowers . . . —at which I looked at my poor darling, and she hung her head. —But the dinner went brilliantly. Dr. Faustus was impressed with my cleverness; the husband and I were jovial to one another, as meanwhile under the table I caressed the wife's soft thigh . . . What a man I was!

They all begged me to stay, but she looked tired. I took the bus home, prouder than a lord. I had won every victory. It was not until the following morning, when I woke up crying, that I realized how much my heart ached.

9

Epitaph for

OLD FRIENDS

* U.S.A. *

We fell to speaking of old times (that being both the excuse and even the purpose of my visit). He sat across from me; she sat beside me; the waitress believed that she was mine.

He said: Remember those lectures of Dr. Faustus's, when I did the doodles and xeroxed them so that we all laughed? And then I wrote that song: "It's Ever So Clear in the German," but Bertrand kept refusing to set it to music?

She laughed happily to remember. Her voice was much deeper than I remembered, due to the smoking. There were two new lines in her face.

Yes, I said into the snow, embarrassed.

I had never heard of this song before.

The gentle decay of their memories had permitted me to be included. My recollection was of sitting alone with them and others in the front row of the lecture hall. Then I got up and left by myself, or else they went off without me, I being alone and despised (why, I couldn't remember). Although we all lived together, I had sometimes failed to exchange words with them for days. Thanksgiving found them eating the turkey she'd cooked, while I sat in the attic with the lights out, waiting for them to finish so that I could rush out unseen to scream. But possibly my memory was as bad as theirs.

She always walked a little bent. She held herself in a peculiar way. It was not until the very end (they both walked me to the station, which I had not expected them to do, and which touched me) that I realized she felt the cold.

You're shivering, I said.

I never remember to buy mittens, she sighed.

Here, I said. I don't need mine.

When we got to the station, she sought to give them back, but I was searching the board to find the gate to my train, and the gloves fell to the floor.

I said: You can keep them

and she said: no no

and I said: I have another pair at home

237

and she said: are you sure?

I said yes.

It was time for the train. I embraced him; I started to embrace her; I had wanted to kiss her goodbye as I'd kissed her hello, but she had already stepped back. I held out my hand to her, then withdrew it in confusion, but by then she had held out hers and I was about to take it, but I felt shy, and also worried about missing my train, so I ran away.

X
DIALECTICS

Why should he not personally take part in
greeting the tsar, for whom the French
socialists now have no other name than hero
of the gallows . . .?

LENIN, *What Is To Be Done?*
(1902)

1

The old man with the cowboy face owned something grand:
cancer of the duodenum!—although when he'd first brought
himself to the attention of the professional hopefuls they laughed and
shook his hand and announced that inside him was a worm, only a
worm, because a lump had formed on his neck, and lumps were the
children of worms in Central America. Just to be sure (it was nothing to
alarm oneself about), they sliced pieces off him, packed them in ice,
and sent them to Mexico, to Guatemala, to the U.S.A., to Canada.
When the results came back they greeted him with even more love than
before. There was nothing to be done, they said. They sat him down
and explained to him that every rule had an exception. He really ought
to take comfort in the fact that it should have been a worm. So every
month he took the Batty line bus into Belize City to buy his hundred
dollars' worth of ground-up snake powder (but not from the head or the
tail, which were poisonous), and he put this powder into capsules before
he swallowed it because it tasted terrible. It eased the pain. His stupid
daughter-in-law, who thought that snakes and worms were the same,
had repeatedly stated her conviction that he swallowed the capsules in
hopes of transforming the cancer into a worm after all, but it was useless

241

to reason with her. Anyhow, he was past the stage of dreaming of worms. His duodenum was full of bat-faces and shadows. He had a refrigerator, so sometimes he would buy two months' worth of the medicine, which would preserve that long if kept cold. When it was used up he put on his sweat-stained cap and caught the Batty bus again. Wind whispered past the windows. He looked out at the road and Guatemalan women stared back at him, their dirty-pale dresses glowing in the dark. It was hot and dry. The women were like those jungle trees that you cut with a machete and hot white milk spurts out. It can burn you, blind you. It makes you swell up and break out. There's a white kind of milk and a black kind. The black kind is not so bad. When they sent pieces of him all over the world he had still been hoping that his cancer was the black kind, but now he knew that it was the white kind. Every answer is tied to a following question, so when the answer was *death* the question was *why?* His son asked why. The professional hopefuls asked why (for they were more chagrined than they had let him believe, that their claims had been repudiated). He asked why again. Even his daughter-in-law asked why, praying for him in her sea-green shirt.

2

Having studied dialectics in the School of the Celestial Whore, I know why, and I will tell you.

His son executed four thousand chickens a day at the chicken factory. Of course his son did not end a single one of these bird-lives himself; he was too important for that. He bought and sold and supervised thirty-two girl assistants within the dusty shady treewalls of his kingdom. The girls came in giggling and sulking and singing songs every morning. They hung the struggling chickens upside-down, and cut their heads off with machetes. The chickens sprayed blood all over the place when they died. Chicken heads fell into the bloody muck blinking, opening and closing their beaks until the busy girls squashed them underfoot, running to take down the dead things and elect live ones to their places. They did this all morning. In the afternoon they rested for an hour, and then the son of the old man with the cowboy face blew a whistle, and they went back to work. By then it was very hot, and the smell made some of the girls tie bandanas over their noses. The smell spread like a stain, growing and thickening beyond the factory and into the ethical world, the immaculate world, as Hegel called it, over the hot greenish-brown river where vultures were flapping their wings; black vultures were sitting on trees, weighing down the branches, so many of them, rows and rows of those black birds. They were too prudent to come to the chicken factory now. They would come in the evening. They waited, smelling the blood as happily as their neighbors the iguanas sunned themselves in the trees, ripening like greenish fruits of a squat oval shape, gathering heat in their ridged and spiny backs, paying no heed to the vultures as the vultures paid no heed to them. —When the girls went home they were black with blood from head to toe. It took them a long time to pick the bloodclots out of their hair before they could go dancing. —It was to inflict necessary and consequent retribution for these murders that the cancer chose the old man.

Idealists might demand that the son be executed instead, but this only proves the shallowness of their conception of justice. Since we are all related, we are all responsible; and the son was but an evanescent particularity in his loud tie anyhow, pinching the girls with fingers which they hated for that evanescence; no, the existence of the son was a matter of indifference to the universal realm of which the vultures were a part. The father in and of himself was equally unimportant; it was purely good fortune that by being made a sacrificial victim, by leaving the worm for the snake, he was permitted, in a sense, to overcome his natural being. Although he trembled and prayed against his elevation, much as the chickens squawked, God made him the placeholder.

3

And why was it the destiny of the chickens to be decapitated? From a formal standpoint we can reply: Because Carmen's dog bit the priest. — But to rush ahead in that way subverts the wisdom of Nature. Permit me, therefore, to present you with the determining chain link by link.

[A] One of the girls at the chicken factory had a brother, a dark black boy with a pitted face whose job it was and had been for six years to pump-spray DDT into the jungle swamps, night after night, sleeping on village porches, bitten by mosquitoes. Wherever he did his job the Americans came and said: I can buy land here for twenty-five, thirty dollars an acre!

[B] Ten of these Americans were businessmen together. For them the essence of life was defined as the perfecting of subsistence. On a flight out of Minneapolis you might see a whole row of them in matching sky-blue suits.

[C] They all went down the dirt lane to the lighted house, and upstairs past the porch to where it became Carmen's stuffy little restaurant with fresh-squeezed O.J. in quart bottles. The choices were fried fish and steamed lobster that night. It was a blue plank room with half a dozen tables. A case of Coca-Cola was on the floor. It was very bright inside. Fat and beautiful Carmen came through the screen door with the platters of fish in her arms. She had huge arms; she wore a blue print dress. She gave each businessman a plastic plate bulging with mashed potatoes, cole slaw, and haddock fried gold and crisp in coconut oil; and a side plate of five slices of white bread.

[D] She owned a dog. His name I forget, but his name was less significant than his character, which was that he was a biter, eternally, essentially and for himself.

[E] It was this dog that attacked the priest late one night when he came by for lobster. The dog ripped off all his clothes. You should have seen that priest move! He pulled himself into a sour lime tree even though it was prickly. For the next few days he was pulling the spikes out of his ass.

It was the mission of the chicken factory to avenge this insult. Year after year, long before and long after the night in which the priest was dishonored, chickens spattered the girls with blood as part of the atonement. Carmen's dog was never punished. He didn't need to be. He too was but a particularity, no more and no less to be blamed than you or I. The girl whose brother's Americans once had dinner at Carmen's left the chicken factory when another girl accidentally cut her with a machete and the cut became infected. She went home and died. God took her. But the chickens kept getting their heads cut off. We may be sure that any excess balance of retribution was applied wherever it might be needed.

Because the old man's death paid for the murders of the chickens, and because the murders of the chickens paid for the assault upon the priest, we might wonder why any one of these required punishment, since each was a punishment of something else, and therefore might be thought to have a justification. But this is not the way that the Great Banker thinks. Money makes money as sin makes sin, and who would want that to stop?

4

There was a witch doctor whose magic could bring out an iguana from inside a girl's stomach. *Any girl, any time!* he shouted proudly. He showed me how he did it. The young lady lay down (she had no choice). He made a pass with his hands and mumbled something; in seconds the flat brown belly would swell, while the mouth split into a grimace, groaning so pitiably, as if she were having a baby, which in a sense she was, for pretty soon she'd vomit the lizard right out of her mouth! —I make it hoppen like *bam!* the witch doctor shouted.

I said: But why do you want to do it? and he started to laugh.

If I don't do it, he said, how I know what gonna hoppen now?

As soon as he said that, I knew that the cancer was saying the same thing inside the old man.

5

Duck under a bush, and your neck and chest will be black with crawling ants. Leave your mother's mouth or belly, and your birth will be an act of vengeance for something you never saw. Something else will get even with you for that. You'll skitter through life like an iguana, biting off men's fingers without even knowing it, swimming those hot slow tropical rivers of your desire that resemble green coffee, scaring the boys in bright shirts leaning in doorways without understanding that you've scared them, and the old ladies in print dresses will see you and call to their sons to come and kill you because you're delicious, and one boy will say to another (extra loud for his girlfriend to hear): This is *nothing*, mon! Lizard nothing! I be bock right now! —but you'll skitter safely over mounds of Mayan ruins and between white poison trees, black poison-trees which frighten the boy away so you'll get away without even knowing why, but someday from behind the edge of the clearing you'll see the two figures coming—first close, then not so close, then very close: the boy with the rifle, which he raises when he sees you, the girl in the sea-green shirt, grasping the machete a bit uncertainly.

10

Epitaph for

SIXTY DOLLARS

* U.S.A. *

A very pale woman sat smoking and working her lips like an octopus. She sucked at her cheeks. She looked over her shoulder. She kept brushing her hair out of her mouth. She tapped her feet. When she got up, I saw that she limped gingerly, as if she had taken walking lessons from pet cats who had recently been declawed. She hobbled through the park, clopping along the left brick path, then left, left and left again. She came back to her bench and sat down. She kept looking over her shoulder. She had long skinny legs.

The sunlight was as brassy as the mating of golden flies.

I could distinguish the people who belonged from the people who didn't, because both sorts left the park, but the people who belonged kept coming back and sunning themselves innocently, as if this were their first time here. Miss Octopus took no such trouble. Day after day she fled here from whatever was behind her.

Even with her face turned away from me, she did not seem right. Her head was too thin, and it moved too much (from side to side, very rapidly). As the afternoon drained away, her face became whiter and whiter. Her eyes were dark downward-turned slits, like her mouth. She kept moistening her lips. She got up and sat down again and listened to a weary blonde who told her,   *Sixty bucks. Sixty bucks.*

She slid a cigarette into her mouth and immediately pulled it out, jerking her arm down.

Brian, you're a *fucking* buttercup!   said the blonde to a little boy. She standing there, I slap her, too. If her mom don't like it, I says, you wanna start a fight?

I didn't wanna fight her,   said Brian.

I can't believe you came out of me,   said the blonde in disgust. You're a pansy like your father. Ain't that right, Miss Octopus? I said ain't that right?

Miss Octopus twitched.

The blonde whore walked barefoot to a low brick wall and leaned up against it. Miss Octopus limped to the sandbox and then sat back down. She kept staring over her shoulder.

Mama! shrieked the little boy. Lookit this! That nigger's hurting me!

Shit, she said. Brian, I can't be bothered with you. Now you kick his ass or he'll kick your ass. Now I'm gonna take your sister away. Now, Miss Octopus, you know where you can get that sixty bucks.

She lifted her baby out of the carriage and walked around, raising it high and kissing it. It was very pale and listless; it scarcely moved. It had no pupils in its eyes. The blonde whore put it back in the carriage and wheeled it away.

A little later, when shadows began to crawl down the faces of the buildings that crowded round the park, Miss Octopus took Brian by the hand and began to lead him away with divine wordlessness, so that I thought that she finally knew what she wanted. But after a few steps she let him go and sat down on the brick wall, staring back and forth. He hung his head. Suddenly she jumped up and snatched back his hand, which fell into her keeping with the same listlessness as the baby had lived. Miss Octopus sank down once more and pulled him onto her lap, clutching him until he began to cry half-heartedly. At this she snapped herself upright and towed him down the path. Long after her hair and dark blue coat had blended into one shade, the white splotch of her face could be seen as she turned her head left and right.

She was proclaimed dead on a rainy day, when the world was an oval circumscribed by my camouflage hood. My head was bent down against the rain, so that I saw mainly the red-brick sidewalk, the canes that blind men tapped. The only person in the park was a woman in a black raincoat, sitting all alone on a wet bench. It was the blonde whore. She held an umbrella patiently over herself. I did not dare to look into her face. Suddenly she told me: Miss Octopus is dead. She just died.

What did she die of? I said.

You *know* what she died of, the whore said.

Yes, I said, I guess I do.

Then I walked on. I stopped when I saw a woman come out of the Hotel Windsor. She wasn't wearing a raincoat. The front of her blouse was unbuttoned so that her heavy breasts could be seen swinging. She had big pink thighs and firm buttocks that bulged inside her skirt. She stood under the awning, smiling at me.

Did you know Miss Octopus? I said. The junky who died?

Sure I knew her, the whore said. Better believe I did. They called her Miss Octopus 'cause she could suck the money right out of you. Shit, she was a *sick* one! I'm glad she died, too, 'cause I owed her sixty bucks.

XI
IN OMAHA

Punishment is a sort of medicine.

ARISTOTLE, *Nicomachean Ethics*

1

My grandmother had begun to have trouble walking the year before I was born. The family doctor said that he couldn't find any problem, but my mother said   Daddy there's something *wrong* with Mother!   and my grandfather took her to see a high-priced neurologist who pricked her and poked her and took my grandfather aside and said   well sir it's Parkinson's.   The family doctor said   I knew that years ago; I never had the heart to tell her.   —You know,   said my grandfather,   maybe he was right. Maybe it's better not to know if there's no cure.

That was thirty years ago. They gave her five years to live then.

This visit is not going to be fun,   my mother said.   Poor Grandma is really failing, and with your Grandpa getting so feeble I'm afraid that pretty soon she's really going to have to go to a home. Your uncle was out there last weekend, and he finally got them to agree that the time has come to visit some homes and put her on the list.

My mother was very nervous and miserable.

2

My mother and my grandfather went to visit homes on Friday afternoon while my grandmother was sleeping. I sat in the living room. It was breezy outside, and the brown leaves scuttered in the driveway. At three-o'-clock I heard my grandmother ringing her bell. I went into her bedroom and said   how did you sleep?   and I knelt down very close to her to hear her and she said   not too well. Could you tell Arnie I need a bath?

He's not here,   I said.   I'll give you a bath if you like.

Where is he?   she said.

He and Mom are out looking at nursing homes,   I said.

My grandmother didn't say anything.

She's not ready,   my grandfather said to me.   All the ladies who help take care of her say that. I can take care of her! I always have.

But all night I heard him coughing in his room.   I don't feel so good, he said. All day he sat resting.

3

In the morning I raked leaves and fallen apples in the back yard until my hands blistered, which did not take very long because I had not worked a lifetime with my hands the way that my grandfather had, so I borrowed some gloves from him and kept working as he said beaming, *well* isn't that *wonderful!* and   Bill, you're *all right;*   and the apples lay so heavy in the grass like sleeping faces and the smell of apples was sweet and strong.

In the afternoon my poor grandmother sat in her wheelchair by the TV, leaning forward to see a little better, looking ahead and a little downward with her fine tired face, her wrists gripping each other so that they wouldn't tremble. In profile she kept much of her beauty. But she was tired. —We watched a French lesson program together. Then the children's program came on, which my grandmother liked because it was so peaceful.

I don't want to go to a nursing home, my grandmother said. I'd rather die.

I can't blame you, I said.

My grandmother wanted a glass of cider. When I brought her one, it was too heavy for her to hold, so I got her a smaller one, which made the cider very elegant like some expensive cognac, and then it was time for her blue pill, and I said you know, Grandma, we need to fill up the bird feeder soon and she said in her weak voice that you had to strain to hear yes I believe the cardinals and robins have been eating there quite often and I said have the varieties of birds changed over the years? and she said there aren't nearly so many of them now; we used to get hordes of goldfinches but now we never see them; the grackles are their enemies, and then also all the insecticides. —It took her a long time to say this.

Later she fell asleep over her book, and her hand slid back and forth in spasms across the open page.

It was usually in the evenings that the twitches began and my grandmother seemed to become almost frolicsome the way her feet would tap as if to some music, the way her legs would dance—but her head was sunken weakly on her shoulder and she strove to hold her knees together to stop the twitching; she pulled feebly at her legs with her hands, but that made no difference.

4

My grandfather sat down by the TV to rest. —We'll watch the scandal in the news, who got killed and the crooked politicians, he said. We gotta watch that.

I wanted to please everyone. I kept getting beers for him, cider and tiny Halloween candy bars for my grandmother; my attentions whirled unhappily round and round, reminding me of the days when my grandfather was a boy and his friends kept great horned owls in cages; he said that when those owls looked at you their heads turned all the way around on their necks. There had to be some way to help these two people whom I loved—but of course there wasn't. My grandmother tried to read her James Michener book, which she was halfway through, but after half an hour she hadn't turned the page.

5

My mother made a nice meatloaf dinner, but my grandmother didn't want to eat it because it wasn't on time.

Carol doesn't understand,   said my grandfather.   If Evelyn doesn't eat at six-o'-clock she can't eat; she's not hungry.

My mother went into my grandmother's bedroom for a very long time, and finally persuaded her to come out. It was time for her yellow pill, her red pill and her two white pills. Her legs danced and danced. I lined up all three of my grandfather's shot glasses with water in them and said now Evelyn don't drink too much   and my grandmother laughed and my mother smiled and my grandfather laughed and said   well how original!   and my grandmother began eating her salad in tired little bites and then she choked. My grandfather had to leap up and pull the lettuce out of her throat.

I'm not very hungry,   said my grandmother.   I want to go back to my room.

What's that, Mother?   said my mother loudly.

I'm not hungry,   said my grandmother.

Well, you know, Mother, you've slept so much today that if you go and lie down you won't be able to sleep tonight.

I want to go lie down,   she repeated.

I wheeled her into her bedroom.

I'm so terrible for everyone else,   she said to me.

It's a lot worse for you than for us, I said. Do you want me to keep you company, or do you want to be alone?

I want to be alone.

6

My grandfather had been passing blood for three days. Friday was the worst, but he didn't tell us until Sunday because he didn't want to spoil our visit. We made him call the doctor at home. The doctor was half asleep. I went with my grandfather to the hospital and he lay on the examination table. We went home; he sat and rested in his favorite chair. I wheeled my grandmother into the chair beside him. My mother made bloody marys; my grandfather got up very slowly and brought two Old Milwaukees from the refrigerator—one for him, one for me.

Couple of beers make you feel better, he grinned. Kind of make you forget how bad you feel.

Soon he had turned on the TV and leaned back with a beer in his hand, yelling happily: I *hate* this lying sonofabitch! You don't know *nothing*, you sonofabitch. I'd like to kick you in the teeth!

I'm pretty middle of the road myself, said my grandfather. What makes me see red is all those jerks that want to take away handguns. Pretty soon, they'd take 'em away from all the people and give it to the animals.

Say, what do you think about all those lawyers? my grandfather asked me. Don't you think we'd be better off if we shot half those bastards?

Shoot 'em all, I said.

My grandfather chuckled. Yessir, Evelyn—Bill and I are solving all the world's problems. But we got to get those liberals out of the Supreme Court. That Warren Court was the biggest disaster that ever befell this country. Now we have so many *rights* we don't have any *freedoms*. Why, just think of all those murderers that get off! Doesn't that make you mad? What about the victims' rights? You know, when it comes down to actually killing somebody, you hate to do it. You really hate to do it. But that Manson, I'd do it myself. What do you say, Bill?

Have to agree with you there,   I said.

A tire commercial came on the TV.   —Aw, go hang yourself,   said my grandfather. He pressed a button on the remote control to kill the sound.

7

The next day the sun went slowly across the sky, and then we had company.

A wind was whirling leaves in the front yard. It was time for my grandfather to make margaritas. I read him the proportions off the ancient recipe card, and he poured in the tequila and triple sec and margarita mix more solemnly than any hanging judge. My grandfather and I had three margaritas apiece. My mother had two. My grandmother had a small one.   —Now, Grandma, don't get too boisterous,   I warned her sternly, and she laughed.

Whenever there was company at dinner my grandfather still said grace in Norwegian, very soft and low, but that was about all of his language that he remembered. When he was a boy his parents made him understand that Norwegian stopped at the front door. It had been that way with all of them. One of his schoolmates started swearing at the teacher in Norwegian once, so she crammed a bar of soap into his mouth and made him swallow it.

I didn't give you any salad tonight, Mother,   my mother said.   It didn't seem to agree with you.

Later, my great-aunt Vi said to me   Evelyn has had such a hard life, I never could have stood it. But she's a very determined lady. I admire her for what she's accomplished. I know they'll give her an extra big gold star in Heaven.

After dinner, Vi sat beside my grandmother on the couch, rubbing her shoulders very gently for a long time as my grandmother leaned against her like a little child.

As I wheeled my grandmother into her bedroom she said: Last night I had a dream that I was walking.

That must have felt wonderful, like flying, I said.

Yes, like flying, she said.

She was too tired to say anything else.

8

There was no virgin prairie left anymore in Omaha, where my grandparents lived, where the houses were small and the yards were narrow like graves. Their old place was like that. They had moved out of it in the fifties because it was too close to the racetrack. The yard they had now was quite wide. In fact, these days it was too big for my grandfather. Soon he would have to hire someone to mow it for him. He had already cut the garden by half; the old garden was more work than he could take on anymore. Practically all he raised now was flowers and tomatoes. I looked around me, and all I saw was houses and little yards, but the county extension agent said that he had a great opportunity for me because there was a place where the indigenous grasses had been reintroduced two or three years ago. My grandfather and I got lost at first trying to find it in his big car that ran so smoothly and quietly even though my grandfather had become dissatisfied with the transmission and said to me I want to have one more new car in my life although I probably won't on account of the nursing home bills, and it was a yellow windy Nebraska day as we rolled steadily along watching with great vigilance for the exit, which we missed, so we ended up on the Iowa side where there were many small farms, and my grandfather said Hell! (he got angry at my grandmother when she said Hell instead of heck), but when we crossed the bridge back into Nebraska we saw the turnoff and we drove along the edge of the Missouri River just past the golf course until we found the dirt road.

There used to be a lot of horse farms out here, my grandfather said. Still a lot of beautiful saddle horses in the west. Used to be a red apple farm, but the big freeze of 1940 ruined everything.

Not very far away, I heard repeated shots, although my grandfather didn't hear them. It was pheasant season. When they were younger, my grandfather and grandmother used to go hunting together, and once my grandmother came running to him through the sunny grass with a pheasant in her arms and she was laughing and the living bird trembled in her arms with its feathers shining a thousand colors of purple and my grandmother said   I didn't have the heart to kill it; it's such a beautiful bird;   and when my grandfather took it from her to wring its neck it got away from him and spread its wings and flew away, so free and high above the grass.

On a bluff overlooking the river, golden grass rose head-high, and so did golden cockleburrs like fruits, and the silver down of seed-thistles, everything dry and precious and bright. When the breeze blew, great golden stalks rustled together and bowed. The grass reached up to the sky; you could see sky through it. I saw six-foot switchgrass with its lacy seedheads; I saw eight-foot Indian grass waving its golden plumes very slowly. On the hills below, the bare black trees of autumn rose like taller stalks. The sunlight was very gentle. The tips of the grass were crowned with golden and white. They glowed against the darker shade of the stalks like jet-trails in the sky. Down low the grass was paler and thinner; sometimes it was speckled. Wind-songs and birdsongs and grass-songs filled the afternoon; the grass-songs were the loudest. The rustlings were stiff and gentle. Nothing was being whirled and scraped like dry leaves in a wind; nothing was being hurt like my grandmother; grass was bowing against grass, and grass-crowds were whispering; that was all. You could bend a grass-stalk double without hurting it; but when you bent it sharply against itself it snapped in two. The breeze never bent it like that.

11

Epitaph for

PRESIDENT JOHN F. KENNEDY

* U.S.A. *

The extra bullets left darker streaks in Zapruder's movies than any deeds of cracked loyalty that we could explain. They hurtled at you like comets from Enigma, so when Oswald got death, Ruby got life, but he died before he talked. Castro got a breather; you got the privilege of not having to undo yourself; you outlived the vulgarity of survival. I was four years old. When your icon began to shine, the radio was talking to the steering wheel (I remember that, but not what it said) and my mother said   our President is dead   and my mother was crying and I looked out the window, crying because my mother was crying, and I saw so many cars creeping slowly along the freeway and everyone in every car was crying.

XII

TROPICANA

Thus there are reasonable persons who,
without a high polish on their shoes, are
almost incapacitated.

I. A. RICHARDS, *Principles of
Literary Criticism* (1925)

When he was six years old, Nicholas Wright wanted to be a
clown. The white cheeks and shiny red rubber noses of these
laughing beings enthralled him step by step into a garden of smiles
whose puckered roses suddenly gaped to laugh *haw-haw* as wet tongues
wriggled like delirious caterpillars so that Nicholas shrieked with mirth
and his parents looked at one another, embarrassed. The circus went
away, and Nicholas forgot clowns entirely. He was now working for
SIDEWARP, a secret arm of the United States government which
"protected" our sources of raw materials in Latin America, so that quite
frequently, in some pleasant restaurant in Tampa or New Orleans,
Nicholas could be seen in company of one of the many nodding
approving career women, saying   I just got a million dollar deal sewn
up with Dole!   and the career woman lifted her wine glass and set it
down as Nicholas went on   I'm almost *there* with the citrus deal in
Belize!   and the career woman thought   jeez what a boring asshole.
—Finally they sent him to Tropicana.

Nick, you are *so* lucky,   said his secretary.   Tropicana is supposed to
be a *wonderful* place. Susan downstairs, you know, the one who used to
be in the Peace Corps, was there about ten years ago, and she just *loved*
it. She never stops talking about it. What will you be doing there?

Raw materials,   said Nicholas.

It must be beautiful there,   she said.   Although I suppose it's changed
a lot since Susan was down in Tropicana City.

Nicholas went to the conference room for his briefing, where he learned that the Kingdom of Tropicana had been discovered by the Portuguese, conquered by the Spaniards without a single (Spanish) casualty, liberated by the French, surveyed by the English, and civilized by the German and American tourists who now gorged themselves on its tan beaches, sitting on mahogany chairs in octagonal thatched huts open to salt and light not sunburn, where, tapping their toes in the sand, waving at surfers and snorkelers, they drank Tropicali Amber or Tropicali Stout in the long-necked brown bottles that the native children would later lay out in empty rows in the sand, as if to imitate the pilings of the rickety piers that stretched long distances into the shallow water, past the glowing greenish stripe of sunny water to the deeper green depths where fishes as big as your arm casually swam, and speedboats with Tropicali pilots rushed tourists from caye to caye for a very reasonable consideration. Beyond them, on the horizon, were little segments of whitecaps where the barrier reef began. Sailboats rode parallel to this line, although (to be sure) a safe distance from it.

Two Collectors

Are you having a good time?   he said.

Yes,   the secretary said,   are you?   —Without waiting to hear his answer, she wandered away and squatted on the sand, picking up the perfect miniature shells.

He watched her kneeling in her bathing suit, one knee higher than the other, churning sand busily with her fingers. Her face was alight with the joy of incipient possession. Later she returned to her towel and scooped with the side of her hand. Her expression never changed, whether she found a shell or not. The tranquilly gloating look on her face much became her. So did everything else. She had small, perfect breasts that never quivered.

Nicholas's Mission

It was a very strange sight to see the mangrove-islands, whose land was nothing but roots between which lapped ocean flows, water blue and green.

How come we're not doing anything?   the secretary said.

I have to wait for further instructions,   Nicholas said.

You didn't get fired, did you? I mean, you didn't just bring me here for no reason?

I thought you said I was *so* lucky,   said Nicholas.

Well, did you get fired or didn't you?

The mangrove lagoon was shallow and creamy-coffee-colored. Low tree-islands bore their darknesses between roots. A yellow bird chip-chipped somewhere in the rubbery forest.

We'll have a good trip. You'll see.

Oh my *God*, Nick. You must feel terrible! What happened?

You're pretty snoopy.

I think I have a right to know if you brought me down here. I mean, do I have a job to go back to? What did you tell them, anyway? You pulled that confidential business, I guess so nobody knew if you were going or coming. I see it all now, Nick, but what's going to happen to me? Nick?

Decay

She was stretching out her shirt like a sail and inspecting it with the lovely remorselessness of a plaster angel. The little shells were clean and white in her cupped hand.

That's a fine little sailboat,   she said. —Neither of them said

271

anything for a moment, and then she said   I wonder if you could rent sailboats here. Probably not.

She put moisturizer on her legs.   —That boat there's a little bit bigger than the size I learned on,   she said.

When he looked at her, he could never catch her unawares. If her eyes were closed, the second his gaze fell upon her she opened them. It was as if his attention stretched over her like a shadow.

She was going away from him with the same delicate assurance with which she picked her way through the shallow water, stepping between sharp corals.

Sabotage

After a certain number of sips of the Extra Strong Rum, which was sold in brown glass bottles half-full, as if to permit continuous distillation to occur, and a clipper-shape label was plastered over another label which was not itself the first—after a certain number of sips, and a number more—and I say only "a certain number" because it quickly became impossible to verify—the island began to contract for Nicholas, drawing in on itself like the lobes of a pickled brain, and the rapid green-grey streaming of the channel to the other island, the mangrove island, seemed part of a more momentous counterclockwise current that whirled round the island washing sand away and tightening it, as meanwhile the wind also did its part by blowing the coconut frond the way the ocean was going, and birds flew that way, too:—west. Only a single snorkeler made paddlewheels of his arms to go against current and tide, away from the direction that the German tourists were facing in their beach chairs (the girl, he saw, had pale white buttocks; the panties of her bathing suit had ridden below the tan line), and when he looked at the snorkeler again, he saw the green stream bearing the fellow backward, as a pair of dark birds wheeled over him watching.   —Raw materials,   thought Nicholas to himself. —The secretary's curly hair was trembling in the wind, like clusters of rich brown berries. Her sunglasses stared from her face pitilessly. Later the ground seemed to tremble.

Small island, isn't it?   said Nicholas.

She bit her lip.

Then he knew her mind. He was very quick that way.

It was a hot night, even on the boat dock where Nicholas stood watching the water lapping at the stretch of tan sand called a street, the lights on in hotels and bars, the Pepsi sign swinging gently, coconut fronds rustling around the streetlights, men with their shirttails hanging out standing in the street because it was the coolest breeziest place, and the boats pulled up in the sand to sleep; the fan blades shimmering in the lighted upstairs window of the Hotel Mira Mar where the secretary was not. Music blared from the Reef Bar (he liked the Reef Bar). Seaweed swirled saltily in and out, and a shirtless boy bicycled down the street. —Now Nicholas activated his STAR scope and peered into the darkness of the Reef Bar's doorway where he saw a girl in a T-shirt and sweatband standing on the porch looking out at the street. Something glittered like sparks in her hand.

He strolled down Air Strip Road, and found the secretary trying to hitchhike.

After a long silence she said   that palm tree looks like a big Indian headdress.

· Looks like a stop sign to me,   said Nicholas.

She let him take her hand and lead her back to the hotel. She seemed as exhausted as a little girl at bedtime.

He heard her in the bathroom brushing her teeth. There was a coarse horsey sound to it that he hated.

The Interrogation

The next day they went snorkeling together. They were spending Nicholas's money. Anyhow snorkels were cheap like the motorboat that waited for them with the bored Tropicali boy sitting in it. She jumped in first; Nicholas followed. There were fishes like lemons and limes. There were corals like beehives, termite nests, fleshy trees that snagged the folds of his shirt, purple sea-fans, dry and rubbery to the touch, and he flew weightlessly over the blue sand (which was not really blue, probably, but he would never know because it was underwater), the corals like orange brains with purple feelers . . .   —These colors,   he said to himself,   are mainly khaki and toilet-water blue.   —Now the fishes were stone-colored, with blue and green scale-flakes; they were black with violently blue spots; they were black and yellow, yellow and black, working their fins to carry them away.

The secretary was swimming close to him. He saw light shimmering pink and red and pale upon her rosy arm, as the sun shimmered blue and green on the sea. It seemed to him that he could see her blood running in her veins. At once desire seized him.

She was flying in the water ahead of him, flying with her long white arms (which were outstretched with such vulnerable yearning sensitivity), soaring with her white legs, her sleek blue belly. Her fingers were spread ahead of her; she was feeling her way. Suddenly she turned and faced him. He waved to her when he saw her eyes upon him behind the mask, so big and blue, and she raised her fingers and waved back. Although he could not see much of her face, he knew that she was smiling. A school of bright-eyed fish blew like pale green leaves through the coral.

That night in the hotel room, pulling her shorts on over her bathing suit, tilting her head to towel her hair, she said: I guess you always wanted to fuck me, didn't you?

Have I?

What do you want me for then?   she said, very low.

Nicholas smiled.   Prudential considerations,   he said.

Support of Healthy Tendencies

Evening again, and in the Reef Bar they were yelling again, and the sky was pink and white above the soft blue sea.

The bar was crowded with men like dark sharks swimming in green water.

He'd taken her there to buy her a drink; it was something to do. She ordered a Tropicana Squeeze and then another. She drank rather too fast. Pretty soon she was dabbing at her eyes with a kleenex. He had expected this: after all, the relationship must mature. He kept watching her. It was only a matter of time before she signaled some other man. With his trained eyeballs he watched every corner of the bar with its bamboo walls and open windows through which street men leaned. The fan spun wearily. On the ceiling hung a fishnet crammed with sea-junk like dead starfish and sand-polished beer bottles and conch shells, all around which ran a loop of winking Christmas tree lights. There was a plastic Christmas tree by the ladies' room, with a dried starfish on top for a star. Men in tank tops strode around, laughing in high voices. Men stood at the bar. A woman with a cigarette in her hand went out to the porch and stood there looking at the ocean and then came back again. She was the one he had seen through his STAR scope before, when he forestalled the secretary's escape. He decided that he wanted to fuck her.

There was nothing to it. He made contact with one of the informers, his imperfect images. They all thought that he was still affiliated with SIDEWARP. He described the girl and asked the informer to take him to where she lived. (The secretary was lying in bed with a wet towel over her face and the fan roaring; she had a headache.) —Sure, Nicky, the man said. I take you to her. Is she a Red? I hate Reds.

Take me there at sunrise, Nicholas said. Don't alert your squad.

Last Rites

Later that night, when her headache was better, he and she went walking on the beach where coconut palms with their pale twisting trunks grew together in shade-clusters, beneath which spread the broad-lobed grasses and trees dark green and light green. Clapboard houses stood on stilts. Dogs lay in the sand. A man in a white shirt shot through the channel in a motor skiff. His shirt fluttered half up to his armpits. Nicholas and the secretary walked to the farthest pier and then back to the Reef Bar and got drunk again. The secretary said something's going to happen soon isn't it? and Nicholas said   probably not.   The secretary said   how long are you going to keep me here? Nicholas said   do you want to go home? You can go tomorrow if you want.   The secretary said   I may as well stay another couple of days.

The night was long and furry like a dog. They lay still. Nicholas got out of bed quietly but at once the secretary's eyes flew bluely open and she said   where are you going?

I'm just taking a walk,   said Nicholas.   I'll be back in a few hours.

Do you want some company?

You're just saying that because you know I don't want you to come with me,   Nicholas said.   You're good at knowing things. Whenever I want your company you try to get away from me.

Fine,   the secretary said quietly.

Nicholas took his key and went out. The informer was waiting at the pier. He was grinning.   —We are always happy when the Americans do something!   he whispered, touching Nicholas's shoulder.   —It is hard for us to have faith otherwise. But tonight again you are looking out for us.

That's right,   said Nicholas.   Let's go.

Deception and Influence

Slowly the darkness dissipated, as the insects chirred and the howler monkeys made slow noises like giants breathing. Grey clouds retreated slowly along the horizon, and the sky glowed white as pearl. Now the white trunks of trees could be distinguished, and the nearer leaves stood out, although farther away the jungle was still an interminable block of shadow. Halfway up a dead tree, the crescent moon still shone more brightly than anything. Flies buzzed around Nicholas in circles. To his right, the informer sat smoking, cupping his hand around the glowing butt as SIDEWARP had taught him. The slow cupped sounds of howler monkeys came to him like the jungle breathing. Now the sky was orange above the cashew trees, and flies circled around.

Ahead was the beach, and the woman's house.

276

Nicholas and the informer waited for a long time. At last the door opened.

The woman stood barelegged in the sand, in a white shift with her fingertips resting lightly on her hips like spiderlegs. He admired her façade. She had a little son; she took him on the dock and squatted down with her hand on his shoulder. He toddled, and he peed in the sand. Nicholas stared at her knees. He stared again when she stood, and this time he could see the hair in her armpits, and the outlines of her breasts in the shift.

Slowly, he lifted the STAR scope to his eye and rotated the filter until her clothes became transparent. He had already lost interest. He said to himself: what am I looking for? What's wrong with me? If this were an assignment I'd like it.

To the informer, to avoid disappointing him, he said: Tail her. Give me a report in three days.

He looked back. She had lit up a cigarette. As always, she held it in her hand but did not smoke it.

Fallback Strategy

The guy in the big black shirt that said BEACH said you wanna girl good face I'm telling you mon good ass listen to me mon this girl good nice.

How much? said Nicholas, thinking to himself operational expenses.

Ten dollar U.S. mon I take half now half when I bring you the girl.

At low tide, the seaweed made islands with little sand-channels between.

Let me see her first.

You no trust me motherfockah I come bock *bod* I come after you.

Ever heard of SIDEWARP? said Nicholas.

Oh brothah don't tell me you be a spook! That's okay mon that's okay. I get her for you.

277

Partners

What's your name?   Nicholas said.

   Conchita. Conchita Liquado. My stage name, sir.

   You like her?   said Mr Beach.   I *tell* you you gonna like her!

   Here's fifty,   said Nicholas.   I'm going to keep her all week. Get lost.

Friends

Here's a friend for you,   Nicholas said to the secretary.

   The girls flexed their legs on the dock,   putting suntan lotion on, rubbing, smoothing, shaping, slapping. The secretary crossed her arms against her buttocks and looked at the map, saying   now where's Antigua?

   In the back of the limousine it was very hot, and Nicholas and the secretary rolled their windows down. The hot breeze blew down the front of the secretary's shirt, so that her small breasts seemed suddenly to be lush and straining.

   The pure white walls of the police station shone in the dust of the market.

   Conchita sat between Nicholas and the secretary. She kept giggling. —I don't know what to do,   she said.   Nicky, what you want me to do?

   Put your arm around her,   said Nicholas, staring out the window.

   So now you think I'm a lesbian?   said the secretary.

   I know it,   said Nicholas.   I've always known it. I read your file.

   Why does that woman with the cigarettes attract you?   parried the secretary.   You see, I know things, too.

278

Of course you know things, said Nicholas. You work for SIDEWARP.

Stop here, he said to the driver. Pick us up in four hours.

You pay now, sir?

Bill to the Embassy, said Nicholas. But don't submit the bill until next week. They won't honor it before they get a chit from me. New procedure.

Oh so it's a week then, said the secretary.

Conchita put her arm around her nervously. —You have such soft soft skin, she said.

The secretary bit her lip.

They waded to an island in the river, an island of hard round rocks like heels. Conchita carried a sixpack of Tropicana Stout, which she had bought with Nicholas's money. She never stopped holding the secretary's hand. When they got to the island, they lay down on the rocks and drank. Very slowly Nicholas slid his hand between Conchita's legs. Conchita's grip on the secretary's hand tightened. The secretary was silent.

Why don't you two go fuck, said Nicholas. That's your vital interest.

How can you give orders when you don't even— the secretary began, but Nicholas cut her off by saying *security six!* at which she fell silent.

He drank a beer then. —Go ahead, he said.

That's what you want?

Yes.

While the girls crossed the river, he could see their hips undulating. A little snake of light connected both their arms, outstretched upon the water. He lay low on the island, behind a clump of rubbery grasses. Then their dark bathing suits became a part of the shade of the immense trees on the opposite shore. For a moment he could see their white bodies. Then they vanished.

The Crisis

At half past six, the morning sunlight made brilliant triangles on the green walls of the hotel room. Nicholas opened his eyes to a steadily increasing feeling of misery, which might have been joylessness exacerbated, or weariness, but was probably simple sadness. The secretary lay beside him, naked. Her eyes had been open for a long time. He looked into them and saw transparency as in the blue-green channels between the mangrove-islands, but only for an instant, since as soon as she saw his gaze her eyes became translucently turquoise like water behind the sliding plastic door of the shower. Conchita was in the bathroom. He heard the toilet flush.

I have some business to do today,   he said.

What kind of business?   the secretary said.

I need to see someone,   he said. He stared at the fan suspended above his head with its three dull and massive blades.

Well, I'm going to go out with Conchita,   she said.   Don't think you can just leave me to wait around for you.

I don't think that,   he said.   I never did. Go and do some shopping.

There was sand on the floor. Her sweet pink toes were like rosebuds in the sand.

As soon as she was gone he went out into the hot sun. The light was very soft and serious, like a tweed suit. It was eight-o'-clock. In the bamboo bars men were already drinking and gambling.

In the plaza he met the informer. He said to him: Wait a minute. Let me leave my wife a note.

The informer did not ask his permission; he accompanied him into the hotel room. She had left her pearl necklace out on the bureau. Nicholas looked at it. The informer looked at it. He sidled toward it with the hip-dance and tail-dance of a nurse shark. As yet he did not touch it. He waited. At last, Nicholas nodded. Still the informer waited. His arm twitched, as jerkily as a pigeon moves its head. Nicholas took the necklace and kissed it, at which it became activated. Then he put it into the informer's hand.

They went out together and tailed the woman who never smoked her cigarettes. The informer was happy, Nicholas morose. —When are we gonna hit her, Nicky? the informer whispered. —Nicholas sucked in his cheeks. —Next week, he said.

When he returned, she was sitting on the bed crying. The necklace had been her mother's. He knew that from her file.

Conchita was not with her anymore.

So you fired her for this, he said. Didn't you?

I guess your week's up today anyway, isn't it, Nick?

You mean Conchita's week or SIDEWARP's week? he said, kneading her shoulders very slowly.

I mean—

They're both seven days, and they both began on Sunday, but they're not the same. That's your mistake.

I don't know what I mean. You know what I mean.

Don't worry, he said. We can keep them all off balance, you and I. They don't know the key goal.

The Initiative

The secretary stood in the doorway of the hotel with her blue swimsuit-breast in perfect profile. Very carefully she made up her face. The breeze was cool and steady. It was evening, and little brown girls rode their bicycles across the sand while black birds like pterodactyls flapped wings sharply down, watching the pier where men cleaned groupers and a big barracuda (whose teeth were almost unbearably sharp). The woman who never smoked her cigarettes stood on a balcony, brushing her teeth and rinsing from a Coca-Cola glass and spitting. One grouper in the bucket was still alive because it had been in the livewell of the fishing boat, so it tried to flip itself sideways out of the bucket, and meanwhile the shallow sea was orange and blue and rippled like women's breasts in the shallows between piers and boats and pilings and seaweed islands;—but farther out the reef-breakers made a broken white horizon half an inch below the horizon.

I see the shadow of a shark, the secretary said.

Are you having fun seeing it? said Nicholas.

The reflections of the pilings were curlicued like telephone cords. Above the sea was a single cloud like a rosy fist.

Want a drink? said Nicholas.

At the Reef? Okay.

I though you didn't like the Reef, he replied very quickly. She could almost hear the nervous whirring of his eyes.

That's why you take me there, isn't it, Nick?

The grouper was black and yellow-spotted. It had not escaped from the bucket. A man picked it up and slit its guts.

Nick?

What?

What's SIDEWARP going to do?

He laughed. Put up a monument to me, probably.

They walked past the informer's house, where she stopped to look through the picket fence, once white, now grey, at the yellow-green vegetation in the cemetery, whose white and black crosses were canted in the sand, whose palms girded the far side of the enclosure, framing grey-green sea and a dingy white fishing boat at anchor halfway to the reef. The boat was more interesting because it was half hidden.

The informer was not in.

They walked past the shuttered building that said **REGISTERED PHARMACIST – LICENSED TO SELL DRUGS AND POISONS**, and there was music in the dirt streets, and couples were dancing, and there was music in the bars where couples danced so close, and the music went *doo-awp-bup-buh-doo-wap-uh-bub-doo-wop-do-bee-do-wap-a-do-bup*, and the sea was blackish amber and foamy and very salty with a trail of moonlight on it, and the stars were very bright. —The secretary walked to the end of the dock and turned on her flashlight. Standing beside her, Nicholas saw that the sea had become a suspension of millions of little dark fishes like seeds in guava jelly. She looked at her watch.

They lay back on some hotel's beach chairs and looked up at the stars through the radiating fronds of the palm trees. She looked at her watch.

Are you waiting for something? said Nicholas.

Oh no.

SIDEWARP won't ever trust *you* again either, darling,   he said.
Don't think you can doublecross me. They'll take you into that little
dark room with the white, white fish . . .

. . . and they returned one last time to the Reef Bar, where the perky
chirp of some unknown bird always turned out to be nothing but a man
scraping his toenail against the wall. It was very hot. And yet as soon as
he had escorted her inside, a sense of refreshment stole over him like
coolness. He saw the woman who never smoked her cigarettes. She
came over to him and shook her breast in his face. It was a fat papaya,
pitted and soft like a rotten pumpkin. The secretary was smiling sadly.
Waves of green shadow broke on his skin. It was as if he had fallen into
the shark aquarium at the American bar down the beach. All around
him the men drank, their voices rising murderously. There were turtle-
shells on the walls. He saw the limousine driver drinking alone in a
corner, lifting up his big turtle's reddish freckled face in greeting; the
secretary fluttered her fingers, and he subsided. The blades of the fan
drew shadows across the secretary's face so that it became a turtle's shell
mottled like water. Beside him, a sea-turtle lifted up its mottled yellow
head like a leopard's and drank beer; the heads of the men were sea-
turtles' heads, like coconuts, like swollen fungi. He swam in Tropicali
Stout. The woman who never smoked her cigarettes was standing in the
doorway unmoving. Her T-shirt had four stripes, like the fish called
sergeant-major. Having made this observation, Nicholas felt more at
peace than ever. The tension of the drinking men made eddies that
surged across his face with sweet foamy coolness. One of the men was
staring at the secretary, although he could not see who; he felt the gaze
from somewhere behind him, fixating on her in much the same way that
a lemon shark scarcely moves its blunt bullet head although its tail whips
powerfully from side to side, its front fins almost rigid like the wings of a
bomber. Someone wanted her.

I wonder if any of those bottles have messages in them,   she said in a
very low voice. She had draped her shirt loosely around her shoulders
and was leaning on the bar, looking down at a barracuda. The nipples
stood out like little buttons under her swimming suit.

A manta ray scuttered up to him, almost invisible in the night-lit
water, dark green against dark green. A manta ray curled itself against
the bamboo pilings. This was the informer, who was now at his right

hand, drinking a Bombshell. He had not sat down. He had come to bear witness, to give warning of the shark; that was his nature. He crooked his hand at Nicholas; his hand was as flexible as a sea-turtle's flippers.

I know about you now, he said. You do nothing with her. See how she cries all the time. Look at those red eyes! You give her to me now.

The secretary slid her shirt off her shoulders, and he saw that she was wearing the necklace.

I'm going with him, Nick, the secretary said. —She had stood up. Her salty-wet hair clung deliciously to her long neck, her bare freckled shoulders.

Nicholas laughed. With *him?*

Now the informer's fist came shooting at his face like the wide blunt head of a nurse shark. Nicholas blocked the punch and stood up and smashed a bottle over his head. —That bottle had a message in it, now didn't it, sweetheart? he said, breathing heavily. The informer was roaring. Blood trickled out of his eyes. But somehow he had Nicholas's STAR scope and he was raising it high above Nicholas's head and the secretary was screaming and Nicholas lunged forward to rip the shark's teeth from that grinning underwater mouth but the STAR scope came down on Nicholas with all the weight of a planet.

Somebody was saying into his ear: *They eat each other, any fish, but they can't cotch it. The only reason those little fish come in is 'cause the sharks can't cotch 'em. But you cotch one, you squeeze the life half out of it, then the big ones gonna eat it.*

They were standing over him, and the limousine driver was splashing water on his face, smiling apologetically because he was an old man. SIDEWARP had hired him during the Korean War.

Nicholas stood up. His head hurt.

He took the driver by the collar. —Where are they? he shouted.

Gone, said the driver. I do not know where. I think to take an airplane.

Well, then, where's Conchita Liquado? She'll do, he laughed.

The room was very hot. Nicholas's head ached.

He remembered now that he still had his ambush pistol, "to enhance defensive posture." He took it out and cocked it and held it to the driver's head. —We're going to play checkers, he said.

He threw the driver down onto the floor. He grinned at the barmaid. —Get a checkerboard, he said.

Repeat please sir?

Get a checkerboard, bitch! he shouted. He reached behind the bar and threw a bottle of rum on the floor. The bursting of the glass was like music.

A boy went running and came back with a checkerboard. —Oh, you are *strong* man! he said respectfully. You drink good, you fight good—that white woman no good! I kill her for you? Five hundred dollar!

Get out, said Nicholas.

He pulled the driver to his feet. —No, no, the man said. Nicholas saw that he was waving his pistol in the man's face. He dragged him to a table in the corner and put his gun down beside him so that it became the precious gamepiece that would win him every inning. —Sit down, he said.

All night he made the driver play. From time to time the driver strove to look into his face, with the awkward effort of a sea-turtle craning its head above water for a breath. When Nicholas saw this, he smashed the pistol butt against the board until all the pieces jumped. The driver was a very old man who wanted very much to sleep. Sometimes he nodded off over the checkerboard, but whenever that happened Nicholas punched him and yelled: *Play!* —None of the men had left. They were as still about him as sleeping nurse sharks. But Nicholas was a lemon shark.

Now it was almost dawn and the barmaid turned off the fan. —Sir, we closed now, she said, trembling. —Nicholas leaped up and slapped her in the face. *I'm going to bruise your ass!* he shouted. Someone hit him with a bottle, once, carefully.

When he came to himself it was midmorning and his face was sunburned and he was lying on the beach, which was riddled with flowers of coral. The tide was out, and seaweed lay like combed-out grass. He stared for a long time at a piece of pink coral on the beach and slowly he began to laugh because it reminded him of a clown's tongue.

12

Epitaph for

A FORD LTD.

* GUATEMALA *

I n Guatemala (which is to say the land of limping dogs, sunshine, dust;—I mean the land of unsmiling soldiers with gun-muzzles low, trudging down white dirt roads; or, rather the land of palm trees like crazy green suns), in Guatemala dead things had life.

You, having done thirty years' service on our magnificent highways (peace be upon them), passed away at last. Your radiator burst. Your block cracked. Your carburetor choked in lead poisons. Your tires sagged. Your hood opened and closed convulsively. Then your headlights dimmed (they're only sleeping).

Tanned Charon with his white smile came to drive you across the spirit bridge to Guatemala.

It was easy. Charon took the international driver's license test and passed it because he had written all the answers inside his sleeve. They took his picture: *zzzt!* Later, if Charon himself decided not to go, his brother used the license instead. No gringo could tell the difference. Sometimes the Ambassador was in a bad mood and yelled   NO VISAS TO THE STATES THIS MONTH!   and Charon's brother only laughed at him and said   I go without visa then!

Charon's brother (whom like the Ambassador we'll call Charon) stayed in the States as long as he wanted. He became a doorman and a supermarket checker and a janitor. Although the other employees came to work broke and borrowed against future paychecks which they had already spent, he saved his money. He knew how to live on nothing. Although the cool grey shells of buildings rose spinally into the grey sky, though the windows of a million hospitals and apartments watched him (some glaring with incandescent tubes, others slyly dark, still others curtained), although gringo taxicabs and motorcycles and buses honked at him on every wet street, Charon only did his work and whistled to himself, gazing at the terraces of highrises as if he were home looking idly up at the crazy grey sun of a cotton tree's branches festooned with cottonballs. The lobbies of the hotels he scrubbed were the same to him as the Mayan soccer courts, the places where the three virgins used to be sacrificed. To him there was no difference between the toilet-stalls he cleaned and the small square caves of coolness with squat god-figures hidden inside them (their features barely seen in the glow of his cigarette lighter).

Finally he went to the used car lot with his pocket full of cash. He knew exactly what he was looking for. He was looking for you.

He got underneath you and inspected your under-carapace inch by inch, seeing, as always, by the flame of his cigarette lighter; he came out and dusted himself off and opened your hood; his fingers told him every pathology of your engine beneath.

You wanna make a deal or what? said the salesman.

Okay, said Charon, smiling brilliantly, ducking his head. He paid in hundred-dollar bills.

He held your steering wheel so gently . . .

If a policeman stopped him he promised that he was going home TOMORROW at the very latest. Home, at last, he went. Home to Guatemala.

Here between black Mayan temples worn white, past the straight and terrible ramp of knee-high steps, Charon had his village. Temples rose up above the jungle. Here Charon and his brother (whom we'll call Charon), his sons and nephews, zombied your innards to endless reliability at low speeds. They all knew how to tap the life hidden in your block like bucketfuls of sweet water inside the limber water-tikai vines, but Charon understood you best. At his touch your gas tank became tuned to the square cave halfway up the highest temple.

Then Charon sold you. —Good American car! he shouted. Lots of power!

A Belizean tour guide bought you (most Guatemalans couldn't afford cars). Actually, the Belizean didn't own you; it wasn't his money. He worked for an American tour operator. Funny business. Americans made you; Americans sold you; Americans bought you; Charon got rich in between.

(Charon celebrated. Prostitution was legal in Guatemala. There were whorehouses at the border. It was two dollars for a Guatemalan; ten dollars for a Belizean. Charon spent two dollars. He was not an extravagant man.)

So you began your days of rolling inexorably over the white gravel. You went past the lake of reeds and white birds, where brown girls washed clothes, wringing them against rocks. You went slowly past villages whose hut-roofs were like square grass skirts. It was hot. Your belly grumbled steam. You went past the yellow-green trees fringily leafy over chalky ground. You passed soldiers (roundfaced, young, cruel: the guerrillas called them the Yellow Men). Long car, you went through this land of red and green, light green and dark green, dead and living, and which were you? Not even Charon knew anymore.

The guerrillas saw you. They lay patiently resting gunbarrels on the canted altars and shattered altar-pieces between the smooth naked toes of trees; they were silent among the shrillings of insects. Dully you rolled past them day by day. You understood nothing, not even the loud liquid flash of the yellowtail bird stunning the sun from its black body.

Look at that bird!   cried the tourists safe inside you.   Beautiful!

You rolled steeply up dirt roads. Guatemala was nothing to you but gravel and dryness.

Later the tourists wanted to remember everything. They even remembered you.   —*Good car, very 'liable,*   said a Korean girl.   *I think it was brown. And dusty. Big tires. Amazing enough, we made it through the trip. More amazing thing, I'd say, is that the other car made it through the Pine Ridge trip! Very old looking.*   Read it on your tombstone.

Every day, more tourists. You never complained like the waterbugs clamoring for rain (it was the dry season). You carried tourists from tree-mound to tree-mound, rolling quietly between bay leaf trees. Who could not be proud of you, you old American car?

After the tourists had made their sunburned way through the temple carvings that were black and white like salted lava, they went into eat a sandwich with white bread and American cheese and Guatemalan catsup. The tour guide sat outside. Lunch was too expensive for him. He drank a Coke and refreshed your thirsty radiator with dirty brown water. You steamed   *ahhhh*   like a happy ox.

Back to the hotel. You rolled calmly over the white stones that villagers put on the road to make speed bumps—they called them "policemen" or "dead men." The villagers did not want anyone to drive too quickly; that raised dust-clouds.

The guerrillas watched you as they watched all things.

They lived on the far sides of fig-tree rivers (the figs rained into the water to feed fish and iguanas). They lived in mud and shade. Mothers and fathers, sons and daughters, they were all guerrillas. In Guatemala you can turn a dog mean by cutting off his tail and making him eat a

291

scorpion's tail. The Yellow Men had been doing that to the guerrillas for ages.

The tourists liked the idea of bandits in the jungle. It made them feel adventurous.   —Do they want to take our money?

No, no,   said the tour guide.   They are not like that.

What do they want then?

The tour guide thought.   —They want a better education,   he said.

Deaf, you rolled by patches of jungle being burned to make plantations.

The guerrillas hijacked fruit trucks and supply trucks. They left everyone else alone unless a driver was stupid, or an American tourist became chatty in Spanish. When the guerrillas came it was best to act as if one knew only English.

They were very polite; they always said: Sorry about the delay, Señor.

They said: Something valuable has been lost near the checkpoint; we are just looking for it, that's all.

(But one saw them carrying everything into the jungle.)

They dressed just like the Yellow Men, but if one looked at the faces behind the uniforms one sometimes saw not just little boys but also little girls.

But you never saw or could see them. You felt only the weight of the tourists on your squealing dusty seats, the reverential guidance of the guide's hands on your steering wheel. And sometimes, when the heat of summers made your dead paint begin to blister, you felt the guide hosing you off, soothing you with petroleum salves. As he bent over you, his shadow fell across your hood like the shadow of peace. He was as tall as a hard-plum tree.

XIII

THE GRAVE OF
LOST STORIES

> . . . for the terrible agony which I have so
> lately endured—an agony known only to my
> God and to myself—seems to have passed my
> soul through fire and purified it from all that is
> weak. Henceforth I am strong:—this those
> who love me shall see—as well as those who
> have so relentlessly endeavored to ruin me.
>
> Poe, to Mrs. Helen Whitman
> (1848)

In the Grave of Lost Stories there is neither day nor night, but a stupendous blackness shot through with corpuscles of fluorescence, like droplets of oil in water—an inalienable fact, of which the vulgar minds around him could not conceive. They were too busy writing anonymous articles about him (he knew that Griswold was behind most of it, but not all; there were so many envious scoundrels!) to ever comprehend that the light and dark of Plato's cave might, indeed *must* mingle at the bottom of the universe, as they could see for themselves if they'd but look through a telescope whose power penetrated into the depths of the earth, beyond the graves that honeycombed the clay like the shafts of mines, so far beyond them as to leave them seeming shallow indeed; and the deeper shot the beams of that telescope, the more violently surged the gloom-rays through the eye-piece, staining the world black like bad old memories; but if it were possible to see through these swirling atoms and the cosmos of Ether under them, then at last the darkness would seem to thicken and narrow into a gorge whose cliffs and stones were darkness coagulated into obsidian. Into this chasm no telescope could pierce. This was the center of the majestic circle of planets and suns—so extreme its gravitational attraction that light was swallowed in it forever. There was a stifling horror about the place, about which hovered the most vile and pestilential fumes; somewhere in this pit was Death itself unfolded. But in what form it revealed itself was unknown, because the gulf was roofed with the foliage of night-trees that leaned toward each other on all sides, gripping each other's soft and flabby trunks with branches that terminated in claws, so that every tree gashed every tree to the heart, growing deeper and deeper into each other's wounds until their agony could never end; from their pallid mushroom flesh bled drops of black sap that rained down into the darkness below, and their velvety leaves vibrated in pain, with a sound like a cloud of midges. —A narrow Path of Dead Tales passed through an arch of these leaves and branches, and then spiraled downward into the pit. At first the moistly disagreeable presence of the charnel vegetation polluted every breath, and icy droplets of tree-blood plashed down upon hands and shoulders, but then the descent steepened, so that it was necessary to hug the wall of the pit and feel one's way sideways, and in the course of many downward revolutions the air became ever cooler and drier, like the stale atmosphere of mummy-caves. Meanwhile, however, the smell of mortality had increased, according to the cube of proximity to that concentrated vortex of corruption, the Grave of Lost Stories. —How pitiably foolish he had been, to imagine that his victims would have been reduced to marble-white skulls, to tibiae as clean as tusk-ivory, to ribs like bleached harps! —No, that would hardly be the Demon's *modus operandi*. —So be it. He had looked upon such sights before. —Still, the *foulness* . . . which is why he concluded in his final poem that matter was a means, not an end. At that time he was working feverishly by lamplight, intoxicated with the solution of ciphers that unlocked his pages of darkness with great clicks, so that he did not have to think about how everything he had written would disgust him the next morning; and he went out to the dark black garden to walk to and fro, wearing a deep and narrow path in the snow as he worked out precisely how deep the Grave would have to be to hold those millions and millions of Stories whose white souls had risen upward like a snowstorm of dreamy unhappiness; well, of course the volume of the bodies would flatten with decomposition; therefore the required depth must be the quotient, but the *full* quotient, not the square root of the quotient; as to how tightly they could be packed into that death-house, their structure had to be considered; it was distinctly stated by all authorities that Stories have skeletons, except for the very early embryos and abortions from those times when you wail in the night knowing that something has just been lost forever but not what; you will never know what, because it is gone. Let us conceive these skeletons, then, to be composed of variegated vertebrae the hue and sheen of black crystal, almost like gaming-pieces as he had thought when Mrs. Osgood was moved by his white-skinned sadness and said ah, Mr. Poe, this country affords no arena for those who live to dream and he said do you dream? I mean sleeping dream? and she smiled and said oh yes Mr. Poe I am a perfect Joseph at dreaming, except that my dreams are of the Unknown and *Spiritual* and he said I knew it; I knew it by your eyes then for the first time he embraced her and she took his hand in hers so tenderly but all at once he felt as if something black, steely-cold, cutting, had closed around his wrist and were pinching it to the bone, and the frozen ache of it poisoned him and the veins stood out on his white wrist; as his phalanxes and metacarpi shattered into chessmen he uttered a cry so that she pulled her hand away and said you are *ill*, are you not, Mr. Poe? at which she became so beautiful to him, and he fell on his knees before her saying is the idea fixed in your head to leave me? as his little wife sat by obediently. Later he was seized with inspiration, and sat down hastily to write, but before he had gotten any farther than that weirdly metallic phrase *the Grave of Lost Stories*, it had already left him, and he sat groaning. Somewhere the Story was struggling desperately to breathe; she was smothering, and he could do nothing. In his life he had committed so many murders . . . Maybe he could save her. He wrote very quickly *there is no day or night* and heard the Story draw in a deep gasp of breath and begin sobbing with hysteria and weariness.

He threw down his pen and knelt upon the floor, wringing his hands. —I call on you to live! he cried. Are you going to vanish like everything else? I wouldn't wrong you if I could help it! Please—I— but the shadow is already there on your throat . . .

The Demon came in, chilling his forehead with an ache like ice. He arose at once. The Demon came in smiling.

I *see* that you smile, he said to this enemy, with quick and bitter sensitivity. Well, everyone is out to ruin me. It really doesn't matter that you smile. But what delegation sent you?

Whoever they are, said the Demon, they are very collected in their resolve. Of that you may be sure.

He heard someone struggling for breath.

Live! he shouted hoarsely. *You beautify the earth—live!* Tears streamed down his face.

He sat listening, knowing that the Demon smiled behind him. He heard the Story begin gasping for breath again, choking and weeping. Trembling, he wrote *lost Stories whose shrouds are—are* He scarcely knew what he wrote; one word, one line, might prolong her life a little longer, until he could think, until he could save her . . .

Oh, very few Stories die of their own accord, the Demon said. They are like us; they want to live, no matter how badly they are treated . . . And yet there are some who know—

Help me! she screamed. For a dozen eternities her ragged gasps of breathing tortured him; then he heard her say very faintly *oh, there's someone sitting on my heart.*

He kept expecting some miracle to happen. He kept expecting her not to come sobbing to him saying I'm dead.

He wrote *there is neither day nor night* and desperately crossed it out and wrote *neither night nor day can be found in the country beyond this Vault, which I so call for lack of any better name* and crossed it out and wrote *in this place, which is hideously exempt from the laws of day and night, the horror of one's situation can scarcely be described* and he heard her sweet breathing (yes! she was breathing still!) and he wrote *there they seized me with mildewed hands and held me fast beyond my power to struggle. Then I fell into a darkness that was not yet darkness—oh, would that it were!—for it prickled with globules of magnetism like—like—* he would not write *the Grave of Lost Stories* in this unlucky context; he gnawed at his pen, forgetting the Demon and even her for the moment; he crossed out the last two lines and wrote *I fell into a darkness whose teeming shadow-tides rushed over me, whose waves poured down upon me with soundless weight, pressing down upon me with a force as steady and interminable as my own unsought-for return to consciousness. My thoughts were ticking like death-beetles, like antique watches. As yet I had not opened my eyes. I would not; would not—and then suddenly terror shot through me like a galvanizing current, for I felt weight and narrowness and stifling compression all around me; I smelled fresh pine-wood; I . . .*

Too late, laughed the Demon, and departed.

Where she had been was silence. As always, the Demon was correct. He knew that there would be circular excoriations about her throat, and the black marks of his own fingers. He had strangled her. The arms would be outstretched as usual, the fingers clenched so tightly that blood was oozing from the palms. Blood must be trickling from the opened mouth; the head thrown back, the protruding tongue ghastly blue.

What a young and beautiful Story you were! he screamed. I—I—

Eddie? his wife called timidly from the other room.

Instantly he was beside her. —Are you warm enough, little Sis? he said.

She nodded. The cat purred on her breast. He stooped down and kissed her forehead.

I was . . .

Yes? he said.

I was—worried about you. I heard you shouting . . .

You've coughed none at all today, he said. I'm really in excellent spirits about that. You can't imagine how I—

He felt the familiar *Vulpine Presence* behind him, breathing icy stinking breath into his ear. He must not let it get near her. —Good night, Sissy, he said, rushing out and slamming the door behind him.

So, he said to himself, bringing pencil to paper:— the skeletons of my lost Stories, being for all practical purposes incompressible, must enforce a minimum volume upon this Tomb (the *Vulpine Presence* snapped its teeth together in his ear)—but still more so the coffins. Were *I* the Architect, I would have quarried deep in the slag of subterraneous fires to get those glassy black building-stones, and then I would have laid out the work in *very definite* proportions. —Which proportions? The question was perplexing, like that of the ratio of infinite lines, and yet not insoluble; for in architecture the Vault, or Cavern, or Cloister with its many tiers of catacombs, must surely obey the primordial law of *Grandness*. That this did not constitute proof he admitted, of course; he could not be *certain* of it, but no other possibility could be seriously entertained. Therefore it would be an oblong room of great dimensions— *and here once again* he wrote *let me suggest that, in fact, we have still been speaking of comparative trifles. The distance of the planet Neptune from the sun has been stated; it is 28 hundred millions of miles*— no doubt it was carpeted with crimson silk of imperishable virtue, through which meandered blue veins. Because the influence of death would be at its maximum here, he expected it to be as cold in this tomb as the blackness of space. The walls must be of marble, of course. They would rise like cliffs, tunneled through with crypts in as much profusion as the caves where sea-swallows make their nests; and indeed the twitterings that came from them were birdlike, but they were tormented cries of the dead Stories in the coffins, and the deep square openings went up the wall as far as could be seen, some glowing with green or yellow light, the rest abandoned to their own blackness; thus the walls rose until they were lost in the luminescence of those sluggish globules that swam in the air like glowworms. Surely, then, he must take account of the coffins, and the spacing between them . . . He wrote: *Behind this portal I saw with unquiet eye the black arch of darkness that led to the vaults—a most peculiar and uncanny sort of arch, for not only did the edges of the ceiling curve downward, but the edges of the floor sloped upward as well until they too met the marble wall; thus it seemed to me as I hurried ahead of my echoing footsteps into that darkness that I was at the bottom of a vast bowl. My disorientation was increased by the glittering whitish pillars that had been set into both floor and ceiling; these towered above my head, or grew downward like stalactites; they were as close together as the pipes of a church organ, except for a narrow space or channel at the center of the floor, where it was lowest, through which I could barely pass my body.* In the margin he wrote: *Not only is the foregoing mathematically accurate; but it also rings true to all the harmonies of my soul.* He sat at his desk almost until dawn, calculating the dimensions on blue paper. His mother-in-law (or mother as she had really become) sat knitting and dozing beside him, and every now and then he would read out the results of his calculations to her and say: Do you understand, Muddie? Am I correct in this? and she said how you *do* read out those figures so cleverly, Eddie! and brought him a mug of fresh hot coffee and pulled in a stitch and her head sank down upon her shoulder; he heard her snoring; he heard his wife coughing in her sleep; the ticking of the clock was almost insufferable to his ears. Thank God for Muddie! She never went to bed before he did, out of consideration for his horror of being alone.

Early the following afternoon, as he pretended to sleep, he heard Muddie talking about him in the kitchen with her dear friend Mrs. Phelps, and Mrs. Phelps was saying how could you *think* such a thing Muddie when I see the *depth* of his love for her! and Muddie said with a sad laugh God knows Eddie loves my Virginia that is not what I meant and Mrs. Phelps said in that tone he hated Mrs. Clemm it is *certainly* not my place to pry and Muddie said oh no no I need to open my heart to someone   and he said to himself   *faugh!*   and Mrs. Phelps said   well then what do you mean?   and Muddie said   Eddie is a very dear boy, and Virginia idolizes him; since she is so sick I think it is a great mercy for them both that he is not a man in the full sense of the word and as I say he does love her fondly and faithfully as I do   and Mrs. Phelps said something in a voice that was drowned out by the beating of his heart   and Muddie said   I honestly fear for his reason if Virginia should pass away; he is so devoted to her   and he heard her crying and Mrs. Phelps was saying   sssh dearie sssh.

He dressed and went out silently, trying in his mind to gather the Grave of Lost Stories into visibility so that he could go down to it and harrow it of its agonized souls; if this proposition proved tenable, he could even—ah, to the Devil with it! He went to the theater with his friend J. B. Booth, and the usher said   gentlemen, where are your tickets?   and J. B. Booth took a ticket out of his breast-pocket and the usher bowed and turned to Eddie and said   and you, sir?   to which he replied   for your stupidity I cannot hold you responsible because you were born that way, but your ignorance is an affront: I am a member of the Press. Kindly trouble me no further, do you understand me?

You a member of the Press?   said the usher scornfully.   You—a drunkard in a shabby black suit! Will you leave quietly or shall I be forced to expel you?

He pulled himself rigidly upright. He looked the usher in the eye. He said very quietly: May God have mercy on your soul.

Oh, Eddie, don't be such a character,   said J. B.   I'll spring for your ticket, and later we'll have a glass, eh? Eddie! Where are you going, Eddie?

Later that night, it was raining heavily, and somebody saw him standing under an awning in that frock-coat of his, glaring at something and muttering to himself, for all the world as if he were repeating the occasion when he wrote "The Bells" with Mrs. Shew and started talking to unseen white-shrouded girls until he fell into a swoon and when they had laid him on the bed the doctor fished a massive gold watch from the depths of his waistcoat and took the pulse and said to Mrs. Shew   this man has heart disease and will die early in life   and although the bystander had an umbrella, something other than unkindness, as he later put it, prevented him from offering it to this crazed emperor of disasters, whom, as it proved, he was gazing upon for the last time. The bystander went home and to bed.

What a dreary dismal rain!

When he felt the familiar breath of corruption in his ear, when he heard the shrill voice of the *Vulpine Presence* (whose parchmentlike forehead he could not bear to see), he realized that he had almost been expecting it. How exceedingly it disliked him he measured by the snapping of its jaws.

Overhead, the moon was shooting its meteor-stones from every volcano. He could hear the whizzing fires . . .

It was at that time, as he dated it, that the *Vulpine Presence* began following in his every footstep. When he sat down at his desk to write, it stood behind him, elongating itself and bending over him to whisper odiously in his ear. If he fled into the garden, it pursued him there, striding alongside him with its arm about his waist. Even into Virginia's room it came with him, aping his every movement, so that when he bent down to kiss her lips it did the same, breathing into her nostrils until she whispered that terrible smell, Eddie and he said I I I and she choked with nausea and began to cough, until he rushed back to his desk and struggled not to hear it clacking its teeth in laughter. Every day it grew more distinct, until he knew its hateful visage better than his own face: that ghastly yellow forehead, whose skin was stretched to drumlike tautness over the bones, the oval pits of the eyes, that sank like twin wells into the skull, the hunched white shoulders, the sunken cheeks, whose deep concavities enhanced the effect of abnormal protrusion in the chin, the shrunken lips that split open like a fissure to display to his gaze every one of those vicious little teeth . . . just as they had been a decade before, when he was writing "Berenice," and because he could not write the next word *instantly* Berenice was already clawing at her breast trying to get air and he heard the delicate rustle of her garments as she sank to her knees and her last breath was rattling in her throat when the *Vulpine Presence* appeared and grinned at him so that he could see nothing but its vicious rows of teeth, like a shark and he exclaimed in horror and closed his eyes but he could not stop thinking about *the teeth* and he wrote *the white and ghastly spectrum of the teeth* and he heard Berenice begin to sob on the floor as his Stories did, feebly, hysterically, when they had been saved; and he sprang up, forgetting the *Vulpine Presence* entirely, and shouted to her   would to God you had died!

The Demon appeared and said to him: No, it is *you* who should have died. Write it.

I *will not!*   he shouted.

She lives, does she not? Shall I return with the Black Cat? Shall we wall her up together?

Slowly, he set pen to paper and wrote   *and in a smile of changed meaning, the teeth of the changed Berenice disclosed themselves to my view. Would to God that I had never beheld them, or that, having done so, I had died!*

Good,   said the Demon behind his shoulder.   Very good.

The *Vulpine Presence* worked its mouth into a little "O" and gibbered in delight.

But she lives,   he thought to himself.   At least she lives.

Virginia died in the last week of January. Her death-agony was very protracted; in the end she smothered. For a keepsake of her the ladies painted a watercolor of her dead face to give him and he knelt sobbing and kissing that cold white forehead until her mother put aside her own grief to comfort him and he said   I can't forget the *horror* when her eyes closed forever   and Muddie rocked him in her arms like a baby and later, shaking and shaking because he still saw how those sad eyes had suddenly become hateful, lusterless, he went to his desk and wrote   *the vortical in-drawing of the orbs . . .*   But after that, though he turned his pen round and round in his fingers, there was nothing to do with the anguish save endure it. (Twenty-eight years later, when he himself was dead and the cemetery was destroyed, her remains were rescued by his biographer Gill and stored in a box under his bed. Sometimes other gentlemen would come to visit Gill and they'd sit on the bed together, talking in low whispers because the landlady was a dragon, and Gill would say   how about a spot of sherry?   and Gill would say   can I refill your glass?   and Gill would say   it feels rather warm in here   and Gill would say?   so we finished off *that* d----d bottle!   and Gill would dig the other in the ribs, breathing heavily, and say   well *I* know why you're here you old rounder you!   and Gill would say   all right then!   and he'd reach under the bed and set the box on his lap and undo the black ribbon with a flourish and crow   yessir, here they are: the bones of Annabel Lee!)

It was a dark and snowy afternoon, and he sat listlessly at his desk turning over the leaves of his books. Muddie had gone out with her begging basket again; there was nothing to eat. In the margin of his Livy he pencilled *I believe that Hannibal passed into Italy over the Pennine Alps; and if Livy were living now, I could demonstrate this fact even to him.* In his Bridgewater he wrote *The plots of God are perfect. The universe is a Plot of God.*

What if Virginia had not been dead when he bore her to the tomb? What if she had only swooned, and were coming to life at this very moment in the nailed coffin, shrieking inside her shroud, struggling for life and breath . . . ? He groaned.

On his first interview with Mrs. Whitman in the cemetery, he professed his love, and when it came out that their birthdays were the same, she was sure that the Stars had called them together; later he held her hand; he would have fallen at her feet but for fear of wounding her, as he wrote to her in time, telling her how he felt the touch of her hand even when she laid it on the back of his chair; she for her part thinking, what a chalky clammy forehead that gentleman has!

Helen, he said, my Helen.

But later that night, when he returned to the tombs alone to see them by moonlight, he saw a marble vault incised with the name MORELLA and he fell to his knees in the snow, weeping when he remembered the panicked scratching of his pen twelve years before as the word-tails grew down below the ruled lines like the alphabet-roots of those night-trees in the cleft where the dead Stories went; and she had shimmered in the air like milk in water and then slowly took shape and now he could hear nothing but anguished panting as his pen raced to save her and the *Vulpine Presence* pursed its black lips and blew upon the paper so that it fluttered like an ocean and he could scarcely see the words and lines; and Morella was gasping with asphyxia; and the sweat of terror for her leaped in beads upon his forehead and he felt his heart curdle in him even as he wrote frantically *fate bound us together at the altar; and I never spoke of passion, nor thought of love* and he heard her desperate rasping breaths and he wrote *the notion of that identity which at death is or is not lost forever, was to me—at all times, a consideration of intense interest* and Morella made a little clicking noise in her throat and thrust back her neck until the skin was unbearably taut and sank to the floor as the triumphant Demon appeared with the shroud, but he wrote *a consideration of intense interest; not more from the perplexing and exciting nature of its consequences* and Morella opened her eyes *than from the marked and agitated manner in which Morella mentioned them* and she sought to rise but the Demon seized her shoulders and thrust her back down upon the floor, hissing you may not be dead yet, child, but you are dying; then Morella gazed at him with her melancholy eyes and replied: I am dying, yet I shall live.

Yes! he shouted joyously, writing *I am dying, yet I shall live* on the blue sheet of paper that Virginia would later attach to the others in the roll, using the *almost negligible* proportion of gum tragacanth powder that he had taught her, so that when Mrs. Osgood accepted her invitation to visit she could laughingly unroll the pasted sheets across the floor as *he* behaved shyly and sweetly and waywardly in front of these two women whom he loved; but for now he was suddenly cast into a well of bitter grief when Morella arose and caressed his cheek with her icy fingers, asking him: But *why* did you make me live, when you feel nothing for me?

and he said I I I

and she said does the Demon love me?

He *does not!* Poe shouted. The oppression of his soul now stifled him so much at these words of hers that he wanted nothing more than that the black and sluggish waters should close over his eyes and mouth. — But Morella only smiled faintly and with one pale hand brushed back the lush, blue-black ringlets from her forehead. Her eyes gleamed; her little white teeth glittered. —Tell me, husband, have I sisters?

Yes, he said in a low voice.

And whom ought I to love best?

Well, he said, Berenice was born just before you, so she is the nearest to you in age, but you must be careful when you play with her, as she is sickly and not likely to live long.

And when she dies, where will she go?

To the Grave of Lost Stories.

Oh, that will be the day of days for her, said Morella. Does the Demon live there?

I cannot say. I do not know where he lives. I have never been down to that place.

And Virginia—how about her? she said to him, singing the name like a bitter mockingbird.

He flew into a rage and said: You have no right—you—to mention *her* to me! You are never to mention her, or I shall throw these pages into the fire—do you hear me?

She said nothing.

He bowed his head over the blue paper and wrote   *But thy days shall be days of sorrow.*   A moment later, his heart softened, and he wanted to call her to him, but she was gone. How to write it? She was gone like narrowing passages of dead stories dwindling into hollow veins in which silence beat instead of blood.

And now, here was her tomb.

Then he saw her pallid figure hurrying toward him in the darkness, and he was chilled with dread. What if she touched him and the droplets of brightness came oozing out of her fingers . . . ? (He had thought that he wanted to go down deeper, but now he knew himself to be as paltry as a shallow grave.)

So it was that he found himself at his desk, writing   *"Sepuleth,"* writing   *a terrible disorder beat in my veins,*   writing   *I shrieked aloud,* but the Demon laughed   this time, you drunkard, you won't be able to pull it off   and the *Vulpine Presence* blew a whistling wind from its mouth that swept the papers off his desk, and in a twinkling he heard Sepuleth's heart-rending catchings of breath, the lovely Lady Sepuleth *with whom,*   he bent down to write,   *I would have dwelled in happiness, among all the flowers and brooks of Arnheim . . .*   but it was too late; he knew that it was too late; he covered his ears so as not to hear her awful expiring sounds and Muddie said   poor Eddie do you have a headache? and he said   yes, Muddie   and she said   shall I rub your forehead for you?   and he said   I was thinking of—of—   and she said   I know, Eddie;   and he closed his eyes for weariness and instantly saw Sepuleth's head lolled against her shoulder, with her long blonde locks streaming down her black dress like rays of the sun, and her elbow was drawn in against her breast, like the wing of a sleeping bird;—it was only the extreme angle of the neck that appeared unnatural.

He had proven in his tale "Of One Hans Pfaall" that some sort of atmosphere must extend from the sun to the orbit of Venus and perhaps indefinitely beyond; if not, as he had written there,   *I can see no reason, therefore, why life could not be sustained even in a vacuum*   . . . But now he admitted that he had deceived himself.

I cannot bear this anymore,   he said.   Berenice, Morella, Ligeia,

Lenore, Ulalume, I call on you to mourn for her and for me. I am going to the Antarctic moon.

Are you going out, Eddie?   Muddie said.

Just to her grave,   he said.

A fine rain was falling. The air was very thick and impure. The river was blackish-grey; the reflections of lights gleamed in it like eyes. He wandered through the streets of the city, where the Conqueror Worm reigned in all the theaters, performing its terrible deeds behind stage-curtains the color of puddled blood, and the senile old Man of the Crowd rushed by him like a whirligig and vanished in the fog beyond the gas-lights and then appeared again to wink at him knowingly because they shared the same panic and the same bottle and his breath was the same as that of the *Vulpine Presence* and then he was gone. Dark-windowed houses of palish brick walled the fog in. He saw a woman running into a narrow lighted archway and the door closed behind her. He saw white pillars glittering in the dark porticoes of building-fronts; grand white sepulchers shone against the blackness of the river. A literary lady called to him from her carriage   good evening to you, my Raven!   and he lifted his hat unthinkingly; his eyes had already fixed themselves in the glare of death. His doubles bowed ironically to him from every alley, wearing the gentlemen's suits that he had never had the funds to wear since his guardian cast him off. They said   Mr. *Poe,* Mr. *Poe, whooh-whoosh!*   He trembled to look at them, but when they greeted him with condescension he was filled with rage, and quoted himself to these selves, shouting: For the love of *God,* Montressor!   at which they blanched and fled, knowing that if he but had them in his power he would wall them up alive, and the Demon and the Black Cat would help him. —The streets were slimy with rain. He felt a swelling ache in his chest, and knew that the Red Death was already inside him, speckling his blackened organs with carmine and scarlet. It was unbearable; he needed a drink. His hands searched eagerly in his pocket and found a penny; he went into a tavern and had a glass of wine, and his face flushed and he determined to seek out the Grave of Lost Stories and set those poor souls free; for he *knew* where it was, and though the task scarcely be safe or easy, he thought that he had sufficient boldness to undertake it.

Undoubtedly this Tomb lay in a difficult and eccentric direction. The foolish and superficial cosmographers (to whom he had to confess a glacial coolness, in respect of the unwarranted praise that they had received), would surely choose to locate it at the center of the earth, as if it were the cavern of Avernus—a distance precisely equal to the earth's radius. But this said nothing about where the actual *vortex* was. To repeat: he knew where it was. His prospects now seemed unbounded. —In other words, the attraction of the Vault must now be increasing in an exponential ratio.

He followed the Auber River past the red cliffs of Circassy, and sunset came, and he descended into the Valley of Unrest where the lilies bowed over a grave—he did not know whose; he refused to know; and now it was dark at last, and he was in the ghoul-haunted woodland of Weir; and the water of the Auber was a mottled silver that showed him his own reflection. Psyche met him at the bank and he was glad to see her, but as he wrote   *Our talk had been serious and sober, but our thoughts they were palsied and sere*   and truthfully her unfocused eyes with the glittering whites and the pupils like green marbles disturbed him far more than the barkings of the ghoul-packs who ravaged the churchyards in the misty darkness behind them; and suddenly a star-ball of glowing gases descended through the trees and Psyche said   I fear the pallor of that Star   but he showed his teeth in a laugh and said   don't be afraid Sis I assure you that a star as bright as that can only light our way   but she said   no Eddie I don't want it to.   —*Then* certainly he pacified his sweet Psyche; he had to; I am entitled as a reader to say that he kissed her, still thinking of the crystalline light of that Star that maddened and exalted him; but Psyche still snivelled and trailed her little wings in the dust, so to distract her from her scruples and gloom he asked her   what do you think happens to the dead Stories?   and she said   oh Eddie they're not as unhappy as you think because I see them all around me so brittle and sparkling, blowing everywhere like dandelion seeds, so *many* of them, even here in this horrid dark place, that they're around me in constellations of stars!   but saying this, she remembered the evil Star that drew them both on, and her happy face fell again, so to keep her from dwelling on her fear he said   but aren't these dead Stories restless?   and she said   yes, but they try to be patient because someday someone will write them again and they'll be reborn as new living girls and brides so healthy and happy   and she also said   Eddie you should not destroy the paper of the dead Stories because that hurts them   as they walked deeper down the cypress ways in the direction that the Star was pulling

them, and the ghouls had fallen silent, and Psyche said   please Eddie
don't make me go on with you anymore   and her plumes were dragging
in the dust again, but he put his arm around her and said   what makes
your dead Stories happiest?   and she said   when a child thinks of them!
have you ever heard children tell each other Stories?   and he said   no
and she said   poor Eddie   and he said   but you do grant that they
remain bound to their bodies?   and she said   yes   and he said
triumphantly   well then that's why we go to the graves of our dead
women, because their skeletons are lying there for us to love and treasure
beneath the marble slabs! Don't you admit that a grave and a corpse are
more real than a memory and a lock of hair?   and she said   I never
thought you such a materialist, Eddie   and he laughed and they went on
into the suffocating gloom and the Star set slowly over the black valley
which his reasoning powers in combination with his accurate knowledge
had enabled him to predict in bold relief, and as the Star set it cast a
last beam down through the night-trees that occluded the gulf, and
tenderly brushed the pure darkness below, like the hem of a skirt brushing his lips; and Psyche said   let's go home now Eddie please!   but he
kissed her so many times and fell on his knees and entreated her and made
her laugh by telling her how her cat Catarina had chased her tail and
how Muddie had been so astounded, until again he quenched her tears;
and so hand in hand they walked among the sad-scented night-trees and
descended into that gorge of coagulated darkness, and on the opposite
wall he saw that a face had been carved—a titanic face, whose mouth
could have swallowed armies; and he stiffened like a galvanized corpse
to see that it was the face of the *Vulpine Presence!* Its jaws champed and
it ground its black stone teeth together. Its eyeballs were the size of
millstones, and they rolled to and fro with a sullen thundering sound.
But he would not let poor little Sissy see it. So he talked and talked to
her ever more rapidly and gaily like his pen speeding so desperately
across the paper to save the dying Stories; and Psyche was smiling again
through her tears and saying   oh you're so funny Eddie   and so they
descended hand in hand into that sweet-sulphur stench of concentrated
mortality. They were in a narrow valley of bones and smoldering fumes,
made still narrower by the ledges that projected overhead, comprised of
a pinkish mineral such as chalcedony, into which were set white nodules
of a cuspid shape; from these little drops of moisture unpleasantly
dripped. She continued to grasp his hand, and he was so happy to be

with her even though her face was so ghastly pale and there was black mold around her eyes and lips; and the yellowish greenish smoke that swirled around her made her hair smell singed and he felt the mold growing cold and clammy on his eyebrows and the taste of death was in his mouth and so they came to a gigantic door of tarnished iron. He said Sissy what does it say on the door? And she leaned forward to spell out the letters with her fingers (for in truth the dark air was so thick that despite the globules of light that writhed in the atmosphere like maggots it was very difficult to see); and she said U and she said L and a sudden agony of terror made his heart beat so loudly that he could not hear what she said and he cried yes? yes? with his haunted face uplifted . . . and she said ULALUME! and his heart became as ashen and brittle and brown as a dead leaf. —I *killed* her, he said in a kind of choked wonder. He remembered now how the suffocation had been consummated. —Psyche had begun to walk away. A chilly and rigid magnificence issued from her. She called back over her shoulder: — Yes, she is dead, but *she is waiting for you inside!*

Please don't leave me, he said in a very small voice, as if to himself.

Remember, laughed Psyche from far away (she was almost out of sight), they're all waiting for you!

A key was in the lock, high above that name carved in weeping letters. The lock was thickly overgrown with fungi, and condensation from the reeking mists all about him had scored the iron with a thousand little channels like tear-trails, now choked with rusts and lichens. From the crack where that massive block of iron had been fitted into the doorway of the tomb, a sickening exhalation issued, and he thought to himself it was *thus* in the place where we buried Madeline Usher! — Immediately there came to him a vision of those thousands of wives and daughters of his who waited within, their white bodies puffing outward with the gases of decomposition; which convinced him, by right of the Grave's position as universal vortex, that these horrible vapors might indeed become the *vaporous rings* of the outer planets. —He rose from his desk and rushed outside to look for Saturn. It was a clear night; Mrs. Shew had very kindly lent him her pocket telescope. —Yes, yes! — Indeed, since all the planets were no more than globular condensations of these ring forms, the conclusion was inescapable (despite the laughable ignorance of the astronomers), that the universe was composed of nothing other than this miasma. And in consequence, since the law of gravitation was nothing but the fact of inexorable collapse, one could expect, after untold millions of epochs, all matter to congeal into that jet-black, obsidian-like form of which the Valley of the Grave was comprised! Some might call this rash speculation; as for him, he could not but smile at the numbskulls who thought to confute him.

Standing on tiptoe, he was just barely able to get the tips of his fingers around the key. It would not move. He leaped up and hung from the key with all his weight; he raised his body halfway above it and locked his elbows; he braced his feet against the door; his face glowed with the fiercely radiant joy of self-destruction. He strained and strained to turn the key in the lock, but it would not move. In his anxiety and frustration he began kicking the door, which resounded with sullen hollow boomings like an immense drum; at last he placed one hand over the other, and then, squeezing until the veins stood out on his forehead, he wrenched the key clockwise with all his strength. There came a great squeaking and grinding. Flakes of rust showered him like bloody sparks. Now the key turned with ease. He let himself down to the ground and took hold of it again; the revolution of the circle was completed, and he heard a click. The massive door swung slowly inward. A foul wind rushed out from that dark place. Now he would discover the corpses. Now the tomb would open for him like a vagina. With a cry of joy, he ran inside. Too late, he saw that the interior was a wedge-shaped *cul-de-sac* lined with spikes. In horror and dismay, he wheeled around to escape, but long before he reached it, the door had slammed shut with a malignant boom; an instant later, the wall-jaws closed upon him.

13

Epitaph for

A LOVED BOOK

* VARIOUS PLACES *

I thought I loved you because you waited for me as innocent as water. (You can't cross the same river once.)

You took your own life—in my hands.

I took you in my hands.

I only took, not knowing to give back. Already half-read, you loved me steadily, never holding back.

I'd already confessed to you: The books I keep are empty coffins; seashells. But I still like to open the books I love, find a page, a chapter, like the hair-ribbon of my dead Ulalume.

I did tell you that, as I'd told the others; it comforted them like morphine. But maybe you didn't need that; you never moaned.

So I never hid from you the relics of your paperbacked relations whose pages have gone brittle inward from brownish-green edges. On memorial days I turn them like prayer wheels, even though leaves fall out, and triangular fragments of leaves shoot down like spearheads. I hope you remembered that when the gangrene of reading advanced beyond your thighs.

Now you are finished in the ending that explains all. I lay you facedown by the bed; I switch out the light dreaming your stories' last traceries; in the morning I will entomb you in the Grave of Lost Stories, your spine-pricked title your epitaph.

Epigraphs and Sources

Author's Note

The initial letter A was scanned and electronically edited from a photograph of an ebony English sextant, with ivory movement, *ca.* 1860, in Jean Randier's *Men and Ships Around Cape Horn 1616–1939* (New York: David McKay, 1969), trans. M. W. B. Sanderson, p. 268. Randier credits the Mariners' Museum of Saint Malo for this illustration.

The Ghost of Magnetism

The epigraph is from Bjorn Kjellstrom, *Be Expert with Map and Compass* (New York: Scribner's, 1976), p. 171.

The Bad Girl

The epigraph is from Ariosto, *Orlando Furioso*, re-translated by the author.

The Happy Girls

The epigraph is from Anonymous, *Never Say Die: A Survival Manual* (Boulder, Co.: Paladin Press, 1979), p. 115.

The Bitch

The epigraph is from Robert Harbison, *Pharaoh's Dream: The Secret Life of Stories* (London: Secker and Warburg, 1988), p. 162.

Divine Men

The epigraph is from *National Geographic*, "The Eternal Etruscans" (June 1988, p. 697).

The Handcuff Manual

The "manual" sentences of this story are adapted from the instruction manual for Peerless hinged handcuffs, as furnished by the Peerless Handcuff Company (Springfield, Massachusetts).

Flowers in Your Hair

The epigraph is from Richard Slotkin, *The Fatal Environment: The Myth of the Frontier in the Age of Industrialization, 1800–1890* (New York: Atheneum, 1985), p. 40.

Kindness

The epigraph is from Saint Augustine's *Confessions*, trans. E. B. Pusey, DD (London: Dent, Everyman, 1962), p. 227.

My Portrait, My Love, My Wife; In Omaha; Tropicana

I don't remember anymore, and I don't care.

Dialectics

The epigraph is from Lenin's *Selected Works in Three Volumes*, rev. ed. (Moscow: Progress Publishers, 1977), p. 97.

The Grave of Lost Stories

Poe's "final poem" is, of course, *Eureka* (1848). While I have breathed deeply of its dreamily logical atmosphere, I have also felt free to distort or ignore its arguments. Poe himself would not agree with the hypotheses that I attribute to him. The conversation between Poe and Mrs. Osgood is excerpted from an entry in the diary of Elizabeth Oakes Smith for 1845. Poe's hopeless cries to the first of the dying stories are partly based on a letter of his (I believe the last) to Mrs. Shew. The sentence in italics about the planet Neptune comes from *Eureka*. (The phrase "the vortical in-drawing of the orbs" also comes from *Eureka*, in an astronomical context.) The conversation between Mrs. Clemm and Mrs. Phelps is reconstructed from a brief mention by Mrs. Phelps's daughter. The anecdote about Poe's biographer keeping Virginia's remains under his bed is given in Hervey Allen's *Israfel: The Life and Times of Edgar Allan Poe* (New York: Farrar and Rinehart, 1934), p. 581n. The marginal note on Livy is given in Poe's "Marginalia" (November 1844). The lines in italics attributed to "Berenice" do in fact come from that story (1835). Ditto for "Morella" (1835). Ditto for "Hans Pfaal" (1835). Ditto for "Ulalume" ("Our talk had been serious and sober . . ."). (I have slightly abridged some of the excerpts.) "Sepuleth," however, being one of the Lost Stories, is of course imaginary. For some of the Psyche's views on dead stories I am indebted to Miss Moira Brown, who lost her life-work of paintings in a fire.